Sharon Gosling is the author of multiple middle-grade historical adventure books for children, including *The Diamond Thief*, *The Golden Butterfly*, *The House of Hidden Wonders* and *The Extraordinary Voyage of Katy Willacott*. She is also the author of YA Scandi horror *FIR* as well as adult fiction including *The House Beneath the Cliffs*, *The Lighthouse Bookshop* and *The Forgotten Garden*. Having started her career as an entertainment journalist, she still also occasionally writes non-fiction making-of books about television and film. Titles include *Tomb Raider: The Art and Making of the Film*, *The Art and Making of Penny Dreadful* and *Wonder Woman: The Art and Making of the Film*.

Sharon lives with her husband in a very small village on the side of a fell in the far north of Cumbria.

SHARON GOSLING

The Secret Orchard

**SIMON &
SCHUSTER**

London · New York · Sydney · Toronto · New Delhi

First published in Great Britain by Simon & Schuster UK Ltd, 2024

Copyright © Sharon Gosling, 2024

The right of Sharon Gosling to be identified as author of
this work has been asserted in accordance with the
Copyright, Designs and Patents Act, 1988.

1 3 5 7 9 10 8 6 4 2

Simon & Schuster UK Ltd
1st Floor
222 Gray's Inn Road
London WC1X 8HB

Simon & Schuster: Celebrating 100 Years of Publishing in 2024

Simon & Schuster Australia, Sydney
Simon & Schuster India, New Delhi

www.simonandschuster.co.uk
www.simonandschuster.com.au
www.simonandschuster.co.in

A CIP catalogue record for this book
is available from the British Library

Paperback ISBN: 978-1-3985-1920-6
eBook ISBN: 978-1-3985-1921-3
Audio ISBN: 978-1-3985-1922-0

Typeset in Bembo by M Rules
Printed and Bound in the UK using 100% Renewable
Electricity at CPI Group (UK) Ltd

MIX
Paper | Supporting
responsible forestry
FSC® C171272

For Madge and Barry Shaw, who gave me a Bramley apple tree that will outlast us all, and George and Angela Ritchie, for their endless support. Good neighbours are everything.

Autumn

1839

She was still smarting from his words as she stormed along the cliff edge. There was a stiff wind blowing from a turbulent sea, but it was not responsible for the salt tears that blurred Ophelia's eyes even an hour after their latest disagreement.

'It's absurd,' Milton had said, dismissively. 'But what am I saying? Of course it is, Ophelia — because you're absurd. I'll not hear of it. You'll not go. You're supposed to be my wife, for God's sake, at least pretend to act like that means something to you.'

Ophelia Greville would usually be able to brush off her husband's dismissiveness. She'd learned well enough how to do that over the taut first year of their marriage. This, though . . . this was a cruelty too far. Milton well knew how dear this plan was to her heart, and he would not even begin to countenance the idea. It was spite alone that made him keep her close. There had never been any love in their marriage, only money and his pressing need for an heir.

As she walked, she reached one hand up to her face and wiped away furious tears. She'd been such a childish fool. She should have argued harder, fought for herself more, but no. She'd been bought off with a promise that had turned out to be worth no more than her father's word. One per cent of her father's land! It was a penny thrown into the ocean, she saw that now, and even that Milton had found a way to argue about. She had wanted to sell her share – had offered to sell it to Milton, in fact, because she needed the proceeds for the trip she had been dreaming of since she was a child, to Africa, to see the vast Savannahs, the wondrous animals that roamed them. Lord Greville had laughed in her face. Firstly, why would he pay for what he already owned? Secondly, even if she had money to spend as she liked, what made her think he would let her go? Ophelia had pointed out that she had not intended to go alone, Milton would accompany her, but that plan was also laughed out of existence.

No, it seemed that 'her' land was as much a trap as money and as much of a prison as marriage. Her father had left her nothing, after all.

Ophelia's laboured breath ended in a short sob. She stopped, hands on her hips at the cliff edge, and realized she had no idea where she was. In the wake of Milton's scathing words, Ophelia had walked and walked, fleeing the suffocating rooms that marked the narrow boundaries of her life. After all, she couldn't get lost. All she had to do was retrace her steps along the cliff edge back to the village and then to the house above it.

She looked about her. She was ankle-deep in rich pasture, but ahead the land dropped away down a slope, half-hidden by gorse that had grown across a well-trodden path. It seemed natural to her that she should follow, and so she did. The gorse picked at her skirts as she pushed through it, then finally set her free. Ophelia walked the grooves left by other feet, noting with a faint chill both of exhilaration and fear that she was now very close to the cliff edge. In fact, one wrong step and she'd plunge down onto the jagged rocks that waited in the surging waves below. This thought stuttered her feet and a step later she was in danger of doing exactly that. Ophelia stumbled, uttering a short shriek as she realized there was nothing for her to catch hold of. Her life – such as it was – flashed before her eyes and she shut them.

Strong hands clamped around her shoulder and arm, pulling her back from the brink. Ophelia opened her eyes to find herself on solid ground again, and in the grip of a young man in a tweed cap, heavy jacket and trousers, who was looking at her anxiously from warm brown eyes.

'You all right, ma'am?' he asked, in as deep a Scots burr as she'd ever heard. 'Nearly went a fair cropper there.'

Ophelia opened her mouth to reply but laughed instead, then clamped a shaking hand over her mouth. Her heart was a soldier's drum, thumping far too fast. Her saviour let go of her shoulder but kept a lighter hold on her elbow.

'Come,' he said, shepherding her down the slope. 'You've had a shock.'

She concentrated on not looking down into the water as he steered her onto a strip of level ground. Once there, he let her go. Ophelia looked around, feeling a little dazed, as if she really had fallen. She was surrounded by trees, as small and tangled as knots of wool.

'What is this place?' she asked.

'It's the old orchard,' he said.

3

'An orchard? On the cliff?'

He laughed at her incredulity, but it wasn't the way that Milton laughed. His eyes were hazel and kind. Her heart had stopped thumping, but now it clenched a little, with a sort of grief she couldn't quantify.

'Aye, 'tis a strange thing, I'll grant you.' He regarded her for a moment. 'You're Lady Greville, from the Big House. I'm sorry I did not know you, ma'am.'

'I'm not "ma'am",' Ophelia said, the numbness spreading still further. 'I'm just Ophelia.'

He smiled. 'Well,' he said, into her silence. 'I'm George Crowdie. Wait there a moment. I've something that will settle your nerves.'

Before she could reply he'd vanished into the gathering shadows. Ophelia did as she was told and remained where she was, listening to the wash of the tide against the cliff and the movement of the wind in the branches of the strange little trees. She felt removed from the world, as if she'd stepped through a door and into another place entirely. Presently George Crowdie returned bearing a bottle made of brown glass, which he held out to her.

'I've nothing for you to drink it from but the bottle,' he said, a note of apology in his voice. 'But drink it anyway.'

She was expecting whisky but the taste that filled her mouth was far sweeter. 'Oh,' she exclaimed, in rapture. 'Is it apple juice?'

His eyes twinkled at her again. 'Aye, but it's more than that. We mix it with the juice of strawberries and a little honey from the hives.'

She was an instant glutton for it. It was the best sweet thing she had ever tasted. Before Ophelia knew it, she had gulped half the bottle. She stopped at last, drew the back of her hand across her lips, *feeling restored. George Crowdie was still smiling at her as she held out the bottle for him to take back.*

'Keep it,' he said. 'It is good for the soul, as you see.'

Ophelia looked at the bottle. She could not return to the house with it. She had been out so long, and alone. When she finally went back it would be under scrutiny, and if she had this with her . . . She surveyed the funny little trees, crouched along this peculiar nook in the otherwise unforgiving cliff.

'I cannot,' she said. 'But I thank you for your kindness, George Crowdie.'

She passed him the bottle and turned to retrace her steps, reluctant to leave despite the now swift falling of evening. This time she would be more careful, keep away from the edge. Before Ophelia had gone two steps she spun back.

'Don't ever tell anyone this is here, George,' she said, suddenly impassioned. 'If my husband knew it existed, he would want it. He would want all of it. Keep it a secret.'

A shadow passed over George Crowdie's face, and he shrugged a little, his gaze wandering past her to where the land fell into the sea. 'Tis his land, ma'am. They're his trees. The cider we make goes into his stores.'

'Not forever,' she said. 'I will make sure of it. I will.'

He looked at her, those hazel eyes curious. Ophelia didn't explain. One per cent. It was a penny lost in the ocean, but it was her penny, and it would be enough. Perhaps she would never go anywhere. But neither would this place. Neither would the Crowdies. Neither would this boy with the kind brown eyes.

'And another thing,' she said. 'I believe you should put a railing

5

up along that treacherous cliff. The estate will cover the cost. It will keep me safe when I come to visit.' She risked a glance at him. 'If I may? Sometimes?'

'Aye, Ophelia,' he said. 'You may. Whenever you like.'

'Tomorrow?'

'Yes,' he said. He was smiling again. She wished she could see that smile, always. 'Come tomorrow.'

Chapter One

Now

Nina stood at the kitchen door in a shaft of summer evening sunlight. She watched the branches of the old oak tree that towered over the milking barn as it moved in the warm breeze. She could remember doing the same thing when she was little, mesmerized by the separate flickers of each individual leaf. She had once told her father that she thought the tree was trying to speak to her, to communicate with each minute movement in a kind of leafy sign language that she might be able to decipher if only she paid enough attention. After that, they would stand there together, making up stories for each other from the shapes they saw formed by the leaves. The tall tales Bern Crowdie translated for his younger daughter had never failed to make her laugh, and seeing her laugh would always make him laugh, too, and so there they would stand, two loons cackling at a tree, until farm business took him away into the barn to see to the cows or out into the fields with the dogs to gather the sheep. He'd always made time for her, that was what Nina would remember most about her father. It was the greatest lesson he had given her as a parent, that no matter what he had to do in his day, he could always find time to make her laugh.

A noise came from the kitchen and Nina turned back into the house to see her mother coming towards her. At sixty-two, Sophia Crowdie still possessed the arresting beauty that had stopped the farmer in his tracks (so the family story went) the second they had met and that both their daughters had inherited. Tall, with olive skin, wild dark curls (silver now, but wild all the same) and sharp green eyes, Sophia had been born in Edinburgh to an Irish mother and an Italian father, gifted with the kind of poise that always made her seem as if she'd stepped from the front cover of *Vogue*. Nina loved both of her parents dearly, but once she had been old enough to wonder, she had never been able to imagine quite how either of them had thought the marriage would last. Their union had been a clash of city meeting country, with their mother craving daily the kind of life that Bern could only ever enjoy for weekends at a time. Still, the union had persisted for twenty years, far longer than many had predicted and long enough to produce two children and a caring friendship that had endured despite everything else sputtering out once both their daughters had fledged. But then, no one fell out with Bern Crowdie. He'd understood that Sophia had always missed the bustle of Edinburgh and that she had long harboured the idea of extended travel to climes with more certain sun than Scotland. Sophia meanwhile had understood that this coastal Scottish farm was where Bern belonged. In the end, they had loved each other too much as friends to make each other unhappy as spouses. The reasonableness of her parents' behaviour had fooled Nina into believing that this was how all adults acted when it came to affairs of the heart. She hadn't discovered the truth of that until much later.

'Are you all right?' Sophia asked now, arriving at Nina's side and slipping one arm around her daughter's shoulders.

'Yeah,' Nina said, though a lump had formed in her throat and she could feel tears pricking at her eyes. She hugged her mother back. 'Just thinking about Dad.'

Her mother held her closer and together they looked out at the farmyard that had been Bern Crowdie's life.

'Do you remember,' Sophia asked, her voice growing husky, 'that Christmas it snowed and we woke up on Christmas day to find that he'd built a whole family of snowmen out here in the yard?'

'Oh yes!' Nina laughed. 'One for each of us.'

Sophia shook her head. 'He'd even made the dog. What was it called, the one he had then?'

'Turtle,' Nina said, smiling. 'That was Turtle.'

'Silly man,' Sophia said, with an affection that made Nina smile despite her tears. 'He must have been out there for hours. His hands were frozen. He never did like wearing gloves. I asked him why he didn't wait until you girls were up so that the three of you could do it together and he said

Sharon Gosling

he'd started one and hadn't wanted to leave anyone out, so he kept going. And then we all had to help with the milking because he was running late! Poor cows.'

Nina snickered again, remembering the sight of Sophia Crowdie herding Ayrshires on that snowy Christmas morning so long ago. She'd never been a natural when it came to farm work, much like Bette. Although, Nina reflected, their mother had at least tried in a way that her sister never had.

'He loved you girls so much,' Sophia said, into Nina's hair. 'He used to tell me how he'd never understand how he got so lucky. Thank you for being here for him, for the past few years. He couldn't have managed this place without you.'

Nina smiled through more tears. 'I was the lucky one,' she said. 'Coming back home saved me and Barnaby. I'm not kidding.'

'Best Barnaby Barnacle,' her mother corrected, and Nina laughed.

'Right,' she said, her laugh resolving into a troubled sigh at the thought of her son. '*Best Barnaby Barnacle*. Did he go to bed without too much moaning? I'll go up to him in a minute.'

Her mother squeezed her again and then stepped away back into the kitchen. 'He's up there with *Spider-Man* or some such. I told him he could read until you go to say goodnight. You might be able to persuade him to take that mask off – I couldn't.'

Nina groaned as together the two women began to tidy up the dinner things. 'It's like he's glued inside that costume,

10

Mum. He hasn't worn anything else since Dad died. I'm worried he's going to insist on wearing it to the funeral. I don't think I'd be able to bear a battle over that on Saturday morning.'

'Ach, let him wear it if he wants to,' her mother said, running hot water into the ancient Belfast sink and beginning to wash up. 'Your father wouldn't have cared. In fact, he probably would have encouraged it. The boy's six! No one else will bat an eyelid either, darling, and if they do it's their problem, not yours. Whatever gets you through.'

Nina picked up a tea towel and reached for a wet plate, leaning her head against her mother's shoulder. 'I still can't believe he's gone. I think there was a part of me that thought he'd be with us forever.'

Sophia kissed her head again and went on with the washing up. They were both quiet for a few moments as they continued their task. The farmhouse was empty in a way it never had been before, an essential part of it that couldn't be replaced now missing. They must have both been thinking something similar, of absence and family and the past, because then Sophia said: 'I wonder when your sister will get here?'

Nina screwed up her face as she moved away to stack the clean dishes. 'I wonder if she'll bother coming at all?'

Her mother made a clucking sound with her tongue. 'Of course Bette will be here. She'll arrive tomorrow, I should think. She's probably just got caught up with work.'

'She's always caught up with work,' Nina felt compelled

to point out, although she realized how petulant her voice had become. Talk about her sister had a way of doing that, as if thoughts of Bette created a vortex that crossed time, taking Nina back to the resentment of her younger years. Nina sighed. 'Part of me wouldn't mind if she didn't make it, Mum. She's not going to want to be here, is she? It's not as if she cared about Dad when he was alive, is it?'

Sophia Crowdie grabbed a towel and dried her hands, turning to face her daughter with a troubled expression. 'Don't say that. Your sister loved your dad just as much as you did.'

Nina puffed out her cheeks. 'How can you *say* that? You do know that in all the time me and Barnaby have been living back here, she's only visited once, and that was before the pandemic? That's once in five years, Mum. *Five*. The only other time she's seen Dad in that time was when she had some work thing going on in Aberdeen and he agreed to go and meet her there for dinner. She's met her nephew exactly twice in his life and the first time was because of that trip you and I took with him to London. We had to go to her, with a one-year-old!'

'Nina,' her mother said. 'Please. You and your sister are very different people, that's all. You deal with things in very different ways. Your life is here. Hers isn't.'

'Well, as far as I can see there's only one way of showing you actually care about your family and that's to be there for them,' Nina said, 'which I can't see that she's ever been. How is that anything other than selfish?'

Her mother looked as if she was about to say something in reply, but then didn't. With a rush that made her want to kick herself, Nina felt a pang of guilt – she hadn't meant to tar her mother with that same brush, however alike Sophia and Bette were. Before she could say anything, though, Sophia had moved to the stove. 'Shall we keep these leftovers?'

'Cam will stop by soon,' Nina said, glancing up at the clock. 'He might want them if he hasn't eaten at home.'

'Cam?'

'I told you about him, remember? Our neighbour? He bought the Bronagh farm a few years back. He's been helping out since Dad died, doing the evening milking for me so I don't have to leave Barney on his own after dinner.'

'Really? That's good of him,' Sophia said. 'Doesn't he have enough of his own to do at home?'

'Yes, and that's what I said when he offered,' Nina said, 'but he insisted. I don't know what I'd have done without him, to be honest. I'm going to have to look at getting more help but I just haven't been able to think about that yet. Cam's been a godsend.'

When Nina had moved back to the Crowdie farm five years before, she'd been juggling re-learning farm life and being a single mother with some hefty emotional baggage, all while looking after a father who had aged far more than she'd realized at a distance. It had been Cam who'd had the patience – both with her son and with Nina herself – to show her what Bern hadn't always had the energy or strength to himself.

Nina could feel her mother's eyes on her. She looked up to see Sophia watching her speculatively. 'What?'

'This Cam of yours,' she said. 'How old is he? Is he single?'

'Ahh!' Nina said, raising a hand. 'No. Nope. *No.* Don't even think about it.'

'Don't think about what?' her mother asked, with an innocent expression that Nina did not believe for a second.

'Cam and I are friends, that's all,' Nina said. '*Good* friends. Don't go getting any ideas. I've got enough on my plate without you meddling.'

'I don't know what you mean,' Sophia said, with a studiously straight face.

'You know exactly what I mean,' Nina said. 'And I don't need you and your matchmaking antics getting me into trouble. It's all right for you, you'll be off home again in a couple of days. Cam and I both live here.'

Sophia picked a grape from a bunch in the fruit bowl on the table and popped it in her mouth. 'Exactly. And I notice you've sidestepped my questions about him. Which tells me a lot.'

'Stop it,' Nina warned her. 'I'm going up to say goodnight to Barney. And that is the end of this conversation.'

'That's the problem with the youth of today,' her mother sighed with false drama, as Nina left the kitchen and made for the stairs. 'You're all just so *serious* all the time. When do you get to have *fun*?'

'We can't afford it!' Nina yelled back from the hallway.

Chapter Two

When Nina pushed open his bedroom door she found her six-year-old son sitting propped up against the headboard with his bedside lamp on and a comic book open on his knees. His faithful black-and-white collie dog, Limpet, was stretched out beside him as usual. Limpet had been rescued from farm dog ignominy by Bern as a puppy not long before Nina had arrived at the door with her baby boy. Deathly afraid of sheep despite his obedient nature, Limpet was never going to be a working dog, but as a pet had proven to be a loyal companion for Barney. The two had effectively grown up together and were now inseparable. If her boy wasn't in school, Limpet was there at his side. Nina had given up telling them both that Limpet should sleep on the floor. Barney always looked at her as if she'd told him he had to leave the dog outside alone all night to be eaten by bears or wolves . . . or perhaps even sheep. Besides, she was glad that Limpet was so devoted – Nina knew that the dog wouldn't hesitate to risk its own life to keep her son safe, and that was good enough for her to forgive all manner of minor transgressions.

Despite being in bed, Barney was wearing a knitted black mask that covered his face and head. Nina was relieved to see that Sophia had at least managed to persuade her grandson out of the rest of the costume, which consisted of a black jumper and trousers combo with added knitted cape. He was in clean pyjamas instead and while these did still continue the caped crusader theme, covered as they were in Marvel superheroes, they were at least appropriate bedwear that hadn't been worn incessantly for the past week.

'Hey, you,' Nina said, softly, crossing to the bed and settling in beside her son, dropping a kiss on his covered head. She could feel the heat radiating through the wool. 'You're hot. You really should take this off, bub. You won't sleep well in it.'

She went to raise the mask, but Barnaby grabbed hold of it beneath his chin with such determination that Nina gave up for the moment. The costume had been a favourite ever since Nina had found it in a charity shop, but since Bern had passed away it had taken on a different aspect. Barnaby (who also now insisted on being called Best Barnaby Barnacle, for reasons either too obvious or too convoluted for him to explain to the mere mortal who was his mother) flatly refused to wear anything else, to the point where Sophia had suggested Nina find another just like it that could be worn in alternation for washing. Nina, on the other hand, was hoping that this phase wasn't going to last long enough for this to be necessary. After all, she didn't think it took a child psychologist to work out where this current compulsion had come from or the purpose it was serving. She just wasn't looking forward to the battle she could see coming when it came to putting on his school uniform when he went back to start the new school term on Monday.

'What are you reading?' she asked, moving her attention to the colourful pages on his lap.

'*Spider-Man*. I just finished. He was fighting Hobgoblin.'

'Did he win?'

'He always wins. In the end, anyway. Even if he has to lose something first.'

Nina hugged Barnaby to her. 'Like all good superheroes.'

'Mu-*um*!'

'It's time to go to sleep, munchkin.'

'I want to read the next comic.'

'Tomorrow. Spider-Man will be right here waiting for you when you wake up, all right?'

He sighed heavily, with all the weight of the world. 'All right.'

'Are you going to take that mask off?' she tried again. 'I really think you should. Even Spidey takes his off when he goes home, doesn't he?'

'That's because Aunt May doesn't know he's Spider-Man,' her son pointed out, with the kind of studied patience children reserve for foolish adults. 'Everyone *knows* I'm Best Barnaby Barnacle.'

It took another five minutes to persuade him to remove it,

but once the mask was off he fell asleep almost immediately. Nina brushed Barnaby's dark hair out of his eyes, watching the dreams flicker rapidly beneath his eyelids, hoping whatever adventures he was on were good ones.

She heard voices in the kitchen as she came downstairs and found her mother and her neighbour, Cameron Hayes, sitting together at the table, Cam eating the last of the lasagne Sophia had warmed through for him with a gusto that suggested he'd not had time for lunch. He paused in whatever tale he was telling and smiled at Nina as she came in, his blue eyes twinkling.

'Hi,' he said. 'Is our friendly neighbourhood sea creature fast asleep?'

'Yup.' Nina went to the washing machine and added Barnaby's mask to the load that was waiting inside, starting the cycle before joining them at the table. She noted gratefully that Sophia had poured her a glass of wine.

'Well, maybe you can relax for a little while now,' Cam said. 'The milking's done and I took fresh salt licks up to the top field earlier so you can take that off your list.'

'Dammit – I meant to do that yesterday,' Nina said. 'I got distracted when the deli called about delivery details for the wake. Thanks, Cam. You're a life-saver.'

'What a lovely neighbour to have,' said Sophia, leaning over to give Cam's hand a pat. 'Thank you for looking after my daughter, Cam. How lucky she is to have such a handsome man helping out around the place.'

'*Mum*,' Nina warned as Cam gave her mother a cheesy grin.

'What?' Sophia asked, looking at her daughter with wide eyes. 'You can't tell me you haven't noticed.'

Nina shook her head as her neighbour turned the same grin on her, raising his eyebrows to comic effect. 'You are a nightmare,' she said, to the room.

'Who, me?' Cam asked, the picture of innocence. 'I thought I was a life-saver?'

'She means me,' Sophia said, wryly.

'Both of you,' Nina said. 'You're both as bad as each other. Cam knows exactly how handsome he is, as do his *many* female admirers.'

'Ouch,' Cam said, with another grin. 'Harsh but fair.'

'Well,' Sophia said, getting up from the table and picking up the bottle of wine, splitting the last of it between Cam and Nina's glasses. 'I think I'll turn in. Lots to do tomorrow. You two carry on, though. You won't wake me.'

'Unbelievable,' Nina said, as Sophia slipped out of the kitchen, pulling the door shut behind her. 'Sorry about that. Ignore her. I don't think I've ever met a man in her presence that she hasn't tried to marry me off to.'

Cam laughed. 'I love her. She's about as subtle as a stop sign.'

'Yes,' Nina agreed, 'which at least means I can always see her coming.'

They fell into a few moments of silence as Cam finished his meal. Nina watched him as she sipped her wine. Despite the smiles and laughter, he looked tired and she felt guilty. He had no responsibilities here besides being a good neighbour and friend. And she couldn't deny that her mother was right, he *was* good-looking. Mid-thirties with fair hair, blue eyes, tall and broad-shouldered, Cam's face was tanned by his hours outside on these cliffs he now called home. Her faint teasing of earlier was true: Cam was never short of female company, though his girlfriends never seemed to stick around for long. He'd never tried anything on with her aside from exactly the kind of gentle flirting he'd been unashamed of in front of Sophia. Nina was grateful for that, suspecting that if Bern hadn't already told Cam of her unhappy history with Barnaby's father, he'd inferred it for himself from her deliberately careful distance – and also possibly from the scar she mostly kept hidden beneath her hair but that would forever linger across her left cheek.

Cam chose that moment to look up and caught her looking at him. 'What?'

She shook her head. 'Nothing. Sorry, zoned out there for a minute.'

He looked sympathetic and she felt guilty again. He had done half of her work as well as his own today. If anyone had a right to be mentally absent it was him.

'How are you doing?' he asked.

'Oh, fine,' she said, putting down her wine glass, twisting the stem in her fingers so that it turned in a circle on the old wood. 'The wake's all organized now, the order of service will be ready to pick up from the printers tomorrow and I'm pretty sure I've managed to let everyone know who would want to be there if they can.'

Cam reached across the table and caught his fingers with hers.

'That's not what I meant,' he said, softly. 'How are *you* doing, Nina?'

She swallowed around the lump that suddenly rose in her throat, and had to take a couple of breaths before she could answer. 'I just ... miss him. That's all. I can't believe he's gone.'

Cam nodded and they sat like that for a while, until Nina pulled her hand away.

'Mum was asking about my sister earlier,' Nina said, glancing at the clock on the wall. 'I haven't even heard from her since I let her know when the funeral was going to be.'

'She'll be here,' Cam said, taking a mouthful of wine. 'You'll see.'

Nina snorted. 'That's the problem with you, Cam,' she said. 'You're determined to see the best in everybody.'

'Not everyone,' Cam said, quietly, and she thought he might have glanced at her cheek as he spoke.

Chapter Three

Bette frowned as another Vesper Martini appeared in front of her. At least, she thought it was a Vesper Martini. It was hard to see. The lights had dimmed as the music had taken on a pounding beat, a kaleidoscope of lights coruscating from above the lines of bottles behind the bar. What time was it?

'I didn't order this!' she shouted, to the man-boy behind the bar. He shrugged, indicating behind her as he put another drink down beside hers.

Bette turned to see Mae reaching for the second drink.

'Mae!' she shouted, leaning in so that her friend would hear her. 'I told you, I've got to go!'

'You can't!' Mae shouted back. 'Not yet! I just got you another drink!'

'I told you I was only stopping for one.'

Mae made a 'pfft' motion with her lips, waving her fingers to dismiss Bette's protest. The mistake had been to come out at all, Bette realized. What had she been thinking? She'd never been this person, not even when she'd been young enough for it. She should have gone home, gone over her notes one final time. She needed to pack, too.

'One more,' Mae begged, still battling to be heard against the music. 'It's been forever since you came out! Come and dance! I've got someone who wants to meet you! Couldn't you do with a bit of idle distraction right now?'

'You know what I've got to do tomorrow,' Bette pointed out. 'I need to go home, prepare, get some rest!'

Mae rested a hand on her arm. 'You've had this Locatelli thing sewn up for months,' she said, her voice carrying through the noise of the bar as well as it ever did through a courtroom. 'You should be celebrating. And we both know you won't be doing that tomorrow night, or at the weekend, or next week, and then after that you'll be too high-and-mighty to ever do this with us again.' Mae raised her eyebrows, an oblique reference to the promotion she technically wasn't supposed to know about because it, like the merger, still wasn't official. 'Let yourself have this. Everyone needs a break some time, Bette. Let yourself go — at least for one dance!'

Bette flicked her gaze towards the dance floor. It was heaving. *Who are these people who can party on a Thursday night and still get up for work tomorrow?* she wondered. *Do none of them have families, children to put to bed?* She supposed they all had partners to do that. Mae certainly did — a doting husband who was at home with their two-year-old. And the others . . . Well. They were most likely exactly like the guy Mae was trying to fit her up with. She could see him from where she sat at the bar, looking her way from the midst of the morass. Passing for late thirties but more likely early forties, raised knowing the world was shaped for him, dark hair falling over his eyes, blue pinstripe shirt open at the neck. In finance, without a doubt. Good at betting on odds with other people's futures. He had the look of the perpetual public schoolboy about him, as if he'd watched *Four Weddings* at a fatefully formative moment and Hugh Grant had become an imprint he couldn't – didn't want to – shake. Or maybe that was just how they came out of wherever he'd been made.

She thought of the pages of notes spread out across her bed that she really should take one more look at before tomorrow morning. Why, why, why had she chosen this over that? *Because you didn't want to be alone*, a voice whispered to her from her deeper self. It sounded horribly, hatefully desperate, and Greg was a perfect example of why she should never listen to it. She didn't, most of the time. Work was usually enough to drown it out. But at the moment . . .

'No,' she said to Mae. 'Absolutely bloody *not*.'

'Oh, come *on*!' Mae said. 'He's cute. Isn't he?'

'He is,' Bette agreed, 'and I will bet my imminent new salary that Greg is married with at least one child.'

Mae joined Bette in staring across the dancefloor. 'Really? You think so?'

'Yup.' Bette turned away before Nice Guy Greg could take their attention as an invitation. 'And I don't do that, Mae. Ever. You know that. Not even if they "have an arrangement".'

She picked up her drink as her phone flashed up a message. Bette didn't want to look at it in case it was Nina. Tomorrow was going to be hard enough to manage without thinking about what she had to do straight after it. Her heart constricted briefly as she thought of her father, of her family, of going somewhere that was supposed to feel like home but that she'd scrambled away from long ago and now rarely visited. She gulped her first mouthful of fresh Martini too fast, lemon twist bumping against her lip. She'd have a headache in the morning and really, why hadn't she just gone home?

'Hi there.'

Bette shot Mae a look before she turned to face him. When she did, Bette glanced at Greg's left hand and wondered why serial cheaters never worked out that it'd be a good idea to make sure they didn't have a telltale tan line where their wedding ring usually sat. Or was it just that they didn't care and they assumed the women they went for in bars like this wouldn't either? *Maybe I'm the naive one*, Bette thought. *After all, this is why I make such a good living, isn't it?*

She flipped a business card from her jacket pocket and held it out to Greg, whose eyes took on a sudden glint. He grinned at her wolfishly.

'Give that to your wife,' Bette yelled over the music, standing up before he could speak. 'Tell her to call me when she wants a divorce. Mae – I'll see you tomorrow. Get home safe. I've got to go.'

She downed the rest of the Martini, air-kissed her friend, and left, ignoring the man still holding her card in mid-air as if he'd been an unwilling participant in some sort of magic trick.

Outside, she looked at her phone. The message was there on the screen, stark and brief in the city night.

Don't disappoint Mum, was all it said.

The next day, mid-afternoon, and Bette allowed herself a swift glance out of the window, a breath of relief as the two parties present in the now-concluded meeting began to file out of the conference room. Outside the summer sun was still high over the City of London. From up here on the gleaming glass and steel of the twenty-fifth floor it was possible for her to see the unsettled glint of the Thames, the wide river's surface rippling with the passage of the tourist clippers zipping back and forth. She loved this view – would love it even more from the corner office five floors higher still that she was expecting to take possession of soon. The thought made her smile briefly. Then she felt a stab of grief. Her father was dead. Bern Crowdie was dead, and now this action was settled there was nothing left to stop her thinking about it.

Bette blinked and looked up to see her client, a successful businessman by the name of Arnold Locatelli, watching her with a shrewd look in his cold blue eyes. Behind him, his soon to be ex-wife was already a receding figure as she walked with her own lawyer out of the life the couple had shared for fifteen years.

'It's been good working with you, Ms Crowdie,' he said, as if they had merely been dealing with one of his many hostile takeovers rather than the dissolution of a long marriage. 'You've got my details. You ever tire of this place, give me a call. I might have something for you. I can always use someone like you.'

Bette schooled her flash of surprise at this declaration out of her expression. 'Thank you. I'll . . . do that.'

He nodded, and then pulled open the conference room door to leave. Bette went after him, drawing level as they reached the elevators, shaking hands with him before he stepped inside and the door slid shut.

She saw Mae at the other end of the corridor as she passed from one room into another and waved. Mae waved back, apparently none the worse for wear despite the previous night.

'Oliver!' Bette announced, walking into the office that adjoined hers with an alacrity that caused the young man behind the desk to look up with a start. 'Did you check out that flight for me?'

'Yes, Ms Crowdie,' he said. 'The last BA flight out of Heathrow to Aberdeen leaves at 9pm.'

'Book me on it, please,' she told him. 'The Locatelli action is settled. I'll be out of the office on Monday but I'll be back in on Tuesday morning. Once you've organized my flight out, you should get out of here too.'

Oliver looked a little stunned. Since he'd taken the position as her legal secretary they'd rarely left the office early. Bette wasn't known for short work hours. 'Really? Thank you, Ms Crowdie,' Oliver said.

'Make the most of it,' she advised him. 'I think things are likely to be pretty hectic when I get back. The announcement should be very soon now.'

The joining of the two firms had been rumbling on for longer even than the Locatelli divorce, but she knew the deal was now at the sharp end. In a week or two, Bette's life would change forever. She'd finally have achieved what she'd always wanted – full partnership in a successful law firm – and she was still four years off her fortieth birthday. That's what focus and hard work got you.

She went to her desk and looked at the list of calls that Oliver had taken for her while she'd been occupied with the Locatellis. There was nothing that couldn't wait, except—

14.51, call from Sophia Crowdie. Message reads: Hello, darling. We're wondering when you're going to get here. Please call when you can. I'm at home.

There was that word again. *Home.* Bette knew her mother was in Scotland, at the farm. She wondered how it had been for Sophia Crowdie to return to the place she had raised her children – although, of course, it wasn't the first time in the years that she'd split from Bern. The funeral was tomorrow, and maybe Bette herself should have been there earlier, but there was no way she could leave before closing the Locatelli divorce. It had been so close to conclusion – prevarication would have looked terrible, especially with the merger and her ascendance to partner so close. Besides, the less time she had to spend at the farm the better. She'd return her mother's call later, Bette decided, when she was on her way to the airport.

'You should get a confirmation of that flight in a minute!' Oliver called from his desk.

'Thanks!'

Bette glanced at her reflection in the window behind her desk. There was a slight kink to the ends of her short bobbed hair, the annoying and unruly curl she expended so much energy forcing into submission beginning to fight back. Her make-up remained sharp, though, the discreet hint of eye-shadow in the creases below her neat brows still doing good work of highlighting her dark eyes. Bette looked exactly as she wanted to look – in control, efficient.

Her phone beeped in her hand. Bette looked at the screen as an email confirmation of the flight Oliver had booked for her popped up on her screen. Seeing the destination made her heart pulse. She couldn't think of anywhere she wanted to go less right now than Crowdie farm, above Lunan Bay, Arbroath, Scotland.

Chapter Four

Bette woke early the next morning from a nightmare she hadn't had for years. It had rolled her into a black fug of fear, tied her up and tossed her about for a while before allowing her to wake, and so when she did the sheets were tangled and damp with sweat. It took several seconds for her to remember that she was in a hotel at Aberdeen airport, where she had landed on the last flight from Heathrow the previous night. She lay breathing hard, staring at the ceiling, frustrated to feel the familiar, aching void that was always left in the wake of that particular dream. She hated the way it made her feel so helpless.

She checked her phone, which was still open on the text of the eulogy for her father that she had fallen asleep reading late the night before. Nina had sent it to her days ago, asking if there was anything Bette had wanted to add, but it had been too painful for Bette to read. She had known she was going to have to be on top form for Locatelli that day, and couldn't deal with both. Bette had told her sister she had no time but was sure whatever Nina had chosen to put in would be perfect. She had received no reply to that message, and indeed that was the last time they had communicated since their father's death aside from the curt instruction to not let their mother down. Bette was sure that Nina was irked, but she couldn't bring herself to care. Not today.

She got out of bed, showered and dressed in her best black suit, the jacket worn over a crisp white silk shirt. As she buttoned this up Bette thought again about the nightmare. She hadn't had it for ages, but wasn't surprised it had returned now. It always resurfaced in times of stress, of which returning to the place she'd grown up was top of the list of causes. In fact, the last time she'd had it had been the last time she'd come home for a visit, pre-COVID. Before Nina, good and dutiful daughter that she was, had moved back home to take on the farm in a way that Bette had spent her life trying to avoid.

She was on the road in a hired car by a little after 8am, taking the A90 south from the city with a passable coffee in one hand and wearing a pair of sunglasses to mask the shadows of her unsettled night. Bette had contemplated going straight to the funeral rather than heading to the farm first, but had decided that she didn't want what was sure to be an emotional reunion – one way or another – with her sister to take place in front of a ton of people she either barely knew, didn't know at all or couldn't remember. Bern Crowdie had been a popular man in his long life and the event of his funeral would surely bring many of those friends together.

Besides, Bette wanted to see her mum. She'd not seen Sophia since a brief weekend trip she had taken to Naples back at Easter, where their mother was now living with her new partner. He was rather young, in Bette's opinion, it would never last, but then what did – and if it made her happy, so what?

The Crowdie farm was tucked away on the way to Dundee, above a small seaside town called Barton Mill. Once the A90 reached Stonehaven she would have to leave it for the smaller coastal A92, a journey that wouldn't take much more than an hour.

The sun was strong as she drove, the small towns and fields that stretched either side of the roads once she left the city verdant in the warmth of a late Scottish summer. Bette passed more than one roadside stall selling strawberries, some of the wares of the large soft fruit producers that thronged this area of the country. Beyond Stonehaven her eye was drawn to the dramatic hulk of Dunnottar Castle. In the Saturday morning light it crouched as a huge silhouette over the waters of the North Sea on the promontory it had occupied since the Middle Ages.

Bette tucked a short strand of hair behind her ear and drove on, down through the small town of Montrose, where she had gone to school, and across the estuary of the South Esk. By the time she reached the final turning that would take her up to her childhood home, Bette had steeled herself for the familiar route. This road and what bordered it were seared into her memory. After all, she had walked home every day come rain or shine from where the school bus would drop her off at the end of the lane. The road was shared by two farms, theirs and the Bronaghs', and often Bette would end up with Nina trailing along behind her. She had resented the responsibility of looking after her 'baby' sister but hadn't had much say in the matter. Then, of course, there were the later trips up this road when she was a little older, being dropped off after a night out, or driving herself once she had passed her test.

But no, she wouldn't think about those nights, or the person who had sat beside her on those particular journeys, however sharp his young face still was in her memory, especially after the nightmare that had woken her that morning.

Bette drove on, passing the undulating field on her right that led right up to the farmhouse. It was a large building of two storeys and a full-length attic with windows that as a child she would sequester herself beside in order to watch storms rolling onto shore. To the rear of the house would be a yard laid in concrete that she had walked across each morning to feed the chickens and the goats, a task that had always been Bette's responsibility. The yard connected the farm buildings together around a sort of courtyard that featured, besides the house itself, an open-fronted Dutch barn where the tractor and attendant equipment was kept, a milking parlour and a dairy. Beyond this little knot of structures was the strawberry patch and then more pasture, persisting all the way to the cliffs. Bette wondered what effect the erosion of two decades would have wrought on those unfettered edges. She and Nina had grown up with the mantra that they must never go near the cliffs echoing in their ears.

As the house came into view Bette slowed, the tarmac turning into a sea of toffee-coloured gravel that curved in front to the main entrance, while the tarmac track continued past the building towards the rear and the farmyard beyond. The gravel had been where guests would park – the only time the front door, protected from the Scottish wind and rain by a wooden, steepled porch, would be used. Family and close friends that might as well be family always used the back. Which was Bette now, she wondered? Technically family, obviously, but she wondered quite how her return would be received. After another moment of hesitation, she drove around the side of the house and into the farmyard, parking beside the farm's old Land Rover and a battered, red two-door Fiat – Nina's, presumably.

Getting out of the car, Bette half-expected her arrival to prompt someone to appear in the kitchen doorway, which was standing propped open by an untidy pile of shoes that were spilling over the threshold and onto the old stone step. There was no sign of anyone, although the old farmhouse kitchen had always been the place where everyone congregated when Bette had been young. As she thought this, she became aware of a sound. It was the burble of voices accompanied by music and sound effects – a television was playing inside. As she got closer she identified the sound as children's cartoons. Of course, she thought. Her nephew, Barnaby. Nina's son, whom Bette had only met twice. How old would he be now? Eight? Ten? Until she had tasked Oliver with keeping the date Bette had consistently forgotten the little boy's birthday, which she could acknowledge was one legitimate reason for her sister's persistent annoyance with her.

She stepped over the discarded shoes and pushed open the door further to go inside. There was no one in the kitchen, the sight of which caused another visceral reaction in the pit of Bette's stomach. It looked almost exactly as it had when she had lived here almost twenty years before, except that the old cathode ray television that had always stood on castors at the far end of the room had been replaced by a large flat-screen version affixed to the wall. It was the source of the noise, playing something so colourful and frenetic that it was virtually an acid trip, though there was no one watching it.

Bette suspected that the television was the only really significant change in the décor of her old home. Everything else seemed untouched, including the old sofa with large, sagging brown leather cushions and two huge matching armchairs. One was covered by an old crocheted blanket that jogged something anew in Bette's memory – it had been made by her grandmother, Jean. On the worn stripped-pine floor between the sofa and the television was a low-slung coffee table that might have been a slightly newer addition, though Bette couldn't be sure. On top of this was a slice of jammy, half-eaten toast (no plate) and a scattering of Lego bricks. There was no sign of anyone. It was as if the *Marie*

Celeste as commanded by a crew of five-year-olds had run aground amid the stormy seas of Saturday morning children's programming.

'*Rrrraaaaaarrrrrggggggghhhhhhh!*'

The childish bellow was accompanied by a volley of frantic barks and both made Bette jump despite the loud volume of the TV. She spun around to see a feral pint-sized figure wearing a black mask and cape over a matching black jumper and sweatpants. It was wielding a flashing lightsaber in one hand and there was a small collie dog at its side. Both came charging towards her from the corridor that led to the rest of the house.

'Intruder!' The child yelled, leaping onto the sofa in front of Bette and waving the toy in her face, missing her nose by millimetres while the dog bounced in place, still barking. 'Go away!'

'Barnaby?' Bette asked, taking a step back and raising both hands.

'That's not my name!' The kid shrieked, swishing the toy sword at her again. 'You're not allowed in here! Intruder!'

'Stop that!' Bette grabbed the lightsaber before it really did hit her, pulling it out of her nephew's hands – because it had to be Barnaby, nothing else made sense. 'Barnaby, my name is Bette. I'm your aunt. Your mum's sister. Calm down, for goodness's sake!'

At the loss of his weapon the boy screamed. 'Help! Help! Mum! *Mummy!*'

'Barnaby—'

36

Bette went to reach for him but the dog leapt between them, teeth bared, and for the first time Bette thought it might actually go for her.

The back door of the farmhouse crashed open hard enough to hit the wall inside with a loud bang. Bette spun around to see a young woman with olive skin, a mass of dark curly hair and fiery dark eyes storming towards her. For a strange moment Bette though it was her mother, young again, but no, because in the next second her mother appeared in the doorway too.

'Nina!' Bette exclaimed, still holding the lightsaber. 'Mum!'

The miniature superhero was hauled into her younger sister's arms as Nina looked over Barnaby's head with an angry, defiant look that hadn't changed since she was five years old herself.

'Seriously?' Nina said. 'You finally bother to turn up here the morning of Dad's funeral and the first thing you do is traumatize a child?'

'Me?' Bette spluttered. 'All I did was walk in and your little hooligan attacked me!'

'Oh yeah,' Nina said, indicating the flimsy plastic sword with contempt. 'You barely got away with your life, there. Good job.'

'Girls,' said Sophia Crowdie, coming further into the room and reaching for the TV remote, clicking it off. In the resulting quiet Bette could hear Barnaby whimpering into his mother's neck. The collie was sitting at Nina's feet, anxious eyes fixed on the crying child. 'Now let's all just take a breath, shall we?'

'She can take a breath,' Nina said, jerking her chin at Bette before turning on her heel, still carrying the boy as she stalked back out into the farmyard, the dog glued to her side. 'I've got work to do.'

Chapter Five

'It's all right,' Nina said, as she carried Barnaby out of the kitchen and into the farmyard. It was only just after nine o'clock, but the August sun was already hot. 'That's your Auntie Bette. Mummy's sister. You were just a baby the last time you saw her.'

'She stole my lightsaber,' he mumbled, his words lost against Nina's shoulder and the sound of a car engine as Cam's silver Hi-Lux pulled into the yard.

'She'll give it back,' Nina said, hugging him tighter. 'I think you scared her as much as she scared you.'

'Everything okay?' Cam asked, climbing out of the truck.

'Fine,' Nina said, 'except for the fact that my sister's finally turned up. She and Barney—'

'Best Barnaby Barnacle.'

'—Best Barnaby Barnacle gave each other a bit of a fright.'

'Anything I can do?' Cam asked, ruffling Barnaby's hair as Nina put him down. He was already dressed for the funeral,

Nina noticed, in a dark grey suit she'd never seen him in before. He'd left the first two buttons of the shirt open, but she could see a black tie rolled up in his top pocket. Nina looked down at herself in comparison, dressed in dirty old jeans and a grimy striped T-shirt. Her nails were caked in dirt.

'Mum and I just finished picking the strawberry order for Merson's. Jen will be here at any minute to collect them for the grocery. They're still in the polytunnel – they're in punnets but they need boxing.'

'I'm on it,' Cam said, and then looked at Barnaby. 'Hey, superhero. Seems we've got an emergency. Can I rely on Best Barnaby Barnacle to spring into action?'

The boy nodded vigorously. 'I know exactly what to do,' he said. 'Follow me!'

Nina watched as he and Limpet took off in the direction of the polytunnel behind the barn, relieved that the upset with Bette seemed to be forgotten. It was going to be an emotional enough day for them all as it was. Nina already felt tired, wrung out in a way her body usually saved for the end of the day. She hadn't slept much.

'You go ahead and do what you need to do,' Cam said, heading after Barnaby, who had already vanished around the side of the barn. 'I'll keep him occupied.'

'Thanks, Cam.'

He lifted one hand in a cheerful wave as he went. For the millionth time Nina wondered what she'd do without him.

She went back inside to find that Sophia had put the kettle

on. The sound of boiling water filled the kitchen. The way the two women were standing, so close together, surprised her. She'd never thought of Bette as being willing to be in close proximity to anyone. When Nina thought of her sister, she always imagined her at a distance – from everywhere and everything, an unreachable island in a rushing stream. Bette Crowdie, to her knowledge, never let anyone close, either physically or emotionally. She assumed her sister had friends and partners down there in London, but no one significant enough to tell her family about, or that seemed to last for long.

Bette looked up as Nina came in. 'I'm sorry,' she said, an apology that surprised Nina even more, both for the fact that it existed at all and was apparently genuine. 'I didn't mean to scare him. He didn't know who I was.'

'Well,' Nina said, 'that's not really surprising, is it?'

'Nina,' her mum cautioned, her back still turned as she filled the old teapot. 'Let's not argue. Not today.'

Nina shrugged. 'Fine. Talk to him later, maybe without yelling. And apologize for stealing his lightsaber. That might help.'

A flicker of annoyance crossed Bette's face. 'I didn't steal it. He nearly took my eye out with it! And that dog—'

'Girls,' her mother said in warning, interrupting before Nina could retort. 'Nina, do you want tea?'

'No,' Nina said. 'I've still got too much to do. I need to get showered and changed and then I need to go over to the village hall to make sure the catering's sorted for the wake,

41

and on the way *there* I have to deliver the order of service to the chapel of rest so they can give them out as people arrive.'

'Is there anything I can do?' Bette asked.

Nina stared at her. 'Is there anything you can do three hours before a funeral you've had absolutely zero hand in organizing up until this point? No, Bette, there isn't. You put your feet up and have a nice cup of tea so you can recover from your strenuous journey into the boondocks. I know just making that effort was a nightmare for you.'

She walked out of the kitchen, leaving a silence behind her as heavy as lead.

The funeral went well, or at least as well as these things can. The service was packed with Bern's many friends. Afterwards most of them came to the wake to tell stories of the man they remembered, some as far back as their school days, sixty or more years before. *The place won't be the same without him*, they said, and *Bern Crowdie was one of a kind*. Nina cried and laughed, holding Barnaby, her boy bewildered by the whole event. Bette was calm throughout. Nina wondered whether she was employing some lawyerly trick to disguise her emotions or whether her sister did not in fact have any to display. She was probably counting the minutes until she could leave, and Nina wondered when Bette's flight back was. Tonight? That afternoon even, perhaps. Maybe she'd even go straight to the airport from the wake once it was over. Nina knew for sure she wouldn't want to stick around for longer than absolutely necessary. It was sad, but Nina was relieved. Life was just easier when they were further apart. They had absolutely nothing in common. Perhaps it was as simple as the age gap being too great. Bette had spent a decade being the only child before Nina, whom she had never seen as anything other than a sheer annoyance, came along. Perhaps there was never going to be a way to bridge that. Nina wished she'd been able to understand that when she was little. It would have saved her a lot of wishing and disappointment.

Once the wake had wound down, though, and the guests had begun to make their departures, Sophia revealed other ideas.

'You'll come back to the house with us, won't you?' she asked Bette. 'You'll stay with us until Monday night? I'm here until then and we all have so much catching up to do.'

'Mum!' Nina said, a little more sharply than she'd intended.

Her mother gave her a steady look. 'What?' she asked. 'Have you forgotten that the will is being read on Monday? Bette should be there.'

Nina looked at Bette. 'Do you *want* to be there?'

'I don't *want* anything about this weekend,' her sister said, with a studied patience that just infuriated Nina more. 'But Mum called me last week and asked me to come with you both to the solicitor. It's just a formality, anyway, isn't it? We both know the terms: he left everything physical to you. That was the agreement. I'd just take part of the yearly income instead of getting a share of the farm itself.'

Nina snorted. 'What yearly income?'

Bette frowned and looked as if she were about to open her mouth to speak, but their mother spoke up instead.

'That's why I thought it important that you should be there with us, Bette,' Sophia said, beginning to busy herself with the clearing of plates. The village hall was all but empty now. 'Your father called me a few months ago, to let me know he had adjusted his will. He didn't say in what way, just that he'd been thinking about things a lot over the past year.'

Bette looked as unsettled by this statement as Nina felt. 'I told him he didn't need to do that,' she murmured.

'And when did you do that, exactly?' Nina asked. 'On one of the many times you called to see how he was doing?'

'Nina,' their mother said, more sharply this time.

'What? Have I said something that isn't true?'

'We emailed,' Bette said.

Nina wasn't sure she'd heard that right. 'Sorry?'

'We emailed,' Bette repeated. 'That's how we kept in touch. There were things he wanted to tell me, sometimes.'

This was an utter shock to hear. Her father had never mentioned hearing from Bette. Nina had assumed their lines of communication were as closed off as they'd become between the sisters themselves.

'He was my dad too, Nina,' Bette said, a flash of irritation breaking out from beneath the still facade. 'Maybe he decided he had something he wanted me to remember him by.'

'What things?' Nina asked.

Bette frowned again. 'I don't know. Maybe one of

Grandma's paintings from the wall in the front room? Or some of his books?'

'No,' Nina said. 'I meant, what things did he want to tell you? In these email conversations of yours?'

Bette looked away. 'Nothing much. News about the farm, how he was doing, television he'd watched. General things. I'm going to go out and get some fresh air.'

Nina and Sophia watched her go in silence. 'Did you know about that?' she asked, once they were alone.

'No,' her mother admitted. 'But it doesn't surprise me.'

Nina frowned. 'Really? Well, it surprises *me*. I didn't think Bette wanted anything to do with the farm – or us.'

'That's not true,' her mother tutted. 'Not everything is black and white, Nina. Bette always wanted a different life, that's all. Farming was never for her. And then—' Sophia broke off.

'And then what?'

Sophia sighed. 'And then nothing. She went away and had the brilliant life she wanted to have.'

There was something else her mother had been about to say, Nina was sure of it, but she didn't press the subject. Nina wasn't sure she could take many more emotional revelations on this day. Besides, she had the sense that her mother understood her eldest daughter in a way that would never allow her to see Nina's side of the argument.

'There aren't enough beds for her to stay,' she said, instead. 'You're in the guest room. Barnaby's got what used to be her room and there's no way I'm turfing him out just so Bette can have a bed to sleep in. Which means there isn't one unless she wants to stay in Dad's old room. And I'm pretty sure I know what she'll say to that.'

Her mother patted her arm. 'There's still the camp bed in the attic, isn't there? She can stay up there.'

Nina actually laughed at that. 'Bette? In the attic? You must be joking.'

Sophia smiled. 'She used to love it up there. It was her hideaway from the world.'

'She'll freak out,' Nina said, convinced of her own words. 'She'll want a decent hotel room or nothing at all. Chocolates on the pillows, rainwater showers, all that malarky. The most we've got to offer is an Aldi knock-off Penguin and a leaky mixer tap.'

Her mother shook her head. 'You don't know your sister as well as you think you do, darling. Trust me, if she's staying at the farmhouse, the attic is where she'd choose to be anyway.' Sophia slipped an arm around Nina's shoulders and tipped her forehead gently against hers. 'This is exactly what the two of you need. To spend some time together under one roof. To get to know each other again, as adults.'

'Not sure about that,' Nina said. 'I think it's more likely we'll end up killing each other.'

Chapter Six

When Bette woke the next morning, it was to the dust and cobwebs of the attic and the creak of a camp bed that should have been landfill years before. For a moment she stared up at the gabled ceiling, wondering what had woken her from what had been a surprisingly deep sleep. Then she heard the sounds of voices emanating from outside, followed by the growl of a quad bike engine as it departed the farmyard, the closing of the kitchen door on the ground floor and the fading tramp of heavy boots across concrete as someone else left the house on foot. The light filtering through the curtainless attic windows was dim, the late summer sun only just beginning to rise. Bette looked at her watch and saw that it was barely four in the morning. Even with her habit of going to the gym before work, this was far too early for her, and yet here she was, wide awake. She lay listening to the house, but could hear no other movement from below.

Staying at the farm had been made a little easier because

of where she'd slept. Bette was oddly comfortable where she was, despite the unadorned sparseness of the camp bed and her surroundings. She felt refreshed, notwithstanding the early hour and the circumstances in which she had slept – because, she realized with surprise, she had actually slept. She couldn't remember the last time she'd slept through an entire night without waking. It must be something about this space. Whatever connotations the farm as a whole had for her now, this had always been her retreat as a child, high up here in the eaves. It had been her place to think, to play, to dream among the many boxes of discarded possessions that had been stacked in its dusty corners. It seemed the same was true, even now. Although Bette realized as she looked around that the attic space was far less cluttered than she remembered, as if someone had made an effort to clear the place.

Two nights, she told herself. *This will be fine for two nights. The days . . . you'll just have to cope with.* An uncomfortable emotion skated through her heart as she thought about the will reading. She knew exactly why Bern had wanted to change his will and what he'd wanted to leave her, even though she'd told him he didn't need to. If she was really honest, though, Bette didn't hate the idea of the look on Nina's face when she was told in black and white what her sister had done. It'd make it difficult for Nina to cast her as the villain for once, wouldn't it? That would make a nice change.

The sun continued to rise, the warming light filtering

through the window to illuminate the dust motes floating in the air. It was peaceful here, curled beneath the thick duvet that Nina had silently dragged out of an airing cupboard for her the previous night. Bette thought about getting up and doing some yoga in lieu of the run she couldn't embark on for want of kit, but instead she felt herself drifting back into sleep. As she went, a memory rose around her, of herself at a younger age, pulling something out of the gentle concealment of a box in one of the attic's corners. An old book, familiar and yet not thought of for decades, existing now only on the periphery of Bette's consciousness, and her last thought before sleep was that she would examine this memory more closely later in the day.

Bette woke again sometime later, roused by more noise downstairs, and immediately forgot her half-asleep promise to herself. The sound from below was exponentially louder than before. She could hear the tinny sound of a radio and raucous voices singing along. The sun through the window was strong now and she looked at her watch to discover that it was 8am.

Downstairs, the noise level was absurd. It sounded as if a herd of elephants was playing basketball to the accompaniment of duelling karaoke singers. She walked into the kitchen to see Nina and Barnaby (complete with superhero costume intact) both headbanging to Sisters of Mercy, a risky move for Nina in particular given that she was standing at the stove with one hand on a frying pan, in which she was cooking bacon and eggs.

'Morning, Bette, darling!' Bette jumped as a hand landed

on her shoulder and her mother appeared cheerily from the hallway behind her, apparently unperturbed by the cacophony. 'Ready for some breakfast?'

At the sound of Sophia's voice, which was loud enough to surf the brief quiet between notes, Nina and Barnaby both turned, stopping their frenetic dancing. In one swift movement, Nina flicked off the radio and the kitchen descended into a silence broken only by sizzling bacon fat.

'Morning,' Bette offered.

'I forgot you were upstairs,' her nephew said. 'Nana says you slept in the attic. Did you really?'

'I did.'

'Your aunt used to sleep up there all the time when she was little,' Sophia said, bustling past her grandson to take plates out of the cupboard. 'The first time she did it she was probably only your age. Scared me to death to find her gone out of her own bed in the morning.'

Barnaby stared at Bette with wide eyes from behind his mask. 'But didn't you mind the spiders?'

Bette smiled faintly. 'I like spiders,' she confessed. 'They get rid of the flies, and I hate flies.'

'My sister, the stealth goth,' Nina muttered, from the stove. She threw Bette a glance. 'I've got enough bacon left for a sandwich, if you want one.'

'Ahh,' Sophia said, 'not yet. Bette's got chores to do first.'

Bette felt her eyebrows rising. 'Chores?'

'The chickens need feeding,' her mother told her. 'That was always your job, wasn't it?'

Bette baulked at the idea. 'I haven't done that for years! I'm not sure I remember where anything is.'

'Not a problem,' Sophia said, 'Barnaby knows all that, don't you?'

'Best Barnaby Barnacle,' the boy said, with what would probably have been a look of slight reproach had they been able to see his face beneath the black mask.

'Best Barnaby Barnacle knows where everything is and what needs to be done,' Sophia Crowdie corrected herself without a beat, 'and he will be happy to show you. Won't you?'

Bette watched as her nephew looked from his grand-mother, to his mother, to her.

'Okay,' he said, a little doubtful but determined. 'Let's go.'

He went to the door and wrestled on his wellington boots. Bette threw her mother a look.

'Go on,' Sophia said, while Nina kept her back turned. 'I'm not kidding. And hurry up, because if Cam comes in first, we'll give him your bacon.'

Bette stood there for another moment. Sophia raised her eyebrows and crossed her arms.

'All right, all right,' Bette said. 'I'm going.'

She went out into the yard to find Barnaby and the dog waiting for her. Barnaby passed her one of the buckets he held.

'First we need to go and get the grain,' he said.

'Right,' Bette said. 'Is the grain store still in the barn?'

'Yes, beside the tractor,' Barnaby looked up at her, obviously surprised. 'How did you know that?'

'I used to live here, remember?' Bette told him. 'When I was your age, and when I was older. It was always my job to feed the chickens and goats every day.'

'We don't have goats anymore,' the boy said, as they reached the barn and Bette followed him into the shadowed interior. 'They kept getting out and eating all the strawberries.'

'Yeah,' Bette said, remembering all the times she'd wasted hours trying to catch escapees. 'They're terrible for that. They'll eat anything.'

'One ate my shoe,' Barnaby said in a tone of agreement. 'That's when Mum got really angry. It was a school shoe, too. I had to wear my trainers and take a note to explain why I wasn't in uniform for a whole week until we could go shopping for new ones.'

It was cool inside the barn, out of the rising sun's rays. It smelled of the discarded hay scattered on the floor alongside the patches of oil, stacked palettes, empty feed tubs, broken equipment and assorted other detritus that had no doubt been put there 'for the minute' but somehow never moved on. Bette looked around, seeing how little had changed, feeling the strange stirrings of memories long pushed away. The John Deere had been the only tractor the farm possessed for as long as she could remember, their finances in no way stretching to a replacement or even a lease on a new one. Bette looked at it now, sturdy but worn and out of date. She remembered being her nephew's age, bouncing along on the ancillary seat beside her dad, the skewed angle uncomfortable but inconsequential beside her pride at being essential as they raced to get the hay in ahead of whatever summer rainstorm threatened the horizon. Bette blinked, feeling something stir in her chest. She took a breath.

'Auntie Bette! Over here!'

Barnaby was levering up the heavy lid of the feed bin. Bette went to help him, catching it midway and lifting it out of his hands to tip it against the wall of the barn. Together they dipped their buckets into the dry grain, Bette helping pull the boy's load out and over onto the floor.

'Do you do this every morning?' Bette asked. 'That's a big job for you to do all on your own.'

He was quiet for a moment as together they shut the feed bin again. 'I used to do it with Grandad.'

'I'm sorry,' she said. 'I miss him too.'

Barnaby sniffed. 'Yeah.'

'Have you given all your hens names?' Bette asked, thinking it best to move the conversation on. She'd have no idea what to do if he started to cry. 'I used to name mine after my favourite pop stars.'

'Like who?' the boy asked, as they headed for the chicken coop.

Bette grimaced. She thought it unlikely he'd know all the names of the Spice Girls. 'I'm not sure you'll know any of them. What are yours called?'

'They have numbers instead of names.'

'Numbers?'

'Yeah, like the Doctor in *Doctor Who*. Except that it

doesn't work anymore because I'd have to have another one exactly like Ten and that's impossible unless I can find a chicken cloning machine and I don't think that's practical, really.'

Bette had absolutely no idea what he was talking about but wasn't convinced an explanation would help and so opted for detached agreement. 'Right.'

She saw the coop ahead, in the patch of pasture in front of the polytunnel. It had changed since the last time she'd seen it, but that was no surprise given that would have been at least ten years ago. Barnaby opened the door of the surrounding enclosure and the hens rushed towards him, clucking happily with their funny, rocking gait. The boy looked up at her, a pair of brown eyes blinking at her kindly from behind the ubiquitous mask.

'You throw them some first,' he said, generously. 'Then they'll be your friends, too.'

Bette had never wanted chickens as friends, but did as she was told. The daft birds scattered after the grain, pecking and scratching happily in the dirt. After a moment she realized she was smiling.

'They like you,' Barnaby said.

She turned to find that he'd put the grain bucket down and taken an old iPhone out of his pocket instead. He held it up, framing a photograph of his little flock.

'Grandad gave it to me so I can take a picture every day,' he said, when he saw her watching. 'It's a project. To record how they grow.'

Bette smiled. 'That's a clever idea. Which one is Ten?' He pointed to a hen with a streak of white feathers amid chestnut brown. 'Oh yes,' she said. 'Very handsome. And definitely not cloneable, I'd say.'

Barnaby tossed another handful of grain. After a moment he said, 'I'm sorry I nearly lightsabered you, Auntie Bette.'

'And I'm sorry I scared you. I didn't mean to.'

'Yeah,' he sighed. 'I know. These things just happen sometimes. Truce?'

'Definitely. Do you have any other chores around the farm?' Bette asked. 'I used to help out with milking sometimes, but I was probably a bit older than you when I did that.'

'I help mummy pick the strawberries,' her nephew said. 'And at the weekends it's my job to feed the horses and the donkey in the evening. I help muck them out too, sometimes, but that's stinky.'

'You've got horses here?' Bette asked, surprised. 'Your mum used to ride when she was little, but she always went to a friend's place to do that, we didn't have our own.'

'They're not ours,' Best Barnaby Barnacle said. 'They're Cam's. He says we can ride them whenever we like but mum told me if that was the case I needed to pitch in and learn how to look after them. It's okay – I like it. Also a superhero sometimes needs a steed, so it's a good idea for me to be their friends in case of an emergency.'

Bette smiled. 'Barney—'

'Best Barnaby Barnacle.'

55

Bette paused, and then started again. 'Yes. Best Barnaby Barnacle, can I ask you a question?'

He scattered one more handful of grain before putting down the bucket and shuffling backwards to perch on the coop steps. 'Okay.'

'Can I ask you where you got your name from? Why are you Best Barnaby Barnacle?'

There was a silence, and for a moment Bette thought that she wasn't going to get an answer at all. Then he shrugged, raising both hands and shoulders in an expansive gesture.

'Technically I'm supposed to be Barnaby. Or Barney, for short. But I wanted a superhero name. Do you know what a barnacle is, Auntie Bette?'

'Yes,' she said. 'It's a little sea creature in a shell, isn't it? It lives in salt water and sticks to rocks and boats.'

He nodded, something of the solemn sage. 'That's right. It sticks and sticks and nothing can make it move. Not storms or someone poking it with a stick or something trying to eat it. Nothing. It just stays right there.'

'Okay . . .' Bette said, not sure she understood.

'I'm Best Barnaby Barnacle because I am always here,' he added. 'Barnacles have superhero strength and they always stick. No one can make them go anywhere. They stick, no matter what. That's me. I'm Best Barnaby Barnacle, and I'll stick around no matter what. Limpet's the same. We're not going anywhere, ever. Not like everyone else.'

'Well,' Bette said. 'That sounds like a pretty good super-hero to me, Best Barnaby Barnacle.'

She couldn't be sure, but she thought he might have given her a beaming smile. It showed in his eyes. She smiled back, wondering about all the history she didn't know about this part of her family.

Chapter Seven

'How about I make dinner tonight?' Bette said, a little later, once she and Barnaby had returned from collecting the eggs from the chicken coop and finished their breakfast.

'That's a lovely idea, darling,' said her mother.

Nina, on the other hand, frowned. 'You can cook?'

'Of course I can cook.'

'I just kind of assumed that with your very important life and very fancy job, you'd be too busy for that.'

'Nina,' their mother warned.

'It's fine, Mum,' Bette told her. 'Nina, I know you've had a lot on lately, what with organizing the funeral and looking after the farm on your own. I get that you're angry with me for not helping with any of that. Take a break from one thing today and I'll cook. Unless you really don't want me to, which is fine. It's all the same to me. But I'm offering. It's your call.'

Her sister sighed. 'Fine. Okay.'

'Will there be anywhere open locally where I can get supplies on a Sunday?' Bette asked, opting to ignore the ire in her sister's tone.

'Hang on.' Sophia went over to the month-by-month calendar hanging on the wall beside the kitchen door. The image for August was of Lunan Bay, its grass-edged sand curving into the distance under a pure blue sky full of the white-grey flashes of kittiwakes on the wing. 'I noticed this the other day. There's a farmer's market down in the village today. You could try that?'

'A farmer's market in Barton Mill?' Bette said, surprised. 'I wouldn't have thought it'd be busy enough to draw in much custom.'

'It's changed a bit since you last visited,' her sister said. 'Things tend to do that when you can't be bothered to pay attention.'

'Nina,' Sophia said.

'It's fine, Mum,' Bette said. 'Let her sulk. It's bringing back a lot of memories.'

Nina might have made some kind of retort but Bette wasn't listening. What would being out and about in her old stomping grounds be like? Who might she bump into? There was one person in particular she was thinking about, of course – the same person who always dominated her thoughts of the farm, of home, of her younger years. Bette pushed her worries away. The chances of running into him by accident were slim to zero, so why was she even think-ing about this? *This is the problem with being here at all,* Bette thought, exasperated with herself. *Everything here leads back to him, even now.*

She felt eyes on her and glanced up to see her mother looking at her speculatively from across the table, as if she knew exactly what Bette was thinking.

'Do you want me to come with you?' her mother asked, as Bette got up from the table and carried her breakfast plate to the sink.

'No, I'll be fine, thanks,' Bette said, not keen to give her mother any opportunity to pry. 'Just give me a shopping bag and I'll be off.'

The village of Barton Mill was built around a natural cove in Lunan Bay, at the bottom of a triangular cleft between two cliffs. North Sea storms being what they were, most of the original houses were built gable-end on to the water, with the exception being the harbour master's office, a small square building that stood at one end of the short sea wall, and the Silver Darling pub, which stood at the other. Aside from the large stately Georgian home that stood back from the cliff, still home to the Greville family of gentry that had owned most of the land in the area back in the day, there were perhaps fifty houses tiered either side of the road that led down to sea level. They were connected horizontally by narrow streets that went nowhere and vertically by footpaths that straggled down in haphazard fashion between gardens and homes to eventually end up at the promenade that curved around the tiny marina. Larger modern houses had sprung up since Bette's last visit, looming from the top of the cliffs where there had once been thriving tenant farms. Most of them were likely to be holiday lets doing brisk business over the summer.

Bette squeezed the car into a parking space. Even knowing that there was a farmer's market on, she was surprised by how busy the place was. She remembered Barton Mill as a sleepy, barely-there place with nothing to attract anyone for longer than the time it would take to walk along the short, curving promenade and back again. Today, though, the place was packed with people. She joined the throng and made her way down to the waterfront, following signs that pointed the way to the promenade and market. When Bette reached the point where the road opened out to give a view of the bay, she stopped, taken aback. What she could see bore little resemblance to what she remembered.

The road that divided the village's small promenade from the line of buildings closest to the shore had been temporarily made into a pedestrian-only thoroughfare to accommodate both the handful of white market tents that had been erected on the stone slabs and the people wanting to visit them. There was a butcher, a fishmonger, a bakery, a dairy with an array of cheeses, a florist and a grocer, all stocked with beautiful local produce. Meanwhile, on the other side of the road, Bette noted with surprise that there were several signs outside some of the buildings. All she could remember of this place from when she lived here were an intermittent ice cream van and a paltry post office. But now there was a small café with tables set out to take advantage of the closed road. There was even a gift shop called North Sea Treasures. It was all so far from what she had remembered of the place that Bette felt as if she'd never been here before. It went some way to ease the latent anxiety that had tangled in the pit of her stomach as she meandered past the market stalls.

As she reached the end, though, there was the Silver Darling pub, unchanged. Its appearance took her back into the past with a sharp shock. A large, grey stone building of three storeys, it was where she'd had her first legal drink once she'd turned eighteen, a ritual Bern Crowdie had introduced her to alongside accompanying cheers from the habitual bar-flies. The pub also had tables outside, beneath umbrellas set on the grey granite slabs that edged the turning circle at the end of the promenade road. The sea wall met this small patio, where a series of steps led down to the edge of the marina and the small knot of boats moored in it. Bette wandered closer, remembering long evenings spent sat on this wall, legs dangling down over the water. She also knew that if she searched, she might still be able to find the place where two names had been etched into one of the stones beside each other. She took a breath and made herself go closer, just to break the spell.

After a moment she turned away and headed back to the stalls. Part of her stayed there on that old wall, though. Something in her could not bring itself to move from that little spot – had perhaps, in fact, never moved on at all.

Chapter Eight

'Oh, my goodness – *Beth*?'

The voice was female and came from behind her as Bette considered possibilities for dinner. It wasn't until it sounded again, this time accompanied by her full name and a touch to her arm, that Bette realized the speaker was talking to her.

'Beth Crowdie?'

Bette turned to see a woman at her side. She only came up to Beth's shoulder, but that was not unusual. Her thick blonde hair was cut into a bob that framed round, smiling features, blue eyes, a wide smile that creased a few lines around her mouth. She was dressed in cream linen trousers and a French stripe top beneath a matching linen jacket – smarter than expected for a Sunday outing to a farmer's market.

'It *is* you – I thought so!' the woman went on. 'My goodness, it's been what – eighteen years? How *are* you?'

Bette was suddenly accosted by the memory of a sunny

day – of *many* sunny days, of laughter, of singing along to the radio, of sharing gossip and–– *Allie.*

'You look *exactly* the same,' said Allie Bright, looking Bette up and down. 'I'd have known you anywhere, despite the short hair. Although honestly, I'd forgotten just how tall you are. How's things? I heard about Bern – I'm sorry. I couldn't make the funeral, but I did send flowers. He was such a character, your dad. I loved hanging out at your place more than anywhere else.'

'Allie! I'm so sorry – I didn't recognize you.' Bette was experiencing a moment of pure overwhelm. Allie. Her best friend all the way through school. They'd spent every day together for years, they had been utterly inseparable, told each other everything. And then Bette had gone to university. Then she'd begun to run and she'd left everything behind, even her best friend.

'It's fine,' Allie said, still smiling. 'It's been a long time – a lifetime, in fact.' She glanced across the road, through the milling throng of people. 'Look, I need to get back. I own the shop over there, North Sea Treasures. If you've got time, why don't you pop over when you've finished shopping? I'd love to catch up, Beth. I hated that we lost touch.'

'Yes,' Bette said. 'Okay. That would be great.'

Allie smiled again, warm and genuine, and nodded. A moment later she was crossing the road, dodging between the eddies of shoppers. Bette was frozen in place for a moment, wondering why her instinct had been to say yes to her old friend instead of no. She could quite truthfully say that she was expected back at home, that she couldn't spare the time. And yet something had compelled her to say yes to this person whom she hadn't seen in two decades.

'Excuse me?'

She turned back to the stall to see the butcher watching her.

'Sorry,' the man said, gruffly. 'But if you're not going to buy something . . .' He gestured to the crowd milling around her, and Bette realized she was blocking the way.

'I'm sorry,' she said, flustered again and hating herself for this uncharacteristic uncertainty. 'I'll take a joint of beef, please'.

After the butchers she bought vegetables and apples, thinking that she could make a crumble for dessert, assuming that Nina would have flour, butter and sugar already. Once all her purchases had been made Bette hesitated, in view of the door of North Sea Treasures, looking at the pretty sign painted in blue on the soft sheen of a cream background, and wondering if she could slip past and away unnoticed by her old friend. But then Allie appeared on the doorstep and caught her eye with a grin.

'Kettle's on,' she said, in a merry tone that Bette remembered now as always being a hallmark of her friend. 'Come on. I've got shortbread!'

Allie disappeared inside again and Bette found herself following, stepping over the threshold and into the little shop. Inside, she found a small room dedicated to the display of jewellery, pottery, greetings cards and knick-knacks. As she looked around, Allie busied herself at the back of the shop, where there was a smaller ante-room with rows of clothes that looked to have been chosen for their colours – all toned by the sea and the shore, blue in all its shades, turquoise, azure, sand, stone, rock and coral.

'Come and take a seat,' Allie said, indicating the small sofa and coffee table that sat at the back of the space. 'I'll get up if anyone comes in.' She put a teapot down beside a plate of shortbread.

'Your stock is beautiful,' Bette said, as she did as she was told.

'Thank you,' Allie smiled. 'I only stock local artisans. Well, mostly local – I've stretched the definition a little so that I can have some pottery from a woman up in in Gardenstown. But that's as distant as my reach gets. We have some talented people in these parts, eh?'

Bette pondered the 'we' in that sentence as she joined Allie on the sofa. Was she still classed as a local even though she'd left so long ago?

'Well,' Allie said, as she passed Bette a mug of tea in a hand-thrown mug glazed with the seashore colours of a rock pool. 'Tell me *everything*, Beth Crowdie. What have you been up to since I saw you last?'

Bette took the mug and cradled it in both hands. 'Well,' she said, a little awkwardly, 'I suppose the first thing to say is that I don't go by "Beth" anymore. Everyone knows me as Bette now.'

'Ah,' Allie said. 'That must have happened after we stopped writing? Why did you decide to change, if you don't mind me asking?'

It was true, Bette realized. They had tried to stay in touch via email in the first months after Bette had started university, but then everything had happened, and Bette hadn't been able to cope with anything that reminded her of home. She'd thrown herself into work instead. Then had come the first summer break, and instead of returning to the farm, Bette had found an internship at a law firm in Oxford, and by the time the new year had started, the contact had dried up completely and had never restarted.

'It felt more hard-nosed than "Beth",' Bette said, 'and I realized early on that anything that could give me an edge was worth it.'

'I'll do my best to remember,' Allie said, offering the plate of crumbly shortbread. 'You always seemed like such a perfect "Beth" to me – tall, willowy, beautiful, confident.' She glanced Bette's way with a grin. 'You're still all those things, clearly.'

Bette covered her faint discomfort at this compliment by taking a biscuit. 'To be honest, I can't even remember being Beth now.'

'Well, the name change explains why I could never find you on social media,' Allie said. 'I'd look, every now and then, usually when a memory of one of our daft teenage escapades occurred to me. But nothing ever came up.'

'I've never really done social media anyway,' Bette said.

'I don't really like the idea of just anyone being able to find you.'

There was a moment of silence between them, and Bette was sure that Allie knew exactly the person that Bette wouldn't want appearing out of the past to tag her online.

'Totally understand that,' Allie said, filling the silence, 'although it is a good way to avoid losing touch with people.'

'Bern always knew how to get hold of me,' Bette pointed out.

Allie smiled. 'I've not been here myself much until the last few years,' she said. 'Flying visits to see Mum and Dad, mainly. I moved north after I finished college – like, *really* north. My kids were born in Kirkwall.'

'You lived in *Orkney*?' Bette asked, her astonishment overcoming her awkwardness. 'How did that happen?'

Allie laughed. 'I met my ex at college. He's from there – a vet. He was always intending to go back and where better to be for an aspiring archaeologist than up near the Ring of Brogdar? I headed up the seasonal dig there for quite a few years.'

'Wait,' Bette said, struggling to keep up. 'What? You're . . . an archaeologist?'

'Aye,' Allie said. 'Or at least, I was.'

'But,' said Bette, more and more coming back to her now as she sat here with her old friend, 'you were going to paint, weren't you? Didn't you do a Fine Art course? I remember how beautiful your artwork was.'

Allie's smile shallowed a little and she glanced away, down

into the shop. 'I still paint. And believe me, Orkney was a perfect place for that. I've got a range of cards in here,' she nodded at a turning display on the shop's counter, and Bette saw watercolour images of land and seascapes. 'But ... let's just say my first attempt at university didn't go so well. I ended up dropping out towards the end of my second year. After that I came home for a while. In the end a part–time course in archaeology caught my eye. I'd always been inter-ested in that kind of thing. Don't you remember all the times we spent looking for fossils in Lunan Bay?'

'Oh yes,' Bette laughed. 'You had eyes like a hawk. I re-member your poor mum trying to find room for all those little bits and pieces you brought back.'

'Treasure!' Allie laughed, 'It was all treasure! Anyway, Mum and Dad encouraged me to go for it. I think they were relieved I was showing an interest in something – anything – again.' She shrugged. 'It turned out to be the best decision I've ever made, by far. And the rest, as they say ... is history. Literally!'

The other woman's cheerful tone and wide smile had returned, but it was obvious that Allie had been through something traumatic enough to change the course of her career and with it, her life. And Bette hadn't known about it. She hadn't been around, even in spirit, for someone she had once thought would be her best friend forever.

'I'm sorry,' she said, now. 'For not making more of an effort to stay in touch. I'm sorry that I— that I wasn't here.'

Allie smiled again. 'I won't lie and say I didn't miss you,' she said. 'But I understood, Bette. You already had your own troubles to deal with, why would you want mine as well? And everything else— Life just happens, doesn't it? You were never going to stay here anyway, we all knew that. And hey, it wasn't as if I was here either, after that. Away I went to the Islands and immersed myself in my work and family.'

Bette smiled a little. 'You've got two kids, you say?'

'Aye, two boys. Well – I say boys, but they're both at uni now. Marine biology, both of them – must have been all the time they spent on the beach as kids. I fully expect Tom to vanish off to the other side of the world, or at least back up to Orkney, to do his PhD. And his brother's always been right there in his footsteps. The latter is what their dad is hoping for, anyway.'

'Oh?' Bette said. 'Then you're not—'

'Still together? No, not anymore. The boys went off to uni and then COVID happened, the digs all closed down and Mum and Dad needed me, and ...' Allie sighed. 'Anyway, you don't want to hear all about that.'

'I do,' Bette said, and realized that she meant it. She couldn't remember the last time she'd sat and chatted with a friend, the occasional rushed lunch with Mae notwithstanding. Despite the length of time since they'd seen each other and all the water that had passed beneath the bridges of their lives in the intervening years, there was something about sitting here listening to her old friend that made Bette feel as if it was only yesterday since their last meeting. She'd missed Allie, Bette realized, without even knowing it. 'I'm only here until tomorrow night and I can't leave without knowing *everything*.'

Allie glanced at Bette's empty mug. 'Shall I make another pot, then? Because honestly, Bette – ditto.'

Chapter Nine

'I can't believe that even Bette would be *this* selfish,' Nina raged.

'Nina,' Sophia said, 'I'm sure that whatever's happened, there's an explanation.'

'Yes — the explanation is that my older sister has never thought about anyone else in her entire life.'

It was gone seven and Bette had yet to materialize to cook the fabled dinner she had promised them all, despite having left to shop for it before lunch. Sophia had tried calling her mobile to find out where she was, but there was no signal in Barton Mill and it would appear that either Bette was still there or she had turned off her phone. Sophia had expressed worry, but Nina was just angry. She had made her son dinner to keep his evening routine, but their mother had suggested the two women wait a little longer.

'I have to go up and say goodnight to Barney and then I've got to see to the cows,' Nina said. 'Cam's out tonight, I told him not to worry about doing it himself. If she does turn up, eat without me. I'll have a bowl of soup when I get back.'

'Nina—'

There came the sound of a car engine outside and the flash of headlamps through the dim windows as it pulled into the farmyard.

'There, you see?' Sophia said. 'Here she is now.'

'I'm going,' Nina said. 'If I see her I'll say something I'll regret. Or rather, something I should regret, but probably won't.'

'*Nina!*'

Bette appeared at the kitchen door with several laden bags as Nina headed for the hallway. She looked around to see her sister's happily flushed face and bright eyes and scowled.

'Hey!' Bette said, cheerfully oblivious to her sister's rage. 'I'm just going to get dinner on. I've got a joint of beef and all the trimmings.'

'A joint of beef?' Nina said, incredulous. 'So, what – you were planning that we all sit down to a nice dinner at nine o'clock?'

'It won't take that long,' said her sister, bustling in to dump the bags heavily on the kitchen table. 'Especially if everyone helps. I just need to get it in the oven, quick. Where's Best Barnaby Barnacle? He can help peel the veg.'

'Where is he?' Nina asked. 'It's half past seven, Bette, which means my six-year-old son ate his dinner an hour and a half ago and is now getting ready for bed because he has to start the new school term tomorrow morning.'

Bette stopped and looked up. 'It's not that late, is it?'

Nina shook her head. 'You know, there was a minute there, when you offered to make dinner, that it actually crossed my mind that you were trying to make an effort to be a proper, caring part of this family. More fool me.'

Bette's eyes found the kitchen clock and winced. 'I'm sorry. I didn't realize the time. I bumped into an old friend – Allie. Allie Bright, do you remember her? We haven't seen each other for years and we just got chatting and—'

'And you forgot that you'd made a promise to your family and you didn't care that we'd all be sitting here waiting for you.' Nina interrupted. 'Yeah, I get it – easily done, right? For you, anyway.'

'Nina, please,' Sophia interjected. 'Let's just all take a step back, shall we?'

'Look, I'm sorry,' Bette said, 'but—'

'No,' Nina said. 'There's no "but" in that sentence, Bette. There's just you, once again, failing to think of others *at all*.'

With that she left the kitchen, storming up the stairs to say goodnight to her son. It was the last she saw of her sister that evening.

'To be honest,' Nina told Cam early the next morning, as they picked another crop of strawberries in the polytunnel before she had to get Barney up for school, 'I really wish she'd leave without coming to the solicitors. We don't need her there and I've had enough of her.'

'Ah, don't say that,' Cam said, as he dropped another berry into a waiting punnet. 'You have a right to be pissed off at her about last night – but she's still your sister.'

'Is she?' Nina asked. 'In name, I guess. By blood, yes. But family is more than that, isn't it? She's never wanted to be part of ours.'

Cam was quiet for a moment, concentrating on picking. Nina sighed.

'Sorry,' she said. 'You don't need to listen to me moan about my life. *Again*. How did your date go last night? What was her name? Sally?'

Cam glanced up at her and smiled. 'Yeah, Sally. It was good. We went to the Darling for a pint and fish and chips.'

Nina shook her head.

'What?' Cam asked. 'It was her idea!'

'I didn't say a thing.'

'You didn't have to. It was all in that wobble of your little head.'

Nina paused in her picking and raised her eyebrows at him. '"Little head"?'

'Sorry. I meant "little wobble of your head",' Cam grinned.

Nina snorted. 'Oh, sure you did, yeah.'

'Come on – what's wrong with fish and chips and a pint at the local for a date?'

'Nothing. At least, not if you're both fifty and have been married for years.'

It was Cam's turn to raise his eyebrows. 'Is that not a touch ageist?'

'All I'm saying is that when you're starting out to impress a girl, you should at least *try* to make a bit more of an effort, that's all.'

Cam shrugged, still picking. 'Sally seemed happy enough.'

There was a sudden flicker of something in Nina's chest as she wondered whether Sally had spent the night at the farm. She probably had. They usually did. She pushed the annoying niggle away. What difference did it make to her? None.

'I'll make more of an effort next time, how about that?' Cam added, turning to pull another empty punnet towards him.

The flicker niggled again. Second dates weren't the norm for Cam. 'You're going to see her again?'

Cam shrugged. 'Maybe, yeah. She was fun. And even if not, it sounds as if I should take any suggestions for classier dates, so have at it. What would your ideal first date be?'

Nina cleared her throat. 'Oh, ignore me. I've never even been on a first date, so what do I know?'

Cam stopped what he was doing and looked up at her. 'Barney's dad was never much one for making an effort then, eh?'

She snorted, concentrating on the strawberries so that her hair fell over that damned scar. 'What do you think?'

From the corner of her eye Nina saw him nod silently and then resume picking.

'I think,' Nina said, eventually, 'that it wouldn't matter what the date was as long as I felt as if the guy had made some kind of effort. It wouldn't have to be fancy or expensive. As long as there had been some thought that had gone into it somewhere, some element to make me feel as if the evening mattered . . .' She trailed off, aware that this was a tangent on which she had no business being. 'Anyway, sorry. It's none of my business. I'm sure Sally had a great time and the second date will be even better.'

She finished her last punnet and fitted it to the waiting box as Cam did the same.

'Do you want me to drop these off at the grocers?' he asked.

'Thanks, but I'll take them after I've got Barney to school.'

'What's the schedule today?'

Nina checked her watch. 'We need to be at the solicitor's office by one. I think the idea is that all the paperwork happens at the same time. Mum's flight home is booked at 5pm so the plan is for us to pick Barnaby up from school afterwards and see her off at the airport. I assume Bette will be leaving at the same time. I should be back in time for evening milking, so don't do it. I need to get back into the swing of things – in a few hours it'll officially be no one's responsibility but mine. I'd better get used to it.'

'You can always call on me, Nina,' he said. 'You know that.'

'Thanks.' She let out a breath. If she were honest with herself, the idea of the farm being entirely hers was a daunting prospect as well as an exciting one. 'How lucky am I to have such good neighbours?'

He watched her, his smile returning, the slightly strange

tension of earlier dissipating. The sun had risen while they'd been in the polytunnel. The bright morning light was glinting through a gap in the plastic, the shine glancing off his unshaven jaw, and Nina was reminded with a slight jolt of just how easy on the eye her now-permanent neighbour was.

'I'm lucky too,' he said. 'Because now I know you're going to be staying for the long term.'

A slight pulse of electricity spiked in Nina's chest. *Nope*, she told herself. *Bad idea. Terrible. What's wrong with you this morning?*

Maybe something of her thought process had been visible in her eyes, or perhaps his comment hadn't held any of the connotations that it might have done, because in the next second Cam gave one of his trademark grins, wiping out the last of the tension that probably hadn't been there at all.

'Because,' he added, continuing his thought, 'good neighbours are like gold dust.'

She smiled, forcing herself back onto an even keel. 'Aren't they just. Now, I'd better get going or he'll be late for his first day. The last thing I need is a reputation at the school gates for being a terrible mum.'

'Pfft,' Cam said, 'as if. I'll pop by later? It's always polite to welcome the incoming landlord, isn't it?'

Nina laughed. 'Sure. Come by after eight? Mum will have gone, Barney will be in bed, and Bette will have scuttled back to London. We'll have the place to ourselves.' She only realized what she'd said after the words were already out. 'Not that that's why you should come over then. It'll just be quieter. Not that it needs to be quiet, obviously. I just thought, after a busy day . . .'

'Sounds good to me,' he said, blue eyes twinkling above another easy grin that she felt was more teasing than it needed to be. 'I'll see you then.'

Nina shut her eyes briefly as he left. Why did she always turn into a blathering idiot when she was trying to play it cool? Why was she even trying to play it cool around him, anyway? Cam was a friend. That was all. Anything else was a very stupid idea, and personally Nina felt she'd already had enough stupid ideas to last her a lifetime. She would not make an ill-advised fling with her next-door neighbour another of them.

'Forget it,' she muttered to herself. 'Get over yourself.'

Chapter Ten

The Crowdie family's solicitor, Roland Palmer, had been dealing with the affairs of the farm for longer than either Nina or Bette had been alive. His offices were in Dundee, and he greeted the three women with condolences and coffee before seating them in front of his desk. Nina and Bette took chairs either side of their mother. They hadn't spoken since the previous night, and had driven to the city in separate cars, Sophia travelling with Bette while Nina drove the farm's old Land Rover. Nina sincerely hoped that after this one final formality, Bette would be on her way back to her own life. Surely there would be no reason for her to even come back to the farm. Bette clearly thought the same, as Nina had spied her overnight bag in the back seat of the hired Audi when she'd pulled up beside her sister in the car park.

Palmer was a grey-suited man in his sixties with pinched features that gave him a severe, patrician air. He frowned slightly as he sat down behind his desk and steepled his fingers on the old mahogany of its polished top.

'Now,' he said, 'I am glad that both of Bern's daughters are here today. Might I hope that is because your father had spoken to you both himself about the recent change in his will?'

Nina felt herself tensing slightly. They'd all long been aware of the terms of their father's will – that Nina would get the farm as a going concern, that Bette would take a share of whatever monthly income that generated, and that in the event of it being sold, the two sisters would split the proceeds equally. 'He didn't speak to us, but our mother told us he'd mentioned leaving something else to Bette,' she said. 'Something of sentimental value from the house, maybe?'

'That wasn't quite it, no.' Palmer let out a slow breath and Nina felt the tension in her gut tighten. The solicitor opened a box file marked with the Crowdie name and lifted out two white envelopes, the kind that could hold a three-folded letter. 'He dictated this to me about six months ago. It is addressed to both of you and he wanted you both to read it when it became necessary. If you prefer, I can read it out to you, but there is a copy for each of you here.'

Nina froze for a moment, staring at the last missive from her father, held in the hands of a man she had never before met. She became aware of her mother's hand on her arm, giving a squeeze of reassurance, but she couldn't seem to summon any words.

'I'd rather read it myself,' came Bette's clear voice, as calm as ever. 'Please.'

Roland Palmer nodded and passed one of the envelopes to Bette, who opened it immediately and took out the contents, a single sheet of paper. Nina caught the solicitor's eye and nodded, and he passed the second one to her. She opened it, took a breath, and began to read.

My two brilliant daughters, the letter said,

I know that this new version of my will is going to come as a shock to you both. Bette, I know that you have never wanted or needed the farm, and I understand that the place holds difficult memories for you. Nina, you know that I have utmost confidence in you in all things, and I do not want you to take the decision that I have made here as a sign that this has changed. However, I can no longer ignore the fact that the farm's circumstances are very poor. Bette, you will understand this better even than Nina, because as per your request I haven't told her of the help you provided some years back. Without that help, the farm would be more in debt than it already is. I cannot in all conscience leave Nina to deal with what she is about to discover alone and I know of no one more capable of finding a solution than you.

I also know that the first instinct for both of you will be to seek a way to revert to our original agreement. However, before you do that, I would like you to listen to my reasoning, which is simple and, I believe, sound.

Nina, you will not be able to run all aspects of the farm alone, but there is no money to pay for help. Bette, you may not know farm management, but I know you'll be able to turn your hand — and mind — to saving Crowdie from the decline that is far worse than I have admitted to anyone — so bad, in fact, that it is a huge relief to me that I know you at least do not need to rely on an income from it. I couldn't bring myself to tell either of you plainly how bad things are before now, and I am deeply sorry for that. Call it pride, call it stupidity, call it guilt — it is probably a combination of all of these things. Please forgive me. If it turns out that saving the farm is impossible, I know that I can rely on you, Bette, to get the best possible terms and price for you and your sister. But I hope that both of you will at least try. Try to keep Crowdie in our family, if only for Barney's sake.

With love, always, and in hope of your forgiveness,
Your father

Nina continued to stare at the page once she had finished reading, her thoughts a blur as she tried to take in everything she'd read. It was Bette who broke the silence. Her voice, so calm a few moments before, had taken on a higher pitch, her surprise clear.

'He's . . . split the whole farm between us. Hasn't he?'

'Yes,' Roland Palmer confirmed. 'You each now own an equal share of the Crowdie estate.'

'Right. I . . . see.'

Nina kept her focus on the page still on her lap, trying to assimilate the information within before she could even begin to deal with this new, unexpected reality. She'd known the farm wasn't flush, but she'd thought that was just the normal margins of a modestly sized modern farm operating in today's difficult market. Sure, the equipment hadn't been updated for literally decades, and there had been times when she'd begged Bern to address issues she felt were pressing, but when she had he'd done that, hadn't he? When they'd really needed something, he'd made sure they got it. How had he paid for that if their coffers were empty?

We emailed. There were things he wanted to tell me, sometimes. About the farm.

'You knew about this,' she said, leaning forward so that she could look directly at Bette. 'Didn't you? You knew, and you didn't tell me.'

'I didn't know.'

'You knew *something*.' Nina was growing steadily angrier. 'Dad says you did. Right here. All those cosy little email exchanges you two had. Neither of you ever thought I had a right to know what was going on? You know, the one of us *doing all the work*?'

'Nina,' Sophia said, softly, 'I know you're upset, I know there's a lot to take in, but—'

'Don't "Nina" me,' Nina hissed. 'I want answers.'

'I do too,' Bette said. 'He didn't tell me anything, Nina, not about this.'

Nina shook the letter, limp in her hand, and then quoted from it. '"*Without your help, the farm would be more in debt than it already is.*" Stop *lying* to me, Bette!'

'I'm not,' Bette said, firmly and with an edge of annoyance, as if she thought Nina's reaction to this utter bombshell was in some way disproportionate. 'Three years ago he told me the barn roof needed fixing but that the bank was dragging its feet on lending the money. Winter was closing in, it needed to be done quickly, and if he didn't book the contractors in immediately there'd be no availability until the new year, which was forecast to be bad. He said that was why he was asking me for a loan instead. I told him I didn't lend to family, because that never ended well, but I'd give him the money. He didn't want to do that, he wanted to get Roland here to draw up a repayment agreement, but I transferred the money that day and told him that was the end of it. I told him the farm was a family asset – our only asset – and of course I'd help. I said—' and here she paused for a moment, the only indication of emotion, 'I said that if he was so worried about it, he could write into his will that it would be repaid as a lump sum when he passed, but that it wasn't necessary. I thought – I thought that's what this was going to be about. I swear, Nina. I thought whatever banking glitch was going on back then, it was a temporary one, probably because of COVID, and that everything else was fine. That's what he led me to believe, and he never asked me for money again.'

There was a brief silence as Nina tried to take this in. The barn roof had been literally falling in when she'd told Bern they had no choice but to get it refitted. It was the worst of the running repairs that had been neglected for too long, but it was by no means the only one, nor the only one they had fixed. A cold trickle of apprehension slid down her spine. The bank wouldn't give him money to fix it, which meant he'd reached a limit of some sort. What did that mean? How many loans did they have? Was there a mortgage on the house she didn't know about? That had always been at the baseline of her security, even before she'd returned to Crowdie to live – that no matter how bad things got for her and Barney, she'd always have somewhere to go, because the Crowdie farm had been in their family for so long that there was nothing owed on the property. It was theirs, free and clear, a home that could never be taken away from them. They would at least always have that.

'How bad is it?' she asked Palmer, trying to keep her voice steady. 'How badly are we in debt?'

There was a pause, during which the solicitor looked grave, in the way of a doctor about to deliver a disastrous prognosis.

'I don't know the full extent of it,' he said. 'But I can tell you that ten years ago your father took out a mortgage on the properly of £350,000, and that has been in arrears for at least three years.'

Chapter Eleven

Bette left Roland Palmer's office in as much shock as her sister. The three women stood in the car park as Monday morning Dundee bustled around them, none of them sure what to do next.

'Now, girls,' their mother said, breaking the tense silence. 'I know this isn't what either of you expected or wanted. This is a terrible shock – for me, as well. But try not to think too badly of your father. He would have been doing everything he could to leave things in a better state for you. In fact, perhaps they are better than you think? Perhaps things had improved.'

Bette rubbed a hand over her face. 'Maybe,' she said. 'But honestly, Mum, it doesn't sound that way. A £350,000 mortgage? And it's been in arrears for three years? I'm amazed the bank hasn't repossessed already.'

'I can't believe you both kept this from me,' Nina said, her voice hollow with an anger that was directed at Bette. 'How could you both lie to me like that?'

'I told you,' Bette said, with as much patience as she could muster, 'I didn't know any more than you did.'

'How can you say that?' Nina asked, still clutching the letter. 'You told him not to tell me about the money you gave him. If he had, I'd have known something was wrong. I'd have made him tell me what was going on.'

Bette wasn't so sure about that, but thought it pointless to argue. 'I asked Dad not to tell you when I put money into the farm because frankly, it wasn't any of your business,' she said, bluntly. 'It was between me and him, and I knew you'd find some way of turning it into a negative about me, the way you always do.'

'I don't—'

'You *do*, Nina,' Bette said, cutting her off. 'You would have accused me of doing it to have something to hold over you, or because I wanted to show off how much money I could spare, or to make you feel inadequate – something like that. And it really had nothing to do with you. At all. I wanted to help Dad and the farm and I could, so I did. That's it. And because I didn't think there was any kind of enduring problem, there seemed no need for you to ever know.'

Nina looked away, staring across the windswept car park. 'How much did you give him?'

'£50,000.'

Her sister made a disgusted sound in her throat. 'And you just had that lying around?'

Bette felt herself reaching the limit of her patience. Nina

had always seemed to know how to push her to the edge quicker than anyone else. 'No, I didn't. Those were savings I'd built up. Actually, at the time it was pretty much everything I had.'

That made Nina cast her a glance. 'Not anymore though,' Nina said, her voice still scornful. 'Because a divorce lawyer can always make more money, right?'

'Nina,' their mother said – she'd clearly been trying to stay neutral until now, let them work it out themselves, 'that's not fair.'

'You know what's not fair about this situation, Mum?' Nina said. *'Anything at all.'*

Bette rubbed a hand over her face. 'This isn't getting us anywhere,' she said. 'We need to go through everything and work out exactly where we are with the farm's finances, and we need to do it as soon as possible.'

Nina looked at her watch, 'Well, right now I need to go and pick up Barnaby from school and then get Mum up to Aberdeen or she's going to miss check-in. Then I have to get back to give him dinner, get him to do his homework, get him to bed, feed the animals, clean the lines, place the feed order I didn't have time to put in this morning, look at the strawberry orders I need to pick to-morrow morning—'

'All right, all right,' Bette said. 'I get the picture.'

'Do you?' Nina asked. 'Because what I really need right now is someone who pulls their weight, not dumps yet more on me.'

'I'll deal with it all, then. Can you send me access to the farm's finances?'

'You mean online?' Nina shrugged. 'If I can find the log-in for the bank account.'

Bette grimaced. 'What about everything else? Supplier accounts, stuff like that?'

'I have no idea. I haven't even started going through the office. In case you haven't noticed I've been a bit busy. Dad looked after all that. He always said he didn't want me to have to worry about the paperwork on top of everything else.'

They were silent again and Bette thought they were probably both thinking the same thing. That above all, Bern Crowdie hadn't wanted Nina to find out the truth about the hole the farm was in. Bette felt a yawning chasm opening up in her gut as Nina pressed her fingers to her lips.

'I have no idea where any of that stuff is. I never even really went into the office. He looked after all the post, and paying the bills – all of that,' Nina said, the tone of her voice suggesting that the true gravity of what she was saying was only just dawning on her. 'Oh, *God*.'

Bette shut her eyes. All she really wanted to do was leave all of this behind and go back to London. This was exactly the kind of nightmare she had never wanted to have to deal with, the reason she'd found a stable profession that had nothing to do with the farming life, so often precarious. But if she didn't pitch in now, there was probably no hope of salvaging anything – certainly not that lump sum of money that had seemed at the time, if not disposable, then at least something she could contribute without missing, with the added bonus of assuaging her background guilt at not being there to help her family physically. What else could she have done? Said no, and proved her sister right about her selfishness where family were concerned? Made it a loan, and added to the farm's monthly burden? How would either of those options have made a difference to where she stood now?

'All right,' Bette said. 'I need to make some calls. I'll cancel my flight and let work know I'm going to be out of the office for longer than I planned. I'll stay another day or two and gather all the information I need to help us figure all this out. There's no point in panicking until we know the extent of the problem. Maybe Mum's right. Maybe it's not as bad as we think. Okay?'

'Okay,' Nina said. 'All right.'

'Good,' said Sophia, taking a breath and running a hand through her hair. 'I am glad I will be leaving you to face this together.'

'Can't you stay too?' Nina asked, and one glance at her sister's face told Bette what she was thinking. That having their mother there would at least provide a mediator between them.

Sophia smiled, as if she knew what her younger daughter was thinking. 'I'm sorry, my darlings,' she said. 'I'll be on the end of a video call if you need me. And in a real emergency, I will come back. But I have my own life and my own commitments. This you will need to deal with by yourselves.

I know you can do it. My brilliant girls, together again. You are going to figure this out. Everything will be fine.'

Bette looked away as Nina hugged their mother, pulling her phone out of her pocket, busying herself because she by no means had the same conviction but really didn't want to start another argument right now. She stepped away and dialled the number for Spencer Coulthard's secretary. Coulthard was founding partner in the firm; he had brought her in as an intern and had always been her mentor and advocate. He'd never said so, but Bette was sure that her imminent ascension to partner herself with the advent of the merger was down to his advocacy.

'Bette,' he said, as he took her call. 'How's things? How's the family? How did the funeral go?'

'Hi, Spencer. It went well, thank you. But look – something unexpected has come up here. I'm going to have to take a few days. I'm hoping it'll be no more than two, but either way I'll definitely be back as usual on Friday. I just wanted to let you know that I need to take more leave.'

There was a pause. Spencer's voice, when he spoke, had taken on a subtle tension that Bette picked up on despite the wind whistling past her on the street. 'You're still in Scotland?'

Bette frowned. 'Yes. Is there a problem?'

'No,' he said. 'I'd just expected to see you tomorrow morning, that's all. With everything going on, it's perhaps not the best time to take a leave of absence.'

'I'm sorry,' she said, a little puzzled by his attitude. Spencer knew how dedicated and hardworking she was – Bette had never taken a day sick and rarely used all her holiday allocation. 'But it can't be helped, I'm afraid. A family matter that can't wait.'

'Of course, of course,' he said. 'I understand. Do whatever you need to, Bette, and we'll see you when you get back. Take care of yourself.'

Bette ended the call, a little unsettled by the exchange, and called Oliver to tell him of her changed arrangements and to let him know what would need doing in her absence. She watched her mother and sister talking quietly between themselves as she spoke, and wished that Sophia would stay, too. She didn't want to go back to the farm at all. With just her, Nina and her nephew there it would seem far too quiet. There were ghosts in those walls and she had an inkling they would rise if the place was silent for too long.

'I should go straight back to the farm rather than coming with you to the airport,' she told her sister, once she had hung up. 'The sooner I can get started, the better.'

'Fine.' Nina pulled her keys out of her bag and wrested the back door key from the ring, holding it out to her. 'We'd better get going,' she said to their mother. 'I don't want Barney waiting by the gate on his first day of school. And I don't want you to miss your flight.'

Sophia pulled Bette to her, the two women hugging each other tightly. 'Call me,' her mother said.

'I will,' Bette promised.

Bette slid into the driver's seat of her hire car as Nina

backed the Land Rover out. She waved in her rear-view mirror, and then they were gone. She glanced at her overnight case on the passenger seat, let out a breath of disappointment, and started the car for the drive back to Crowdie.

Chapter Twelve

Bette tried to make sense of everything as she made her way back to the farm alone. She wasn't surprised that her father hadn't told her his plans for his changed will – he would have known that she'd not have been happy about them if he had. But he had also known, and she had thought he at least respected, her desire not to be tied to the farm any more firmly than she already was. She'd thought he'd agreed with it, too, especially since one of his two daughters had actively wanted to be involved in the family business.

She and Nina were vastly different people and always had been. This split in interests had widened in adulthood, and had been reflected in their respective responses to heartbreak. Nina's instinct had been to go home and stay there. Bette's had been to never willingly go back. Not that Nina had known Bette's reasons back then. She probably still didn't know them now. Nina had been just nine the year it all fell apart for Bette, then nineteen. There had been light years dividing the sisters and their interests even at the time. A whole universe had expanded between them during the intervening period.

At first, Bette's desire to never return to this place had been a purely visceral reaction, a way to survive an emotional blow that had been so monumental at the time that she'd thought the world was ending. Then after a while it had become practical. She'd thrown herself into her studies and was busy, determined and ambitious. That focus had at first been a way to keep her afloat emotionally as she tried to heal her fractured heart, but it had gradually become genuine and all-consuming. She'd regained the dream she'd always had. Bette liked the law. She liked the orderliness of it, which seemed like such a stark opposite to what she felt was the utter chaos of a farmyard.

Then she had discovered the divorce courts, and her path had been set. By then she had decided that the idea of love the whole world was sold on from an early age was nothing but a farce. She dated here and there throughout university, mainly because people seemed to think she was weird if she didn't, but none of those connections had held any lasting (and in most cases even short or medium-term) interest for Bette. She had reached the depressing conclusion that, as young as she had been when she'd met the person her heart had been entirely fixated on, and as awful a mess as that had become, he had indeed been The One, or as close to such a thing as was possible in this imperfect world. And look how that had turned out.

Bette did not think of herself as a poetic person, but there was something of the cosmic come-around in the idea of her making her living from separating failed couples as advantageously as possible for a client. Love was a fallacy, marriage was in Bette's view usually a mistake, and if her bastard of a fiancé hadn't cheated, she'd probably have ended up stuck in a bad one herself. If that had happened, she liked to think she'd have been able to find someone as efficient and capable as herself to get her out of it when it inevitably failed.

The saying goes that the best revenge is a happy life, but to Bette's mind it didn't hurt if one could be helped along the way to that end by a healthy dose of 'What's yours is now solely mine, you cheating bastard'. In facilitating this for others, she had achieved her own form of happy life. Bette had left behind Barton Mill, her family, her home and all the memories that accompanied them for a new life so distant that nothing about them could follow her. And now here she was, back again, and for the worst possible reasons.

Bette pulled into the farmyard and killed the engine but sat there for a moment with her hands gripping the steering wheel as she contemplated her old family home.

'Dad,' Bette murmured, as she looked up at the dilapidated window of her old bedroom, 'why didn't you *tell* me?'

She knew the answer, of course, though it didn't make it any more comprehensible to her. He'd asked her to help with the barn roof because he'd had no choice. They had to have a barn, and it had to have a roof. He couldn't get a loan from the bank and in the end he'd been forced to ask his daughter for the money instead, but woe betide him ever doing so again. It seemed that even Bern Crowdie, good man that he was, could fall victim to pride at its most foolish.

Bette got out of the car and went inside. She knew where the farm 'office' was, a small room whose door was at the bottom of the stairs that led to the second floor. She'd rarely been in there. As a child it was out of bounds, though it had held little interest for Bette anyway. Now she made herself tea in the kitchen and attempted to steel herself for whatever she might find inside it.

The hallway was somewhere else she hadn't paused to contemplate during her return. It had seemed unchanged since her childhood, when she hadn't paid any attention to it either. Now, carrying her tea, Bette paused as she made her way through it. It was narrow and dark without the light on despite the brightness of the day. It bisected the house, leading from the kitchen to the lesser-used front entrance, passing on the left a glass-panelled internal door that led to the living room and to another, smaller parlour beyond that had its own external door, even more rarely used.

The hallway walls had always been covered in photographs – a project that went back further than her own grandparents. There were generations of Crowdies arranged in varying degrees of formality over the faded flower-patterned wallpaper. If she were to look hard enough, she'd probably find some of herself here somewhere, along with her parents, and Nina too. There would be some of her father here, progressing from boy to teenager to young man, although Bette did not remember ever being shown them nor searching for them herself. This hallway had simply always been here, part of the house, a fixed point never thought about, even when she had lived here. More photographs had been added during her lifetime, but to Bette this had seemed to happen organically, as if the house had sprouted the images itself, fully formed, fully framed, new flowers blooming on the old vine-patterned paper in the remaining spaces on the wall.

The collection ended above the old telephone table that stood beyond the door to the sitting room, next to the front door. Here the light was a little better, the sun shining in through the small diamond-paned window in the old oak door. Bette saw that here there was a new photograph. The quality of it wasn't particularly good, and Bette got the sense that it had been snapped on someone's phone. It was of Nina, Barnaby and Bern. It had been taken out in the yard, on a summer's day not unlike this one. Barnaby stood in front of his mother with Nina's arms around him. She had tilted her head against their father's shoulder, and they were all laughing at a joke Bette could not hear. Bern Crowdie was leaning on his walking stick, his other arm around his daughter. It was not an expertly arranged photograph, because behind them was only the unkempt background of the empty barn. The bright sunlight was flaring, and they were all in movement, hence the slight blurring, as if the picture had captured the very energy of the moment itself instead of only its image. No, it had not been well planned, but taken by someone who had spied something in that second and decided to immortalize it. Cam, perhaps, the new neighbour? Bette peered closer, feeling as she did so an unexpected pang, a renewal of grief. Her father looked happy, she thought, and she was glad that whatever worries he might have had about the farm, he had not been alone here at the end.

After another moment Bette turned away from the wall and crossed the hallway to open the office door. Beyond, the room was small and the air was musty. A large, solid oak desk dominated the space. On the desk was an old Toshiba laptop, and Bette was surprised by another twinge of sorrow as she imagined her father sitting here, writing her emails and reading the ones she had sent in return. It was open, but switched off.

Bette sat down, taking in the old galvanized filing cabinet that stood in one corner and a series of bookcases, all full to bursting. Besides the computer, the desk was piled with paperwork, though none of it seemed to be in any particular order. A quick check showed that the drawers were similarly full. She would have to go through it all and try to form some sort of useful order from the chaos. There were bank statements, bills, invoices, orders and God knew what else all piled together. Everything needed to be examined and filed, in case something vital was missed. As Bette began the dizzying task, she searched for the passwords that would allow her to get out of here and back to her own life. There she could at least deal with this mess remotely, in both a practical and emotional sense.

Chapter Thirteen

Nina had completely forgotten about the arrangement for Cam to drop by that evening. He knocked on the kitchen door at about five past eight, as Nina was making herself beans on toast, having no appetite or patience to bother with anything more complicated.

'Hey,' he said, pushing open the door with the promised bottle of fizz in one hand. 'Congratulations!'

He was holding an actual bottle of champagne, she noticed, as she stared at him blankly for a moment before her memory kicked in.

'Ah,' she said. 'Yes. Well. They may be a little premature, as it turns out.'

Cam came all the way into the kitchen, a puzzled look on his face. 'Oh?'

Nina looked down at her lacklustre dinner and realized she wasn't hungry anyway. She reached for two tumblers instead (she didn't think they even owned champagne flutes), setting them on the counter beside Cam's offering. Opening the bottle probably wasn't really appropriate in the circumstances, but there wasn't anything else to drink in the house besides her dad's collection of single malt.

'Long story,' she said, 'but I can regale you with the outline if you like.'

He popped the cork, frowning. 'Sounds ominous.'

'Oh, you don't know the half of it.' Nina looked at her glass as the bubbles died down and wondered whether she should get him to pour another for her sister. Bette hadn't emerged from the study at all since Nina had got back to the farm with Barnaby after dropping Sophia at the airport, but she'd heard her on the phone a couple of times, an unfamiliar voice rising and falling in the background. 'Bette's still here. Turns out we are now equal owners of the farm. But actually, we might both end up owning nothing at all in the very near future.'

'Ahh,' Cam said, setting the bottle down. 'Well then. Story time it is.'

He sat quietly as she recounted the unexpected events of the day, and Nina found that retelling them in her own way to a third party helped take a little of the panic and confusion out of the tale. She felt better for having someone to talk to, and Cam was a good listener.

'It's such a mess,' Nina said, eventually. 'And I feel so ... not betrayed, that's not the right word. Not let down, either, because I know that Dad would never have done this intentionally. But still, I'm *hurt*, I suppose. For so many different reasons. That he didn't tell me about all this. That he confided in Bette, but not me . . .'

'I totally get where you're coming from,' Cam said, as she trailed off, 'but from what you've said, I don't think he did confide in Bette, did he? This sounds like she was blindsided, too.'

Nina sipped from her glass. Her natural reaction was to baulk against what Cam was saying, because if this wasn't Bette's fault then it was Bern's, and she didn't want to put that blame on her dad. But that really wasn't fair, was it? Even she could see that. And Bette had given their father £50,000, without which the farm would be in an even worse state. She'd given it, not lent it, and yes, it was galling that her older sister had had that amount in savings when Nina barely had a pot to piss in. *But*, Nina asked herself, *whose fault was that? You were the one who dropped out of school before you'd even finished your Highers. You were the one who went off with an abusive moron instead of pursuing your education. You were the one who had a child on your own without first working out how to provide for him.* She knew all of this rationally, and yet still there was that knot of resentment beneath her feelings for her older sister that she had just never been able to untie. If Bette had been here for her when she was a kid, the way older siblings were supposed to be . . . if she'd ever been the kind of person whom Nina could have turned to for advice, to tell her problems, to lean on when she was at her lowest, maybe Nina would have found herself on a different path. Everything had always come so easy to Bette in a way it never had to Nina. Nina had never been academic, not in the way Bette had been right from the word go. School had seemed like such a waste of time for Nina, especially when, however hard she tried, her grades never even came close to matching Bette's. And by the time she needed help with the really important exams, her brilliant older sister had left and rarely returned. Then Nina had left herself and her life had continued to spiral out of control until she'd come back to Crowdie and found Bette even more absent than before.

'Yeah,' was all she said. 'I'm sure you're right.'

'And you say she's in there now, trying to piece everything together? Wasn't she supposed to be flying back to London tonight?'

'She told work she had to stay an extra couple of days,' Nina said. 'She's gathering what she needs so she can deal with this from there.'

Cam nodded. 'Does that mean that everything carries on as normal, for now?'

'Yup,' Nina said. 'No news is good news, I guess.'

'In that case, have you seen the forecast?' he asked. 'There's a storm blowing in from the north. I think this one's called Ida. Due to hit the coast late on Wednesday night. They've had it on the long-range radar for a while but it's changed course and now the Met Office says it's heading right for us.'

'You're joking,' Nina groaned. 'I haven't even started baling yet.'

'I know. That's why I thought I'd better let you know. Will you make it?'

'I'll have to. It doesn't sound as if we'll have money for any extra winter feed – I can't risk losing what we have.'

Cam nodded. 'I can call around, see if anyone else can lend a hand?'

'I can't afford the plant hire, or the labour,' Nina said. 'I'll just have to manage it, somehow.'

'Well, I'm halfway through mine,' he told her. 'I've still got the top field to do. I'm aiming to be finished by tomorrow mid-morning. Once it's out of the way I'll come over and help here.'

'You don't have to do that, Cam,' Nina said. 'This is my responsibility. Well – mine and Bette's.'

'I know I don't have to, but I'm offering because I want to help,' he told her. 'And I think Bette will have enough on her plate.'

Bette herself appeared a little later, looking as tired as Nina felt. It was after nine o'clock, and she had her mobile in her hand, as if she'd just finished a conversation. She looked surprised to see Cam there.

'Sorry,' she said. 'I didn't mean to interrupt.'

'You aren't,' Cam said, offering a smile. He gestured at the bottle. 'This was going to be for a celebration but it we decided to open it anyway. Can I pour you one?'

'No – but thanks,' Bette told him, with a faint smile. 'Nina . . . I'm sorry, but we really need to talk about a few things.'

'Say no more,' Cam said. 'I've got an early start tomorrow anyway. I'll get out of your hair.'

'Sorry, Cam,' Nina said. 'I'll catch up with you tomorrow?'

'Sure. I'll be over as soon as I can.'

Nina saw him to the door and waved him off into the twilight before turning back to Bette.

'Sorry,' her sister said again. 'I didn't realize that you and he—'

'We're not,' Nina assured her.

'Okay.'

They stood there, an awkward tableau, two strangers who should be anything but.

'Have some,' Nina said, indicating the bottle. 'It'll go to waste otherwise. I can't drink it all myself – it always gives me a horrible hangover.'

Bette relented with another faint smile that didn't quite reach her eyes. 'All right then.' She noticed the now-cold plate of food. 'You haven't got an appetite either, huh?'

'Not really,' Nina said. 'It's been that kind of day.'

Bette gave a heavy sigh. 'It has.'

'Come on then,' Nina said, passing her sister a tumbler of champagne. 'What do we need to talk about? Besides the obvious . . .'

Bette wandered over to the old sofa and sank into it. 'I've called in a couple of favours, spoken to a couple of people,' she said. 'A property lawyer and an accountant. They can't give me much concrete advice until I've got the full picture on the farm's finances and current debt, but one thing they both said is that we need to get an independent valuation on the property as a whole as soon as possible.'

Nina froze with her glass to her lips. 'Like ... from an estate agent? As if we were going to put it on the market?'

'Exactly like that, yes,' Bette said, her voice weary.

'That's a bad idea,' Nina said. 'News around here travels fast. If anyone knows we've had a valuation done on the farm it'll be everywhere within a day.'

Bette frowned. 'Why does that matter?'

'Because I don't want anyone gossiping about the farm being in a mess,' Nina said. 'You know what people around here are like.' She paused. 'Or maybe you don't, not anymore. Anyway, the last thing I need is for anyone to think we're selling when we're not. Especially not any of our customers. All it would take is for the dairy or the strawberry sales to fall through and we'd lose most of the little of the income we have.'

'Why would they do that?' Bette asked.

'Because no one wants an unstable supply chain,' Nina pointed out. 'And it's not as if there aren't plenty of other replacements for us. I've worked hard to keep us where we are, Bette. I don't want it undone just like that.'

Her sister rubbed a hand over her face. 'We don't have a choice,' she said. 'We need to have the full picture in case the bank decides to call in the debt. If they do, and we let them go by their own valuation, we could lose everything and still end up in debt. Besides, if we're going to have any hope of getting out of this mess, we need to know what we'd be refinancing.'

'Refinancing? Loans, you mean?' Nina asked. 'It sounds

as if Dad had already exhausted that idea, so who would give us a loan? We're barely keeping the lights on as it is, how am I going to find money for a monthly loan payment? Especially the kind it sounds as if we're going to need?'

Bette spread her hands. 'We've got to find some solution. That means looking at all our options, even the ones we don't like, even the ones we don't go with. A valuation is a good place to start. It'll also tell us things we need to be aware of that I haven't even realized need addressing yet.'

'And it'll give you a head start on getting it ready to put on the market, regardless, won't it?' Nina said. 'Don't tell me you haven't already thought about cutting your losses and running. I know you'd sell this place without a second thought, but this is my home, this is Barney's *home* and—'

'I don't want us to have to do that,' Bette said, interrupting. 'Really, I don't. But if we are going to have any hope of keeping Crowdie, we have to consider every other option. And I'm telling you, the first thing we need to do is a valuation. You asked me to handle this side of things. That's what I'm doing, and this is how it has to be done.'

'Fine,' Nina said.

'Good,' Bette said. 'Then I'll call around tomorrow to find a land agent who can come out as quickly as possible.'

'Don't use anyone from Montrose or Arbroath,' Nina said. 'It's too close. Ask someone in Dundee.'

'Okay,' Bette said, although Nina could see she found this an unnecessary request. 'Can you show them around?

They'll probably have questions that you'll know the answers to better than me.'

'Not if it's in the next few days,' Nina said. 'I'm going to be baling flat out until the storm hits.'

Bette sighed. 'Right. Okay. What about a map of the farm? Of the boundary? Dad must have had one of those somewhere.'

Nina pointed to the wall beside the window that looked out into the farmyard. 'You mean like that?'

Bette looked blank for a second, staring at the glass–framed schematic, and then laughed. 'I'd totally forgotten that was up there,' she said. 'I must have looked at it every day when I lived here and since I've been back, but it just . . . blended in.'

Nina nodded. 'It's always been there, for as long as I can remember. I don't think I've ever really looked at it, either, not since Dad used it to teach me the names of our fields when I was a kid. It won't have changed though, will it?'

Bette had got up and walked closer to the framed map, a festival of thin ink lines and italic names written across the blank fields. 'Not unless he sold or rented out land without telling either of us about it.'

Nina actually shuddered at that thought. 'Don't.'

Bette lifted the frame from the wall. 'I'll take this out and scan it. I'm sure the solicitor's got a copy on file but it'll be as well to have one to hand. I'll look at the deeds the Land Registry hold to make sure it hasn't changed, too.'

'Sure.' Nina rubbed a hand over her face. 'I'd better go to bed. Tomorrow's going to be tough.'

'Okay,' Bette said. 'I'm going to do a little more sifting in the office. I'll try not to wake you when I come up.'

'Do you want fresh sheets for the guest room?' Nina asked. 'I can get you some.'

'No,' Bette said, a little absently, still studying the map. 'I'll be fine in the attic.'

Nina watched her sister for another moment, trying to work out what was going through her head, and then wondered why she thought that would be any clearer to her now than it had been for the first twenty-six years of her life.

Chapter Fourteen

The next day, Bette looked up a land agent in Dundee and arranged for a visit on Wednesday morning. She spent the rest of the day struggling with more of the farm's messy paperwork and doing battle with the bank, trying to gain access to her father's account. Everything was taking too long and was shockingly analogue. Most of the supplier invoices were on paper, and nothing looked as if it had been filed for at least six months, probably more like a year. She was trying to get a handle on annual expenses, but without easy access to bank statements, which seemed to be the only data that was kept digitally rather than physically, it was extremely difficult. She was loath to resort to calling up individual companies if she could avoid it, but if she couldn't get the bank to co-operate by close of play on Wednesday she was going to have to do just that.

She kicked herself, increasingly annoyed that she hadn't seen this coming, that she hadn't insisted on having a handover document ready with exactly these kinds of details on them. Hadn't she seen colleagues and their clients battling with this issue enough to know how difficult such a hiccup could be when dealing with estates? She'd blithely imagined that this wouldn't be something they would need to deal with for a long time to come – or rather, that she herself wouldn't have to deal with it at all. But she should have checked, nonetheless. She should have made sure Nina and Bern had straightened such things out between them.

There was no point saying any of this to Nina. Besides, her sister was barely in the house at all for the whole of Tuesday, the sound of the old tractor rattling up and down the farm's uneven tracks at a speed that made Bette think it might shake itself to pieces before Nina managed to get the hay baled and stacked. She remembered how tough and long hay days were. The term 'Make hay while the sun shines' never made more sense than on a day like today, when it blazed dawn until dusk in a blue sky but the forecast was counting down to biblical rain and wind.

Nina finally stumbled in at ten o'clock, so tired she could barely speak. Bette had cooked herself Bolognese earlier, using penne rather than spaghetti so that she could quickly reheat a portion for her sister when she finally appeared.

'Thanks,' Nina mumbled, as Bette set it and a glass of the red she'd bought earlier in front of her at the kitchen table.

'Sure.'

It was all the conversation Nina could muster, and the only words they exchanged that whole day. Bette sat at the table with her sister with her own wine, and in the exhausted silence there was an odd harmony. Bette remembered hay days when she was younger, when there would have been extra hands to help and they'd all come crashing in at the end of the day with Bern, ready for the huge pot of pasta that Sophia would have waiting, all of them sitting down to eat it around this very table.

Nina was already out when Bette got up early on Wednesday morning. She'd heard her sister leave at least an hour earlier, the tractor rumbling out of the yard well before the sun was up. Barnaby had spent the previous night at a schoolfriend's house, where he was due to remain for the next two nights, to take a little off Nina's overflowing plate as she completed baling. Bette showered and dressed and stood at the kitchen door with coffee, listening to the distant rumble of the tractor and squinting up at the sun, already hot.

The land agent, Martha Carr, reached Crowdie promptly at 9am, arriving in what Bette found to be a faintly clichéd black BMW coupe.

'Shall we start with the house?' she asked, once she'd greeted Bette and turned down the offer of coffee.

Carr was a small woman with neat, prematurely white hair, who emitted an air of brusque efficiency that Bette would have found reassuring had she encountered it at work in London, but for some reason found vaguely threatening in the context of her broken-down family home. Having invited her to come, Bette suddenly found herself reluctant to open up the Crowdie farm to what she felt sure now would be a critical eye. Still, it had to be done.

It was also only as she began to show the woman around that Bette realized she was walking into a domain that she had barely reacquainted herself with since her return. The living room, for instance, which was the first room they went into. As soon as she stepped inside, Bette understood that she was about to subject herself to the reawakening of more memories, which perhaps explained why she hadn't done this kind of deliberate walk-through before. The living room was a warm space: low-ceilinged, rectangular, with two small windows that admitted little light set in the external wall, opposite a large hearth swept clean. Around this was arranged a square of armchairs and an old sofa with the fire as their focal point, a coffee table standing on an old oval rug in the centre. There was a crammed floor-to-ceiling bookcase against one wall, a large and equally untidy sideboard lining the other. Above this the wall was as busy with framed images as the hallway, though these weren't photographs, but watercolour paintings. They were all landscapes, lovingly rendered images of the local area, all made by her grandmother. Jean and Murray Crowdie had moved into accommodation in Montrose that was easier to maintain when they had retired and Bern had fully taken over the farm, though a day rarely went by without them dropping by. Bette could remember Jean Crowdie standing out on the cliffs with her easel and paints whenever she could, especially in summer. It was a vivid image in Bette's mind, probably because that was the only time that she'd been allowed near the cliffs as a child. Those pastures closest to the cliffs were off limits to any children.

'That was a hobby of my grandmother's,' Bette explained, as she saw the estate agent taking them in.

'She was very good,' the woman observed. 'These are beautiful.'

Bette had to agree. It was a realization that took her by surprise, another aspect of her childhood that she had forgotten.

Across the living room was another door, which Bette remembered as a formal dining room the family only ever used when they had company for dinner, which was almost never. Most of the time they all ate in the kitchen. Pushing open the door now, Bette saw that it had been converted into a playroom for Barnaby. There were toys scattered across the faded and threadbare rug. There was a child-sized desk strewn with coloured pens, some of which had rolled from the table top onto the floor. The old dining table that Bette remembered had been moved to one end of the room, pushed up against the wall.

The tour continued, Martha Carr taking silent notes as they moved upstairs to examine the bedrooms one by one. Bette did her best to answer her questions, all the time feeling like an interloper, a voyeur peering into private places. When they reached her father's bedroom, the room that had belonged to both of her parents at one time, she very nearly waited outside.

Back downstairs, Bette heard the rumble of the tractor as

Nina raced by with another load of hay, fast enough and close enough to the house to make the windows rattle.

'Well, then,' said Carr, briskly, once she had assessed the kitchen, the parlour, the pantry. 'Time to walk the boundary, I think.'

Outside, the sun was high and hot, the sound of birdsong overlaid by the noise of the tractor. The boundary between the Crowdie farm and the land now owned by Cam Hayes was marked by an intermittent fence – broken in places, possibly never existent in others.

'That'll need to be fixed for any sale,' the agent said, making yet more notes on her iPad. She looked ahead as they headed for the pastures that edged the clifftop. 'What's the erosion rate like, do you know?'

'I don't know about recent years,' Bette had to admit, 'but I've got a map here that shows what was always the worst when I was a kid.' She brought out her own iPad and displayed the scan she'd taken of the farm's layout. 'At some point a long time ago, there was a significant incident that closed off the cliff edge of this pasture. I think there must have been a storm or something like that.'

Carr peered at the screen. 'Could it have been the Great Storm of '53? That did a lot of damage all along this coast.'

'Possibly, but I always got the impression it was much earlier than that. I never thought to ask, to be honest – when we were children we were always just told to stay away from the cliffs and that was that. There's a fence that runs all the way along the boundary at the cliff edge.'

'Well, we'll walk as close as we can,' Carr decided. 'I can look up trends later.'

Bette felt compelled to lead the way, heading for a five-bar gate that marked the very edge of their farm's limit at the track that ran between the cliff pastures and the inland fields. She did brief battle with it to persuade it to open – she'd forgotten how those chain and hook affairs worked and it had dropped on its hinges, too – and pushed it open through overgrown grass dotted with a curlicue of molehills as it sloped towards the shoreline. Ahead, it was just possible to make out the glint of the North Sea, shimmering in the summer light. The salted scent of it was in the air and Bette could hear it rolling in to crash against the cliffs. She'd always loved that sound, though she rarely got to hear it now.

They headed through the pasture to the swelling sea, walking right up to the fence at the cliff edge, and both women paused to lean over it. Beyond was a few feet of pasture grass that ended in a ragged tear of soil and rock, in some places much closer to the fence than others.

They continued walking through pasture along the fence line, which grew increasingly overgrown with gorse, hazel and blackthorn until it was impossible to keep close to it or to see the cliff edge any longer. They cut across the pasture instead, the agent still trying to skirt as close to the farm's furthest boundary as possible.

'There seems to be a lot of land beyond this overgrowth here in particular,' Carr said, attempting to peer through the brush. 'But the fence cuts it off. Any idea why?'

'The erosion, I should think,' Bette said. 'Like I said, whatever happened was pretty catastrophic. I can't think of another reason.'

Carr stopped and brought up Google Earth on her iPad, and then keyed in the post code for the Crowdie farm. Bette stood at her shoulder as she zoomed in on the pasture where they were standing. They both looked at the edge of the field, where it turned into sea. They were zoomed in so far that the resolution was sketchy, but the estate agent pointed to the fence and what was beyond it.

'That's where we are, right?' she said. 'It doesn't look like erosion beyond that fence to me. Is that a path, there?'

Bette frowned, trying to make out the patterns in the landscape. 'It can't be,' she said. 'There's nothing down there. At least that's what I was always told.'

Carr looked up from her screen to the haphazard hedge in front of them. 'Let's see if we can take a closer look, shall we?'

They walked on, tramping across grass that seemed not to have been grazed for some time. Then the pasture dipped. At the bottom of this short incline the fence appeared again, although it was hidden between two large gorse bushes and would not have been visible from the track at the top of the field, or even from the middle of the pasture. Beyond it, squat bushes, tufts of cow parsley and the bright blue of harebells crowded the edges of an overgrown path that vanished straight over the cliff edge.

'That's it,' the agent said. 'That's what we could see on the aerial photograph. 'Where does it go?'

'I have no idea,' Bette said. She had no memory of this track. It was possible – probable, even – that she had never seen it before in her life.

'Well,' Carr said, tucking her iPad back into her bag and heading for the fence. 'I'm all for finding out.'

Chapter Fifteen

Her hands were sweating – all of her was sweating, her T-shirt stuck to her like a wet rag and really, why was it that no one had invented a bra that wicked moisture away from your skin instead of plastering it right against you in the worst way? Even the sports bra Nina wore seemed incapable of actually providing this service. What about one with removable gel pads you could put in the fridge, or the freezer? *Chill Your Tits: Cool Underwear for Hot Women.* Boom! Now there was a good business idea, she thought. She heard the ringing of her phone over the noise of the tractor and pulled over. As Nina wrested the mobile from her pocket she briefly pondered a change in career to solve this problem for all womankind, but then she remembered that the last time she'd tried to use a sewing machine she'd ended up almost throwing the thing across the room in frustration, and that idea departed as quickly as it had arrived.

'Bette?' Nina asked, sweeping back her hair and holding

the device to her ear. She'd snapped yet another hairband, a common frustration. *I really should learn to keep a whole bloody bag of them in here.* 'What is it?'

She listened as her sister spoke, but still didn't understand what she was saying, partly because Bette appeared to be standing directly in the wind and partly because even when she could hear the words Nina couldn't make sense of what she was being told.

'What? *What* about the cliff?' Nina rubbed a hand over her face, which did nothing to dislodge the feeling that she was about to suffocate in her own steam. 'Look, I'll come, all right?' she said. 'Tell me where you are.' The answer she got to that question made no sense, either. 'What ledge? I don't know what you mean. Send me a location pin,' Nina said, eventually. 'I'll be there as soon as I can.'

The requested locator pinged as she restarted the tractor. Nina rattled her way to the hay pile, deposited the bales that she'd loaded when Bette called, and then headed for the farmhouse, parking in the yard and taking the opportunity to grab a cold can of Coca Cola from the fridge before striking out to find her sister. Frowning at the blinking blue dot on her map screen, Nina noted that Bette appeared to be on or perhaps even over the edge of the cliff. But she hadn't been screaming on the phone, so presumably neither she nor the land agent she was with had fallen onto the rocks.

The route she followed took her across the farmyard, past the barns and the chicken pen and on past the strawberry polytunnel. Beyond this, the pastures were split by a roughly rutted track wide enough for the tractor to pass down. Nina crossed this, reaching the fence line of the fields that ran directly along the cliff edge. Looking up, she expected to see her sister and the land agent standing at the far edge of one of these fields, but there was no sign of them. The blue dot was still there, though, blinking insistently on her screen. Were they stuck in the bushes that ran along the fence? What on earth were they doing?

Nina climbed over the gate and into the pasture. Like Bette, she'd never been allowed near the cliffs when she was little, and she held the same rule for her own son. Barnaby was under no circumstances to come into these fields, the track was as far as he was allowed to go. At the centre of the field she stopped, utterly confused. There was still no sign of her sister.

'Bette?' she shouted. 'Where *are* you?'

'Down here, Nina!'

Her sister's shout was faint and distant, as if it were coming from underground. For one crazy second Nina wondered whether Bette had slipped through a faery ring, tales of which their parents' elderly neighbours, the Bronaghs, had once delighted in teasing her with when she was little. But no, Nina realized that she was inside the mess of bushes right at the cliff edge. Was she mad? One wrong step out there and Bette would surely fall to her death on the rocks below, or else drown in the rough swell.

'What are you *doing*?' Nina asked, as Bette's head and shoulders appeared around a gorse bush that was pushing its way through the fence.

'Did you know this was here?' Bette asked, cheeks a little flushed by exertion and the wind, too.

'Did I know what was—' Nina stopped speaking as she got close enough to see the old path beyond the border fence on which her sister was standing. It had been almost entirely obscured by the gorse, hidden from view unless you happened to walk right up to it. 'What—'

'Come on,' Bette said. 'You've got to see this. Watch your step.'

Nina climbed the fence as Bette headed off down the path, pushing her way through branches and holding them out of the way for Nina to follow. After a few feet of battling vegetation, the bushes suddenly gave way to open air and an unexpected slope that made Nina lose her footing. She stumbled forward, righting herself against a waist-high wrought-iron fence that had been driven into the cliff edge.

'You okay?' Bette asked. 'Don't worry, it's not much further. The going is easier from here.'

'I'm fine,' Nina said, a little short of breath. 'What's this fence doing here?'

Bette shrugged. 'I'd be willing to bet that someone once wasn't as lucky as you just were. Can you imagine it *not* being there?'

Nina looked. Bette was right. Without it her misstep would have sent her plunging over the cliff. Beyond it the earth dropped away into an absence that sheered straight down to the jagged rocks and roiling water below. Beside it, the footpath twisted left, sloping down in uneven steps as it worked its way north.

Bette went on and Nina followed, treading carefully in the sandy indentations left by other feet. A few steps ahead the path opened out a little more, sloping down still further, and then, abruptly, it became a wide oblong of land clinging to the cliff edge, as if half the field they'd just made their way from had sunk down the side of the cliff and settled here, above the reach of the crashing waves but beneath the rest of the Crowdie pastures. Bette stopped beside a huge, towering boulder of grey stone that stood like a sentry at the bottom of the track. Nina came to a standstill beside her, her hand on the old fence.

'What the hell is *this*?'

'I don't know,' Bette said. 'I've never been down here before. I never even knew it was here. Are you saying you didn't either?'

'No!'

'Well, someone must have known about it,' Bette said, gesturing to the fence that had saved Nina from certain death. It continued down the side of the path they had followed and ran all the way along the cliff edge. 'It goes right to the other end of this— I don't even know what to call it. Forest?'

Nina could see what Bette meant. The field before them – Nina thought it was probably about half an acre in size – was full of small, gnarled trees. They all looked ancient, bent by the constant battering of the sea winds and wizened by years. Some of them looked dead, lichen spattering their bare branches and bark like paint. Around them grew long grasses, reaching up as far as the lower branches, adding to the strange, otherworldly aspect of the place. Nina was reminded of her earlier suspicion that Bette had been sucked into the faery realm. Maybe that wasn't too far from the truth after all. This didn't feel like their farm at all, which Nina knew inside out after a childhood spent growing up on it and five years of her adult life looking after everything that lived and grew within its boundaries. Almost everything, anyway. These trees looked as if they'd been left to their own devices for decades.

'What a curious place,' called Martha Carr, as she waded her way back to them from the other end. 'Details about it would be welcome. That fence looks Victorian, but there are bee boles and a sheltered stone bench carved into the rock wall at the far end that look far older.'

'Bee boles?' Bette asked. 'What are they?'

'Alcoves they would have put beehives in over winter back in the day.' She reached them and looked expectant. 'How long has this orchard been here?'

'Orchard?' Bette asked.

'Yes — there are a few trees with apples on them. I've no idea what variety, I'm not a fruit person. But an orchard could be a real point of interest for any potential buyer — especially, I have to say, one with such an unusual aspect. Assuming this does actually belong to the Crowdie farm?'

'I guess so,' Nina said. She turned to indicate the path.

'That leads straight up to our pasture. And it's below our fields, isn't it?'

'Yes,' the land agent agreed, 'but I'm not sure it's quite that clear cut. Look at this.' She lifted her iPad to show them both an aerial satellite grab of the farmland. Nina saw that she had been drawing a line in to mark their boundary with Cam's farm according to Bette's scan of their old family map. 'You see here? Do you have a relationship with your neighbour? I wonder if he knows this is here?'

'I know him pretty well,' Nina said. 'He only bought the place a few years back, but he's a friend. We knew the old couple who used to own it far better, but I can't remember them ever mentioning this place either. And Cam's started an orchard at the front of the property since he moved in. Why would he have done that if he knew this was here?'

'We'll have to check the original deeds and boundaries,' Martha Carr told them. 'We need to be sure. I've learned from experience that these things aren't always simple. It's probably worth asking your neighbour to look at his boundary lines, too, so you're all on the same page. Now, I think there's still some of the property I need to see, and time is getting on.'

The two other women started making their way back up the path, but Nina hung back for a moment, surveying this strange, secret orchard. She would have liked to spend more time here, to look around at this patch of land that until this moment she'd had no idea existed. But out over the water she could see black clouds beginning to gather. The promised rain was edging its way towards land, and before it reached them she had to get the last of the hay baled and stacked. It was going to be a race against the weather as it was, even with the promise of Cam's help.

Chapter Sixteen

Bette and Martha Carr concluded the tour of the farm's boundary, but Bette's mind was firmly back amid those strange, tangled trees. The land agent promised to be in touch soon with a valuation, although as she'd pointed out, until they knew more about the patch of land on the cliff and specifically who owned it, it would be incomplete.

She watched as the woman pulled away, the wheels of her BMW spitting dust into the dry air. Then she went inside to call Nina again, the quickest way to get hold of her sister, who had gone back to baling.

'Is Cam coming over to help?'

'He said he'd be here after lunch,' Nina said, sounding out of breath. Bette could well imagine what the heat in the tractor's cab would be like this close to midday. 'Shall I tell him about the – I don't know what we're calling it? The orchard?'

'Yeah, we need to get that boundary question answered as

soon as we can. I'll call the solicitor and make sure the map we have is the most up-to-date one.'

Nina was silent for a minute, and Bette imagined her thoughts were in the same place as her own. 'Maybe Mum knows something about it?' Nina said. 'I can't believe neither she nor Dad had any clue that place was there. She might be able to tell us about it?'

'I was thinking that too,' Bette agreed. 'I'll message her, see if we can Zoom about it?'

'I don't think I'll be able to do that today,' Nina said. 'This is taking longer than I thought and the wind's already up. The storm's going to blow onto shore before dark.'

Bette considered saying she'd talk to Sophia herself, alone, but thought better of it. 'Tomorrow, then?'

There was a pause. 'I thought you were planning to go back tomorrow?'

'I was, but I haven't heard from the bank and I've still got a mountain of paperwork to go through in the office and now, with this as well . . .' Bette shook her head. 'I think I'll have to tell them I'm taking the whole week. I can be back on Monday and it shouldn't make any difference.'

'Okay,' Nina said. There was another pause. 'You really shouldn't carry on sleeping in the attic, though. Not with this storm coming. Who knows how badly that roof leaks?'

'Oh God, don't say that,' Bette said. 'A new roof is the last thing we need to be thinking about right now.'

'Exactly,' Nina said, 'so don't be up there. What you don't know can't worry you, right?'

Bette snorted a slight laugh at Nina's dry tone. 'Right. I see. I have a feeling that kind of thinking is how we've ended up where we are, to be honest, but I see your point.'

'Trust me,' her sister said, 'a blind eye will help you a lot around here. I've got to get on.'

After they hung up, Bette went back into the office to call the bank again, but all they could do was assure her that her request was 'in progress'. Then she called Oliver to tell him that she was going to take a little longer away from the office.

'Okay,' her secretary said, his voice doubtful. 'I can sort that out for you, of course.'

Bette frowned at his tone. 'Is something wrong?' she asked.

'I don't *think* so. At least . . . no one's said anything to me. It's just . . .' he trailed off. 'I feel as if there's something going on here, but I don't know what.'

'In what way?'

His sigh surfed the line. 'I don't know. Maybe I'm being paranoid. Something just feels . . . off. Muttering in corners. Sideways glances. That kind of thing. You know?'

Bette did know, and she didn't like it. Office politics were always her least favourite thing about being part of such a big firm. And it was about to get exponentially bigger. 'It's probably something to do with the merger,' she said.

She wasn't sure how to interpret the silence that followed from Oliver's end of the line.

'Maybe,' he said, eventually. 'Anyway, I'm sure there's nothing for you to worry about. I'll see you on Monday?'

Bette told him he would and they said their goodbyes, but she was left unsettled in the wake of the call, remembering feeling the same after her brief chat with Spencer Coulthard just two days before. Could something be going wrong with the merger? She considered calling and asking him directly, but surely whatever it was could wait until Monday. Any time she spent chasing down Oliver's probably unfounded discomfort would take away time she had to deal with sorting out her father's estate. Once she was back in London, she could deal with whatever was going on there with no distractions, but until then, better that her focus was fully on the task at hand.

She was about to call Roland Palmer about the land deeds when her mobile pinged with an incoming message from Allie.

Can't remember when you said you were heading back to London and wanted to make sure I said goodbye. Let's try to stay in touch? Let's not leave it so long again! A xx

Bette smiled as she sent a message back.

Actually, I'm staying until Sunday now. And we must def keep in touch, yes!

Oh, came the almost immediate reply. *I hope everything's okay?*

Getting there, Bette said, *just discovered something a bit unexpected about the estate, that's all.*

She hit send and then something else occurred to her. Allie had spent plenty of time on the farm when she was younger.

Come to think of it, Bette added, *you don't know anything about an orchard on the side of the cliff, do you?*

The three dots that indicated Allie was typing blinked for a few seconds, and then disappeared. A moment later Bette's phone rang.

'Hey,' Allie said. 'I thought it'd be quicker to call. What's going on? What's this about an orchard? I didn't know Crowdie even had one.'

'It seems like no one else did, either,' Bette said. 'It's a really strange little place, hidden away right on the cliff. It was obviously used at some point, though, because there's an old wrought-iron fence down there, and there are bee boles in the cliff, as well as a bench cut right into the rock.' There was a pause that dragged on so long that Bette wondered if Allie had been cut off. 'Allie? Are you there?'

'Sorry,' her friend said. 'That's just rung a very faint bell.'

'Really?' Bette leaned forward. 'Then you *do* remember it?'

'No,' Allie said, sounding vague, as if she were straining to pull something from the depths of memory. 'No, I really don't think so. Sorry. There was just a split second there that I thought— but no, it's gone. I can't imagine I'd have forgotten going to a place like that at yours. And we were never allowed near the cliffs, were we?'

'No,' agreed Bette. 'And the path had been fenced off completely. We were always told that the area had eroded into the sea, but apparently not.'

'Sounds fascinating.'

'I bet it's right up your street, actually,' Bette said. 'I'm about to go back down there to take some photographs for reference. I'll send you some.'

'Well,' Allie said, 'I'd love to come with you to see it. Can I? The shop's shut on a Wednesday afternoon, so I'm free.'

Bette made lunch for Nina and herself while she waited for Allie to arrive – sandwiches that she wrapped in cling film and left in the fridge, texting her sister where to find them when she had a moment to break.

Thanks, Nina texted back, and Bette was surprised by the appended *xx*, something she could never remember her sister including in any message to her before.

When Allie arrived she was flush-faced, pulling into the farmyard and parking beside Bette's rental car in a flurry of heat-stirred dust. Her excitement made her look younger, as if she were still the teenager Bette remembered rather than the mother of two young men.

'I've got it,' Allie said, by way of breathless greeting as she climbed out of the driver's seat. 'I've realized why your description of this orchard rang a bell. Do you remember that old book we found in a box in the attic one summer when we were kids? It was about a secret orchard, wasn't it? An orchard hidden away on the side of a cliff.'

Bette drew a complete blank. 'A book?'

'You must remember it!' Allie said, as she followed Bette back into the kitchen. 'It was about a young woman who had married this awful older man who only wanted her so that she could give him a son and heir, because he was the master of this big estate and none of his previous wives had produced children. But she didn't love him and couldn't get pregnant and ended up falling in love with one of the estate labourers, who managed this strange little orchard on her husband's land. We were obsessed with it. We took turns in reading bits of it to each other whenever I stayed over that summer.'

'Are you sure you're not getting confused with *Lady Chatterley's Lover*?' Bette asked. 'Didn't we read that at school?'

'Yes, and I remember that too,' Allie said, 'but this was different. It was written like a novel, but it was set out like a diary, with dates and everything. You really don't remember?'

Bette stood for a moment, looking out into the shaft of sunlight and farmyard visible out of the open kitchen door. Did she remember? There was something there, for certain, but it was too ephemeral to catch hold of.

'Maybe,' she said, eventually.

'Could the book still be in the attic?' Allie suggested. 'It had been there for years when we found it, just sitting in a box.'

'I don't think so,' Bette said, thinking about the first night on this visit that she'd spent up in her old haunt of the attic, remembered the feeling that there was something missing from the corners, something that had been cleared away. 'It's pretty empty up there now. I can look – but it might be better to do that another time. I want to get down to the orchard and take these photographs before the storm comes in. I don't think it'd be a good place to be in bad weather.'

The sun was still high and hot when they reached the orchard slope, but the wind had risen, thinning into a knife edge that cut across the water from the gathering clouds scudding towards them. Bette took photographs as Allie waded about amid the long grasses, fascinated by everything she saw.

'The fence,' she said. 'It's got a monogram entwined amid the design, have you noticed? I think it's an O and a C – look.'

Bette bent down to see what Allie was pointing at, parting the long grass that tangled through the filigree of wrought iron to see that she was right. She framed a photograph and snapped it, zooming into the image to look closer.

'I wonder who that is?' she said, as she and Allie looked at the letters together.

'It must be one of your ancestors, mustn't it?' her friend pointed out. 'A great grandparent, maybe?'

Bette shook her head. 'No idea. I'll add it to the list of questions to ask Mum.'

'Show me these bee boles,' Allie said, then. 'This fence doesn't look that old, at least not in the grand scheme of things, but looking at the rest of this place . . .'

Bette looked at her as she trailed off. 'What?'

Allie scanned the strange field of wizened trees. 'It *feels* really old – doesn't it? As if it's been here for a long, *long* time.'

Bette laughed. 'Is that the archaeologist in you speaking?'

Allie smiled. 'Maybe. That's why I want to see what's in the cliff.'

'Come on then,' Bette said. 'I haven't had a proper look myself yet, either.'

They stuck to the fence rather than fighting their way between the trees. As they tramped through the long grass, Bette thought she felt the first drops of rain alight against her cheek. Reaching the far end of the orchard, they were confronted by the cliff. It towered over them, looking as if it had been neatly cleaved, like an apple cut in half. The bare rock face was almost straight, on top of which was the very edge of Cam's pasture. Looking up, Bette could see that there were bushes hanging over the edge – probably as dense as they were on the Crowdie side, which would mean even someone walking right up to them wouldn't see over the edge and down into the orchard. Had that been deliberate, she wondered? Had whoever had established this place wanted to hide it? It certainly felt hidden.

'There are the bee boles,' Allie said.

She pointed to a series of five shallow alcoves cut into the wall. They were at about waist height, a couple of feet deep, and shaped a little like a church window, with the stone curving to an arch at the top.

'Pretty amazing, aren't they?' Bette said. 'They look as if they were cut by hand.'

'Yeah,' Allie agreed. 'They must have taken some doing.'

They walked past each, all empty except for a few caught leaves and twigs. At the end of the line of alcoves was what looked like a larger version of the same, but twice the height and filled with stone.

'This isn't a bee bole, is it?' Bette observed. 'I wonder what it is? It looks as if it's been deliberately blocked up.'

Allie reached out to lay one hand flat against one of the tightly packed stones. 'A larger place for storage, perhaps?' she suggested. 'Like a shed, so that whoever looked after this place didn't have to bring equipment down from above with them every time?'

They both contemplated this statement, and Bette thought they were probably each thinking about that story that Allie had outlined, about the lonely young woman falling in love with the keeper of an orchard.

'You know, this isn't really my area of expertise,' Allie said, 'but I'd like to do some research, see what I can come up with from a historical perspective?'

'Sure,' Bette said, as another gust of wind cut across her face, this time bringing with it the definite sting of rain. 'That would be great. Any information we can find out about this place will be more than Nina and I know now, that's for sure.'

Chapter Seventeen

Nina only managed to have a snatched conversation with Cam about what they'd found. The baling had to take priority, and even with both of them working at full pelt it took them until well after eight o'clock before they were finished. By the end they were working in the dark and the storm had descended, the hard rain already beginning to patter onto the dry dust of the farmyard as she'd stowed the tractor in the barn. She'd waved Cam off with the agreement that they'd talk more about the orchard when they saw each other next.

The storm worsened as the night wore on, the wind rising to gust against the farmhouse, making the old windows of Nina's bedroom rattle and creak. Despite her exhaustion Nina had lain awake after collapsing into bed, listening to the squall batter the farmhouse until eventually it resolved into a downpour that soothed her into a fitful sleep. She was woken by a text ping arriving as the dawning day was still murky, and rolled over to reach for her phone. It was from Cam.

This is crazy it said. *How could we not know this place was here?*

She smiled at his incredulity and sent a text back. *Are you there now?*

Yes, he replied. *Hope you don't mind?*

Of course not. Wait for me, she wrote back. *I'll bring coffee.*

Nina got up and dressed quickly before going down-stairs. Bette had done as Nina had suggested and moved from the attic into the guest room. Her door was still closed, so Nina moved quietly about the kitchen, making strong coffee in two insulated mugs before she made her way outside. She had thought the rain had stopped, but in fact it had only lessened, a drizzle falling from a grey dawn sky. She splashed across the farmyard puddles, clucking to the sleepy chickens. Nina hunched her shoulders, wishing she'd paused to put on her coat, but she couldn't be both-ered to go back now.

She found Cam leaning on the fence blocking the way to the hidden footpath. Nina grinned at the look on his face and the dishevelled nature of his hair, knowing that hers – far longer, far harder to tame – likely looked even more un-kempt. Cam had been just as exhausted as she was the night before. Nina held out the coffee she'd brought as she reached him and he took it gratefully.

'Thanks.'

'You've been down there, then?'

'Aye,' he glanced back towards the narrow path. 'I prob-ably should have waited, but—'

Nina dismissed his concern with a waved hand. 'It's fine.

I'm glad – it's too crazy to explain without you seeing it with your own eyes. Come on – I didn't have time to have a proper look myself yesterday.'

She climbed over the fence to join him and then led the way. This morning the path was slippery as well as uneven, the rain turning the indentations into mud. Nina concentrated on her feet until she reached the boulder that marked level ground. Then she stopped and waited for Cam, a couple of steps behind her.

The rain slowed further and then ceased altogether. From above the turbulent water there came a bright gleam of Godlight shining through the breaking clouds, gold splitting gunmetal as the new day continued to drive out the night's storm. It shone upon this strange, hidden piece of land, upon the small, peculiar twists of trees that were growing hunched beneath the cliff, shaped by the constant battering of the winds. It gave Nina the same strange, dislocated feeling of being somewhere *Other* that she'd had the day before.

'Bette said that neither of you knew this was here?' Cam asked, as he came to a stop beside her. His voice was hushed, the kind of tone one uses in a cathedral. Nina understood the sentiment. There was no wind, no rustle of creatures in the undergrowth or birds twittering in the branches of the trees. 'Do you think your dad knew?'

It was something she'd wondered about herself as she'd lain awake listening to the rain the night before. 'I can't believe he didn't. But why wouldn't he have told us about it?'

'What about your mum?' Cam asked. 'She might be able to shed some light?'

'Yeah, Bette's scheduled a Zoom call with her later today. I guess we'll find out then.' Nina gulped her coffee, glad for the burst of caffeine. She groaned slightly as her back twinged.

Cam looked concerned. 'You okay?'

Nina laughed a little ruefully. 'Getting old, I think. Yesterday was tough. How did anyone ever get away with making farming look all gentle and pastoral?'

Cam smiled. 'I'm sorry I couldn't help more than I did.'

'Don't be daft,' she said. 'Without you I'd have been totally scuppered and probably still baling now. Anyway, you've got your own place to worry about. I'm grateful when you do help out, Cam, but I don't expect you to make your own life harder to do that. The last thing I'd want to do is make myself a nuisance.'

'You, a nuisance?' He smiled, fine lines crinkling around his eyes. 'That you could never be.'

Nina looked away, taking another large mouthful of coffee as she surveyed the trees. It really didn't look like much of an orchard. 'The land agent said there are apples. Did you find them?'

'I did, actually. This way . . .' Cam led her further into the orchard. Nina had to step carefully as the unkempt grass tangled around her feet and legs. The wash of the sea was louder today, the wind stirring the waves to crash against the cliffs in a constant rolling boom. The air was still wet from the downpour, the heavy smell of petrichor after such a long period of dry weather perfuming the air.

'Here,' he said, as they reached one of the little trees.

It was barely as tall as the top of Nina's head, branches wizened. But it had leaves in abundance and between them she could see the fruits here and there. There were a few windfalls scattered amid the grasses beneath, too, a product of the previous night's storm. Nina bent to pick one up and held it in her hand with a frown.

'Is this definitely an apple?' she asked. 'I don't think I've ever seen one this yellow. And it's a bit of a strange shape.'

'I know,' Cam agreed. 'It's not a variety that I've ever seen either – not that I'm an expert, obviously. At first I thought it might be a quince, or something like that, but no – I'm pretty sure it is an apple.'

Nina weighed it in her hand. Even as a windfall it was surprisingly big, almost filling her cupped hand. It was also oddly conical – wider towards the stalk and narrower towards the bottom. The example she held in her hand couldn't have been on the ground long, because although it bore evidence of insect attack, it wasn't really bruised at all – probably not surprising given the deep cushion of grass beneath the tree. She wedged her coffee mug against the tree trunk and retrieved her utility knife from her jeans pocket, handing the apple to Cam so that she could open the blade.

'I want to know what it tastes like,' she said, taking back the fruit from her neighbour's hand and cutting a slice of the least nibbled area she could find.

Cam watched her as she chewed for a moment. 'Well?'

Nina was trying to analyse the taste. 'It's . . . quite sharp. I don't think it's an eating variety. Although actually, it does have an underlying sweetness there, too. It's definitely apple, though.' She cut another slice and held it out for him to try.

Cam took the slice and tried it. 'Hmm. Yeah, that's not like any apple I've ever had before. It's almost . . . salty?'

'Well, it is growing right by the sea,' Nina pointed out. She looked at the other trees around them and then at the half-eaten apple in her hand. 'I'll take this back with me to Bette so she can try it, too.' She rested the apple on the lid of her mug so she could fold the penknife shut before picking it and the coffee up again. 'I guess we'll see what Mum says later and take it from there.'

'I was thinking,' Cam said, as Nina swallowed the last of her coffee. 'There's this guy I know. He's part of the darts team and he knows a lot about fruit trees, including apple. It's what he does, he's a freelancer who does consultancy for people with orchards. He's been working with the Grevilles – you know, the big estate that owns most of Barton Mill?'

'Yeah,' Nina laughed. 'It's not really possible to live around here without knowing – or at least knowing of – the Grevilles.'

Cam nodded. 'Well, we've been talking about him coming up here to Bronagh to see the saplings I've planted over at my place. I'm such a novice and he really knows his stuff, so he said he'd be happy to take a look and give me whatever advice he could. Maybe I should ask him to come and take a look at what you've got here too, while he's at it? If anyone's going to know what type of apples they are, it'd be him.'

Nina considered. 'Hey, if he wants to come, why not? The land agent said she'd like to know more about the place. I know Bette would too. It's so . . .' she looked around again, '*weird.*'

Cam laughed, following the line of her gaze. 'I know what you mean. Not creepy, though.'

'No,' Nina agreed, realizing that he was right. There was a sort of natural peace to the place. 'It's probably because despite being right on the cliff, it's actually quite sheltered, isn't it? Even though one end is on a slope, it's basically a wall. And the other end is *literally* a wall. It's sheer rock. Speaking of which, that's the end that might be yours depending on how the boundaries line up. We should go down there and look at it.'

They walked together to the end of the orchard, both of them fascinated by the traces of life still extant in the cliff. The bee boles seemed as if they might be ageless, their sandstone edges weathered but still sharp enough to appear untouched. The stone bench was inviting despite the pools of water that had gathered on its surface thanks to the lashing storm. Who else had sat there, Nina wondered, and when? Who had made it, and for whom?

'Let me know what your mum says, won't you?' Cam asked, as they parted at the field gate, both with their own days to start. 'And I'll give Ryan a ring, see when he might be able to come have a look.'

'Ryan?'

'Apple guy,' Cam clarified.

'Okay, you do that – thanks. I'll text you later. I'd better go sort out the cows.'

Chapter Eighteen

'Oh yes, that'll be the old orchard,' said Sophia Crowdie, her voice echoing a little through the Zoom connection.

'Then – you and Dad *did* know about it?' Bette asked, incredulous. It was mid-afternoon and she and Nina were sitting beside each other at the kitchen table, looking at their mother on the screen of Bette's iPad. 'Why on earth didn't either of you ever think to tell *us* about it?'

'Didn't we?' Sophia asked, vaguely. 'That doesn't seem right.'

'Pretty sure we wouldn't have forgotten you and Dad telling us about a secret orchard stuck on the side of the cliff, Mum,' Nina said.

'Well, to be honest I'd forgotten all about it. It was abandoned before I even met your dad, I think. He might have shown it to me once, but that was probably the only time I went down there. I remember it being kind of spooky.'

'Mum,' Bette said. 'Is there *anything* you can tell us about it?'

Sophia Crowdie blew out a breath. 'Not much. Like I said, it had stopped being used before I even became part of the family. I think there was some story about a child falling from the ledge, or something like that.'

'What?' Nina asked. 'You mean – a sibling of Dad's?'

'No, no, this would have been a very long way back,' their mother said. 'In the 1800s sometime, I think, or maybe even before that. Anyway, from what I remember the family didn't want to use it after that and it just . . . fizzled out.'

'The 1800s?' Bette mused. She thought about the wrought-iron fence. It did look Victorian, or perhaps even Georgian, but . . . 'That would make it really very old, wouldn't it? There are trees down there still producing fruit right now. Could they really last that long?'

Sophia shrugged. 'I don't know, darling, I'm sorry.'

'Maybe Cam's friend can tell us,' Nina said. 'He called earlier and said that they'd arranged for him to come up tomorrow morning.'

'Oh?' Bette was surprised. 'He must be keen.'

'I think he's already got a day of work booked in the area, so he's coming before he starts that. And he's supposedly an expert on fruit trees, so maybe he'll be able to shed some light for us.'

'Well, between him and Allie maybe they can tell us something, or give us some place to start with more research, at least. That reminds me,' Bette added, 'I'm sure there used to be more up in the attic than there is now. I mention it because Allie remembers a book that she and I read when we were kids that sounds as if it might have had something to do with the orchard, but there's nothing like that up there now.'

'That was probably Dad, in COVID,' Nina said. 'He kept having these big clear-outs. I think it was because he was bored – he couldn't go out for his usual pint at the pub and he couldn't do as much on the farm by then, either. He sent lots to the local auction houses when they reopened.' Bette watched Nina as her sister fell silent, a thoughtful look on her face. Then she sighed. 'Thinking about it now, I guess he was finding ways to raise money, too, although none of it can have fetched much, can it?'

The thought of this twinged something painful in Bette's heart. Is that what Bern had been doing? Searching for some forgotten treasure hidden away in a dusty corner of this old house? It was terrible to think that things had got so desperate without either of his daughters knowing. On the other hand, she could well believe that he was bored out of his mind and looking for ways to keep busy during those lockdown months. Either way, it seemed likely that the book Allie remembered, and that Bette thought she could now vaguely recollect too, had gone. Who knew where it had ended up.

'It doesn't matter,' she said. 'I just wondered, that's all.'

'There's your grandmother's paintings,' their mother said. 'I haven't thought about this for years, but I remember her taking her easel down there when she had time. It's possible that she was the only person who ever went down there at all, in the end.'

Bette blinked. 'How did I not know that? I used to love watching Grandma paint. Why did I never go with her?'

Her mother shrugged. She was holding a glass of white wine and wearing a cream sundress that set off her tanned skin while sitting against an open window that looked out onto a backdrop of brilliant azure blue sky. She looked perfectly at home, an ideal advertisement for the Italian tourist board. Meanwhile, outside the Scottish summer had sent another squall of rain.

'Your dad was very strict about you girls not going anywhere near the cliffs, remember? Your grandparents were, too,' Sophia reminded her. 'Probably a family memory from that poor little child lost all those years ago.'

Bette saw Nina look at her watch. 'Okay, well, I've got to go and pick Barney up from school,' she said. 'I haven't seen him for two days, I'm missing him like crazy. So is Limpet.'

'Go, go get my beautiful grandson,' Sophia said, waving a hand as she took another sip of wine. 'Give him a big kiss from me. I have to go too. Sorry I couldn't tell you more about the orchard. Let me know if you find out anything else.'

Once they had said their goodbyes and ended the call, Nina turned to Bette. 'That book you mentioned – there's still a pile of them that Dad had in his room. I think he was getting ready to send another lot to sale. It might be worth looking there?'

'Really?' Bette hadn't been back into her father's bedroom since she'd showed Martha Carr around the house. 'Okay, thanks. I'll have a look.'

Nina got up from the kitchen table with a sigh. 'Dad's room is another thing that really needs sorting out,' she said. 'I just haven't felt up to it yet.'

Bette nodded. 'There's no rush. But maybe I can help you before I go back to London.'

'Yeah,' Nina said, after a pause and with a faint smile. 'That would be good. Thanks.'

Once Nina had left to collect Barney, Bette went up to their father's bedroom. Looking around, she spied a pile of books and papers against the wall in one corner. Bette sat cross-legged on the old carpet and picked each volume up one by one, but none were the book she wanted. She was about to put them all back where they had been when she took note of the stack of papers at the bottom. There were several sheaves of very old, yellowing paper laid flat on top of each other, all in clear plastic folders. It was obvious that they weren't what she was looking for, but they caught her eye nonetheless. Bette collected them all and took them back to her father's study for closer examination.

She looked through the folders, peering through their covers to see what was inside. As far as Bette could make out, she'd found the original deed for the house and land. The deed was dated to 1839, which came as a surprise to her, as she'd assumed the Crowdie ownership went back further. She could make out that it was between the Greville estate – the major landowners of the area since the Clearances, and still the owners of the manor house that stood sentry above Barton Mill – and the Crowdie patriarch of the time, who had been called George. Beyond that Bette found it impossible to decipher much else from the dense paragraphs of hand-inked text, which were in the typically florid style of the period. Still, it was a curious document to have, and it would be interesting to compare it against the land deeds held by the solicitor, Roland Palmer. Bette wondered if there was a map that matched the period included somewhere in the pile and whether, if so, it would be different from the one on the wall in the kitchen. She searched for any mention of the orchard, too. Anything that would give her some context for that strange patch of land and whether it really did belong to them.

A little later there was a brief knock at the door and her nephew stuck his head into the study. He was wearing his superhero costume, as usual, and Bette wondered whether he'd taken it with him to stay at his friend's house, or whether he'd changed into it as soon as he'd got home. Limpet was at his side, living up to his name, the collie seeming far happier than he had since his little owner had been away.

'Best Barnaby Barnacle!' she said, genuinely pleased to see her nephew. The house had been so quiet without him. 'You're back!'

'Hey, Auntie Bette. Did you miss me?'

'I did,' she laughed. 'Did you have a good time at your sleepover?'

He nodded, coming further into the room and peering with interest at the sheets of old paper spread out over his grandfather's desk. 'Yes, but I'm glad to be home. I missed

Limpet. And Mum,' he added, quickly – and then, pointing to the papers, 'What are those?'

Bette shifted so that he could join her beside the chair. 'Really old documents all about the farm. I was looking to see whether there was a map that went with them, one that would show us what the farm looked like back then.'

'Like the one me and Grandad were making,' her nephew said, 'as my summer project, before he died.'

Bette looked down at him. 'Were you?'

Barney nodded, his eyes taking on a solemn look behind his mask. 'We were supposed to make a map of where we live for school over the summer holidays but I was doing it with Grandad and Mrs Dalston told me she'd heard what happened and that I didn't have to finish it if I didn't want to.'

'Do you want to?'

He considered, tipping his masked head to one side. 'Yes, because having a map of the farm means I can look out for potential trouble,' he said. 'But I don't think I can do it on my own and Mummy is too busy to help. Plus, I need to add the orchard now that we know it's there, and I don't know what it looks like.'

'Maybe I could help you finish it instead?' Even as she said the words, Bette wasn't sure what had compelled her to offer such a thing. She was only going to be here a few more days and anyway, crafting was decidedly not her thing. Neither were children, as a rule.

'Yes!' he said, excited. 'We could start after dinner. I've still got loads to do. And you know what the orchard looks like!'

'Best Barnaby Barnacle, did you forget what I sent you in there for?'

It was Nina's voice, and it sounded as if she was calling from the doorway of the kitchen.

'Oops,' Barney said, and looked at Bette. 'Would you like to have dinner with us? Mummy's made risotto. She says there's plenty for you, too.'

Bette smiled and stood up. 'That sounds like a very good idea.'

Later, after her nephew had gone to bed, Bette sat back down at the desk, taking out her iPad so that she could make notes about the papers she'd found. Outside, the rain started again. She could hear it pattering as it fell, a rhythmic, soporific beat.

When she finally went to bed herself the house was silent but for the sound of rain still falling outside. Bette fell asleep quickly and found her dreams full of strange twists of trees. When she woke the next morning it was still with thoughts of the orchard in her mind.

She got up, threw on the pair of jeans and the sweatshirt that Nina had lent her and went downstairs to the living room, flicking on the old Bakelite switch beside the door. She went to the wall above the sideboard to look at the gallery of her grandmother's paintings, searching for something she couldn't quite remember but knew would be there. As she did so, she realized just how much of the farm her grandmother had recorded with her paintbrush. It was almost a time capsule, this wall, she thought. Amid this painted history was plenty of evidence of the orchard. Having been there herself now, Bette could easily recognize it.

One picture in particular caught her eye. It was the one she had woken thinking of, that matched so distinctly what she had seen in her mishmash of dreams. It was a small watercolour painting of a single gnarled apple tree dotted with fruit so yellow they looked almost golden against a craggy background of grey stone, windfalls scattered amid the grasses beneath it. In the corner she could clearly make out her grandmother's signature, the little flourish she had proudly added to every one of her works once they were finished. There was a date, too. August 1963. An apple tree in its entirety, small and tangled, painted by her grandmother long before Bette had even been born. Bette took the painting and went into the kitchen, glancing at the clock on the wall to see that it wasn't even 6am. She paused, wondering if she should wait a little before going down to the orchard. But when she opened the kitchen door the rain had stopped and the dark clouds were parting to reveal a bright, sun-washed dawn. The air was so clear it almost chimed, the birds were singing, and Bette was already in the pair of old boots and raincoat Nina had given her to wear. She tucked the painting into a pocket and stepped out into the farmyard, pulling the kitchen door shut behind her.

Chapter Nineteen

Outside, the air was fragrant with the herbaceous scent of grasses as Bette made her way past the chicken coop and the polytunnel. She could hear the lowing of cattle in the distance, the Crowdie herd beginning to make an orderly queue for morning milking.

The wet grasses brushed Bette's jeans as she made her way through the pasture towards the concealed dip in the earth. She'd become better at finding her footing on the way down the path, but this time it was wet and slippery. She stayed as far away from the fence as she could, not wanting to tempt fate if she slipped. Below her the wash of salt water against the cliffs was gentle in the morning sun, worn out after a night of being buffeted by wind. There were bees abroad, meandering between the laden blossom of the bushes that hid the orchard path. This made Bette think about the bee boles. There would have been hives among the trees once, resident colonies that would have helped with pollination every season. She wondered when they had been taken out. When the orchard had been abandoned, presumably – when whoever it was who had taken care of the place and the bees had decided never to return.

Bette bent to pick up a windfall and smoothed a thumb over the yellow skin. The fruit was far from perfect, its skin marred by the vagaries of the weather. It looked different from the pictures of the fruit in her grandmother's paintings. Was that an artist's eye simply wanting to put a gloss on reality? Or was long neglect taking its toll?

Bette put down the windfall and searched for what she'd come looking for. She walked the rough line of trees closest to the rear cliff, taking out the painting she'd brought from the house. She was beginning to think that she must just have dreamed her waking conviction because she had glimpsed her grandmother's painting when she and Martha Carr had looked at the wall of pictures together. But then, there it was. Bette stopped, knee-deep in wet grass, a strange feeling tingling down her spine. She held up the small canvas in her hand.

In front of her was the same tree that her grandmother had painted, she was sure of it. Not a figment of imagination, but a painting taken as much from reality as the rest of Jean Crowdie's works. Bette looked between the watercolour and the tree before it. There was no fruit on the tree now. It looked decrepit, a tangle of branches, some of which had been lost since Bette's forebear had set her easel here to capture it in paint. But the shape of the trunk was the same: there was the same fork, and there, an ancient knot grown over into a knobble. It was the same tree. And it was alive – there were still leaves on some of its branches. They were sparse, but they were there. Raindrops from the night before glinted on their green curves.

Bette's heart thumped a little in her chest, though she couldn't really understand why. She knew nothing about apple trees. Perhaps this was nothing unusual? But the sensation she felt was about more than just the seeming impossibility of the longevity of this tree. She looked at the painting again. The date her grandmother had inscribed there was 1963. Sixty years ago. This tree had been old even then, or so the picture in her hand suggested. Could it really be the same tree? Bette knew there were trees that could live for centuries, but *apple* trees?

Voices drifted to her from the other end of the orchard, shaking Bette from her reverie. She turned and peered between branches to see two figures carefully making their way down the path into the orchard. It was only then that Bette remembered what Nina had said about their neighbour bringing his friend to visit this morning. Her first thought was that this was perfect timing – she could ask this guy about her recent discovery. Her second thought was that she must look an absolute mess – she hadn't even bothered to run a comb through her hair before she'd headed out, and thanks to the humidity of the recent rain her curls were at full insanity. She dragged a hand through her short hair, but it was too late to worry about it now. There was no way to avoid them and what was a man who spent all his time looking at apple trees going to care about her hair anyway? He was probably ancient. As for Cam, he clearly only had eyes for her sister. Neither of them would even notice what a mess she was.

'Morning,' Bette called as she waded towards them through the grass. 'Cam, when you said you would be here early I didn't think you meant *this* early!'

'Morning, Bette,' Cam said, smiling as they both came into view. 'Well, Ryan's got a full day so he wanted to pop by first. I didn't think anyone would be about down here!'

Bette registered the visitor's name just a split second before she saw his face. She was mid-stride and was so thrown that she stumbled to a stop.

'*Ryan?*' she said, aghast.

He stared at her, the colour draining from his face. '*Beth?*'

'Oh – do you two know each other?' Cam asked.

Ryan Atkins. He looked exactly the same. It was almost twenty years since she'd last seen him but he looked *exactly the same.*

Bette couldn't breathe. She stared at him, horrified. He couldn't be here. How could he be here? *Why* would he—

Painting and questions forgotten, she waded past them and kept going. She couldn't stay here. Not now. Not when—

'I have to go.'

'Beth,' Ryan said, again.

'It's Bette,' she called back, shakily, not even turning. She couldn't look at him, not again. 'I haven't been Beth since I was nineteen.'

It was undignified, running away, especially when the grasses tangled against her legs, determined to trip her. Bette didn't pause and didn't turn, praying he wouldn't come after her. He didn't. There was a buzzing in her ears, but she thought that was just because her heart was pounding hard with the shock. She reached the path and scrambled up it as fast as she could go and didn't look back until she was sure the gorse would have hidden the orchard – and him – from view.

Chapter Twenty

Nina had assumed that her sister was still in bed asleep. She knew Bette had been up late in the study again, and had heard her move quietly past her room to her own at almost one in the morning. Which meant that when Bette came crashing through the kitchen door from the farmyard as she was making Barnaby's breakfast, Nina nearly had a heart attack. She dropped the bowl of cereal she was holding. It fell to the floor where it smashed on the old ceramic tiles, scattering cornflakes and shards of pottery everywhere.

'Bette! What the—'

'Did you know?' her sister demanded.

Nina got down on her knees to start clearing up. 'Did I know what?'

'That it was him?'

Nina looked up at her sister. 'What are you talking about?'

'Cam's fruit expert friend,' Bette said. She looked wild, Nina thought. Not bad, just not her usual perfectly coiffed lawyer self. Hair all over the place, no make-up, scruffy in Nina's old cast-offs. It was kind of cute, actually. Her uptight sister, all undone. 'Did you know it was *him*?'

'Who?'

Bette stared at her. 'I have to go,' she said. 'I have to get out of here.'

Nina, still kneeling on the floor, watched as her sister grabbed her bag from the table and made for the door again. 'Bette—'

But Bette was gone, the kitchen door banging shut behind her and her footsteps echoing heavily on the concrete of the farmyard. Then came the slamming of a car door. A second or two later Bette was driving away.

She heard footsteps on the stairs and Barnaby came into the kitchen from the hallway, dressed for school but with his superhero mask pulled down over his face. He came around the table and stopped when he saw his mother and the remains of his breakfast on the floor.

'What happened?' he asked.

Nina thought for a second, but came up with nothing. 'I . . . really don't know.'

Her son considered the broken bowl, decided it wasn't a superhero situation, and pulled off his mask, revealing hair about as messy as Bette's. 'I'll get the dustpan and brush.'

Nina got to her feet, her hands full of smashed crockery. At least, she reflected, she hadn't added the milk yet.

Half an hour later, Barnaby had successfully had his replacement breakfast and was back upstairs brushing his teeth. Nina was washing up while mentally listing her tasks for the day when Cam stuck his head around the kitchen door.

'Hey,' he said, his face holding a trace of anxiety.

'Morning,' she said, automatically reaching out to fill the kettle. 'Did something happen with Bette earlier? She came in here as if she had the devil at her heels, then jumped in the car and headed for the hills.'

Cam leaned against one of the cabinets with his arms crossed. 'I don't know what happened,' he said. 'She was in the orchard when I got there with Ryan. She was fine until she saw him, then she completely freaked out. He did, too. I had no idea they knew each other.'

A dim light went off in Nina's mind. '*Ryan*,' she said, thoughtfully.

'He called her Beth,' Cam went on. 'But by then she was away. They both looked like they'd seen a ghost. I thought Ryan was going to go after her, but then he said he'd better leave and was there another way out of the orchard? Presumably he didn't want to risk bumping into her again. I said there wasn't, so he said he'd stay long enough to make sure "the coast was clear" and then he'd go. I said he might as well look at what he'd come to see in the meantime, so he had a look around the orchard and took some photos, but it was obvious he was messed up – like, really shaken. He's just gone so I thought I'd better come and see if Bette was all right.'

The light in Nina's mind grew brighter. 'Ryan,' she

162

mused. 'I think we might have had a farmhand who worked here when I was little with that name. Dad had a few kids who used to come in and help at the weekends and during holidays for a while, usually students at agricultural college . . . I think there was a Ryan among them at one point.'

'Do you think it could be the same guy?' Cam asked.

Nina shrugged. 'I guess? Bette acted as if I should know him – but I would have only been around Barney's age. It wasn't as if I hung out with the farmhands all the time when I wasn't at school and Bette was always way too cool to want her baby sister tagging along with her. I used to go riding on a Saturday morning, so most of the time I wouldn't have been here anyway. I might have met him a few times in passing, but that's about it.'

They were both quiet for a moment, until Cam said what they were both thinking.

'Maybe they were a couple?' He suggested. 'Might explain why they were so shocked at seeing each other again. You know, if they had a bad break-up, or something?'

'But we're talking years ago!' Nina said. 'They both would have been teenagers – kids! Bette's reaction was really extreme.'

'First loves can be pretty intense,' Cam pointed out.

'I suppose,' Nina agreed, thinking ruefully that she knew that for herself first-hand.

Cam sighed. 'Well, whatever it was about, I'm sorry if I put my foot in it with Bette. But honestly, I had no idea. If it is the same Ryan, he didn't say anything about knowing the place. He just said he'd grown up in the area.'

'I wouldn't worry about it,' Nina said. 'If it was a romance, I'm sure it's just like you said – they were both shocked at seeing each other again. It was probably one of those things where they'd forgotten the other even existed and then – bam! It hit them both at the same time and it was a bit overwhelming, that's all. It'll blow over. My sister really isn't one to be swayed by emotion.'

'Okay,' Cam said. 'I'm not sure how to deal with Ryan now.'

'Did he tell you anything about the orchard?' Nina asked. 'Did he know what kind of apple trees they are?'

Cam shook his head. 'He didn't seem to know – although he was so distracted that it was hard to tell. His head definitely wasn't in the game after he'd seen Bette – or Beth, as he called her. What was *that* about?'

'Oh, that's her birth name,' Nina said. 'That's how I knew her growing up, as Beth. Then about a year into university she suddenly decided she wanted to be known as Bette. No idea why. After that it was like she just decided she didn't want anything to do with her old life, or us, or the farm. She never came home for holidays, not even Christmas. She always went travelling, or worked as an intern, as far away from us as possible. If we ever wanted to see her, we had to visit whenever she could "fit us in". That was why she and I grew apart, really. She was never here when we might have actually been the right age to be friends. And even when

I needed her the most, when having her to talk to might have made a difference, might have made me not feel so alone and trapped—' Nina broke off, not wanting to relive those months when she had discovered she was pregnant and thought her only choice was to stay with a man who so clearly only wanted someone he could control completely. Bette would never have let herself get into that position, would she?

Cam, oblivious to Nina's inner turmoil, looked thoughtful. 'Sounds to me as if she was running away from something.'

Nina snorted a slight laugh. 'Bette's never run away from anything in her life. That's not her style.'

He looked at her. 'Are you sure? Obviously you know your sister better than I ever could. But she never came back, even for Christmas? That for sure sounds like she was avoiding something. Or someone.'

Nina thought about it and realized Cam was right. She'd always assumed that Bette just thought farm life wasn't good enough for her and ditched everything about it at the first chance she got. She saw now how simplistic that view was – and how extreme her sister's leaving had been.

There came the thundering of footsteps on the stairs, and Barnaby arrived in the kitchen. 'Mummy!' he said, out of breath, 'I've got to feed the chickens!'

'You do indeed,' Nina agreed. 'Shall I come with you?'

'No, I can do it,' he said, as he jammed on his wellies. 'Hi, Cam.'

'Hey, champ. Be careful out there, it's slippery.'

'I will,' the little boy promised. 'Mummy, when I come back can Cam take me to the orchard?'

'I don't think there'll be time, bub,' Nina said, glancing at the clock. 'You don't want to be late for school.'

'Okay,' said her son, with a disappointed sigh. Then he was out of the door, making for his beloved flock.

'He wasn't wearing his superhero costume,' Cam observed.

'Nope. We've agreed that he only needs to wear it when there's an actual emergency, rather than just in case of an emergency.'

'Nice,' Cam smiled. 'How did you get that one to stick?'

'I pointed out that superheroes don't wear their costumes all the time, and said it was because if they did people wouldn't take as much notice when there was an emergency, a bit like the boy who cried wolf,' Nina said. 'That seemed to work.'

'Good mum tactics,' Cam said. 'I'm impressed.'

'Anything that means I'm not having a battle with him every morning before school is worth it,' she said, checking her watch. She didn't want him to go quite yet. If he did, she might start thinking of things best not dwelt upon. 'I've got time for a coffee before I take Barney to school – stay for one?'

When Bette still hadn't returned by mid-afternoon, Nina started to wonder. Had her sister been so spooked by her encounter that morning that she'd actually taken off back to London without saying anything? Perhaps the shock meeting with this Ryan guy had given her the impetus to up sticks and head back to her real life?

Ryan. Nina had dredged her memory and come up with the hazy image of a burly young man who had maybe been around more than his counterparts. She had no idea whether her mind was making something up to fill a gap, but then she thought about the photographs in the hallway. Thinking back that far, had she at some point posed for a group photograph, out there in the farmyard? She had a foggy memory of being herded into a small crowd, and laughter as someone leaned out of an upstairs window, trying to snap an image of them all. If that wasn't her imagination playing tricks, could Ryan have been there in the group too? Nina went to look, more out of idle curiosity than the idea of solving a mild mystery involving her sister; even if Ryan was in such a photograph, she thought it was unlikely she'd recognize him.

There were three group photographs of the sort that Nina vaguely remembered being taken. Taken in consecutive years, they showed a gathering of all the casual workers that had once converged to work on the farm. From the pictures they looked mostly like teenagers. Nina thought they were probably all still in their final years of school or at college, picking up a little money and experience, helping out in their spare time. She could only find herself in one of them. It was the last one, which was labelled 'Crowdie Weekend Farm Crew, Summer 2006'. Nina searched it, looking for any faces she recognized. There were a few that popped out, people she hadn't thought of for years and whose names she couldn't remember, but none that she connected with the name Ryan.

Then she found her sister. Bette, or Beth as she had still been then, because Nina realized that 2006 would have been the year her sister had turned eighteen, the year she left for university. There in the past, Bette's hair was long, her natural dark curls tumbling over her shoulders. She looked as if she'd been hard at work with the rest of the 'crew' – she was in work boots and worn jeans, a baggy old band T-shirt tied up around her waist. She was clearly as happy as the rest of them, her face lit with laughter.

Standing beside her was a young man – tall and broad-shouldered, with dark hair, a wide smile, and chiselled model looks. He had an arm around Bette's shoulders, and her head was crooked against his neck. They were clearly comfortable with each other, as if this was a common stance. They made a handsome couple.

Nina looked at the other two group photographs and realized that Ryan – if that's who it was – was in both of them, smiling and happy in each, although the last one was the only picture where he and Bette were standing together. That meant he'd worked at the farm for at least three years. It seemed clear to Nina that at some point during those three years, he and Bette had been in a relationship. But then her sister had left. She had, as Cam had pointed out earlier, run away.

She looked at this image of the past for another moment, and then pulled her phone out of her pocket to send a WhatsApp.

Mum, she typed. *Do you remember a worker at the farm from the mid-2000s called Ryan?*

She could see that Sophia was online and was blessed with a swift reply.

You mean Bette's fiancé? Of course I do. Lovely boy.

Chapter Twenty-one

When she'd left the farm, Bette had no idea where she was going. She had only known that she couldn't stay a minute longer. Not with Ryan right there, embodying all her worst nightmares. Her fight or flight reflex had kicked in and she'd chosen to flee, just as she had all those years ago. Part of her thought she'd been running ever since.

Once she'd calmed down, Bette realized two things: that she was on the road into Dundee, and that she hadn't had any coffee. Putting the latter right at least gave her something to do, a task to accomplish that would occupy her mind for a while. Of course, when she found a coffee shop and parked up to enter it, she'd looked in the mirror and remembered all the other things she hadn't done yet that morning, some of which included having a shower and combing her hair. The hair she managed to tame in the car because she'd at least had the presence of mind to snatch up her bag before running out of the house and so had a brush with her, but the shower was beyond the capabilities of her hire car. Bette contented herself with reasonably tidy hair and a touch of mascara and lip gloss and gave the rest up as a bad job.

Coffee and a croissant settled her nerves somewhat. She consumed them in the car, thankful for the caffeine, while she worked out what to do next. As usual when Bette needed refuge from anything, including herself, she decided that work was the answer. First off, she called Roland Palmer.

'Do you have copies of the deeds to the Crowdie farmland?' she asked. 'If so, can I come and take a look at them with you? There are some queries I need to discuss.'

'I do and you can,' he said. 'When were you thinking?'

They arranged a time that morning. Bette then called the farm's bank – also based in Dundee – and requested a meeting with a manager to discuss the issues involved. She employed her best lawyer tone to make sure that happened sooner rather than later, which ended up being that afternoon at one o'clock. Bette checked the time as she rang off. It was still only just after 9am, which gave her time to find something more appropriate to wear. She needed more clothes anyway – the small suitcase she'd brought with her for the funeral was not enough to sustain her unexpected extended stay. She went into the town centre as soon as everything opened and found something suitable – a simple but smart combination of navy pencil skirt, white fitted shirt and a pair of tan wedges with an open toe.

After that it was a case of finding somewhere she could change and prepare for both meetings. Her iPad was another item that had been in her bag. All she needed was somewhere quiet to sit and work. The car would do at a pinch, but she was already craving more coffee and she didn't really want to eat up all her phone data by slaving it to her iPad and sharing the 4G. She didn't have much hope that she'd find somewhere with decent WiFi, a café and somewhere quiet to sit and work, but then Google pointed her to the V&A.

Bette had no idea that a second branch of the Victoria and Albert Museum had been established in Dundee, but apparently it had opened in late 2018 and indeed, there it was, an impressive building worthy of housing the designs it had been created to contain.

Once in her new outfit, she found a corner in the café, bought another coffee and settled down with her iPad. Anything that got her past the shock of seeing Ryan again and the inevitable foray into her memories of the past that the encounter had brought up was worth the time. Busy, busy, busy. Too busy to think about her own past and the heartache therein. It had always helped before. It would help again. After all, it had all happened eighteen years ago, hadn't it? She had lived half her life since then. It couldn't hurt her now. Or it shouldn't, anyway. As the day passed in activity, Bette's spirit settled. There were plenty more important things for her to think about than the meeting of an old ex.

The session with Roland Palmer was straightforward. Bette told him of the papers she'd found, and although she'd left the house in too much of a hurry that morning to bring them with her, she did have the photographs of them she'd taken. Together they compared these with what the solicitor held himself, which reassured them both that the boundary line of the orchard was the natural limit of the cliff beneath Cam's furthest pasture: the orchard did indeed belong to Crowdie.

'I'd love to see this place for myself one day,' Palmer murmured, looking through the photographs that Bette had taken. 'What an extraordinary location.'

'My father never mentioned it, either in person or in any documents you held for the farm?' Bette asked, and was rewarded by a shake of that greying head.

'No,' said the solicitor. 'I've worked with your family for decades and this is the first I've heard of it. Do let me know what you turn up about it, won't you?'

Bette assured him that she would, and then they entered a more painful discussion about what she was likely to be confronted with at the bank and how to deal with it.

'Even if I can persuade them not to call in the loan immediately, that's only going to be a respite, and they'll at the very least want the arrears paid,' Bette said. 'Now that I can be sure that the orchard land belongs to Crowdie I can get a full independent valuation on the land, but ... that's only really useful if we're going to sell. And that's still the absolute last resort, as far as I'm concerned.'

Palmer nodded as he passed back the iPad and steepled his fingers. 'Difficult. I think you're right about the bank. They've been extremely forbearing thus far, but now that the original signatory to the mortgage is deceased I think it likely they'd want to call in the loan, especially considering the length of time on the default. You could downsize, sell some of the outlying land.'

Bette took the iPad and flipped to the map of the farm she'd known since childhood. 'Even if I could find a buyer, I don't think that would be enough to cover what we're likely to owe in arrears, let alone keep up with the payments going forward.'

'Then I think your only option is to offer another security against the deficit.'

Bette looked up at him with a frown. 'Another security?'

Palmer spread his hands. 'It's not ideal and they may not go for it anyway, given that at this point they can legitimately demand full repayment because of the default. It's also, of course, very risky if you don't have a clear way out. But given their previous willingness to cut your father some slack, they might give you a short period of time if you can secure an extension against another surety. Say, for the amount of the arrears only. Do you have anything that you could provide as additional security against that? Farm equipment, perhaps, or even livestock?'

Bette stared at the framework of her childhood home, drawn in bare lines that seemed so ephemeral between her hands. What did Crowdie have that a bank would want? A new roof over an old barn. A tractor as old as the hills it ploughed. A half-herd of cows that had already been slimmed down, same with the sheep. A coop full of happy chickens. She could offer it all and it wouldn't be enough. Even if it had been and even if the bank would give them more time to catch up with the arrears, how could they ever hope to do that, no matter how much time they were given? She'd never wanted the farm in the first place and the sensible thing to do would be to let it go. But now, now that she was here, now that she'd spent time beneath that old roof again, now that she'd met her nephew and knew him as a person instead of a strange, incidental fact disconnected from her ... The thought of giving up and letting the bank take her family's land and with it their history wasn't so easy to contemplate. Especially with this new, additional mystery of the orchard which, it seemed, had been there her entire life and yet she knew nothing about.

Bette couldn't let it go, not like this. Not without trying everything, and not knowing that she was in a position to do more. Could she really return to London and her comfortable life knowing she'd done anything less than everything she could?

She looked up at the solicitor, who was watching her with a sympathetic gaze. It would mean telling work that she needed even more time here in Scotland, but ...

'Yes,' Bette found herself saying, despite her trepidation. 'I do have something else I can offer them.'

Chapter Twenty-two

'Believe me, Oliver, I really don't want to do this,' Bette said, talking via her handsfree kit as she sat in the car, about to make her way back to Crowdie. 'But it can't be helped. I can't do this remotely, so I'm going to have to stay. I can work over the weekend, if that's what's needed. Email me anything you need me to see.'

'It's not that, Ms Crowdie,' her secretary said. 'Mr Coulthard has been trying to schedule a meeting with you. He's been quite insistent.'

'Really? Well, you can tell him I'll be back on Tuesday. Make it first thing, if you like.'

There was a pause. 'I wonder if it might be a good idea for you to conduct it via Zoom?' Oliver suggested.

Bette frowned. 'Oliver, is there something you're not telling me?'

'No, no,' he said, a little too quickly. 'I just thought . . . I have a feeling the merger announcement is going to happen next week, and he wanted to talk to you before then.'

She sighed. 'All right. That makes sense. In that case, can you schedule something for Monday afternoon? The business I need to complete will be taking place as early as possible that morning, and without sorting that out I can't return to London, so I have to make sure that's done.'

Another pause. 'I'll arrange it, Ms Crowdie.'

'I'll be on a late afternoon flight back from Aberdeen, so make sure you don't schedule it after three o'clock.'

'Will do. I'll let you know as soon as it's booked in.'

'Thanks, Oliver. I'm sorry for the hassle. I'm looking forward to being back at my desk and more readily available, believe me.'

They rang off and Bette drove for home, taking the road via Arbroath as she tried to gather her thoughts after what had turned into an unexpectedly momentous day at the end of a crazy week. It was a beautiful early evening, as if the rain and the storms had never happened. The sun shone out of a bright blue sky not yet tinged with the colours of sunset. It occurred to Bette that she hadn't been down to the beach at all since she'd been back. It had been a favourite childhood haunt that had held its appeal right through her teens for its soft golden sand edged by sloping grassy dunes. Thinking about the beach inevitably took her back to the unexpected encounter early that morning, and as the sign loomed ahead Bette made an impulsive decision.

She was over Ryan. She'd been over him, and the life she'd

thought they were going to have together, for a long time. She'd been a child then, she was an adult now – a *successful* adult, because she had made sure that what he did to her would not ruin her life. That part of her past no longer held any significance, and what she had been able to accomplish today was proof, if any had been needed, that the decisions she had made after Ryan had broken her heart had been the right ones. Today had demonstrated that materially, and now Bette decided that walking in the footsteps of her younger self would go a long way to proving that to herself emotionally, too. Seeing him this morning had just been a shock, that was all, and she was over it. He no longer had any hold over her.

When she parked up, Bette realized that walking on the damp sand in her new wedges was a sure way to both ruin them and turn an ankle. There was no one around, so she did a quick-change out the back of the car (she hadn't done *that* since she was a teenager, either) and replaced the skirt with the jeans again before pulling on her boots. She glanced around, but the handful of cars dotted around the sandy tarmac were all empty. There was a slight wind as she crested the dune path that led onto the beach, and then there was the North Sea, stretched out before her in an expanse unbroken between where she stood and the shores of Denmark. Bette shut her eyes and breathed in, sucking in the salt air. This felt so different from the cliffs on which the Crowdie farm stood, perhaps because this was the coast that she remembered from her childhood – when she saw the sea close up, it was usually because the family had come here to walk and play.

She began to head south from the car park, towards the ruins of the Red Castle, looming over the estuary waters like something out of *Game of Thrones*. This was somewhere else she had played as a small child, although now it seemed there had been a landslip, and the ruins were out of bounds. The weather here could be merciless.

Thinking of this made her contemplate Ryan again, a memory resurfacing from the depths. It had been a stormy day, low clouds scudding overhead, heavy with rain yet to fall. The wind was already up when they'd got there, gusting along the curve of beach, stealing their breath. They'd debated turning tail and going home, but Bette hadn't wanted to. She'd grabbed his hand, teasing him about the big rugger lad being afraid of a bit of rain, and tugged him into a run. They'd dashed straight into the wind, and not to be outdone Ryan had pulled ahead of her – he was a little taller, so obviously his legs were longer: this was how she'd excused it later. In the next moment it was he pulling her along, both of them laughing, charging towards some unnamed, unseen finish line. Then the rain had started, not gradually but like a wall crashing from the sky. It fell as if it would never stop, so heavy that when they drew to a halt Bette couldn't catch her breath, and not only for the running. Ryan had pulled her to him, shucking his jacket up over his head and holding up his arms, cocooning them both from the worst of the downpour. She'd pressed herself against his chest, wrapping her arms around him, head under his chin. He'd been warm, chest heaving as he filled his lungs. They'd stood under that downpour soaked to the skin, buffeted by the wind, but somehow entirely untouched by anything but each other. They were all that existed and that little space under his coat was the whole world. It was a moment out of time – a moment of perfect happiness, Bette remembered thinking at the time. She had thought Ryan felt the same, especially since it was the very next day that he'd asked her to marry him. But she must have been mistaken. Because young or not, teenage impulse or not, he could never have felt the way she did at that moment and then broken her heart so callously, so completely.

It wasn't meant to be, she told herself. *We were just children, playing at being adults. If we had married then we would be divorced by now anyway.*

This was what she told herself, despite the niggling voice at the back of her mind that whispered something different, something that echoed the hopeful optimism of who she'd been back then. *Beth*. Such a soft name, for a soft girl. Beth Crowdie was a silly child who let people take advantage of her good nature, who fell in love and mooned about like an idiot. Bette Crowdie, however, was no one's fool. She got what she wanted out of life. And she never fell in love. Lust, perhaps, yes. There was always a way to make room for that. But love? All consuming, life-changing love? No. Never again.

Really, Bette reflected, breathing out into the wind as she turned and began to walk back the way she had come, *Ryan did me a favour, didn't he? I learned all that early enough that it didn't impact my career. In fact, it was why I was so driven so early.*

The sudden flurry of rain took her by surprise. The wind had driven clouds towards the coast, and here was another downpour, although it seemed set to be a brief drizzle rather than a full cascade. Still, she had no jacket and so Bette picked up her pace, making for the car along with the few other dog walkers and families who were on the beach. As she glanced up, squinting her eyes to see where she was going, Bette saw a single figure going against the flow of people escaping the sudden change in weather. A tall figure with broad shoulders and dark hair with his hands stuffed deep into his jeans pockets was making his way determinedly in the opposite direction, away from the only exit despite the inclement weather. She couldn't see him clearly but something about him made her heart turn over. Bette cursed herself – it was only that she'd just been thinking about Ryan again, that's all, she told herself. That's why her mind immediately took her there. It wasn't him.

Except that as she got closer, Bette realized that it *was* him. Impossibly, here was Ryan, the Ryan she had just been thinking about, the Ryan that she had now seen twice in one day after not seeing or speaking to him for eighteen years. There was no escape – there was no other way to get to her car but to walk past him. Perhaps he hadn't noticed her, she thought, perhaps she could put some distance between them as they passed so that he wouldn't even know she was there. But even as this thought crossed her mind, Ryan's own step faltered. He stopped, looking right at her, and Bette realized that even though there was still some distance between them and despite the falling rain, he had recognized her in the same way that she had recognized him.

There was nothing to do but keep walking. Hadn't she told herself that this morning had just been the shock, and nothing more? What had happened between them – both good and bad – was in the past. There was no need to be embarrassed or distressed by this meeting. In fact, it was good. They could clear the air. After the meeting she'd had with the bank and after what she had been forced to do to stop it being taken from them immediately, Bette and the Crowdie farm could use all the help they could get.

She drew a deep breath of wind and rain, squared her shoulders, and moved on.

'Ryan,' she called, as she drew nearer.

He blinked, a tint of colour on his high cheekbones as he looked at her. 'Beth.'

She didn't correct him. There was no point getting off on the wrong foot again. 'I'm sorry about this morning,' she said. 'I . . . hadn't expected to see you. It took me by surprise, that's all.'

He gave a slight, lopsided smile that was instantly so familiar that it shivered something in her heart, though she clamped down on that immediately. 'Yes. It was the same for me. I'm so sorry. If I'd known you would be there, I wouldn't have come. I thought you'd be gone by now, back to London. After the funeral, I mean.'

Bette glanced away. 'I . . . was surprised you didn't attend, actually.' She'd prepared herself for that in advance. If she'd seen him then, it would have been fine. 'I thought you might come.'

'I would have,' he said. He was watching her face, she could tell without even fully looking at him. 'I didn't want to ... cause extra upset on a terrible day. I'm so sorry for your loss, Beth.'

'Thank you.'

They fell into silence. Bette looked up and found him studying her, his face peppered with rain that he didn't seem bothered about wiping away. Despite herself, her heart clenched painfully, because she'd been right that morning. He really did look exactly the same. A few more lines around his eyes, perhaps, but still the same. And when she'd been a teenager he'd been the most gorgeous boy she'd ever seen in real life.

Bette cleared her throat. 'Look. I'm only going to be here for another day or two anyway. And whether I'm here or not shouldn't stop you from doing whatever you need to do in the orchard.'

'Right,' he said, after a pause. 'The orchard.'

She looked up at him again. 'Did you know it was there?'

'No,' he shook his head. 'It's ... something.'

That she had to agree with. 'Do you know what kind of apples they are?'

He looked away, out over the sea. The rain had stopped, Bette realized, but the wind was still blowing. It mussed at his thick hair, forcing him to push it out back of his eyes. 'I need to take another look. If you're sure you're okay with that?'

'Ryan, it's fine,' she said. 'What happened was years ago, anyway, wasn't it? We were children. It doesn't matter now. Now we've got the awkwardness out of the way, we can forget about it again.'

He let out a breath, a troubled look crossing his face. 'Beth, there's something I've always wanted to explain to you. Something I should have told you years ago.'

'No,' she said, cutting him short. 'Really. There's no need, Ryan. It's in the past. It's done with. We might as well have never met before today, for all it means now. All right?'

He stared at her for a moment. 'All right,' he said, eventually. 'I won't be able to come back tomorrow, I've got commitments elsewhere. But I could make it on Saturday?'

'Yes. Actually, that could work well,' Bette said. 'Allie's coming back to take another look then, too.'

Ryan looked at her askance. 'Allie?'

'You remember Allie Bright? Did you know she trained as an archaeologist? She's doing some research for us to see if she can turn up anything about the orchard.'

At the mention of her old friend's name, Ryan smiled. 'Allie. Wow. That takes me back.'

Bette found herself returning the smile, a moment of shared memory. The three of them had hung out together plenty. It had always been another source of happiness for Bette, how well her best friend and her boyfriend had got on.

'I haven't seen her for years,' Ryan added. 'We lost touch, after—' he stopped, abruptly, realizing what he'd been about to reference. He looked away.

'Well,' Bette said, opting for nonchalance, 'it seems as if this week has become a time for reunions. She's coming up after lunch on Saturday. Why don't you join us then?'

'Okay,' he said. 'I'll do that.'

She walked away, wondering if he'd follow, but he didn't. When she reached the path over the dune Bette turned back. Ryan was still standing where she'd left him, hands in his pockets, looking out across the waves. He cut a lonely figure in the wind, and she wondered why he'd come to this place. She wondered what he was remembering as he stood on the wet sand, staring out to sea.

Chapter Twenty-three

'I can't believe I didn't know, that's all,' Nina said. 'I was young, but not *that* young. And at the time I thought Bette was the coolest big sister on the planet. I would have been obsessed with a wedding if they had been planning one. Which means they can't have told me about it.'

Cam frowned a little over his coffee mug. 'It doesn't sound as if it lasted very long, whatever happened, does it?' he said. 'Maybe they didn't tell anyone. Maybe they didn't get far enough along to even start planning. Like you said, they were both very young at the time, right?'

It was early evening and he'd popped back in to see if she needed help with anything – and also to see how Bette was. Nina had had to tell him that her sister still wasn't back yet, despite the hours since they'd both last seen her. Nina had tried to call a couple of times, but Bette's phone had been turned off. After that bombshell of a text conversation with her mother, she had spent the day trying to remember more about Ryan, but was still drawing a blank.

'Maybe,' Nina sighed. 'But *Mum* obviously knew.'

'What did she say about the break-up?'

'Nothing. She wouldn't talk about it. Said that if I wanted to know anything I'd have to ask Bette about it.'

Cam nodded. 'Sounds sensible. After all, whatever happened must have been bad – because that kind of explains why Bette left the farm and never came back, doesn't it?'

Nina blew out a breath. 'I suppose so, yeah.'

'Are you going to ask her about it?'

'I don't know. It's not as if my sister is the most forthcoming of people at the best of times, or at least, she isn't with me,' Nina said. 'I'm not even sure how I'd bring it up.'

They were quiet for a moment or two. Nina was glad to have him there, and reflected that with Cam, she never felt compelled to fill silences. They were always as companionable, as comfortable, as the conversation itself. They were seated together at the kitchen table, as if this was what they did every evening after work, sharing stories of the day, of people they knew, unwinding together, decompressing from the rest of the world. It was, Nina told herself, a dangerous habit to get into. And yet . . .

'Anyway,' she said. 'Have you eaten? I was going to—'

There came the sound of a car pulling into the yard, and a moment later Bette appeared in the kitchen doorway. Her sister looked between Nina and Cam.

'I'm sorry,' Bette said. 'Am I interrupting?'

'No – I've got to go, actually, or I'm going to be late,' Cam said, making to get up. He grinned at Nina. '*Someone* told me I needed to make more of an effort on first dates so I'd better get home and scrub up before I head out for this one, eh?'

Nina smiled, ignoring the slight pang that passed through her chest at her neighbour's words. 'Aha. No second date with Sally, then?'

Cam gave a dramatic sigh. 'She hasn't called me back. I know when I'm not wanted.'

'I told you,' Nina said, getting up from the table herself. 'You should have made more of an effort in the first place.'

'I know, I know,' he said, still grinning as he headed for the door, both hands raised. 'Hence here's me about to go take a shower and get my glad rags on! I'll catch up with you both soon, okay?'

'Cam,' Bette said, as he passed her, 'Ryan's going to come back on Saturday afternoon to take another look at the orchard.'

'Oh,' Cam said, glancing back at Nina in surprise. 'Well, that's . . . great.'

Nina watched Bette, trying to gauge her mood, but her sister only smiled at their neighbour. 'I'm sorry about this morning. We've got a bit of history, Ryan and I, and neither of us expected to see each other. It was just . . . a shock, that's all. But we're both over it now.'

Cam smiled. 'All right. Good. As long as you're really okay with it?'

Bette returned the smile. 'I am. Night, Cam. Have a good one.'

He nodded a goodbye to both of them, and was gone. Nina looked down at the mugs on the table, only one of them still half full.

'He's really going on a date?' Bette asked.

'Yes,' Nina said, getting up to put both mugs in the sink. 'Why is that a surprise?'

'Because you two seem to be getting closer by the day.'

Nina sighed. 'I told you, we're just friends. Do you want a glass of wine? I think I need one.'

There was a moment of silence and Nina looked over her shoulder to find Bette watching her. 'Yes,' her sister said, 'that's probably a good idea. There are a few things I need to talk to you about.'

Nina made a face as she pulled a bottle of wine from the rack and two glasses from the shelf. 'That sounds ominous.'

'Well, it's a good news/bad news situation,' Bette said, sliding into the seat that Cam had vacated a few moments before. 'The good news is that the orchard is definitely part of the Crowdie farm.' She paused. 'I should have told Cam that before he left. Damn.'

'I can let him know,' Nina told her, putting down their now-full glasses and joining Bette at the table. 'But I'm not surprised by that, to be honest. Cam won't be, either, I think he was already assuming it was. Which means the bad news must be *really* bad.'

She watched as Bette took a large mouthful of wine. 'The

bank is threatening to repossess if we don't come up with the money in arrears . . . well, pretty much immediately.'

Nina's heart froze in her chest. 'But . . . we can't do that. There's no way we can do that. It must be a huge amount of money, right?'

'Right,' Bette agreed. 'Close to £95,000.'

Nina rubbed a hand over her face, feeling sick. 'Then . . . that's it. We're going to lose the farm. We're going to lose *everything*. Aren't we?' What was she going to do? Where was she going to go? Panic began to rise in her throat.

'No,' Bette said, attention on her wine glass, a pensive look on her face. 'Or at least, not yet. I've bought us a respite. We've got three months to come up with the money before they make any more moves to recoup it.'

Nina blinked. 'How did you get them to do that?' she asked. 'Dad must have tried every trick in the book to stop them repossessing before now. Why would they give us another chance?'

'Well, because I can be pretty persuasive,' Bette cleared her throat. 'And because I used my flat as collateral.'

For a moment, Nina wasn't sure she understood. 'Your flat . . . in London?'

Her sister gave her a slightly wry smile. 'That is the only one I've got, yes.'

Nina drew in a breath. 'Then, if we can't find that money in three months . . .'

'I'll be the one in hock for it.' Bette shrugged slightly. 'It was all I had to offer them that would stop them calling in the whole loan straight away.'

'I—' Nina didn't know what to say. 'Bette, I don't know how three months is going to help. That amount of money . . .'

'I know, but it was either that or start packing up to-morrow,' Bette said. 'And I know you think I'm heartless, Nina, but—'

'No,' Nina said, stopping Bette mid-sentence. 'I don't. I *don't*. And *thank* you. But if we can't at least find the arrears, you'll be the one losing your home.'

'No,' Bette said. 'It won't come to that. I've essentially taken out another mortgage against the flat, with a three-month grace period. Will it take a huge chunk out of my salary to pay both? Yes, absolutely. But I'm about to become a partner in one of the biggest law firms in London, so I can just about manage it. But Nina,' she added, scrubbing one nail against an invisible mark on her wine glass, 'it doesn't solve all our problems. With the best will in the world, I can't do that indefinitely. And there's still the rest of the mortgage to pay. If we can't find a way to make the farm not just viable but profitable in the next three months . . .'

'I know,' Nina said. 'We're screwed anyway.'

They lapsed into quiet for a few minutes. The kitchen was warm, familiar. Nina wondered how many conversations between various family members had taken place at this very table, over however many years, decades, *centuries*. She gave a heavy sigh at the thought that this might be one of the most important – and also one of the last.

'Are you hungry?' she asked. 'I haven't eaten yet. I could make us an omelette? Basic, I know, but—'

Bette smiled. 'I'm starving. An omelette sounds great.'

Nina got up from the table and was surprised when Bette got up, too, evidently planning to help. She couldn't remember the last time the two sisters had cooked together. It was possible it had never happened at all.

'I was worried about you today,' Nina said, as she tipped the beaten egg into the pan. 'I tried to call.'

'Sorry,' Bette said, diligently chopping onions far finer than Nina herself would ever have bothered. 'I was flitting about, here and there.'

'But you spoke to Ryan again?'

'Yes.' Bette finished the onions and began on a slightly sorry-looking red pepper she'd dug out of the fridge. 'I went for a walk at Lunan Bay on my way home and bumped into him again.'

'I didn't remember him,' Nina told her. 'The name Ryan didn't mean anything to me when Cam first mentioned him. If it had . . .'

'It's okay,' Bette said. She gave a slight laugh. 'It's funny. I've been dreading a meeting like that – avoiding it – for years. Literally, years. But now . . .' she shrugged. 'It's done with. The worst has happened. We're both adults, we can deal with it. Water under the bridge. It really is fine, Nina.'

Nina let out a breath. 'Well, that's good.' She scattered the onion across the egg, then the pepper and the cheese Bette had grated.

'You really didn't remember him?'

Nina looked up at Bette's question. 'No. I had to search those old photos in the hallway. And . . . I had to ask Mum.'

Bette nodded, refilling their wine glasses. 'Ah. And what did she say?'

'Not much,' Nina said, truthfully. 'But . . . I had no idea you'd been engaged.'

There was a brief silence as Bette tipped her wine glass to her lips, turning to look out at the darkness beyond the kitchen window as she leaned back against the counter. 'Well,' she said, eventually. 'It wasn't something to be particularly proud of, in the end. He asked me before I went away to university. We agreed we'd wait until I graduated and he'd finished agricultural college, by which time I'd be twenty-one and he'd be twenty-three, which seemed . . . an impossibly adult age, at the time. We had a year of trying to be long-distance, and then he confessed that he'd been cheating on me. And that was that.'

'Bette,' Nina said. 'I'm so sorry.'

Her sister turned to her, eyes a little glassy but with a wry smile on her face. 'It was a long time ago. And honestly, looking back now, I wonder what on earth I was expecting. He was a teenage boy and he was gorgeous. He could have had anyone he wanted.' She gave a brief, slightly bitter laugh. 'I guess he did. Anyway, it was a valuable lesson learned early.'

'The first cut is the deepest?' Nina asked.

'Hmm. Something like that.'

Nina said nothing more. She wondered how all their lives would have been different, if Bette had married Ryan.

Would her sister still have ended up in London? Presumably not, if Ryan's profession had remained in agriculture. One thing was for sure, she wouldn't have disappeared from Crowdie for so long.

'What about you and Cam?'

Nina looked up. 'What do you mean?'

'Neither of you have ever made a move?'

'No, of course not. I told you, we're just friends. And we're neighbours, Bette.'

'What's that got to do with anything?'

'Have you never heard the expression "Don't crap on your own doorstep"? It would be too complicated if it didn't work. And I've got Barney to think about. It's not worth the risk of it going wrong. Even if he was interested. Which,' Nina added, deftly splitting the omelette between two plates, 'he's never given any serious indication that he is. Come on, let's eat before this gets cold. We've got more important things to talk about than my love life – or lack of one – haven't we?'

Bette's phone pinged. Nina seated herself back at the kitchen table as she watched her sister check the notification. Then she looked up, laden plate in one hand and her phone in the other.

'That's my solicitor, confirming they'll have the papers I need by first thing Monday morning,' she said.

Nina nodded, a feeling of relief flooding through her as Bette slipped the phone back into her pocket and joined her at the table. *Disaster averted*, she thought. *For now, at least.*

Chapter Twenty-four

Saturday dawned bright, the sky streaked with white clouds so high and fine that they looked as if they had been delivered by the strokes from a painter's brush. Bette helped with the early strawberry pick but then disappeared back into their father's study. Since finally gaining access to the farm's accounts, her sister had sequestered herself there again, dissecting the further probability of their demise. Nina had been too afraid to ask for an update. They were already in dire straits; finding out anything worse at this point seemed like overkill. She was still struggling to assimilate the events of the past week, which seemed to have taken place over the length of a year rather than seven short days.

'Can I come to the orchard today?' her son asked, looking at her over his lunchtime sandwich, which on Saturdays he was allowed to eat while sitting on the sofa in front of the television. It was currently tuned to Disney+, which had been a Christmas surprise from Bern. It was only at that moment that it occurred to Nina that this was another expense they could not afford. 'I've been really good at school this week, and I'm the only one who hasn't seen it yet. If everyone's going, *please* let me come too.'

'Okay, kiddo,' she said, with a smile. 'You're right, you've been super good, and this is the perfect time for you to visit the orchard. But you have to promise me that you'll stay where I can see you at all times and you won't go anywhere near the edge, all right?'

'I promise,' Barnaby said. 'Can Limpet come too?' At the sound of its name the collie at his feet pricked up his ears and huffed a little.

'Of course,' Nina said. 'You two are a package deal, right?'

'Should I wear my superhero costume?'

'I don't think you'll need to do that,' Nina said, as the sound of footsteps echoed across the yard. A second later Cam appeared in the doorway.

'Hi Cam,' Barney said. 'I'm coming with you to the orchard!'

'Excellent,' said Cam, crossing the two steps to the table and leaning on it with a grin. 'Then we shall be fully prepared in case of emergency.'

'There will be no emergencies while my son is on the side of a cliff, thank you very much,' Nina said, sending Cam a warning look as the sound of a car rattled into the farmyard, pulling to a stop outside.

'Er— no, of course not,' Cam said, backtracking. 'It's all very safe down there, very secure, no need for superhero activity of any sort.' *Sorry*, he mouthed to Nina.

There came the crunch of footsteps and then a knock on the door just as Bette appeared from the hallway, having heard the car arrive.

'Nina,' said the woman that Bette introduced as Allie, 'my goodness, look at you. You won't remember me but I remember you. And this is your little boy?'

Barnaby had got up from the sofa to join them. Nina smiled, pulling him to her.

'I'm Best Barnaby Barnacle, and I'm very pleased to meet you,' Barnaby said, formally, putting out his hand for Allie to shake.

'Well, aren't you the cutest,' Allie said, smiling as she shook his hand and giving it a slight squeeze, too. 'Just the way I remember your mum being when she was a little girl.'

Barney looked up at Nina. 'Can we go now?'

'We're just waiting for Ryan,' Bette said, as another car pulled into the yard. 'But I think this must be him now.'

Nina attempted not to be too obvious in the study of the man who had once broken her sister's heart. *And Ryan Atkins could definitely break hearts*, she thought, of the man who swung easily out of the cab of the Ford Ranger now parked outside. He must be nearly forty now but his features were still chiselled, his thick hair still dark despite the odd spattering of silver.

'Hi,' he said, with a smile that seemed to be mainly directed at Bette. 'Sorry I'm late.'

'You're not,' Bette said. 'I'd have said you're right on time.'

Allie stepped forward to pull him into a hug. 'Ryan! Bette

said you were coming. It's so good to see you. It's been too long!'

He hugged her back, warmly and with another smile. 'It has. Hello, Allie.'

'Well, look at this – the old gang all back together,' she went on, as they parted and she turned to Bette with a smile. 'Like old times.'

'Come *on*!' Barnaby said, impatiently. Tired of waiting, he and Limpet set off across the farmyard. 'Let's *go*!'

They all trooped together towards the orchard: five adults, a child and a collie dog, surely the most activity that strange, secret place had seen for decades. Nina called her son to her as the party made their way down the slope beside the cliff, making sure he stayed as far away from the iron fence as possible. Barnaby took out his old iPhone and began to take pictures of anything and everything.

'Great idea,' said Allie. 'I'm glad to see that we've got an official photographer on hand. Every expedition needs one!'

'Did you see the monogram on the fence?' Bette asked, as she fell into step beside Nina. 'We think it's an O and a C – C for Crowdie, presumably. Although I don't know where the "O" would fit in, the patriarch at the time was George.'

'His wife, perhaps?' Cam suggested.

'What about the child that Mum told us about, Bette?' Nina suggested. 'The one that fell from the cliff and was supposedly the reason this place was abandoned? Could it be in commemoration?'

'Maybe,' Bette said, though her voice was doubtful.

'Although if they were planning not to use the site again after that happened, why would they put up a fence? And also – if the fence was put in when the Crowdies bought the land – and Allie has already said she thinks it fits the date on the deeds, 1839 – it suggests that the orchard was either already established, or had just been established, doesn't it? But if it's been abandoned since then, that means the trees were already here.'

They toured the orchard, slowly making their way through the tangles of trees towards the cliff face at the far end. Here and there, Ryan paused, examining one of the gnarled trees. He seemed to be deep in thought, and when they stopped at a tree that still had fruit growing amid its sparse leaves, he picked up one of the windfalls and contemplated it with a frown on his face.

'Nina and I tried one when we first found this place,' Cam said. 'It's pretty sharp, but then I guess they're not quite ripe yet?'

Ryan nodded thoughtfully and pulled a penknife from his pocket, repeating the same action that Nina had performed just a few days earlier. She watched him eat a sliver of the apple.

'I didn't think it was an eater,' she said, as he chewed. 'Even if it's not ripe yet, it's too sour for that, don't you think?'

'I think you're right,' Ryan said. 'Actually, my feeling is that it's a cider apple.'

'Well, now, that's interesting that you should say that,' said Allie. She was standing close to the tree, one hand against its bark in a strangely reverent gesture. 'As it chimes with some-thing that I came across when I started researching this place.'

'Oh? And what's that?' Bette asked.

'I'm going to hold off any pronouncements for a while longer,' Allie said, somewhat enigmatically. 'At least until I've had another look at the cliff workings.'

'Wait,' said Bette, pulling something from her pocket. 'There's something else I'd like to show everyone before we head for the cliff. One of the trees.'

As they waded through the orchard after her, Nina realized that what Bette held in her hand was one of their grandmother's paintings. When she stopped in front of a par-ticularly twisted tree that seemed to be leaning back against the rock of the cliff for support, Bette held it up so that they could all see. The painting also depicted a tree.

'I'm not mad, am I?' she asked, a general question that encompassed the gathered group. 'It's the same tree. Isn't it? Look at the way the trunk forks there, you see? And that branch there, even, the one that's touching the ground. It's in the painting. Isn't it?'

They all looked between the two: the image of the tree on the canvas Bette held, and the little tree bent across the stone before them. It did look remarkably similar.

Ryan, who was closest, blew out a breath. 'It certainly looks like the same tree. And that's not all.' He ducked be-tween and beneath branches until all they could see were his jeans. There was a slight snapping sound, and then he backed out again. There was an apple in his hand, small, knobbly, yellow-green – but definitely an apple. 'It's still producing fruit.'

'Our grandmother painted this in 1963,' Bette said, of the image she held in her hand.

Standing beside her, Cam made a surprised sound. 'Is that really possible?'

'It depends how old it is,' Ryan came back towards them. 'The original Bramley apple – the first one ever grown – is over 200 years old and that's still producing fruit. It's down in Nottinghamshire.'

'Well, if this is the tree in my grandmother's painting, we know this one is at least sixty years old,' Bette pointed out.

'A lot older than that, surely,' Nina said. 'It looks ancient even in the painting.'

Cam had been watching Ryan as he ate another slice of the windfall he'd carried with him. 'What do you think?' he asked. 'Any more of an idea of what variety it could be, if it's a cider apple?'

Ryan shook his head. 'It's not one I've come across before. It's certainly not one of the common varieties.'

There came a shout, and they all turned, startled.

'Where's Allie?' Bette asked.

'Over here!' The shout came again, and they moved towards it until the cliff at the end of the orchard came into clear view. Allie was standing beside one of the bee boles. 'Sorry,' she said, a little breathlessly. 'But I couldn't wait any longer. Not after hearing how old these trees potentially are.'

She indicated the bee boles. Barnaby ran up to take a

photograph as Allie pointed to something at the apex of one of the arches. They all gathered closer, leaning in to look at what she was pointing at.

Where the tip of the archaeologist's finger rested there was something etched into the rock, definitely manmade rather than a natural indentation. Bette raised her hand and traced her fingers along the stone. Lichen had crept into the carving – but it was definitely there.

'It's a fleur-de-lis,' she said, as she traced out the stylized three-petalled detail of the flower. 'Isn't it?'

Allie nodded, her eyes bright. 'It is.'

Bette shook her head. 'I don't know much about them. But I do know they've got religious connotations. Because of the trinity, maybe? Is that significant?'

'I think so,' her friend said.

'Were you expecting to find it?' Nina asked.

'I thought it might be here,' Allie said. 'Hoped, really, I suppose.'

'What does it mean?' Nina asked. 'What made you think it would be there?'

Allie let out a breath, looking back at the bee bole. 'What I'm going to tell you now is really all conjecture,' she said. 'But for many years historians have been searching for the site of a lost monastery that once stood somewhere in this region. It was destroyed during the Scottish dissolution of the monasteries that began in 1560, so successfully that no trace of it has ever been found.'

'Then how do you know it existed?' Bette asked.

'Because what we do have is a very early treatise on bee-keeping, written by a monk who was one of the first people to study them methodically. It's been in the archives at St Andrews University since it was found in the library of a stately home in Northumberland decades ago, for which it was acquired in an auction and re-bound sometime in the 1800s.' She indicated the bee boles. 'It's why it's so fantastic to find these. It will take more research, but I'm already sure these are the very boles referenced in that book, which means all his observations on the life cycle and habit of his honey bees were developed in this very spot.'

'Who was he?' Bette asked.

'His name was Brother Alphonse,' Allie went on. 'He was a Benedictine monk and very little is known about his life, although reading between the lines of his manuscripts it is possible he was Italian or French. In his earlier years he was apprenticed as an apothecary, but by the time of his death, which we assume was in 1560, the year the monastery was razed . . .' Here she paused, and took a breath before continuing. 'He was responsible for what was renowned as the best cidery in Scotland and perhaps in the whole of the British Isles.'

Chapter Twenty-five

'Wait,' Bette said, into the slightly stunned silence that followed her friend's words. She looked back into the trees behind them, packed so closely together, looking so very neglected. 'You're not saying that you think that that's *this* orchard? That it's been here since the 1500s? That's impossible, surely.'

In answer, Allie looked at Ryan. 'That's your area of expertise, isn't it?' she asked. 'What do you think?'

Ryan surveyed the trees with another frown, and then looked at the remnant of the apple he still held in his hand. 'There has always been a fable among cider producers in this area,' he said. 'A story about a secret orchard that produced perfect apples.'

Bette watched as her nephew took the apple held in Ryan's hand and looked at it critically. 'It doesn't look perfect,' Barney said, with typically childlike incisiveness. 'It's all knobbly and a weird colour. It doesn't even look like an apple, really. Not a *proper* one.'

Ryan smiled down at him. '"Perfect" in cider terms doesn't mean the fruit is like a person's ideal version of an apple,' he explained. 'When you drink cider – or in your case, Best Barnaby Barnacle, an unfermented apple juice – it's usually a blend of juices from different apples. Most orchards have at least two, more likely three or four, varieties of apple trees. That's partly to do with pollination, but also because, especially in the case of cider production, to make a good cider the maker has to balance out the sugars and acids in the juices. If you made it all from one apple, the chances are it would have too much of either and would taste terrible. One major skill of cider making is in the blending of the juices to make a good end product. Unless you have a "perfect" apple – one in which the acids and sugars in the juice are perfectly balanced for cider making without needing any modifiers. They're rare, and they're not always easy to grow – they mature more slowly, might not produce reliably year by year, and often need specific environmental conditions.'

Bette looked out at the apple trees again. 'You can't really think that's what we have here, though? That . . . lost orchard of perfect apples? It can't be, can it? That would mean it had been here, producing apples, for almost five hundred years.'

'It doesn't seem likely, no,' Ryan admitted.

'But if it is Brother Alphonse's orchard, it must have been maintained for a long time after the monastery itself disappeared,' Allie pointed out. 'These trees probably aren't five hundred years old, but we know from the evidence of Bette's grandmother's painting there that at least some of them could be getting on for a century old, and maybe even older. And there's that fence, which is a later addition to this place, suggesting that it was in frequent use well into the 1800s. In which case, these trees could be the last cultivars of that ancient orchard.'

'How would we be able to tell?' Nina asked. 'Can we look at apples produced by the same variety elsewhere and compare them?'

'That's the thing,' Ryan said. 'If these are the apples from the myth, then there aren't any other trees like this anywhere in the world.'

'Exactly,' said Allie. 'A monastery's orchard was guarded jealously by the monks, because sales of the cider would have been a hefty part of their income. In this case that would have been especially so if the cider really was as good as the stories suggest. They would not have allowed grafts to be taken from the trees so that they could be grown anywhere else. They would have controlled every tree as well as the fruit they produced very carefully.'

It was Nina who asked. 'Grafts?'

'Well,' Ryan said, taking a breath. 'Putting it as simply as I can and leaving out millennia of apple-growing history . . . Every distinct apple variety in existence is a hybrid, and each tree of that variety is a clone. If you wanted a new Golden Delicious tree, for example, you wouldn't take the pip from a Golden Delicious apple and plant that. If you did that, you couldn't guarantee what you would get. It would likely revert to its wild apple forebear, or some entirely new variety that would be a mix of that wild apple and the apple the seed had come from. To be absolutely sure to get the exact Golden Delicious fruit you want, you have to take a cutting from a Golden Delicious tree and graft it onto another tree, or quick-growing rootstock. That way you'll know that the fruit that tree will produce will be what you were expecting when you decided you wanted more Golden Delicious.'

'And what *I'm* saying,' Allie added, 'is that no one was ever allowed to do that from the trees that produced those perfect apples. If this *is* Brother Alphonse's orchard, then we're looking at the last existing trees of a lost variety that was extremely rare in the first place.'

There was a silence as everyone tried to take in this information.

'I guess, if you're right about this orchard originally belonging to the monastery, it explains why the orchard was planted here, on the side of the cliff, doesn't it?' Cam said, eventually. 'It seems like such a crazy place to put anything at all. But it would be easy to defend, wouldn't it? Or to just keep a secret. After all, none of us ever knew it was here.'

Allie nodded. 'Yes – it's not a stretch to imagine that theft of both the fruit and the trees would have been a worry. And of course, the salt air probably had a hand in giving the apples their unique taste. At several places in the bee book Brother Alphonse refers to the bees pollinating his "salt apples". It's possible that even taking a graft wouldn't yield the same results as growing the fruit so close to the North Sea.'

'Brother Alphonse was a superhero,' Barnaby said, his tone a little awed. 'This was his secret hideout *and* he saved all the apples from the bad guys.'

Allie laughed. 'Do you know what, Best Barnaby Barnacle, I think you're spot on there,' she said. 'He even would have had an outfit that looked a bit like a cloak with a hood – his monk's habit.'

'What does any of this mean, though?' Bette asked, trying to work out how this could help them. 'I get that the history is phenomenal, if both of you are right. But even if we can prove for certain that this is the secret orchard – what then? All that's here now are a few last dying trees and some empty bee boles.'

'Well – that's not quite all,' Allie said, turning to look inland towards the cliff. 'There's that doorway, too, which I'm really curious about. The archway has been strengthened in a way that the bee boles haven't, which suggests it was built to allow safe access. It makes me wonder how far back into the cliff it leads. At the very least, with your permission, I'd like to look at that a little more.'

Bette looked at Nina, and she could see that her sister was thinking the same thing as she was. What harm could it do? In any case, until they knew exactly what they had here, what they had found so far meant nothing. 'Okay,' she said. 'Of course, you're welcome to do whatever you need to do.'

'As for the orchard,' Ryan said, 'I think a good start would be to test the apple juice to determine the balance of acids, sugars and tannins the fruit has. I've got all the equipment, if you're happy to let me do that.'

'Sure,' Bette said, looking at her sister again. 'I mean, I don't have a problem with that, but it's Nina's call, really – I won't be here, I'll be heading back to London on Monday afternoon.'

'I'm fine with it,' Nina told Ryan.

'Great,' he said, with a faint smile that was directed at Bette. 'I can't pretend I'm not fascinated to see what the results are.'

They spent a little more time in the orchard before they all began to make their way back up to the cliff top. Bette found herself pausing beside the huge boulder at the base of the path as the rest of the group moved on ahead. She turned back to take one last look at the place, knowing that it might be a while before she got back here. Tomorrow, Sunday, she'd be busy gathering up everything she needed to take back to London, and then on Monday she intended to be in Dundee as early as possible to sign and hand over the papers to the farm's lawyers. By evening she'd be back in her flat in Wapping. It seemed a world away, that small piece of real estate not far from the river, the glass and steel and brick of her open-plan wharf conversion, clean and tidy and uncomplicated compared to the frenetic tangle of greenery and rock she looked at now. Her return to Crowdie had been even more difficult than she'd expected, but in a strange way it had been compelling, too. She wasn't going to miss the place, exactly, but the past week had revealed to Bette that she had more of an emotional connection to it than she had realized. The discovery of this little unknown corner of it niggled at her and leaving it with so many questions to be resolved left her feeling unsatisfied.

'Bette?'

She turned to see Ryan standing a few feet away. He was watching her cautiously, wary of interrupting. She glanced up the path to see that they were alone, the others having forged on ahead. He had waited for her.

'Are you all right?' he asked her.

'Yes,' she said, turning towards him, his shadow reaching out to her as the afternoon sunlight cast him slightly in silhouette. 'Just still taking it in, I think. Thank you for coming today.'

He smiled slightly, glancing towards the old trees. 'Thank you for letting me come. To be honest ... if this does turn out to be the lost orchard, it'll be the fulfilment of every cider maker's dream.'

'How did you end up being the fruit tree expert guy?' she asked, suddenly curious. 'Didn't you originally want to farm?'

'I did, but some friends and I started making cider in college and got the bug.' He looked down at his hands. 'It was ... a good distraction.'

Bette looked away.

'We started our own cidery and it was pretty successful straight away,' he went on. 'You might have heard of it, actually. It was pretty big there, for a while, Applejacks?' When Bette shook her head, he carried on. 'Anyway, we sold it to Stu's Brews a few years back and that's when I decided to go into private consultancy instead. At the time I thought it would make life easier to be flexible for the family.'

'Family?'

This time it was Ryan who looked away. 'My wife and I were planning to have children, but ... well, to cut a long story short, it didn't happen.'

He was married, then. Bette waited for this news to spear her, but it didn't. She probed her heart a little, quiet for a moment as his gaze found her again, but there was no explosion of pain, or even of anger. It was what it was. He had moved on. Bette was relieved to discover that, in fact, she was entirely detached from this news, because it had no bearing on her at all. He was just someone she used to know.

'I'm sorry,' she said. 'That it didn't work out, I mean.'

He glanced away again with a faint smile and a nod. 'Anyway, by then my business was established and there was no reason to abandon it. In actual fact, it's been far more successful than I ever expected it to be.'

'I'm glad.' Bette took a breath. 'Ryan, it's been really good to see you, and to have this chance to ...' She was going to say 'clear the air', but that wasn't quite right. And yet for her, something had changed. She'd always expected that seeing him again would throw her into turmoil, but in fact the opposite had proven true. The dense, dark cloud that had lingered for so long over the memories of her early life had lifted. The monster under the bed that she had always feared had turned out to be nothing but a shadow.

Whatever she'd been trying to say Ryan apparently understood, because he smiled.

'Yeah,' he said. 'Me too. It's been good to see you again. Really good.'

Chapter Twenty-six

On Monday, Bette left for Dundee at about the same time her nephew was leaving for school.

'Don't worry, Auntie Bette,' he said. 'I'll take lots of pictures of everything so you don't miss us too much. Especially the hens.'

She laughed and hugged him. 'Thank you, Best Barnaby Barnacle, that would be great.'

She hugged Nina, too, though this one was briefer and significantly more awkward, the two sisters still not entirely at ease with each other. 'I'll call,' Bette said. 'And I'll text when I get out of the bank this morning.'

Nina nodded. 'Thanks.'

The plan was for Bette to hand over the papers in Dundee and then stop at Crowdie for her meeting on the way back through to Aberdeen airport, but Nina wasn't sure where she'd be at that point and Bette would be on a tight schedule, so better for them to say their goodbyes now. They had discussed all they needed to the previous night.

Bette waved them off, then got into her hire car and headed for Dundee. She watched Crowdie recede in her rear-view mirror with mixed feelings. The farm now felt more like home than it had for half her life. Yet she couldn't deny the huge feeling of apprehension at the thought of what she was about to do. But she'd gone over and over everything in the past two days, and still couldn't come up with any other option. There were so many reasons why cutting their losses and putting Crowdie on the market immediately was just unfathomable, and her own newfound reconnection with the place was just one of them.

It took remarkably little time for her to sign over a chunk of her life to her father's bank.

'Thank you, Ms Crowdie,' said the financial manager. 'We truly appreciate the sincere efforts you are making to underpin the farm's debt. And as a family bank we understand how important the heritage of home is. Please do contact us if you need to discuss anything further.'

Bette shucked the anxiety from her shoulders as she walked back out into the sunlit street. It was done. Now she and Nina had three months to make sure her signature on those papers wasn't either a horrendous mistake or an utter waste of time. Besides which, all of that needed to take a back seat to her work. From tomorrow morning, she'd be back at her desk and back in the swing of things, preparing for the merger which she assumed was going to be announced later today, as that was the only way Spencer's insistence on the meeting she was now heading back to Crowdie to take made sense.

She got back to the farm with plenty of time to make sure that her father's study was dressed properly for the meeting. Bette had spent time the previous evening hanging a blank grey curtain behind the desk as a neutral backdrop, and ensuring the lighting was appropriate. She thought it was likely that she was about to be introduced to her new fellow partners in the conjoined firm and wanted to make as good an impression as it was possible to make through the medium of the computer screen. She'd straightened her hair for the first time in days and wore the suit she'd been wearing when she arrived in Aberdeen, which now seemed like a lifetime ago. She'd even put on a full face of make-up, or at least as full as it ever got for Bette.

She had no inkling there was anything wrong right up until the moment the remote meeting began and the video of the boardroom in London appeared on her screen. Even then, it didn't surprise her that all six partners, three each from the two firms, were arrayed around the table. Then Spencer Coulthard – the man who had sponsored her internship when she had still been in training, the lawyer who had put his faith in her, who had welcomed her into the firm and who had always been her biggest supporter – began to speak, his forehead creased into a frown.

'Bette,' he said, the gravity in his voice pushing a knife of ice into her heart. 'I'm afraid we have something difficult to talk with you about.'

*

The call ended up being ninety minutes long, and by the end of it, Bette was a wet rag. When the meeting concluded she sat staring at the screen, her mind blank as a terrifying feeling of hopelessness began to creep into her limbs, a chill of horror inching towards her heart.

Redundant.

It was such an ugly word, one Bette had never for a moment thought she'd be confronted with. She still couldn't work out how everything had fallen apart with such spectacular speed. Hadn't she always worked harder than any other associate at the firm? Hadn't she brought in excellent clients who were always happy with her work? Look at Arnold Locatelli – Bette knew for a fact that she was the third divorce lawyer he'd hired, and the only one he'd stuck with. And yet here she was, apparently surplus to requirements not only as the partner she had expected to be, but even as a colleague. There had been a lot of talk about why, and the fact that she was not the only one, but Bette had barely been able to listen properly, too stunned and humiliated by the disaster unfolding around her. How had she not seen this coming?

Bette's heart quailed and she pressed her fingers to her lips. What was she going to *do*? In a flash she saw herself signing those papers that very morning, shaking hands with her father's bank manager. Besides her own exorbitant mortgage on the flat she loved so much back in London, now she was also liable for the farm, and she couldn't afford either. Not now. She'd been banking on her fat new salary, not on losing even the one she currently drew. She'd get a decent redundancy package, but that would barely keep her going for three months, especially with the additional burden of the farm weighing her down.

The idea of having to go cap-in-hand to another firm filled her with dread. The finalizing of the merger and its consequences would get out soon enough and it would travel like wildfire around the City. Bette Crowdie, redundant. Who would want to take her on in light of that? What new clients could she possibly attract — who would want a divorce lawyer that not one, but two major firms had decided was surplus to their requirements going forward?

It's not a reflection on you, Bette, Spencer had said. *It's not personal.*

But how could that possibly be true?

What was she going to *do*?

Bette stood up so suddenly that Bern Crowdie's old office chair rocked on its rickety wheels and almost fell. She had to get out of there. The walls were crowding in, as if the entire farmhouse were collapsing in a concertina of brick and rubble that would crush her, grind her into dust beneath its weight. She stumbled out of the office and along the hall, beneath the gazes of all those generations of Crowdies who had kept the farm going, kept it in the family, kept it whole. In the kitchen, still in her suit, she pushed her feet into the pair of her sister's hiking boots that she had been wearing since she arrived. *Nina.* Bette had to get out of there before her sister reappeared; she couldn't talk to her now, what on Earth would she say? The horror of having to explain herself and what had occurred was another terror lurking on the horizon. She crossed the farmyard and made for the track, heading for that secret pocket of land on the side of the cliff where no one would find her. The orchard.

The sky was incongruously blue, the sun shining on as if Bette's world hadn't suddenly spun off its axis. She held herself together as she slipped and slid down the path. Around her there were birds singing – not only the sea birds wheeling and screaming along the rocky cliffs, but smaller visitors to the orchard flitting between the branches. Bette struggled through the long grass, eyes blurring as she made for the cliff wall, as she went as far as she could to the very edge of this nowhere place, as if there would be somewhere further to hide from the world there. When she reached the stone bench that had been chipped out of the eternal, unmoving rock she collapsed onto it. Bending double with her hands over her face, she sobbed.

Redundant.

Work was her *life*. It was all she had. It was *everything* to her. She didn't have close friends outside work, she didn't have a partner, she didn't even really have a family she felt close to. She'd dedicated everything to her career. Bette had wanted to be successful, she'd wanted to be secure, and most of all, she'd wanted to be *respected*. Bette had wanted to make herself the kind of person that no one would ever think about crossing. *Bette Crowdie, she's the best. Bette Crowdie, she's who you want.* She'd thought she'd got there. She really had. But now, here she was, and—

'Bette?'

She looked up, shocked, her face streaked with tears.

Ryan was standing in front of her, carrying a basket laden with apples.

She tried to turn away, tried to swipe away the tears, because she didn't need to be humiliated twice in one day and particularly not in front of him, but it was too late. Ryan dumped the basket on the ground and in two swift steps was crouching in front of her, reaching for her hands.

'Bette, my God – what is it? What's happened?'

She shook him off and wiped her face again. 'Nothing,' she said, 'I'm fine.'

He moved to sit beside her on the old stone. 'You're not fine. What's going on? I thought you were going back to London today?'

At the mention of London the tears started again – it was as if, now they had started, she was powerless to stop them. It was infuriating, and it was unwanted, so now she was angry as well as heartbroken, and the last time she had felt this so entirely at odds with herself *he* was responsible for the mess she had briefly become. *Eighteen years*, she thought, *have I really achieved nothing in almost two decades? Have I really worked so hard to come full circle and end up right back where I started?*

This thought didn't help with the tears and in the end she just let them come. Ryan sat beside her, quiet, until the worst had passed.

'Whatever it is,' he said. 'There must be something I can do to help?'

She looked at him then, this stranger she had once thought she would spend the rest of her life with but who had betrayed her in such an awful away. '*You?*'

He flinched a little at that, but didn't turn away. 'Bette,' he said again, his voice soft.

She looked away from him, out towards the sea far below them. It was calm today, incomprehensibly so, a gently rippling expanse of blue that shimmered with the sun. In the silence between her breaths she could hear the bees buzzing in the orchard, the birds singing in the trees, as if nothing had changed here for decades, centuries.

'I've lost everything,' Bette said, in a voice she almost didn't recognize as hers. 'What hasn't gone yet will vanish soon enough. My flat, this farm. My career. It's all gone.'

She told him briefly what had happened during the call. That the merger had meant an imbalance at the top of the tree, that they couldn't have as many partners as they'd originally negotiated. And Bette hadn't been there to fight her corner, to make the incoming firm understand why she was so vital. It seemed that the dominoes tumbled by Bern's death had still been falling, even when she hadn't been there to see them.

'Bette,' Ryan said, reaching out again to take her hand. 'I'm so sorry. I know how important your career is to you.'

She looked at him, the irony of his statement echoing around her head. '*Do* you?'

The pulse that passed through his eyes told Bette that he knew what she meant. Instead of letting go of her hand, though, he squeezed it tighter.

'Even when I knew you all those years ago you were the brightest person I'd ever met,' he said. 'A shooting star, Bette, that was going to go so high and so far that none of us would be able to keep up with you. And you're still that person. I can see it. There'll be other positions, won't there? Other law firms who would be lucky to have you.'

She didn't answer, not wanting to have to explain the details of the depths of this failure. In any case, even if he'd been right, there was no other firm who was going to pay what she would need to keep both her flat and this place going.

'This morning I took on the arrears for this place,' she said. 'It's going to sink me, and we're going to lose everything. I'm going to have to tell Nina that we're done, that I've failed Dad. That I've failed *her*. I tried. I thought I could make it work. But by Christmas we're going to be left with nothing. We don't have anything else to sell. We don't have any other assets. There's *nothing*. We're done. Crowdie's done.'

Ryan squeezed her hand again. 'Maybe not,' he said.

She looked at him. Her tears had finally dried up, and now she'd been left with an intense feeling of weariness, as if she'd been emptied out and left a hollow husk of what she used to be. 'What do you mean?'

Ryan looked at the trees in front of them. 'I've got a suggestion to make,' he said.

Chapter Twenty-seven

When Nina got home with Barney after school later that day, the last thing she expected to find was her sister, still at the house. Bette was sitting at the kitchen table with a mug of tea, and looked up when her nephew ran in through the door to say hello. She was smiling, but Nina's internal alarm bell went off at the sight of her pale face. Bette looked wan and exhausted, and her eyes were rimmed in red, as if she'd been crying.

'Auntie Bette!' he said, giving her a hug. 'What are you doing here?'

'I missed my flight,' Bette said, returning the hug but looking at Nina over his head. 'And it turns out there are some more things I need to talk with your mum about. So here I still am.'

'Great!' Best Barnaby Barnacle said, with genuine enthusiasm. 'That means we can finish our map of the farm. Can you help me now?'

'Why don't you go up and get changed first, bub?' Nina said.

They both watched as the boy and his faithful hound bounded out of the kitchen, along the hallway and then thundered up the stairs. Nina pulled out the chair opposite Bette.

'What's happened?'

Bette dropped her gaze to the mug clutched between her hands and Nina's heart sank further.

'Bette? Is it the bank? I thought everything was all right for now – I got your text this morning, telling me that—'

'It's not the bank,' Bette said, quietly. 'Nina, I've lost my job. That's what the meeting was about this afternoon. To tell me—' she stopped and took a breath before going on. 'They've made me redundant.'

'Oh Bette,' Nina said. 'I'm so sorry.'

Bette looked away, and despite knowing what a huge blow this must have been, Nina was shocked to see tears in her sister's eyes. She couldn't remember ever seeing Bette cry. She tried to focus on that, on feeling sympathy for her sister, who was so clearly devastated, instead of the thoughts that had immediately turned towards the farm. *Now what do we do?* she thought. *In three months, without Bette's income . . .*

Bette sniffed and wiped her eyes quickly. 'Anyway,' she said, 'obviously this leaves us with a rather large issue. Because while the bank isn't a problem at this moment – it will be.'

Nina rubbed a hand over her face. 'Right. But . . . you'll

get another job, won't you? Another firm will take you on. I bet you could walk right into somewhere else tomorrow morning if you wanted to.'

'I'm not so sure about that,' Bette said. 'And even if I did, then it's unlikely my salary would match what I've just lost at the firm, let alone what I expected to get as a partner.'

'But—'

'Please, Nina,' Bette said. 'I can't talk about that right now. I can't. Okay?'

'Okay,' Nina said. 'Then what do you want to talk about?'

Bette looked down at her tea, her fingers squeezing the mug hard. 'I've been speaking to Ryan.'

'Ryan?'

'He was down in the orchard, gathering up the windfalls. I went down there, after . . .' She trailed off, as if it were too painful to enunciate the details of her sudden joblessness. Bette shook her head, and went on. 'Anyway, he thinks he can regenerate the orchard.'

Nina blinked, blindsided by this sudden, nonsensical change of subject. 'The *orchard*?'

Bette turned a watery gaze on her. 'He thinks it could be worth something, Nina. In fact, he thinks that if he can get it back to full production, it could be worth a *lot*. If they are the apples he was telling us about on Saturday – these amazing "perfect" cider apples – he thinks he could find plenty of people who would be desperate to either buy the apples from us or purchase the entire orchard outright. Which isn't an impossible proposition, if you think about the location.

224

It's already separate from the rest of the farm in all practical senses. All we'd need to do is determine access rights that we're willing to either share with the buyer or sell outright. The rest of the farm could continue as we've known it all our lives.'

Nina tried to take this in. 'But most of the trees are dead, aren't they? Even the ones that are still alive look as if they might not last the next big storm, let alone another winter.'

'I know, but Ryan seems convinced that they can be saved. Or at the very least that we can cultivate new saplings from the trees still there.'

'But it would take years to grow trees big enough to produce fruit, wouldn't it? And we don't know the first thing about fruit trees.'

'He's offering to help us while we learn. He also says that if we're willing to sell them, the grafts themselves could be a valuable income stream. Not to mention one that would be ready to go almost immediately. Grafts are taken in autumn and spring, so from that point of view we found the orchard at the perfect time.'

'Wait, wait,' Nina said. 'I can't ... I'm having trouble keeping up with this, to be honest.'

To her surprise, Bette smiled a little. 'I know. But the way he explained it ... Nina, if he's right, that weird little patch of land on the side of the cliff might be the only thing we've got left that's worth anything at all.'

Nina blew out a breath. 'You know, I'm not usually the cynical one, but that sounds like a big "if".'

'It does. I know it does. But what other options do we have?' Bette asked. 'Surely we should at least try?'

'It depends on what we're going to have to put into it to find out, doesn't it?' Nina pointed out. 'Because I don't think I have to tell you that we were already running on empty, Bette, and after today . . .'

Her sister nodded. 'I know that. And so does Ryan. Which is why he's offering to help us free of charge. He's going to be working at the Greville place in Barton Mill over harvest season anyway, and all the time he's there during the day, he's willing to help us get the orchard back on its feet whenever he can around that.'

'That's . . . very generous of him,' Nina said.

'It is,' Bette agreed.

'He knows that we've only got three months?'

Bette squeezed the mug between her hands again, her knuckles whitening with the grip. 'He knows enough about the situation to understand what's at stake. Obviously we can't have the orchard back to full health in that time. But he thinks we can get it to a place that would make it an attractive proposition for sale, at the very least. And we can take the grafts we need to grow new saplings. That could be something.'

Nina leaned back in her chair. Overhead, she heard the sound of Barnaby playing with Limpet, some game that seemed to involve galumphing about on the old farmhouse floors in a way that made it sound as if there were a herd of elephants above their heads. She thought about what it would mean for her son, being able to stay in this place, the only real home he'd ever had. She thought about what it would mean to feel secure. Had she ever felt that as an adult? She had. Here, for a brief time at least, she had.

'We don't really have a choice but to try, do we?' she said. 'If we can sell the orchard without having to sell the rest of the farm . . . If Ryan really thinks that could raise enough to clear the debt . . . That would be amazing.'

Bette actually smiled a little at that. 'It would be. And no, we don't really have a choice. But I told him I needed to talk to you about it before agreeing to anything.'

Nina frowned a little. 'What's in it for him? It's going to be a hell of a lot of work to get that place up to scratch, isn't it? And he's willing to do it for free? Why?'

Her sister's gaze slid away again. 'I think he's genuinely interested in seeing whether the orchard can be revived. It would be a big feather in his cap, wouldn't it, if he can bring a place that's been no more than myth for centuries back to life? And anyway . . . he's not proposing to do all the work himself. There's too much for one person and he's got full-time work of his own.'

Nina sighed. 'That's my worry, Bette. We can't afford to hire labour, and I'm already stretched thin as it is.'

'I know. That's why, if it's okay with you, I'm going to stay here and work on whatever needs to be done.'

Nina stared at her. 'You're not going back to London?'

Bette shrugged. 'I can't just take the first job that comes along, for the same reason as you didn't want anyone around here thinking this place was going to go on the market,' she said. 'I don't want to seem desperate. I need to find a way to make this redundancy seem like a positive for me, at least on the surface. I need to appear to be assessing my options before making a move.'

'Yeah,' Nina said. 'I can see how taking time out to deal with your father's estate would be a good cover story for a gap on your resume.'

Bette looked at her, as if trying to work out the meaning behind her words. 'That's not the only reason for me to stay,' she said. 'I want to pull my weight, especially if the orchard really does turn out to be as vital for us as Ryan thinks it could be.'

Nina nodded. 'This place is yours as much as mine,' she said. 'In fact, legally it's probably more than half yours now, isn't it?'

'I don't see it that way,' Bette said. 'I'm not trying to take anything from you, Nina.'

'I know you're not,' Nina said, but all the same, there was a bad taste in her mouth.

Chapter Twenty-eight

'I know I'm being unfair and ungrateful,' Nina said. 'I know that without her I'd be in a far worse position, and that the farm would probably have already been repossessed.'

Cam turned from the stove to look at her over his shoulder. 'But . . .?'

She sighed. 'But she hasn't had anything to do with the farm for two decades, precisely because of the guy she's now throwing in everything with to save it. I'm the one that's been here, and I suppose I just feel a bit . . . Oh, I don't know, really. Ignore me, I'm just blathering.'

'You can blather all you like,' Cam said, 'as long as you also get those bowls out of the oven. This is ready.'

Nina grabbed the tea towel that was draped over Cam's shoulder and bent down to open the oven door, retrieving the bowls that were warming within. She'd come over to update him on everything – which, if she were to be honest, was also an excuse to get out of the house for a while. Not that she and Bette had fought, or that her sister was in the way, or being abrasive in any way. But this time last week Nina had expected that Crowdie was going to be hers, that she and Barney would finally have a home of their own and to themselves. She hadn't realized how important that idea had been to her until she'd seen Bette sitting there at the kitchen table, when she'd expected the house to be empty. It was an adjustment, that was all. Cam, true to his kind soul, had recognized exactly what Nina had needed as soon as he'd opened the door to her knock, and had asked her in not only for a beer, but also to share the curry he was midway through cooking. And, it went unspoken, so he could listen to her offload about her worries.

She'd been able to say yes, she reminded herself, because Bette was back at home with Barney. *Think of the positives, Nina,* said a voice in her head that sounded suspiciously like her mother.

They sat down at Cam's kitchen table. 'What's unsettling you most about the orchard proposition?' he asked, as they began to eat.

'I don't know that I'm unsettled, exactly,' Nina said. 'And even if I was, what difference would it make? If I want to have any hope of keeping the farm as we know it, we have to find a way of clearing the debt. If the orchard can do that, it will be a godsend. Honestly, I think it's Bette that I'm finding hardest to handle.'

'In what way?'

Nina thought for a moment, trying to frame her

complicated feelings about her sister. 'She's been a pretty nebulous figure in my life ever since I was born. She never wanted me around or to spend time with me – she made it very clear that I was just a nuisance when I was little. She was always getting told off for calling me a brat and refusing to take me with her when she went out. And once she left for university, she basically vanished. She wasn't here in the aftermath of when our parents split up, and even though they always stayed friends, that was a lot. I felt alone. That just got worse as I got older. I did stupid things because I didn't have anyone to talk to. I was only nineteen when I got pregnant with Barney, and I can't help thinking that if Bette had been here, if she'd seen what was happening, she'd have made me realise that I didn't have to stay with Barney's dad. Dad and Mum tried to tell me that, but Bette had gone off and was living her own life, wasn't she? She didn't need them, so I shouldn't either, I think that's what was at the back of my mind. That I'd be a failure if I couldn't make it on my own, the way my sister had. She never even called me when the baby was born. I just got a text. One word: Congratulations. I thought she didn't care, or maybe that I wasn't worth her time. Now, here she is, maybe permanently. I'm essentially living with a stranger, except that she's a stranger with a huge say in what happens in my and my son's life going forward.'

Cam nodded. 'I can see how all that would be tricky to navigate.'

'It's not only that,' Nina admitted. 'I've been angry with her for a long time, Cam. Or at least, I've been angry with who I thought she was. And now . . . I guess I'm discovering she's not actually like that at all. Yes, at times she can be aloof and infuriatingly calm. But the thing with Ryan really did seem to throw her for a loop. It made her seem . . . I don't know, more human, somehow? I know that sounds weird. It just seems so *unlike* her. Or who I thought she was, anyway. And she's so good with Barney. He really loves her.'

Cam chewed silently for a while, contemplating her words. 'She really was thrown that first time they saw each other, that's a good description of it,' he said. 'He was, too. Totally overwhelmed, both of them.'

'Right,' Nina said. 'And now she's saying she's giving up the idea of going back to London to stay here and *work* with him.'

'Or maybe,' Cam said, 'it really has nothing personal to do with Ryan at all and she wants to help because she really does think it's the only way to give the farm a way out.'

'Yeah,' Nina sighed. 'Maybe.'

'You don't think there could still be a spark between them, do you?' Cam asked.

'Between Bette and Ryan?' Nina asked. She found the notion oddly shocking, but couldn't really pinpoint why. Another weird twist in her relationship with her sister: she'd always thought of Bette as distantly old, and yet now that she was here in the flesh it was clear that wasn't the case.

'Yeah,' he said. 'I mean, the way they were both so affected by seeing each other again tells me that whatever they had back then was pretty powerful. And they were going to get married, right? They haven't seen each other for almost twenty years and now suddenly here they are, thrown back together ...'

'No,' Nina said. 'I don't believe that. I can't. He cheated on her. She was obviously really heartbroken by it.'

'I know,' Cam said, quietly. 'But the heart isn't always rational, is it?'

He fell into silence as he took a long draft of his beer. Nina watched him for a moment. She'd caught the slight edge to his voice and wondered whether he spoke from experience, and if he did, just how bitter that was. She hadn't asked about his past or how he came to be single and childfree at the age he was, why he'd come to the Bronagh farm with plenty of knowledge of how to farm but no family close by. It wasn't her business to ask, but she wondered whether this little observation was a hint.

Cam glanced up and caught her watching him. Nina didn't immediately look away, caught on the cusp of asking the question. Cam didn't look away either, and he didn't smile. Instead a slight tension entered his eyes and his gaze flickered away from hers for a moment, but only far enough for him to study the rest of her face, until it rested on the small white scar over her cheekbone, the creation of which she barely thought about anymore, except in nightmares that were few and far between and yet even now still persisted.

'The past can be a pretty heavy weight,' he said, still in the same soft voice. 'Sometimes heavy enough to stop us moving forward, however much we might want to.'

Nina felt her heart turn over at his tone. She wondered again if Cam were talking about himself as much as he seemed to be hinting that he was talking about her, but she didn't have the courage to ask. Although there were all those many first dates, she reminded herself, all those various Sallys who came and went. Cam never had any problems moving forward, did he? She picked up her own beer and swigged it, taking the moment to step back from whatever line they had been approaching.

'Bette's never had trouble moving forward,' she told him. 'In fact, I think that's all she's been doing since she left home. It's only *now* she's stopped moving.'

Cam nodded. 'That's quite a rug she had pulled from beneath her, wasn't it, losing her job? Especially so soon after your dad dying. I get the feeling that work has been her security for a long time. And now here she is, having lost both, and your dad pretty much made her directly responsible for getting you out of the hole he'd left you both in. Which, by the way, was a pretty heavy responsibility for him to drop on her without warning. When you think of it like that, it's kind of easy to see why having Ryan turn up out of the blue right now as well is such a curve ball.'

Nina was quiet for a moment, swirling her drink around in her glass. She hadn't thought about it like that. She was used to thinking of Bette as the successful one, Bette as the high-flyer, the sister who had been unstoppable and who had always known exactly what she wanted and would do anything to get it. It was inconceivable, surely, that her sister's work situation was as difficult as she'd suggested. Nina's assumption was that Bette could walk into another position as soon as she wanted.

'God,' Nina complained, only half-joking. 'You're making me feel like a terrible person.'

Cam laughed. 'You're not. *Of course* you're not! You've got a lot on your plate, too, and you're also still grieving Bern. And I absolutely understand why you were so hurt by Bette as a child, and why that's difficult to let go of. But it's always easy to be hardest on those close to you – and you and Bette are close family, even though I understand it doesn't feel that way right now. When it's all right in your face, it's hard to take a step back and see the bigger picture. Especially when, as you said earlier, you've had this image of who you thought your sister was in your head for so long. I think if you could see it from where I'm standing, you'd find it easier to be sympathetic to her.'

'Yeah,' Nina sighed. 'I'm sure you're right.'

Cam drained his beer and indicated her glass as he got up. 'Another?'

Nina realized that she'd be completely happy to stay here in his company for the rest of the evening, which was exactly why she shouldn't. She gave a reluctant smile and finished her meal.

'Thanks for the offer,' she said. 'For dinner too, that was delicious. But I should really get back, it's Barnaby's bedtime and though he might be a good boy, there's no way he'll tell Bette that of his own accord. And also,' she added, with mock approbation, 'now you've pointed out what a heartless cow I've been, I probably need to play extra nice with my sister. Cheers for that.'

He grinned at her, and Nina tried not to wish she could stay.

She'd been expecting to find Barnaby and Limpet squashed together on the sofa in the kitchen watching TV when she got back, but they weren't. She'd also expected to find Bette in the study, but there was no sign of her sister either.

Nina could hear the murmur of voices from somewhere, and eventually located it as coming from Barney's playroom. She leaned in through the open door to find Barnaby and Bette sitting side by side at the old dining table, heads bent over something spread out across it, a scatter of coloured paper scraps around their feet and even over the collie dog who was lying with his nose on his paws beneath the table.

'Hello you two,' she said. 'What are you up to, hiding away in here?'

'Auntie Bette is helping me with my summer project,' her son explained, as Nina got close enough to see what they'd arrayed across the table. 'I have to add the orchard now that we know it's there, don't I?'

It wasn't until she saw it that Nina remembered the 'Map of Where You Live' homework assignment that Barnaby had been given to complete during the summer holidays. This had been another project that her son and her father had been making together: a large cut-paper collage representation of the Crowdie farm. Nina had left them to it and the pair had gone at it with gusto. They had started with the farm and the farmyard, cutting coloured shapes to represent each individual element – the farmhouse, the barns, the fields, eventually the blue-green tumble of the North Sea itself – and then filling in details with pencil and pen. Even objectively it was beautiful, and Nina had said nothing about her worries of how she was going to actually transport the thing to Barnaby's school when the time came. It was only now that she realized that Barnaby hadn't mentioned the map to her at all since his grandfather died, and felt a sharp pang of guilt that she'd been too caught up with work on the farm to even remember that it existed.

'Well,' Nina said. 'That's very nice of Auntie Bette. And I love how you've done the orchard! I can even see the fence! And are those the trees?'

'Yes,' Barnaby said. 'We've done them with green paper because that's how they will look once they're all healthy and have grown properly again. Next we're going to add lots of apples because Grandad and I already decided that the map is what the farm looks like in summer, and by next summer there will be *loads*.'

Nina laid a hand on her son's head, amid his thick dark hair. 'That sounds like a great plan. But I think you're going to have to save finishing this for another day, bub. It's past your bedtime.'

'Five more minutes?' he suggested, hopefully. 'And then I promise I'll go and wash my face and brush my teeth. And Auntie Bette can tuck me in.'

Nina glanced at Bette and realized that her sister was just as surprised by this as she was.

'Okay,' Nina said. 'Five minutes. Then it's time for bed, superhero.'

Chapter Twenty-nine

Ryan told Bette that the first thing that needed doing at the orchard was clearing the tangle of grasses that had grown up unchecked around the trees. It would be a tough job, not least because some of the trees were packed so closely together and the ground as a whole was distinctly uneven. First thing the next morning, Bette dug out the farm's ancient petrol mower from the barn and stood contemplating it in the yard. She couldn't ever remember using it herself – or indeed ever needing to use any mower. It wasn't as if she had ever had a garden in London, or at any time during her student days. She told Allie this when her friend called to ask if she could come down and do some work in the orchard later that day.

'My mum says she's okay to mind the shop for a few afternoons,' Allie explained. 'It'll give me time to spend at Crowdie, if that's okay with you?'

'Sure,' Bette said, peering at the workings of the machine with her phone against her ear. She thought it might be rusted beyond use. 'Ryan's coming up as soon as he's finished at the Greville place to help for a while so he'll be here at some point, too. Fingers crossed I've got this thing working and actually made a start down there by then.'

'Ryan, eh?' Allie said. 'I'm glad you two have worked things out. He was always such a sweet guy.'

'Not *always*,' Bette pointed out.

'Hmm,' Allie said.

'We're off, Bette!' Her sister's voice rang out from the kitchen doorway, and Bette turned to see Nina hustling Barnaby into the car, the little boy waving. 'Best Barnaby Barnacle's going to be late for school!'

'See you!' Bette waved them both off and then turned her attention back to the mower and her phone call. 'Allie, can we catch up properly later? I'd better get on.'

Bette loaded the mower into the back of the farm's Land Rover, added a rake, a flask of coffee and a packet of biscuits. Then she paused and looked at Limpet, sitting forlornly on the step of the farmhouse, bereft now that his boy had vanished for another day. 'Limpet, do you want to come with me?'

The dog pricked up his ears at his name and trotted across to jump into the passenger seat. Bette headed right into the clifftop pasture above the orchard, figuring it'd make her life easier to drive as close to the cliff edge as she could. The fence blocking the way to the orchard path proved a challenge and she wondered whether it would be wise to open up the access going forward. But eventually, there she was, in the orchard alone and about to begin the long process of attempting to bring it back to life. She paused before she pulled the cord on the mower, contemplating the wind- and water-washed quiet of the cliffside, suddenly proud that she was going to be the one to take this first small step, a practical measure that might yet secure Crowdie's future. Limpet sat beside her, looking up at her quizzically.

'Well then, pup,' Bette said. 'Here we go.'

She started at the far end, with the reasoning that the ground directly in front of the bee bole cliff was the most level the ledge had to offer and would make for good practice until she got used to the mower. It was still heavy going, not least because every few feet she had to pause to gather up obstacles in her way – rocks and fallen branches, mainly, although there were a few windfalls too. These she added to the basket that Ryan had left in the bench alcove. He'd told her that they'd need to find somewhere to lay them out to soften for a while before he could press them and test the juice. Limpet opted to stay out of the way of the catastrophically noisy mower, and slotted himself into the space left on the bench beside the apple basket.

Bette managed to push the mower up and down parallel to the cliff face twice before she had to stop, her arms aching as if she'd attempted to bench-press a truck. She paused when she got to the fence, Limpet looking at her from worried chocolate-brown eyes as she hefted the basket of apples onto the ground and collapsed onto the hewn stone beside him. The dog immediately shifted so that his chin was on her thigh, and Bette rested a hand on his black-and-white head as she caught her breath.

By the time Allie arrived at about two o'clock, Bette had got the hang of the mower and begun to navigate the trickier parts of the orchard, although she soon realized that shears were going to have to be used directly under the trees. She located a pair during a quick lunch break, trudging wearily back up the coast path and across the pasture, making the decision that yes, it would definitely be a good idea to remove the fence that blocked her way if she was going to be making this journey multiple times a day for the foreseeable future.

She was kneeling with the shears at the base of what Bette had come to think of as her grandmother's tree – the one Jean Crowdie had painted so painstakingly that it was still recognizable sixty years later – when she heard Allie's voice behind her.

'Hey! This looks great already!'

Bette clambered to her feet as Allie reached her and the two friends regarded her work of the morning. The trees she had freed from the overgrown grasses and weeds looked far less wizened than their counterparts. They were still small, of course, still windblown. But they also appeared healthier. Without the overbearing wall of green, it was also possible to see how many of them still bore leaves. And without the thick mat of undergrowth around each, it would be possible to walk among them unencumbered. Bette found herself cheered by the worth of her efforts, which had so far left her aching, sweaty and exhausted in a way that not even a Sunday morning at the gym managed to accomplish.

'Thanks for letting me come,' Allie said. 'I don't want to waste any time. This is a find worth throwing as much effort as possible at before the season turns. Can't excavate during the winter. I'll try to stay out of your way.'

'I'm looking forward to seeing you work,' Bette said, with a smile. 'There's coffee in the flask on the bench if you want it. Biscuits, too – just ignore Limpet. He'll beg for one, but I'm under strict instructions from his owner.'

'Right you are,' Allie said. 'Then tomorrow, the coffee's on me.'

Bette went back to her task. Limpet periodically appeared at her side to see what she was doing and toured the orchard, checking out each nook and cranny, though he never went far. Then, as Bette was trying to shear the worst of the overgrowth from beneath another tree and wishing for a fresh barista-made coffee, Limpet got up from where he'd been lolling beside her and gave a sharp bark, his ears pricked and looking at her expectantly.

'What is it?' she asked.

Limpet turned in a circle and barked again, and then again, sharp little urgent yips, staring at her with his head cocked, as if he expected her to know what he wanted.

'I don't know what—' Bette began, and then a thought occurred to her. She looked at her watch to see that it was exactly 3.30pm. 'Ah,' she said. 'Best Barnaby Barnacle's on his way home from school, isn't he? Do you want to go back to meet him?'

The dog yipped again in answer, bouncing a little on his four eager paws. Bette really didn't want to walk all the way back to the farmhouse again, only to have to immediately return.

'You know the way home, don't you, boy?' she said. 'Run home, Limpet. Home!'

The dog took off, charging through the trees and up the track without hesitation, and Bette reflected on her nephew's good fortune at just how loyal a companion he had.

By the time Ryan appeared Bette was flagging again. He arrived earlier than she expected, just after five o'clock, and he came down the path carefully pushing a loaded wheelbarrow over the old worn ruts in the soil. By this time Bette had mowed right the way along the gap between the trees and the fence.

'Hi,' she said, turning off the mower as he approached, suddenly painfully aware that she was a sweaty mess, when he looked . . . really good. She waved at the barrow. 'What's this?'

'Hey,' Ryan smiled, apparently unconcerned by her dishevelled appearance. 'It's an apple rack. We need a shed for it to go in, but I already had one of these I can spare on a loan, so I thought I'd at least bring it down. We need to get the windfalls racked as soon as we can.' He looked around at the orchard, taking in its changed appearance. 'Wow, this looks great already.'

Bette followed his gaze. 'It does, doesn't it? It's hard work, though. Or I guess it's probably more that I'm just out of practice,' she added ruefully, rubbing at one shoulder, which was beginning to seize up. 'I'm definitely not the farm girl I was. Too many years spent behind a desk – my knots are getting knots!'

'It'd be tough for anyone,' he assured her. 'Especially working on their own. I'll take over – I can spare an hour or so. You should head back, have a sit down.'

'I can't do that if you're here working and we're not even paying you for it,' Bette said. 'But I'll let you mow for a bit. Not sure my old bones can take much more shaking today.'

'Old?' he said, his dark eyes twinkling a little. 'You must be joking. I don't think you've aged a day. You look exactly the same as you always did. Apart from the hair, that is,' he added, studying her closely for a moment. 'Beth Crowdie with short hair. It suits you, but it's strange – I never once in all these years thought that you might have changed it.'

Bette wasn't sure how to respond to that. Why would he have thought of her at all? She looked away, wondering what his wife would think about what he'd just said.

'Sorry,' he said. 'I didn't mean to—'

'It's fine,' Bette said. 'I'm just going to—' She waved vaguely at the orchard and went off to find the shears she'd put down earlier.

They worked on together, chat mercifully rendered impossible by the roar of the mower. Bette gathered broken branches, piling them up beside the wheelbarrow containing the apple rack. Perhaps they'd have a bonfire, she thought, and wondered if her nephew had ever toasted marshmallows over a flame. As kids they had done that down on the beach sometimes. She remembered a little party of her friends, Allie and some of the farmhands included, one summer Saturday night. Ryan had been there too, though this was before they were a couple. She could remember that night so clearly: the electricity she'd felt every time she looked at him, the absolute certainty that all she would need to make her life complete was for him to look her way, to notice her the way she'd noticed him.

And then he had.

That velvet night under the stars had held their first kiss, she realized now, with a jolt that turned her heart over with the memory of that moment of pure teenage passion. She'd been laughing over something with Allie, their faces bright in the flamelight, and then she'd looked up to see that Ryan was there, sitting down beside her. Time had slipped sideways as they talked about everything and nothing, and the next thing she knew Allie had gone to talk to another friend, tact-fully absenting herself from the duo, because she knew better than anyone how hard Bette had fallen for Ryan. *I'm going to go for a walk*, he'd said, eventually, getting up and dusting off the battered jeans he wore, which on him seemed far more stylish than on anyone else. *I want to see the Red Castle by starlight. I'll come too*, she'd said, and off they had slipped together. They'd only gone a few steps before he'd twined his fingers gently around hers, and a few steps after that he'd said, *You're the most beautiful girl I've ever met, Beth Crowdie.*

It had been a line, of course, Bette knew that now. But back then, doused in moonlight beneath the stars, his words had turned her legs to jelly and she'd known for sure she was in love. And that was even before he'd pulled her to him, kissed her, and said, *I've wanted to do that since the moment I saw you,* as if they were characters in a movie and this was their happy ending. Because back then she'd been too young to know that in real life, there are no happy endings.

She was still thinking about these things when behind her the sound of the mower cut out, leaving in its noisy wake the shocking hush of sudden quiet. Bette came back from the past with a jolt, and when she turned to look at Ryan there was a moment in which it seemed inconceivable that she wasn't still back there, on that beach.

'I'm sorry, but I'm going to have to go,' he said. 'I've got somewhere I need to be.'

'That's fine,' Bette said, dropping her last load of branches and walking back towards him. 'I think I'm done, too. I'm considering dragging Allie down to the Darling for a drink, and I'll get barred if I walk in there smelling like this. I'd better have a shower first.'

Ryan laughed, and then a thought appeared to occur to him. 'Hang on – aren't you both *already* barred?'

'What?'

'You *are*!' his eyes widening as he teased her with a memory Bette hadn't thought about for decades. 'You *and* Allie. For that stunt you both pulled with the dartboard and the door of the gents' loo on Christmas Eve . . .'

'I don't know what you're talking about,' Bette scoffed, with a laugh of her own as she pretended not to remember that particular teenage escapade. Her heart was still consumed with the one she'd just been reliving. 'Must have been one of your *other* girlfriends.'

She realized quite what she'd said the minute it was out of her mouth. She'd meant it in the same light tone as Ryan's own teasing, but perhaps it had hit the mark with a sharper edge than she'd intended. Ryan's laughter faded and she looked away.

'Can't have been,' he said, quietly, after a moment. 'There was no one but you, Beth Crowdie.'

She felt a stab of cold shock and looked up at him, but before she could ask what he meant, a voice called to them and there was Allie coming towards them.

'I thought I heard voices,' she said cheerfully and then paused, as if she'd just noticed something. 'Oh – I'm sorry, was I interrupting?'

Bette felt a need to cover her moment of confusion with something positive and smiled. 'No, no. We were just discussing next steps for the orchard. Listen, do you fancy a drink down in the village?'

'That,' Allie said, emphatically, 'sounds like a great idea. I'm parched. Are you coming too, Ryan?'

'No,' Ryan said, and Bette found it impossible to look in his direction. 'No, I need to get home. You two have fun, though. And stay away from the dartboard.'

Chapter Thirty

Allie managed to secure a table beside a window despite the pub's early evening throng. Outside, the sun was just beginning to set, casting a golden glow through the window beside them. The wind was up, waves dashing against the sea wall to send fizzes of white foam spray high onto the air.

'Sounds as if it's been a fruitful first day – no pun intended,' Allie said, hoisting her pint of beer in a grateful salute as Bette sat down with their drinks.

'Well, I've made a start,' Bette agreed. 'How about you? I should have come to have a look at the end of the day, sorry.' She'd been too preoccupied by that strange moment with Ryan, too eager to get out of there.

Allie shook her head. 'There's not much to see so far. I'm hoping I'll be able to loosen one of the stones without causing too much damage so we can see what, if anything, is behind it. It'll be slow going.'

'Any sort of archaeological investigation always is, isn't it?'

'Yes. And it's been a while since I was in the field,' Allie sipped her beer. 'It's nice to be back out there, though. I'm hoping working in the orchard is going to help me realize I'm not quite as crocked an old lady as I was beginning to feel.'

'You, crocked?' Bette laughed. 'Come off it.'

'I don't know,' Allie said, wistfully. 'Maybe it's having you back, Bette. I swear you haven't changed a bit, while the rest of us . . .' she shrugged.

Bette stared into her pint. 'Ryan hasn't changed either.'

'That is true,' Allie agreed. 'And I have to say, seeing you two together earlier made me feel like I'd stepped into a time warp.'

Bette thought about that statement Ryan had made, and wondered whether to ask Allie what she thought. *There was no one but you, Beth Crowdie.* She gulped more of her drink, instead. What was the point in dredging up the past? They'd both moved on, and he was married. No point in prodding that sleeping dog.

'Oh,' Allie said, fumbling for her phone as if she'd just remembered something. 'There's something I wanted to show you.'

Bette put down her drink and leaned closer as Allie opened a photo album on her phone.

'It's the fence,' she said. 'It's easier to see now it's clear of overgrowth.' She zoomed in on an image of the intricate design incorporated into the wrought-iron panels. 'I had another look at the initials visible in the ironwork. Tell me if you disagree – but I think that's a G, rather than a C.'

Bette looked at the enlarged image. Allie had found a panel less patinated with rust than the others, making the small, curlicued letters more visible. 'I think you're right,' she agreed. 'I suppose that makes sense – as I said, George Crowdie was the signatory on the deed. I'm still no clearer on who the "O" might be, though.'

Allie peered at the image, then looked up at Bette. 'Did you have any luck finding that book?'

'The diary one? No,' Bette said. 'Why, has that photo reminded you of something about it?'

Allie made a face as she looked at the picture again. 'I'm not sure. Maybe? I wish I could read it again, see whether anything I think I remember about it is real or just my mind playing tricks.'

'I think that's a lost cause,' Bette told her. 'Nina reckons Dad cleared out tons of stuff during the lockdowns, including out of the attic. It probably got shoved in a box that went to auction.'

'If it was about the Crowdie orchard, it could be a gold-mine of information,' Allie mused. 'I wonder where it ended up? Perhaps it's worth contacting the auction house. They might be able to help. Or, failing that, there are a few archives and private libraries that collect material of that sort – diaries, handwritten accounts, social history. After all, that's how we found the Brother Alphonse manuscript. That was sold by auction and bought by an archive specifically looking for such material.'

'That sounds like a long shot,' Bette said, doubtfully. 'We

might be completely misremembering this book. It might just have been a paperback potboiler that Dad ended up using for kindling, for all we know.'

'It might,' Allie agreed. 'But I don't know ... the more I think about it the more I have a feeling it was more than that. We always thought it was just a story, but now I wonder if it was an *actual* diary. I can't remember any real details about it, though. Not even the writer's name. Still, if you want to give the archives a go, I can put a list together.'

'I guess it's worth a try,' Bette said.

The conversation moved on, and by the time the next morning rolled around Bette was doubly sure that it was pointless to dwell on that moment with Ryan, or to bring it up with anyone, least of all Allie. The only possible meaning Ryan's statement could have had, given their history, was that there hadn't been anyone else for him but her *at the time*. Which was probably true. After all, he'd been happy for a while, hadn't he? He must have been. It was just later, when she wasn't there, that he'd decided he couldn't wait for her. Besides, Bette reminded herself yet again, this was all two decades in the past.

It took a week for them to completely clear the trees of undergrowth. Bette spent every available hour down in the orchard and had never slept more soundly in her life, finishing each day in a blur of tiredness that felt squarely earned. Ryan joined her each evening, somehow fitting in his time to help her despite his own full days. After the strange tension of that last conversation, they drew an unspoken line between them, retreating to a vaguely professional distance and sense of formality, as if they hadn't once agreed to spend the rest of their lives together.

'I've got a suggestion to make,' Ryan said at the end of the week, as they stood contemplating the orchard, the trees now cleared of every scrap of tangled undergrowth. 'The next task is going to be the removal of the trees that are definitely dead. There are quite a few, it's a specialist job, and it's not something to do alone. I'm working with Lucas Greville up at the Greville estate – he's the youngest son, and he's got his heart set on starting his own artisan cider company. That's what my job over there is – helping him set it up and teaching him the ropes. What would you say to my asking him if he wants to give me a hand down here? He's doing a forestry course and he knows his way around a chainsaw.'

Bette frowned. 'I'd have to talk to Nina and look at our finances, see what we can afford to pay. It'll be pretty tight. Not sure any Greville will want to work for minimum wage.'

'I think I can get him to help out for free,' Ryan told her. 'He's got the knowledge but he needs experience, and working down here is a good chance to build that. I can ask, anyway, if you're interested. If not, I'll look elsewhere, but the advantage of persuading Lucas to help is that he's got his own chainsaw, so there'll be no equipment hire, either.'

'I guess it's worth asking,' Bette said. 'Although . . . what's he like to work with? When I was a kid that family didn't exactly have a good reputation for being decent neighbours, landlords – or employers, for that matter.'

'Well yeah, he can be a bit of an arrogant prick,' Ryan admitted. 'I think his parents have had trouble keeping him on the straight and narrow – or whatever they consider that to be. But he is only eighteen and to his credit he is actually putting in the graft for this orchard of his. He seems really serious about making good cider, whatever it takes – which is why I agreed to take the job. It's also another reason I think it'd be a good idea to get him involved in this place, and the earlier the better. If you need a serious buyer quickly, you could do worse than have him on side. After all, they've got the money and I can see Lucas being keen to corner the market in this part of Scotland. I'd imagine being able to say he's the owner of the secret orchard would be massively appealing to him.'

'If we can prove this is actually the secret orchard,' Bette pointed out, and Ryan smiled.

'That's another thing,' he said. 'There's an old shed up at the estate that I think the groundsman might let me have. It's in bits, sitting in a pile waiting for burning at the moment. It's rickety but I think it's all there. Once we get that set up, we can rack the apples for a couple of weeks and then take a look at the juice.'

Bette put her hands on her hips. 'All right. Thanks. I'll talk to Nina about Lucas, but I can't see that she'd have an objection to it. We need any help we can get, we can't turn down free labour – if he's willing.'

'I'll ask him. I think he will be.'

'Will you tell him we're thinking of selling in the

not-too-distant future? It would be good to gauge a reaction there, see whether I should be thinking about finding an alternative buyer if it turns out he's not interested.'

Ryan considered for a moment, and then shook his head. 'Personally, I think we should wait before putting that idea in his head. Let him put in some graft first. I can see the thought of some other cider producer benefitting from any hard work he's done biting Lucas hard, especially if the place's potential has become obvious and he's been part of getting it there.'

'Sounds like a plan,' she agreed. 'Okay, we'll wait a bit, and we'll just hope he hasn't spent his trust fund by then.'

Chapter Thirty-one

'It looks so different, doesn't it?' Nina said, surveying the changed orchard from where she and Cam stood beside the boulder at the bottom of the track.

It was early evening, the tail end of August, with the sun dipping in the sky overhead and the spindly indigo shadows of the trees beginning to lengthen across the newly mown grass. The sound of the sea was gentle against the cliffs, the seabirds wheeling along the rocky outcrops above the water. Barney was in his full superhero costume, zooming along ahead of them with Limpet at his heels. Any photograph Nina could have snapped of them then would have looked like a frame from *Calvin and Hobbes*, two friends on an endless summer adventure. Best Barnaby Barnacle had promised to stay away from the fence, but had insisted that he had to check on every single tree.

'It really does look good,' Cam agreed, as they left the slope and began to stroll among the trees, unencumbered by undergrowth. 'If I hadn't seen it the way it was before, I don't think I'd believe it had been abandoned for so long. And you say Allie's found something interesting?'

'According to the text I got from Bette earlier, yeah,' Nina said. 'It was a photo of the walled-up doorway with one of the stones missing. She said something like "Allie says there's a bigger space than she expected behind here". Come on, let's go and take a look.'

As they made their way towards the cliff, Barney came chasing after them, flush-faced and out of breath. His super-hero skills didn't seem to extend to stealth. 'I counted all he trees, Mummy,' he declared. 'They're all there.'

'That's good,' Nina told him, privately wondering if her son was expecting that someone could have slipped one in a pocket and snuck away with it in the night. 'Come on – we're going to see what Allie's been up to.'

There wasn't really much to see. It looked exactly like the photograph that Bette had sent, no more, no less. A void where there had once been a whole, a small dark space that led straight into the cliff. The stone that Allie had removed was inside the nearest bee bole.

'She needs a finds table,' Cam observed. 'That's what they have in *Detectorists*, isn't it?'

'I'm not sure taking a rock out of a wall counts as a "find", really, does it?' Nina asked, standing on tiptoe to look into the hole. 'She's right, though. There's a space behind there, it's not just more rock.'

Cam leaned in closer to take a look, his shoulder pressing

against hers. She could smell his aftershave, lingering in the summer evening air. 'Yeah,' he said, thoughtfully. 'I can't see anything in there, though. Or how far back it goes.'

'Can I see?' Barnaby asked, appearing beside them.

'Sure,' Cam said. 'Come here, champ, I'll give you a boost.' He hooked his hands under the boy's arms and lifted him high enough to see into the gap.

'Wow,' said Best Barnaby Barnacle, with absolute wonder. His voice echoed a little into the dark space beneath the cliff. 'I bet it's Brother Alphonse's secret hideout!'

Nina laughed. 'Not very secret, if that's the case,' she pointed out. 'The door's here for everyone to see!'

'Some secrets are so secret they look as if they're not secrets at all,' her son said, with lofty patience, as Cam put him back on the ground. 'Come on, Limpet! Let's go and check on Great-grandma's tree!' He scampered off, the dog matching his every move.

'Out of the mouth of babes,' Cam observed, as they watched him go, before turning to look at the ancient doorway again. 'I wonder how much further Allie's planning to go? Will she remove the whole wall?'

Nina stood on tiptoe to look through the gap again. 'It probably depends on how much time she's got, doesn't it? It took her nearly a whole week to get that one out. And maybe she doesn't need to? She could probably get a camera in there already, don't you think?'

Cam bent forward again and this time he rested one hand lightly against her back as he leaned in beside her. The touch was warm through her shirt, and his bulk behind her felt so solid, so inviting, that for a split second Nina felt a very strong urge to lean back against him and turn her nose into his neck. She didn't move, and neither did he, and so they remained there for a moment, neither of them speaking or moving. Nina wondered if she was imagining the tension, or whether Cam's thoughts had strayed in the same direction as her own. She didn't want to move unless it was closer to him.

'Yeah,' he said, after what seemed like a very long time. 'A Go-Pro or something, with a light on it, I guess. It'd certainly be fascinating to see more.'

Cam dropped his hand from her back, breaking the spell as he turned away. Nina pushed away her sudden pulse of disappointment.

'When I ran into Bette yesterday, she mentioned that Ryan was going to be putting in a shed?' Cam asked, sliding his hands into his pockets as he looked back at the orchard again.

'Yeah,' Nina said, swallowing her rush of embarrassment. He was clearly oblivious to her sudden fluster. It made her feel like a fool. 'Ryan and this boy Lucas will be bringing it with them when they come up after work. I think it's going to go at the other end of the orchard, between the boulder and the cliff. They need it to store the apples.'

'It's really remarkable what they've done already,' Cam said. 'It looks like an actual orchard, doesn't it?'

Nina realized that he was right. This place was no longer an abandoned patch of wasteland. She could feel the potential in it, even though the work to restore it had barely started.

Since the day she'd discovered the huge weight of the debt attached to her childhood home, Nina had felt a growing sense of hopelessness that had not been mitigated either by the discovery of this orchard or by Bette's hope that it could solve their problems. Privately Nina had thought it a desperate, ridiculous proposition. Who out there would want to pay them what they needed for this desolate ledge of land clinging to the side of a weather-beaten cliff? But now, looking at the orchard from this new perspective, she felt a sudden spark of hope ignite. There was potential here, she could see that now. Maybe this plan that Ryan had talked Bette into, this scheme to sell the orchard and only the orchard — maybe it wasn't such a crazy idea after all.

She was quiet for so long that Cam looked at her askance. 'Hey,' he said. 'Penny for them? You're miles away.'

'Sorry,' Nina said. 'Cam, I'm so terrified of having to leave the farm. Of having to find somewhere else to live, some way else to live. Of having to tell Barnaby that we've got to move — and that he might not be able to take Limpet. Because how am I going to afford the kind of place that'll allow a dog? There's nowhere around here that'd be in my budget. Without this farm, I don't even *have* a budget. Without Crowdie, I don't have a job, or a home. Ever since I found out about the state this place is in financially, I guess I've just been waiting for the axe to fall. And when Bette told me Ryan's plan, I couldn't see how the orchard could possibly ever sell for enough to mean that we can stay. But now . . .' She felt tears prick at her eyes and blinked them back. 'Seeing it now? Maybe she's right. Maybe there is a chance. Maybe Best Barnaby Barnacle and I won't have to leave after all.'

Cam reached out and touched her arm. 'I hope so,' he said, quietly. 'I can't imagine not having the two of you living next door. I don't want to think about not seeing you every day.'

Nina looked up at him. Around them, the evening sunlight gilded the world, melded their shadows with the landscape around them, as if their two figures were part of the orchard itself, as if the two of them had been here as long as the oldest trees, as if they would always be here. They were standing close together, and Cam's eyes were fixed on her face, watching her with an intent that made Nina's heart stutter but that she couldn't be sure wasn't just a product of the changing evening light. His hand lingered on her arm in the same way that it had against her back a few minutes earlier.

A noise echoed to them from the orchard. For a moment Nina thought it was a swarm of bees, so loud and angry was the buzzing that arose around them. Then she realized that the echo was bouncing off the cliff behind them, thrown from the waters of the North Sea.

'What *is* that?' she said, as the noise grew louder still.

'I don't—' The noise grew even louder and they both looked out over the water as something black and spider-like rose into view from below, close enough for them to see the glassy eye of the camera buried in its body, the rotors holding it aloft. 'A *drone*?'

They watched as the small aircraft lifted above their heads. Barnaby and Limpet came racing towards them, staring up at the noisy aerial invader. It hovered above them for a moment, staring back.

'What's it doing?' Barnaby asked. 'What's it looking for, Mummy? Is it looking for us?'

Nina tugged her son against her, one arm around his shoulders. 'I doubt it,' she said, wanting to soothe the sound of anxiety in his voice. 'It's just some people interested in the coast, that's all.'

Cam moved to the fence and looked down. 'There's a boat. I think that's where it's being flown from. It could be some sort of film crew. It's a great sunset, I can understand someone wanting to film it.'

The infernal noise of the drone rattled to them from the clear sky as it began to drift north and away. Nina and Barney edged closer to the fence and watched as the boat followed it, moving slowly, parallel to the cliffs, far enough out to avoid the treacherous rocks at their base. Eventually the sound faded to a distant buzz. Beside her Nina felt Barnaby shiver and gave him a squeeze.

'There you go,' she said. 'It's gone now. Nothing to worry about.'

His face was still worried, and as she looked at him Nina realized just how long the shadows had grown around them. The sun was setting fast.

'Come on,' she said. 'Time to head back for dinner. Limpet, lead the way!'

The dog trotted off in the direction of the orchard path, and they followed, Cam falling into step beside Nina.

Eventually Barnaby seemed to shake off his anxiety, and ran after the collie.

'Careful on the slope!' Nina called.

Once they were alone, she and Cam couldn't seem to find anything to talk about, the advent of the drone notwithstanding. Nina wondered if she'd imagined that moment between them, if the look she'd thought she'd seen in Cam's eyes was no more than a product of her own lonely mind and wishful thinking. She wasn't willing to risk finding out.

When they parted at the pasture gate, Cam gave her a smile that seemed no more or less warm than any other they had shared, but when he added a quiet, 'See you tomorrow,' Nina wondered if there was a weight to it that wouldn't have been there previously.

Barnaby was preoccupied all evening, eating his dinner quietly but with a slight frown on his face, as if he was contemplating something of dire import. She found out what when she asked him to start getting ready for bed.

'Mummy, from now on I am going to sleep in the attic,' he said. 'Like Auntie Bette used to. I've been thinking about it for a while and it's the most sensible thing to do.'

Nina was by no means as sure of this as her son. 'I don't think that's a good idea, bub,' she said. 'What if you need the bathroom in the middle of the night? You might fall down the stepladder. And what about poor Limpet? He'll miss being able to sleep on your bed, won't he?'

'He can get up the stepladder on his own,' her son told her proudly.

'What?' Nina said, in disbelief. 'Surely not. Dogs can't climb stepladders, can they?'

'Limpet can,' Barnaby insisted. 'We've been practising.'

'They have,' Bette affirmed, coming into the kitchen, clearly on the lookout for a glass of wine. 'I saw them just this afternoon. Very efficient.'

'Limpet is a very clever dog,' Barnaby said proudly. 'Anyway, can I sleep up there, Mummy? Auntie Bette used to all the time, she told me so.'

'It's true,' Bette nodded. 'I did. I loved it. And I always slept really well. I did when I slept up there those first few nights that I—' Then, catching Nina's forbidding look, she subsided, holding up a hand. 'Sorry, sorry.'

'You will let me, won't you?' Barnaby said, pleading.

'But why do you want to?' Nina asked. 'Your bedroom's got everything set up exactly how you want it, with all your comic books and your reading lamp. You can't drag all of those up there, can you?'

Barnaby looked serious for a moment. 'It's the best place for a lookout,' he explained. 'In case any bad guys come and try to steal from the orchard.'

'In case ... what? Where's this coming from?' Nina asked, bemused, and then realized. 'Barnaby, is this about the drone? You don't need to worry about that. It wasn't bad guys, it was someone wanting to film that beautiful sunset. It flew away, remember?'

'What drone?' Bette asked.

'It wasn't anything to worry about,' Nina said, and

explained briefly. 'It just sounded a bit scary, that's all. No need for Best Barnaby Barnacle to go on high alert superhero-style.'

The little boy still looked serious. 'But we have to protect the orchard,' he said. 'That's what Brother Alphonse would want us to do. It's supposed to be a secret location, and he had a secret hideout. We need one, too.'

Nina went over and gave him a hug, kissing the top of his head. 'Look,' she said, 'I really don't think it's a good idea for you to sleep in the attic on a school night. And I'm sure that it needs a clean up there. But if you still want to give it a try when the weekend comes around, you can, all right?'

'All right,' he conceded, with a sigh. 'I'll go and brush my teeth now.'

'Good boy.'

As he scampered up the stairs, Nina turned to Bette.

'What?' her sister asked, with a shrug. 'Never did me any harm.'

'That,' Nina told her, 'is debatable.'

Chapter Thirty-two

On Friday afternoon, Nina was finishing her lunch at the kitchen table when she caught sight of a figure walking past on their way into the empty farmyard. She expected whoever it was to appear at the kitchen door, which was, as usual, slightly ajar. But no one had knocked by the time she'd got up and put her empty plate in the sink. Nina went out to find out where whoever it was had gone and found a young man in his late teens nosing around the tractor, which she had parked in front of the open barn.

'Who are you?' she asked, making him jump out of his skin.

'Christ!' he exclaimed, spinning around to face her. He had sandy blond hair with an undercut, round cheeks framing a slightly snub nose and blue eyes beneath eyebrows that gave the impression of being permanently raised. He wore a cream-coloured pullover and blue jeans, both of which Nina recognized as expensive brands not found on the High

Street in Dundee. 'I didn't think anyone was here. You gave me a fright.'

There was no hint of apology, she noticed. The suggestion that he'd thought the house was empty set alarm bells ringing. Nina glanced at the tractor. The last thing they needed was someone casing the joint for anything worth stealing.

'This is private property,' she said. 'What are you doing here?'

'Working,' he said. 'With Ryan? Down in the orchard. I'm Lucas. Lucas Greville.'

'Oh, I see,' she said, relieved. 'Well, I'm Nina Crowdie. The owner.'

'Right,' he said. 'The *owner*.'

There was something in his tone that didn't sit well with Nina, a slight edge of – what was it? Amusement? Disbelief? Whatever it was, it seemed condescending. She supposed that if you were a Greville, with all the land ownership that went along with the name, the run-down corner of this coast that was Crowdie farm seemed pretty undesirable. She didn't like this boy, or his attitude, and would have been happy to tell him to get lost. But he was working for them for free, and this was not the time to look a gift horse in the mouth.

'Can I help you with something?' she asked, looking at the tractor again.

'We've got a lot of wood to move,' Lucas said. 'I just wondered whether there was an easier way than dragging it up the slope by hand, but there's no hope of getting a tractor down there, is there? Or even a quad bike.'

Nina thought this a strange explanation given the obvious impossibility he'd already observed for himself, but she didn't say so. 'Do you have to move the wood at all?' she asked. 'Can't you burn it? Or tip it over the cliff, even?'

He pointed at her, thumb up and forefinger extended, an exaggerated gesture accompanied by a polished smile that she was sure made younger hearts flutter, and frequently. Probably a few older ones too. To Nina it seemed cynical, insincere and distinctly irritating. In a flash she was reminded of Barney's father, who could be so very charming when he wanted something. 'Now there's an idea – sorry, what did you say your name was?'

'Nina,' she repeated. 'And you're . . . *Luke*, was it?'

His smile faltered a little. Evidently it wasn't usual that anyone forgot *his* name. *Ah yes,* she thought. What was it the kids called it? *Main character energy.* But then again, wasn't everyone the hero of their own story in their heads? Some with more justification than others.

'Lucas,' he said, shortly, and then, 'I'd better get back.'

She watched him go. He disappeared around the side of the barn and down the path that led towards the pastures and the orchard track.

'I don't like him,' Nina told Bette, later.

Barney was at a friend's house for the evening, so Nina had gone down to the orchard after milking. Bette spent most of her time there now, and sure enough, there she was, still working even after Ryan and his rude sidekick had left for the evening. They had rebuilt an old shed between the boulder at the bottom of the track and the rear cliff wall, a large ten-by-eight structure that, though slightly dilapidated, had plenty of use left in it now that it was standing again. It was a dry evening, and Bette was painting it when Nina arrived, racing to finish before the sun set. Nina had grabbed a brush and started to help, and so now here they both were, each painting the side of a shed, as if this was a perfectly normal occurrence in their lives.

'It was the way he was nosing around,' Nina added. 'And his general attitude, as if he had every right to be here.'

'Well – he does. We invited him,' her sister pointed out. 'Or at least, Ryan did. Besides which, he's helping us out for free, Nina. And he gave us the shed. We'd have had to buy one otherwise.'

'I know, I know,' Nina sighed. 'But does that mean he has the right to poke around? I'm pretty sure he'd been nosing into the barn. And the fact that he thought no one was in the house while he was doing it made me uncomfortable, that's all.'

'Sorry,' Bette said. 'But I very much doubt he was looking for anything to steal. What do we have that the Grevilles couldn't buy ten times over? I'm sure he was just being nosy – you know, poking around to see how the hoi polloi live. Marvelling at our antiquated ways.'

'Maybe,' Nina said, with a slight laugh. Bette was right, of course – the idea that Lucas would want to steal anything of theirs was absurd. She'd had to tinker with the tractor again just to get it to start that morning. 'He's probably just never seen something so old still working.'

'Are you talking about the tractor?' Bette said, raising an eyebrow. 'Or me?'

They shared a moment of muted amusement, in which only the rustle of the orchard leaves and the strokes of their brushes against wood could be heard beneath the evening breeze.

'I'll have a word with Ryan,' said her sister. 'Tell him to keep an eye on Lucas and that the house and farmyard are out of bounds.'

'No, it's fine,' Nina said, with a sigh. 'There's no need to make it a *thing*. I'm sure I'm just being paranoid.'

They finished painting and both stood back to admire their handiwork. The shed looked sharper with its fresh coat of paint.

'What's next, then?'

'Ryan's sent me a link to instructions of how to assemble the apple rack he's lent us,' Bette said. 'I thought Best Barnaby Barnacle might like to help me put it up on Saturday morning?'

'I'm sure he'll love that,' Nina said. 'If he gets any sleep, that is. He's going to camp out in the attic tonight,' she explained, off her sister's look. 'He's been begging me non-stop and I promised that tonight he can.'

Bette laughed. 'Bless him. I bet he'll have a blast.'

'He might, but I won't. I won't be able to sleep for worrying that he's going to wake up at some ungodly hour, forget where he is and fall straight through the hatch.'

'I'll keep an ear out,' Bette said. 'And you know that

Limpet would stop that from happening. Tell him to get the dog to sleep at the edge of the hatch to make sure.'

'That's not a bad idea. Is Ryan coming back over the weekend?'

'Yes,' Bette said. 'This afternoon he and Lucas marked the trees that need removing and they're going to come back together on Sunday to start taking them down. There's about half that need to come out.'

Nina tried to imagine what the orchard would look like after this purge. 'It's going to look pretty sparse once they do that, isn't it?'

'To begin with,' Bette agreed, 'but with any luck the grafts will take well and the saplings that go in their place will flourish quickly. Ryan thinks that in five years this place could be back to full production, or close to it.'

'That's pretty amazing,' Nina admitted. 'We still don't know whether these are those perfect apples of his though, do we? He hasn't done the juice test he was talking about yet?'

'Not yet – the apples need to soften a little more. The racking will help with that. Another week or so, he said. We'll need to harvest the rest of the apples now that there's somewhere to store them, too.' Bette paused, an uncomfortable expression passing across her face. 'There's something else I need to talk to you about.'

'Oh?' Nina braced herself. Bette was still combing through the farm accounts. Had she found something else awful that they hadn't known about?

'It's not to do with the farm,' her sister said. 'It's my flat in London. I've been thinking and the most sensible thing to do is let it out. It's just sitting there at the moment, costing me money. Every month I can cover the mortgage without eating into the redundancy payment or my savings, the better for me and Crowdie. It's a good place in a sought-after area, it won't be difficult to find a tenant or let it out as holiday accommodation.'

'Okay,' Nina said, slowly, taking this in. 'I ... kind of assumed that you'd want to get back there permanently as soon as possible.'

'I do,' Bette said. 'But if this orchard plan doesn't work out ...'

'Yeah,' Nina said, with a sigh. 'Contingencies and all that.'

'Would you mind if I was here longer-term?' Bette asked. 'I don't mean indefinitely, but I think I'd probably have to let it for at least six months if I decided to do so.'

Nina gave her sister a genuine smile. 'Of course not. This is your home as well as ours, Bette.' She meant it, too. Since that conversation with Cam about her feelings towards Bette, their relationship had undergone a subtle change. Not that Nina wanted to live with her for the rest of her life, but it wasn't proving as difficult as she'd feared when she'd told their mother they might end up killing each other. 'You're welcome as long as you need to be here.'

Bette smiled. 'Thanks. I'll need to go back and pack up what's there so I can put it with a letting agency. But at least that means I'll be able to pick up some of my own clothes, which will prevent me from going on an inappropriate spending spree – I can't borrow from my little sister forever, can I?'

Chapter Thirty-three

Bette's experience of Lucas Greville wasn't quite as negative as her sister's, though she could see where Nina's dislike came from. As soon as he arrived, his attitude to Bette herself was dismissive, as if the fact that she was there was incidental and she wasn't a fundamental signatory of him having been asked to help in the first place. Bette put this down to his youth and an upbringing that had been steeped in privilege. Lucas listened to Ryan, though, which surprised Bette more than his actual attitude, and given Nina's first meeting with him, made her think there may be a touch of misogyny going on there too. This was nothing new to Bette, who couldn't care less what Lucas thought of her, and didn't feel the least bit diminished by his behaviour. She didn't like him, but she'd had plenty of clients she didn't like, either. Such was life.

'Have you told him about your theory?' Bette asked, the first night after Lucas had been and gone, and it was just her and Ryan left in the orchard. 'That this place is the fabled secret orchard?'

Ryan gave her a guarded look. He'd been wary around her since that charged moment when she now suspected he'd said something he hadn't intended to let out: *There was no one but you, Beth Crowdie.* It also suggested that there was more there for her to learn, which she studiously told herself she had no interest in knowing.

'Yes,' he said, cautiously. 'I'm sorry, perhaps I should have run that by you first? He was reluctant to get involved at first, but that was what swung it. And we do really need his help, Bette.'

'It's fine,' she said, lightly. 'I just wondered how much he knew about our financial situation, that's all.'

Ryan shook his head. 'Nothing from me, I promise. As discussed, I haven't mentioned the idea that this place might be for sale in the future, either.'

Lucas didn't come with Ryan every evening, but he'd pledged to spend a few full weekend days in the orchard in order to take down the old trees. Bette didn't have much to do during these sessions aside from finding ways to dispense with the wood.

'Applewood chips are good for smoking,' Ryan pointed out, and so Bette found a restaurant in Dundee that would buy what they had. She carted it down there herself, which meant driving the Land Rover, as she'd dispensed with her hire car on the basis of expense. She kept the thicker trunks to dry for Nina to use as firewood for Crowdie later in the season.

It was as she returned from this expedition that she came across Lucas examining the wrought-iron fence at the edge of the orchard ledge. Bette could hear the echo of the chainsaw running elsewhere amid the thinned-out trees, and surmised that this was Ryan, chopping the last of the logs for them. Lucas was crouching beside one of the ornate designs, fingers pressed against the letter that Bette had first assumed was a stylized 'C' but that Allie had suggested could actually be a 'G'.

Lucas heard her footsteps and turned to face her as he stood.

'Hi,' she said. 'It's interesting, isn't it, the fence? We've been trying to figure out who the initials belong to.'

Lucas nodded, a smile on his face, although as usual with the young man's expressions, Bette found it difficult to tell whether what he was projecting was actually what he felt. 'It's a good bit of ironwork. I was trying to work out whether I'd seen something similar before.'

'Oh?' Bette asked. 'Where would that be?'

Lucas smirked, as if she'd asked something amusing, and then said. 'Can't remember. Anyway – better get back to Ryan.'

He walked away, putting his phone in his pocket as he went. Bette watched him vanish through the trees in the direction of the chainsaw's racket, and then crouched by the fence so she could look more closely at the design. She moved to the next panel along and considered the same, then took out her phone and snapped as close-up a picture as she could, thinking. She said nothing to Ryan, either about what Lucas had said or her minor epiphany.

Later, though, Bette brought it up with Allie.

'If it *is* a G, rather than a C, it could stand for Greville, couldn't it?' she said. 'They did own the land before my family bought it, after all.'

'Wouldn't be a huge stretch,' her friend agreed. 'They could have put in the fence before they decided to offload that patch of land.'

'I wonder why they did that in the first place?' Bette mused. 'It's not as if landowners are typically willing to part with their land.'

Allie shrugged. 'Money problems, maybe? It's possible that what became Crowdie wasn't the only parcel they sold at the same time. Or if it was, it could have been because it was right on the edge of their estate.'

'There's the orchard, though,' Bette pointed out. 'If it really was as good as you and Ryan say, why would they give that up?'

'Good question,' Allie admitted. 'Although by then its production may have already significantly declined. Besides, the Grevilles have never had a reputation for producing cider – they're certainly not part of the myth that Ryan talked about. It could be as simple an answer as whoever was head of the family at the time wasn't a cider drinker and didn't care about maintaining the orchard.'

'This is all conjecture, anyway,' Bette said. 'OG or O and G, whoever they were, might have nothing to do with the

Grevilles. It just made me think, because if I could find a name, it might be worth approaching that list of archives you gave me. The more I look at this fence design, the more I think I recognize it. And I think I remember it from a book. The frontispiece, like a design around the title of twisted branches and flowers.'

Allie considered. 'That wouldn't fit with the book being a personal diary though, would it?' she said. 'If this design was printed in?'

'I know,' Bette said. 'But I don't remember thinking the book was an actual diary at the time, do you? From what I can remember it read like a story – like a novel.'

'I think it was written by hand, though,' Allie said, 'which would fit with the idea of it being a diary.'

'Really?' Bette asked, doubtfully. 'It must have been very clear penmanship for the two of us to be able to read it, if that was the case.'

Allie got out her phone, opened the browser app and tapped a few keys. In a few minutes a triumphant look dawned on her face.

'Ophelia Greville,' she said. 'Born Ophelia Marchant in Northumberland in 1820. Married Milton Greville in 1837.'

'When she was *seventeen*?'

'It was the way of things back then, I suppose,' Allie said. 'She didn't live long. Died in 1840.'

'The year after my family bought the Crowdie land and orchard,' Bette realized. 'Mum said there was a story about a child falling from the cliff and that's why the orchard was abandoned. Maybe Ophelia was the child.'

'She wouldn't have been thought of as a child at the time,' Allie pointed out. 'In fact, she was lady of the manor when she died.'

'Maybe that's the way she ended up being thought of as time passed?' Bette suggested, trying to make it make sense in her own head. 'Perhaps the story got mangled in the re-telling over the years. Mum didn't know any other details at all. Does it say there how Ophelia died?'

'No, this is just a basic family tree,' Allie told her. 'Do you think the book might have been hers, or about her?'

'I guess it's possible,' Bette said. 'Lucas did say that he thought he recognized the design. That would fit if it's a traditional Greville pattern, wouldn't it? He might have seen it around the big house.'

'Maybe,' Allie agreed. 'I do think it's worth putting out a call to the archives. Even if none of them have your book, they might have more information about Ophelia and whether she had a particular connection to the orchard.'

'Okay,' Bette said. 'I'll do that tomorrow. How are things going on your end? It looks as if you've managed to widen the gap in the wall.'

'I've got two more of the stones out,' Allie said, 'and I've talked to a drone operator mate who's done cave exploration before. He's not free for another week but I've booked him in to come and take a look inside for us. Trust me, in terms of archaeological research things are moving apace.'

When she got home that night, Bette spent some time searching online for any further information she could gather about Ophelia Greville. There was very little to be had beyond what Allie had already turned up. Her father appeared to have been more significant, a landowner whose wealth had been inherited, in its entirety, by his young daughter's new husband on his passing. Bette compiled a brief email regarding her interest in knowing more about Ophelia Greville and detailing her and Allie's combined memories of the possible diary they had found as children and sent it to the five contacts Allie had given her. The more she thought about it, the more Bette thought it likely to be another dead end. After all, the initial may well have nothing at all to do with poor Ophelia Greville. Bette wondered whether it would be worth asking Lucas Greville if he knew anything about his ancestor. Perhaps she would, the next time she saw him.

She went up to bed at around midnight, treading lightly for fear of waking her sister and nephew. It was strange for Bette, living with a family again. She hadn't done it since she'd left home the first time. The closest she'd ever come was in her student and intern years, sharing dingy flats and even worse kitchens, and she'd left that behind as soon as humanly possible. Now, though, Bette was becoming used to the rhythms of living with other people again. Footsteps on the stairs blended into the background. The sound of Barnaby playing somewhere in the house, or the noise of Limpet's infrequent barking, or the clattering melodies of the kitchen as Nina cooked. All of these factors, so alien to her life before her return to Crowdie, had fast become a familiar soundscape. Strangest of all was that she didn't hate it. In fact, Bette thought that she had perhaps missed it, the simple affirmation of living one's life cheek-by-jowl with family. It made her wonder what else she had missed out on by staying away for so long. Especially since the reason she had left so completely in the first place had come back into her life, and the fear that had dogged her for so long regarding Ryan had proven to be unfounded.

As she reached the top of the stairs she heard a creak ahead of her and stopped. Best Barnaby Barnacle was staring at her, wide-eyed, from the bottom rung of the attic ladder. Limpet sat at his feet, ears pricked.

'What are you doing?' Bette whispered. 'You should be in bed.'

'I'm going to sleep up there,' Barney whispered back, nodding up to the hatch above his head.

'You can't,' Bette told him, keeping her voice at the same low pitch as she crept quietly closer. 'You know your mum only wants you to stay up there over the weekend.'

'But I've been doing it all week,' he protested. 'And I haven't been too sleepy for school once! Mum hasn't even noticed!'

Bette sighed, feeling that this was well beyond her pay-grade. She would usually defer to her sister, who was after all the parent, but it was late and Nina would be fast asleep, exhausted.

'Do you promise to be careful?'

'I've *been* careful,' her nephew pointed out. 'I'm always careful!'

'All right, all right,' said Bette, thinking that it would be best to get him to sleep and confess her part in his subterfuge to his mother tomorrow. 'Off you go, then. Straight to sleep!'

Barnaby surprised her by leaning forward and kissing her cheek, throwing one small little-boy arm around her neck and squeezing hard. 'Thank you, Auntie Bette. You're the best aunt ever.'

Bette knew this not to be true, but didn't correct him as he scurried up the ladder. She watched, incredulous, as Limpet scrambled quickly after him. That dog really would follow his boy anywhere.

She listened for the telltale creak of the camp bed, un-changed from when Bette had snuck up there of a night herself as a girl. Then, satisfied that he was in fact asleep, and pleased that she could see Limpet lying sentry by the open hatch, she went to bed herself.

Chapter Thirty-four

September rolled on towards October, the light hours short-ening as the year sunk deeper into mid-autumn. The weather had turned sultry and humid, the days peppered with rain showers and a late warm spell that filled the air with the scent of damp grasses gone to seed. The bales of hay, piled high and wrapped in their coats of black polythene, had begun gently to ferment into silage, the sour-sweet scent of the winter feed preserving as it settled. The orchard shed, which had become storage for the equipment as well as for the windfall apples resting quietly in rows on several levels of the rack, had taken on the fragrance of the softened fruit.

'We'll juice them and test it when we harvest the rest still on the trees,' Ryan told a fascinated Barnaby, on a day when Bette had brought her nephew with her after school. Every moment he spent outdoors he now wanted to be in the or-chard, and every moment indoors, the attic.

'How do you get the juice out of an apple?' the boy

wondered, picking one up and smoothing his small thumb over it. 'It's not like an orange.'

Ryan smiled. 'It's a lot of fun and the first stage involves buckets and sticks. Then we put them into a special press. I'll show you when we get to it. You can help, Best Barnaby Barnacle.'

'It's a good point, though,' Bette said, as the boy ran off with Limpet to check on Allie's progress at the other end of the orchard. 'There'll be plenty of equipment we'll need, won't there?'

'Don't worry about that,' Ryan assured her. 'I've got a press I can bring with me, and a few gallon storage drums. I've got all the test meters, too.'

'Thank you,' Bette said, relieved. 'You've been so generous, Ryan. With your time and with everything else.'

He glanced away as if faintly embarrassed by her thanks. 'It's the least I can do.'

Bette was about to ask him what he meant when Lucas reappeared on the orchard track, his phone in his hand, where it seemed to be permanently. She couldn't decide whether her personal discomfort around Lucas was purely because of her sister's dislike of him, or something deeper. Her own interactions with Lucas had remained perfectly civil, after all. This sort of uncertainty worried Bette, made her wonder whether she'd spent too much time out here in the 'boondocks', as Nina liked to call them. Was she losing her sharp edges, her acuity? She'd be going back to London in a few days, albeit only temporarily while sorting out leasing the flat, and wondered how it would feel to be in a big city again. Bette wasn't sure if it was the bustle she missed, or the sense of being in control of her own life, a concept that had slid away from her as surely as the passing weeks since she'd been back home.

'I want to be here for the harvest,' Bette said. 'Will we be able to do that either side of me being gone? I'm hoping to only take a couple of days.'

'Let's see,' Ryan said, aiming his next question at Lucas. 'Why don't you go and pick an apple, and we'll take a look at it.'

'Sure.'

Lucas ambled off into the orchard, in no apparent rush. Bette felt Ryan looking at her.

'What?'

He smiled. 'Just wondering how it feels to be moving back here – back home.'

'It's not permanent,' Bette reminded him. 'And the answer is . . . it's not as bad as I always thought it would be.'

A frown creased his forehead. 'Why would it be bad? Crowdie is a wonderful place. I think the three summers I spent working here as a kid were probably the happiest I've ever been.'

Bette gave him a hard look, shocked by the sudden jolt of her heart. 'Ryan. Do you really need to ask me that? You, of all people?'

'I'm sorry,' he said, looking pained. 'Bette, we really should talk about—'

But then Lucas was there, with an apple yellowing in the palm of one hand and an open pocketknife in the other.

'I'll do the honours, shall I?' he said, and sliced the apple in two, opening it up to display the pips inside. 'Looks pretty good to me.'

Ryan took one of the pieces and examined it for a moment. 'To me, too. See the pips?' he said, showing it to Bette. 'They're about as dark as they're going to get. That means they're ripe and ready for harvest. I think we should get them picked and racked at the weekend. Will that be before you go back to London?'

'It can be,' Bette said.

'It won't take long to get them all down,' Ryan said, 'especially if everyone pitches in.'

'I'm sure they'll want to. In fact, I know one little superhero who'll be distraught if he doesn't get to help.'

Ryan laughed a little at that. 'He does seem pretty fixated on this place.'

'It's Allie's fault – ever since she cast this Brother Alphonse character as a medieval superhero, Barney's been obsessed with the idea of taking his place as the orchard's defender,' Bette said. 'Although who he thinks he needs to defend the place from is anyone's guess. He and Allie are as bad as each other – I think they'd both camp out down here if they could.'

As if on cue, a shouted cheer came from the other end of the orchard. Ryan and Bette looked at each other.

'Come on,' Bette said. 'Let's go and see what all the excitement's about.'

They fell into step together, but Bette turned to see that instead of following, Lucas was taking a picture of the half of apple he still held in his hand, raising it up to catch the evening light.

Allie had loosened another stone in the wall, and her shout was to summon anyone who wanted to see it removed from its long resting place. Barnaby was fizzing with excitement, bouncing up and down on his heels as Ryan and Bette got closer.

'It's going to be big enough for me to get inside,' the boy said, excitedly. 'Look! Once Allie takes it out, I mean, and I climb up. I'm small enough to fit inside, I know I am!'

'Under absolutely no circumstances will you be climbing into that hole, Best Barnaby Barnacle, do you hear me?' Bette said, slipping an arm around his shoulders and squeezing his shoulder warmly. 'Your mum would have a heart attack at the mere idea.'

'But—'

'Your aunt is right,' Allie said. 'It won't be safe. The ceiling could be loose. That's why we'll be sending the drone in, so that it can take photographs instead of us risking our own noggins.'

'But I'm supposed to be the orchard's official photographer,' the little boy said, miserably. 'You *said*.'

'That's true, I did,' Allie agreed. 'Wait a moment while I take this out, then, and I'll lift you up for a look-see. You can take the first photograph of the inside, how about that?'

This was enough to cheer him up, but the photograph

showed little beyond the fact that the space behind the wall was larger than any of them had expected.

'You did a great job,' Allie told the disappointed boy. 'It's still a valuable document for us to have. And who knows, the drone may not be able to do any better. You never know until you try.'

Chapter Thirty-five

The day of the harvest was the busiest the orchard had been since it was rediscovered.

'When we're done picking, we'll sort and juice the first batch I collected so we can test it, and depending on what the time is after that, we might be able to start off the first grafts,' Ryan added, indicating a line of young saplings in pots that he and Lucas had ferried down from his truck earlier in the day. 'I brought the rootstock with me just in case.'

'What's that?' Bette asked, of a small contraption that looked a little like a wooden half-barrel with an open top, set on a stand. It had a device like a corkscrew fitted to its top and a small tap at its base.

'That's an apple press,' Cam said. 'We've set that up to use later.'

'And ... the rolling pins?' Nina asked, quizzically, of the pile of black plastic buckets that stood beside the press, the top one of which held several wooden cylinders.

Ryan grinned. 'That's the fun part, which I will also tell you about later. Come on, let's get these apples picked.'

The temperature had begun to drop, and the day was bright but with a chill breeze to it, that bite in the air that is the true harbinger of the year fading. It was only about ten o'clock when they started picking in earnest, with a bucket each that was then decanted into a larger basket back at the shed when full.

Bette got quicker at picking as the day went on. There was a knack to it. She found if she took hold of the fruit and twisted the stalk, it would usually come off cleanly. A few had been damaged, with late-season bees and wasps taking the opportunity to sap the ripe fruit of its sugar while it still hung on the tree.

Once the apples were down from the trees, they needed to be set to soften for a couple of weeks, the way the windfalls had already lain in the apple rack.

'The windfalls we're going to press today, so that we can test their sugar and acid content and get the juice fermenting.' Ryan told them. 'There's less than a bushel's worth, so we're going to extract the juice the old-fashioned way.'

'Like Brother Alphonse?' Barnaby asked, the excitement of the day nowhere near waning for him.

'Yes,' Ryan agreed. 'Actually, Best Barnaby Barnacle, we're going to do it pretty much exactly as Brother Alphonse would have five hundred years ago, using the press I showed you earlier.'

Bette stepped closer to look inside the device, which had

been lined with fine black mesh. 'We just chuck the apples in there and crush them?'

'Not quite. We have to mill them first.'

'Mill them?' Nina asked.

'Basically, we need to break the apples down a bit before they go into the press.'

'Ah,' Allie said. 'Then I guess that's what the buckets and rolling pins are for?'

Ryan grinned. 'Exactly.'

It was a strangely convivial event, crushing the apples. The sound of wood pounding against fruit wasn't really conducive to conversation, but Nina found herself in a sort of meditative state. Once they had enough, the milled fruit was tipped into the netted press. Ryan put another clean bucket beneath the sluice and turned the screw until juice began to pour out of the bottom of the press.

'Now that you've got the juice, you can test it?' Bette asked.

'We can,' Ryan said, looking around for something. 'I've got my kit somewhere . . .'

'Actually, I've got mine,' Lucas said, holding up a toolbox. 'I thought it'd be a good opportunity to practise what you've been teaching me, right?'

'Right,' Ryan agreed. 'Okay then – take it away, Lucas.'

Everyone gathered around the table as Lucas opened the toolbox to reveal, not a traditional array of tools, but a series of glass gauges and meters, some syringes, test tubes and small bottles of chemical solutions.

'Do the sugars first, then the acids,' Ryan advised his student. 'When did you last calibrate the hydrometer?'

'Yesterday.'

'That should be fine, then – just let it stand in the juice for a few minutes to climatize before taking a reading.'

'What does that do?' Barnaby asked, pointing to the gauge that Lucas lifted out. It looked like a long thermometer.

'The hydrometer will tell us approximately how much of the juice is sugar,' Ryan explained, as Lucas got to work. 'That's important, because the sugar is what will turn into alcohol and make the juice into cider. The higher the sugar content, the stronger the cider. It's not one hundred per cent accurate, but it'll give us an idea of how strong a cider made from this juice would be.'

Lucas looked at the hydrometer and then glanced up at Ryan, standing aside so he could look for himself.

'Well, that looks pretty promising,' Ryan said, as Lucas made a note of the number. 'Now the titration, which will check the acid levels.'

They watched as Lucas measured out some of the juice with a syringe and put it in a test tube. He then began adding drops of solution and shaking the tube with each addition, making a note of how much he'd added.

'You see how the juice is changing colour?' Ryan asked them. 'Lucas will keep adding the alkaline solution until that stops and the colour stabilizes. He'll keep a note of the solution he's added and then calculate—'

Lucas made a noise that sounded suspiciously like a curse.

He looked up at Ryan, noted a number down in his book beside the sugar measurement, and held it up for Ryan to see.

Ryan grinned. 'Yeah, I've never seen numbers that balanced before. I'd say that's about as sure proof as we're going to get that these are Brother Alphonse's perfect cider apples.'

'Really?' Bette asked, with a huge sense of relief.

'Really,' Ryan said, still smiling. 'And since that's the case, I think we should get on with growing some more of these trees. Let's get some grafted, shall we? The rootstock I've chosen is a quick-growing variety, so all being well they could start producing fruit as early as the next season if the grafts take. Lucas, give me a hand, would you? These are all three-year-old saplings,' Ryan explained, as he returned carrying several of the small trees, setting them down on the trestle. The saplings looked like little more than bare sticks with a few leaves on them. 'We're going to be bud-grafting from our scions – the part we take from the old trees – to the rootstock. It's a bit more complicated than bark grafting or whip-and-tongue, but it means we can do it now rather than waiting for next spring. Follow me and we'll cut some scions.'

For the next half-hour they all watched closely as Ryan showed them how to find a suitable budding branch on one of the trees that had produced fruit that year. He cut the bud growth from the branch, then grafted it into the rootstock by cutting a T-shape in the young bark and peeling it back and slotting in the scion before wrapping it all in what looked like Sellotape.

'It's grafting tape,' Ryan said, handing the roll to Barnaby. 'It'll help keep the bud dry as the graft takes and protect it from wind, too.'

'Is that all there is to it?' Bette asked, watching with her arms crossed. 'It really does look easy.'

He smiled up at her. 'It's pretty easy, once you get the knack of how to cut the scion and fit it to the rootstock. You've seen me do it. Why don't you try?'

'Oh, no,' Bette said, holding up one hand. 'I'll leave that to you practical sorts. Nina, you do it.'

'I'll do it!' Barnaby shouted, 'I've been watching, too!'

'The knife's a bit sharp for you, mate,' Ryan said. 'Tell you what, though, I've got another job for you. In the shed are some wire frames that'll stop the rabbits munching the new trees when we plant them. You can go ahead and grab those for us.' The boy ran off as Ryan held out the scion branch and the Stanley knife to Nina. 'Here you go. There are more buds you can cut from this branch – everyone should have a go. We'll add several grafts to each rootstock tree.'

In the end, they all pitched in, even Bette. Nina became so engrossed that she barely even noticed the time, and was shocked to look at her watch and realize that Barnaby should really be doing his homework while she made his dinner.

'We'd better get back,' she said. 'Are you going to plant them tonight, too? I don't think I've got time to help with that.'

'That can wait a few days,' Ryan reassured her. 'We'll put them in the lee of the shed, they'll be protected there. I should get back, too. If someone can give us a hand taking the demijohns up to the barn . . .'

'No problem,' Cam said. 'I can do that. You and Barney get back, Nina. We can finish up here.'

'Not yet!' Barney said. 'I've got to make sure all the saplings are safe and accounted for.'

'What do you mean?' Nina asked.

'I've put numbers on all of their pots, look,' the boy said, pointing to a surprisingly neat number '7' drawn on to the pot closest to them. It looked as if it had been put on with permanent marker. 'There are ten. That way I can count them every morning and every evening to make sure there are none missing.' He did a quick count and said, with a frown, 'Where's number ten?'

They looked around, and Lucas said, 'It's here.' He lifted it onto the table from beside him. 'Nothing to worry about.'

Barney insisted on taking photographs of each tree, and only then could he be persuaded to head home.

'We made apple juice from our own apples, Mummy,' he said later that night, as he climbed the attic ladder to go to bed. 'That's kind of magic, isn't it? But I should have numbered all the bottles we filled, too. I'll do that tomorrow.'

'I'm worried that it's become a new obsession,' she said to Bette, later still, as the two sisters sipped glasses of wine in the kitchen. 'All he talks about is the orchard. He's convinced someone's going to steal it from us and he's got to keep it safe. I'm not sure what to do about it.'

'Maybe you don't need to do anything,' Bette said. 'As

obsessions go, it's pretty harmless, isn't it? And it's got him enthused and wanting to be involved – that's a good thing, surely? He's learning a lot. He was watching Ryan like a hawk earlier. Allie says he's interested in everything she's been doing, too.'

'What happens when we have to sell the place, though?' Nina fretted. 'I haven't told him that's what we're going to have to do. It'll break his heart.'

Bette surprised her by reaching out a hand and squeezing her arm. 'One step at a time.'

Nina looked up with a weary smile, surprising herself as she realized how used she'd become to having her sister around. She was going to miss her while she was in London, and that wasn't something Nina had ever expected to feel.

Chapter Thirty-six

It was Sunday morning, bright and chill. The drone that Allie's operator friend, Rohan, brought down to the orchard was tiny compared to the one that had flown over Nina's head a few weeks before. In fact, it was barely bigger than the guy's hand. Allie had succeeded in removing four of the sandstone bricks that had sealed the walled doorway closed, and it was now open by about a third. Nina had milked the cows as quickly as she could, leaving Bette to give Barnaby breakfast earlier than usual so that they could all be there for the event.

'This one really does sound like a bee,' Barney observed, as the archaeologist held the drone flat in her hand and its owner navigated it into the air. It disappeared in through the small gap in the cliff, its whirr echoing weirdly against the old stone. Allie had lowered a strong LED floodlight on a rope through the reopened aperture, the stark white-blue shine uplighting the rock inside with strange, jagged shadows.

Rohan had a screen on the control console so that he could see through the camera mounted on the drone, and they all leaned forward as the device disappeared inside the cliff. At first the glare from the floodlight bleached everything out, but then the image stabilized.

'We're only seeing this in black and white,' Rohan told them. 'The contrast will be better in such a low-light environment, it'll give us more of a chance of picking up an idea of what we're looking at.'

The drone swept slowly to the left, moving into the space Allie knew was there but hadn't been able to reach.

'That,' she said, in wonder, 'really *is* a far larger space than I was expecting. Or at least, a longer one. It looks like a true passageway.'

The drone moved on, curving deeper into the cliff. The picture on the screen darkened as it moved beyond the flood-light's range. Then a few seconds later it fritzed, as if static had interfered with the image.

'Right,' the operator said. 'I'm losing the signal. I did say this might happen, didn't I? I can't go much further, Allie, or I risk it setting down and I won't be able to safely retrieve it.'

'Okay,' Allie said, a little reluctantly. 'Don't risk the drone, obviously, but— wait, is that another doorway?'

A void had appeared on the screen, or what could have been a void, set into the right of the passage down which the drone flew. Rohan turned the camera towards it, the light it carried barely cutting through the darkness, but showing another open space.

The picture fritzed out completely then, and Rohan cursed faintly under his breath. 'I'm going to have to bring it back. I've got thirty seconds before it sets down.'

The whirr of the drone drew louder as it made its way back towards them, and eventually there it was, flying through the gap and out into the air above their heads, a traveller returning from the underworld. Rohan set it down beside the nearest bee bole and picked it up.

'I can't believe it,' Allie said, in a stunned voice. 'There's so much more in there than I was expecting. This opens up so many more questions. If that passage goes much further back, it suggests this is a natural cave system in the cliff that has been augmented, possibly over centuries or even millennia.'

'I'll drop you the footage so you can take a closer look at it,' Rohan told him. 'Thanks for asking me up here, that was fascinating. The season's closing in quickly though, isn't it?'

'Don't I know it,' Allie said, with a sigh. 'There's only a matter of weeks before I'll have to start backfilling.'

Rohan made a 'pfft' sound. 'Can't you get some volunteers up here to help you? Or are you worried about nighthawks?'

'Nighthawks?' Barney piped up. 'What are they?'

'Thieves, basically,' Rohan told him, as he packed the drone away. 'People who aren't so much interested in the history of a place as what they can steal from it to sell.'

Barney puffed his chest out under his superhero costume. 'I won't let anyone steal anything from Brother Alphonse. *Or* from us.'

Rohan grinned and patted the boy on the head as he straightened up. 'That's the spirit. Right, I've got to go. Got to get the big rig up to Aberdeen for a doco scout.'

'Thanks for coming, Rohan,' Allie said, leading the thanks and goodbyes from the group. 'Really, it means a lot.'

'Anything for you, Allie. Glad to see you back at it.' And with a wave, he was heading for the orchard track.

'What will you do now?' Bette asked her friend. 'There's obviously more to explore in there, but if you can't get any sort of remote equipment to operate under the cliff, how will you manage it?'

'I've got to get in there myself,' Allie told her. 'I'll look carefully at the video that Rohan will send through, but there weren't any signs of a cave-in, or even any loose soil on the ground.'

'Still,' Nina said, 'that seems pretty risky.'

Allie shrugged. 'I don't want to seem reckless. This is what I do – or at least, what I *did*. Who knows what might be in there?'

'It's Brother Alphonse's secret hideout,' Barnaby whispered. 'I *told* you he had one!'

Allie smiled. 'I think you could be right, Best Barnaby Barnacle, but it could be even more than that. If it's a natural cave system, there could be traces of Neolithic habitation. I'm thinking of the cave carvings at Wemyss.'

They talked a little more, but Nina and Cam both had work to do, and it was clear that nothing would be happening very fast. At her son's behest, Nina left Barnaby in the care of her sister. Together they were planning to stack all the apples they'd harvested the day before on the vacant rack.

'That's a big job,' Nina observed to her son.

'It's okay,' he said. 'I want to do it. I told you, Mummy, I want to look after the orchard as well as Brother Alphonse did. Which reminds me, we should talk about bees. There should be bees!'

'Bees, huh?' Nina said, feeling that this discussion might end up leading to the news that the orchards wouldn't be theirs for very much longer, which was probably a conversation best left for another time. 'I think you should deal with the apples first. Give me a hug.'

'Who knew Allie Bright was our local Indiana Jones?' Cam said, as they walked together back up to the pasture above.

'As long as she doesn't take Barney in there with her, I'm fine with her being as gung-ho as she likes,' Nina said.

'You would say that,' Cam grumbled. 'It wouldn't be your pasture her skeleton would be mouldering under for all eternity.'

Nina frowned.

'Sorry,' Cam said. 'Bad joke.'

'It's not that,' Nina said. 'But you make a really good point. Are those caves on our land, or yours? Because sure, the access might be on our side, but the cliff is the boundary, isn't it? Your pasture is on top of it. Does that mean the cliff and what's inside it – meaning the caves – is actually yours, too?'

'Hmm,' said Cam. 'Good question. I suspect it's a pretty

grey area, to be honest. After all, that's why people get screwed over with the whole fracking thing, isn't it? They might own the land their house sits on, but there's some bit of legislation that says they don't own what's under the land. I would imagine the same would go for our cliffs.'

'Or *your* cliffs.'

'Presumably at some point in the dim and distant past – when Brother Alphonse was pootling about in his caves, for example – that was a moot point because it was all owned by the monastery,' Cam said.

'I guess so,' Nina agreed.

They had made it to the track, and Cam paused before he struck out in the direction of the Bronagh farm. He looked around slowly, from the distant broken boundary that marked the beginning of his property, along the hidden line of the coast with its cliff and the orchard hidden by gorse and broom, to the furthest reach of the southern horizon, where the Crowdie farm met the land beyond.

'It could be good to revisit that, couldn't it?' he said. 'If it was all one again?'

Nina wasn't sure what to say to that, or what he meant. Was Cam thinking that he could buy the orchard himself? Could he afford that? She wasn't sure and didn't know how to ask. Before she could say anything, however, Cam had thrown her a grin and a wave and headed off towards Bronagh.

'Give me a call if you want company while Bette's way,' he said. 'I'll see you later, yeah?'

Chapter Thirty-seven

'It would be a pretty good outcome, wouldn't it?' Nina observed to Bette that evening, over a glass of wine.

'Cam buying the orchard?' Her sister asked. 'It definitely would. Are you sure that's what he meant, though?'

'What else could he mean?' Nina asked. 'Unless he's got some vast untapped wealth I'm not aware of, he couldn't have meant he'd buy the whole farm. I don't think he'd do that anyway, unless he meant to rent it to us. He wouldn't turf me and Barnaby out if he could help it, and he couldn't run both on his own.'

Bette said nothing, but smiled into her wine in a way that made Nina suspicious.

'What?'

'Nothing.'

'*What?*'

'*Nothing!*' Bette insisted, and then changed the subject. 'Barney and I have just added Brother Alphonse's "secret hideout" to the map of Crowdie, by the way. I think that might be a subject that persists for a while.'

Nina smiled. 'It's good of you to take the time with him. And thanks for putting him to bed – I'll go up and say good-night myself in a minute.'

'It's fine. He's a good boy. And I won't see him tomorrow before school, I'm going to leave early doors.' Bette sighed. 'Not really looking forward to the drive, to be honest.'

'Are you sure about doing it all in one go?' Nina asked. 'That's a hell of a long way.'

'I just want to get it done,' Bette said. 'And I don't want to deprive you of the Land Rover for longer than necessary.'

'It's fine,' Nina told her, 'Cam's already said I can borrow his Hi-Lux any time I need to while you're away.'

Bette gave that little knowing smile again.

'What?'

'Nothing!'

It was strange without Bette in the house. In reality it had only been a few weeks since her sister had returned to Crowdie, but in that short time she had become a firm part of it. In her absence the stillness that had so disturbed Nina after Bern's death returned. She kept walking into the kitchen, ex-pecting Bette to be there, but she wasn't. Barnaby was quieter again too, although still enthused about Allie's continuing work in the orchard. Without his aunt there he wasn't able to visit the cliff ledge as much. He was still sleeping in the attic, and had somehow finagled this to encompass school nights, too.

In Bette's absence, and with both her and Nina's permission, Allie arranged for several former colleagues to come and look at the site, hoping they might be interested enough to volunteer some physical assistance before revealing it to official eyes. Nina couldn't be on hand while Allie showed them around the orchard: two men and a woman, to whom she was briefly introduced when they first arrived.

Bette's friend came to find her later, a beaming smile on her face. 'They're as excited as I am,' she said. 'And given the nature of the site and the potential significance of the find, they're all in agreement with me that the work needs to continue despite how late in the season we are. Really we should already be backfilling the hole I've made in order to preserve whatever's inside from the elements over winter. But what we're hoping is that if we can get inside and map what's there, which all four of us agree is probably proof that this is the site of the former monastery, we can use that to lobby St Andrews to fund LiDAR scanning next season, to locate the actual monastery ruins. That's ground-penetrating radar,' she added. 'It's expensive to arrange but would give us answers almost immediately, once we know approximately where to look.'

After that, Allie spent the next few days with the luxury of help. It didn't occur to Nina to ask her to keep the discovery quiet, and to pass this on to her colleagues, too.

Then, early one evening a couple of days later, as Nina was giving Barney his supper, there was a knock at the seldom-used Crowdie front door. They were jolted out of their conversation about their days by the unfamiliar bang of the rusted iron knocker against the old wood.

'Stay there,' Nina told her son, and went along the hallway to see who their visitor was. She found a man of about thirty with windswept brown hair standing on the doorstep.

'Hi,' he said, with a charming smile. My name is Connor Fitzgerald, I'm a journalist with the *Scottish Argus*. Do you have a moment to talk?'

'I—' Nina began, completely thrown for a loop. 'I'm sorry, but my son and I are in the middle of dinner. What's this about?'

Fitzgerald peered past her down the dim hallway towards the lit kitchen, and Nina felt a strange urge to step into his way, to shield her son from his view. The journalist smiled again, still charming, though she had the slight sense of window dressing.

'I completely understand, I don't want to take up much of your time,' he said, as he pulled his phone from his pocket and she watched as he swiped the screen to show that the voice recording app was already open and waiting. 'I grew up on a farm, it's such a busy life, always something that needs doing, isn't that right? I'm writing a piece about the discovery of the monastery on your cliff, here, as well as a secret orchard. What a find! It's a real piece of local interest, I know people are going to be fascinated by it. What can you tell me about that? Can you give me a tour? You don't mind if I record this, do you? It's just so much easier to make sure I get things right.' He pressed the record button, taking her failure to refuse as an agreement.

'I— no, I can't give you a tour,' Nina said, latching on to something in his stream of words. 'I told you, we're in the middle of dinner.'

'That's not a problem,' he said. 'I'll just have a look around on my own, shall I?'

'No,' Nina said, uncomfortable and wanting him gone without quite understanding why. She wished Bette was here – she'd know exactly what to say. 'Look, it'll be getting dark soon and it's not a safe place to access at night. Why don't you give me your card and I'll call you at a better time?'

'I don't have time for that, I'm afraid,' Fitzgerald said, with a tone of genuine apology that Nina still didn't believe for a minute. 'My deadline's tomorrow. I just wanted to give you a chance to tell your side of the story, Ms Crowdie. We'll be writing it either way, you see. About the discovery of this piece of important national heritage, and the dispute over who owns the land,' he said, watching carefully for her response.

Nina stared at him, the cold fingers of panic gripping her shoulders despite the lack of need for it. 'There's no dispute,' she said. 'My family has owned and farmed this land since the early 1800s. It's *our* land.'

'Is it?' Fitzgerald asked, with a smile. 'That's not what the internet says, Ms Crowdie. Look, I'll just have a look at the place, you know, to get a sense of atmosphere, something I can tell our readers . . .'

'No,' Nina said, more firmly this time, though by now she was genuinely scared. 'If you do that, you'll be trespassing. I am going to shut the door now, and I'd like you to leave. I'm a single woman on her own here with a young child and I won't hesitate to call the police if I feel I need to. You've got that on tape too, right?'

Fitzgerald smiled again, but there was a definite hard edge to it now. 'I do indeed, Ms Crowdie. It was nice to meet you. Be sure to pick up a copy of the *Argus* on Thursday, won't you?'

He turned and walked away to the car parked on their driveway. Nina gripped the door, her hands shaking, watching until he had pulled away, his red tail-lights eventually vanishing into the gathering dust.

'Mummy? Who was that man?'

She turned to see Barnaby standing behind her with an anxious look on his face, Limpet at his side. She forced a smile despite her thumping heart and shut the door.

'Oh, no one,' she said, relieved that her voice held steady. 'Did you finish your dinner?'

'Yeah.'

'Well then, how about an ice lolly? There are some in the freezer. Come on, back to the table.'

All she wanted to do was call Bette, but she didn't want to alarm Barnaby. She held on until he was squirrelled away in his attic hidey-hole and then called her sister.

'I didn't know what to do,' she said. 'Maybe I should have shown him around after all? But it was getting dark, and—Oh, I wish you'd been here, Bette.'

'Don't worry,' Bette said. 'You did exactly the right thing. No one doorstepping like that wants an actual story, they just want to stir trouble.'

'But what about what he said? About a land dispute? What did that mean?'

'I don't know,' Bette said. 'My guess is it's total bollocks, designed to get a rise out of you. It'll be to rile up anyone who wants to take a look at the orchard themselves, a "it's of historical importance, it should be public access" kind of argument. Did you look online?'

'No.'

'Good. Don't. Leave this to me, Nina, and don't worry, because there's nothing at all to worry about. We have the deeds to the land. It's ours. Whatever this is, it's not real. Okay?'

Nina shut her eyes. It was the lack of control that scared her, the feeling that someone else could come along and, just like that . . . 'Okay.'

'Good. Don't look at the paper when it's out, either. I'm going to call Allie, find out which of her archaeologist mates has decided to make a name for themselves by blabbing about our business down the pub. Have a glass of wine, have a bath, and go to bed. By the time I get back this will have blown over.'

Nina did as Bette suggested, but her dreams were

unsettled, full of smiling men who said one thing but meant another. And Cam was there, too, telling her that the land should all be one again, and wouldn't that be the right thing to do?

Chapter Thirty-eight

Bette had been packing the last of her crates when Nina called. The flat had looked halfway empty already, her possessions hidden away in stacked boxes that felt like precarious monuments to a life she no longer had. The larger pieces of furniture were remaining where they were; she'd discovered that it was far easier to let the place part-furnished. She already had a storage company coming to collect what would neither be staying in the flat nor coming with her back to Scotland, and had arranged this with the building's manager and the concierge. She wouldn't even need to be here herself. Next week, someone else would be living here, as if Bette had never really existed in this space at all. In packing up the traces of herself, Bette had realized that life in London had already been so remote that her leaving would go almost unnoticed. She'd tried to see this as a blessing. After all, letting the place would at least remove part of her anxiety over the mortgage. But it had left her feeling unmoored, with only Crowdie as her anchor.

In the wake of Nina's call, the first thing Bette did was exactly what she had told her sister to avoid. She sat on the minimalist grey sofa opposite the glass wall that was her window over the Thames, picked up her iPad and searched for Crowdie online. She'd done this before, after Ryan had first told them of his suspicions regarding the myth of the secret monastery and its 'perfect' apples. She'd been interested to see what mention there was among the throngs of people interested in such historical oddities. That trawl had located only a few mentions of the fable on cider-making forums, along with speculation of where the orchard and the monastery might have been situated. None of the places mentioned had been anywhere near the Crowdie farm or Barton Mill.

This time, though, it was a completely different story. Bette searched and scrolled, at first horrified at what she saw, then slowly becoming utterly furious. She bookmarked as she went. Over the past couple of months, with gathering pace, threads on multiple cider-making Reddit forums had appeared, posted by someone calling themselves 'CiderExpert001'. These posts gave information about the orchard, boasting about how it had been in their family for generations, how only under the person's expert stewardship would the 'best cider in the world' be ready for release in two years' time. 'CiderExpert001' seemed happy to engage with anyone who wanted to know more, answering questions, commenting on discussions. The engagement had been instant and enthusiastic – clearly, there was a true appetite for both the legend of Brother Alphonse's spectacular cider and the idea that the orchard had been found.

The real kicker, though – the aspect that in Bette's book took this from idle chat to a deliberate and calculated hostile action – was the social media account this person had set up specifically dedicated to 'their' orchard. She found mention of it on a new Reddit discussion thread, posted by someone clearly excited by the story this unknown person had spun. The title of the thread was 'HOW YOU CAN PERSONALLY HELP, NO MATTER WHERE IN THE WORLD YOU ARE!' Bette clicked the link and found herself on an Instagram page called 'The Secret Orchard'. There were multiple photographs documenting 'The rejuvenation of this ancient family orchard', posts soliciting sign-ups to a newsletter and website that would both be 'Coming Soon'. The photographs seemed to document all the work that had been done in the orchard, right from the point when Bette had begun to clear the overgrowth, yet nowhere was Bette herself photographed or mentioned and neither, for that matter, was Crowdie. Some of the images were close-up reportage shots – of the shed, for example, with which was included the hashtag #reducereuserecycle, and of the ripe windfall apples in the basket Ryan had used to gather them. There were even photographs of the new grafts and the first pressing of the juice.

Worst of all, though, was the one that had been posted just a few days before. It was a beautiful shot of the orchard at sunset, all its shadows on full display and the trees gilded by the evening light. It had obviously been taken by a drone, and it reminded Bette of what Nina had told her, of the drone that had scared Barney that evening in the orchard. The caption under the photograph talked about CiderExpert001's genuine worries over a 'vexatious claim' when the exact whereabouts of the orchard was revealed because people had been 'squatting illegally' on the land for years. Beneath were hundreds of comments from strangers from all over the world expressing anger over this awful 'injustice' and how they 'wished there was something they could do to help'. *Thank you, it's terrible*, said the replies from the owner of the page, which had been added to every single message. *I appreciate your support. Please sign up to the website and newsletter. Please help me fight for my family's historic rights and hard work. The more support I have, the better chance I have of preventing this theft of my property.*

The page already had over 40,000 followers. It had been active for a month. This was clearly what the journalist who had doorstepped Nina at home had been referencing.

Abandoning her search, Bette went back to packing. She shoved the last of her belongings into the final storage crate and sealed it, her mind racing. She'd already packed two suitcases full of clothes and other essentials ready for her return to Crowdie. Now she went back to the boxes containing her work suits and chose two more of her favourites to take with her as well – her equivalent of making sure she had adequate armour to hand. There was a battle coming, and she was determined to be prepared.

She'd intended to stay until the next day, but now Bette wanted to be back on the road north as soon as possible. She left instructions with the building's front desk and was in the Land Rover within an hour of talking to Nina. She'd drive until she was too tired to continue and find somewhere on the motorway to stop for the night. The sooner she got back to Crowdie, the better.

She called Allie from the services just north of Watford Gap, where she had to stop for fuel.

'My God, I'm so sorry,' Allie said, mortified when she learned of the doorstepping journalist who had interrupted Nina's quiet evening. 'I don't know how that could have happened.'

'It might not have had anything to do with you, or your friends,' Bette reassured her. 'And even if it did, I'd be thankful to whoever it was. It's the only reason we know about this nonsense online, and now we do know we can find a way to deal with it. I just want you to be aware of what's going on, that's all. From now on, we won't be letting anyone else into the orchard, especially not anyone the family doesn't know personally. I know that might make life difficult for you . . .'

'It's fine,' Allie said. 'I understand.'

'And I want you to log every time you see a drone around the property.'

'I'll do that.' Allie let out a long sigh. 'Who do you think is behind this?'

Bette made a scornful sound in her throat, looking out of the Land Rover's window. It was dark now, and starting to rain, the lights of cars bleeding fractured smears of red and white glare into the night. She hated driving in the rain.

'There's only one person it can be, isn't there? Lucas Greville. Every time I've seen him he's been taking a photograph of something. Remember that drone that Nina and Cam saw the day before Lucas first arrived? I bet it was his. He wanted to take a look before he'd even visited the place, as soon as Ryan told him about it. More fool me – I thought his arrogance was harmless, but apparently not.'

'I suppose that makes sense,' Allie agreed. 'But you have proof that your family owns the land, don't you?'

'Yes, although I'll go over that with the solicitor to make sure. But even so, in this day and age the court of public opinion can be incredibly persuasive, however downright wrong its conclusions.' Bette rubbed one hand over her face. She was weary already and there was still so much further for her to go. 'I should have gone with my first instinct and told Ryan . . .'

Bette stopped and stared blindly out of the window as a thought occurred to her.

'Bette?'

'Yes.' She blinked. 'Sorry, Allie. Look, I've got to go.'

Back on the road, Bette let her thoughts coalesce. It was Ryan who had brought Lucas in to help at the orchard, wasn't it? Ryan who'd suggested they wait before they told him about the eventual plan to sell. If they'd discussed the sale with Lucas straight away, everyone's cards would have been on the table. They might even have already had a deal in place. But now, it seemed as if Lucas Greville was making a play to take control of the orchard without having to invest a penny. Was Ryan complicit in this? The more Bette thought about it, the more she couldn't believe he wasn't. The thought sat like a block of ice in her stomach. *Fool me once, shame on you. Fool me twice . . .*

No. There was no way anyone managed to fool Bette Crowdie twice. The Secret Orchard belonged to Crowdie Farm, and if it changed hands, it would be theirs to sell. Neither it nor the farm itself would be taken away by an underhanded trick.

She drove on, the anger sparking in her veins keeping her awake.

Chapter Thirty-nine

'What are you going to do?'

It was the following morning. Bette had arrived at Crowdie in the early hours and had folded herself onto the sofa in the kitchen, unwilling to risk waking Nina or her nephew by stumbling upstairs to 'her' room. Now Barney was at school and the two sisters were huddled at the table over mugs of strong coffee. It didn't seem as if Nina had slept much more than Bette.

'I'm going to go to war,' Bette said. 'If Ryan thinks this is going to work, he's got another think coming.'

'Ryan?' Nina repeated, shocked. 'Do you think he had something to do with it?'

'Of course he did. He brought Lucas here, he advised me not to bring up the idea of a sale straight away, to let him put in some graft first so that Lucas felt connected to the place. He must have planned it all along. He's probably got a stake in the set-up of this cidery of the Grevilles.'

'But – are you sure?' Nina asked. '*Ryan?*'

'I should have known better than to trust him again,' Bette said, and then, at the look on her sister's face, 'What?'

'He just doesn't seem the type to do something this underhanded,' Nina said. 'Maybe we should—'

'You don't know him like I do,' Bette said. 'But I'll deal with it. Neither the Grevilles nor Ryan Atkins nor the whole bloody internet are going to get their hands on the orchard without going through everything I can throw at them. Crowdie is our land, and we've got the deeds to prove it.'

She spent the day on the phone, online, and also trying to go through the final batch of papers left over from her attempts to organize the study. Roland Palmer was baffled by Greville's behaviour, which was reassuring to Bette despite her conviction that there was nothing that could legally stand up regarding a land claim. This sort of dispute wasn't her area of expertise, although it was clear to both of them that what she'd found online was ample evidence for legal counter-claims against the Greville estate for multiple infractions of Crowdie rights.

'I can't imagine Graham Greville knows what's going on here,' Palmer said, speaking of the current head of the family. 'Not that I know him personally and nor have I had dealings with him in business, but he's well-respected in the area for being a decent person to work with. This would seem like a very strange move for him to make. It's not going to be difficult to shut this down, at least not from a legal standpoint.'

'Well, if he doesn't, he's going to get a shock when I come calling,' Bette said, the phone in the crook of her ear as she slowly leafed through yet another stack of yellowing receipts. She gave up with a sigh and squeezed the bridge of her nose, where a nascent stress headache was forming.

'Roland, can I ask you a favour? I don't have time to examine the last of these papers. They're mostly old receipts and to be honest I'm tempted just to burn them, but I've gone through everything else and—'

'Say no more,' said Palmer. 'Drop them in or stick them in the post and someone here will take a look. Lawyers, eh? We've all got the due diligence gene, am I right? You just focus on this new crisis.'

Bette smiled. Over the weeks that she and Palmer had worked together on the farm, she'd grown to like the crusty old solicitor. She'd seen how well he dealt with his clients, how dedicated he was to them. She'd been impressed by the work his firm took on on their behalf, too, far more varied and intricate than she'd realised. 'Thanks. I'll do that tomorrow.'

By early evening, Bette had her pieces in place and was calmly confident about her ability to dismantle Lucas's attempts to take the orchard from them. As she'd worked, though, her fury in another direction had only multiplied. Ryan. How could she ever have let herself trust him again? How could she have let him get so close for a second time? She was as angry at herself as she was at him, along with being shocked at his rank duplicity. Bette had *liked* him. She'd enjoyed his company, all those hours they'd worked together, *laughed* together over the past couple of months. How could he have done all that with a straight face, knowing exactly what he'd set up? He, possibly better than anyone else other than Nina, knew how important the sale of the orchard was for Crowdie. He knew that without the hope of it, they were lost, and yet he'd still gone ahead with this awful, nefarious scheme.

How? she thought, and for a second her rage was subsumed by a sharp stab of grief. *How could you do this to me twice?* Lucas's betrayal was commonplace, but *Ryan's* . . .

She waited until she could be sure that Ryan would be down at the orchard. The last text exchange they'd had had taken place the morning before, while Bette had still been in London packing up the last traces of her life there. He'd told her he'd be back with more rootstock for grafting this evening. She hadn't told him she was back, hadn't given him any warning about the fury she was about to rain down upon him and his plans. Bette left the farmhouse with her iPad in her bag, not speaking to either Nina or Barney. The weather had descended into a light drizzle, the slate-grey sky streaked with seams of imminent rain.

'How *dare* you?' was her opening salvo, delivered to his back as he bent over the workbench set up in front of him. There was a sapling laid out before him; he'd been in the middle of cutting a slot for a new graft. Of Lucas there was no sign, which was lucky for him, at least.

Ryan jerked around at her words. 'Bette?' he asked. 'What—'

'Did you think I wouldn't find out?' she asked, cutting him off, holding up the iPad, on which she had assembled everything she'd found the day before. 'Did you *really* think I'd let you get away with it?'

'What?' He put down the knife in his hand. 'What are you talking about? I didn't know you were back. What's happened?'

'It was *you* who told me not to bring up selling this place to Lucas right off the bat,' Bette went on, gesturing to the trees, flourishing now with the new growth encouraged by the first care they had received for too long. 'And now I see why that was. You and he wanted to make sure that he was the only one with a footprint here. You wanted to help your boss's son establish that as a precedent.'

Ryan came towards her, eyeing the tablet clasped in her hand. 'I can see you're angry—'

'Oh, *can* you? *Really?*'

'—but I swear, Bette, I don't know what you're talking about. Please tell me what's going on.'

'What's going on is that on Saturday night Nina had a visit from a journalist, wanting to know all about the orchard and whether there was any comment from the Crowdie family about its disputed ownership.'

He looked confused. '*What?*'

'My reaction exactly. Nina had no idea what he was talking about and when she called me, neither did I. I had to do a bit of searching on the internet to find out what he meant. Can you guess what I found?'

'No. What is it?' Ryan looked at her, his gaze wary and worried but steady. She had to admit that if he was faking knowing nothing, he was being very cool about it. But then, it wouldn't be the first time, would it? He'd been proficient at hiding his true nature even in his teens.

Bit by bit Bette confronted him with everything she had bookmarked: all the threads on the multiple cider-making Reddit forums by 'CiderExpert001' giving information on the orchard, boasting about how it had been in their family for generations. Ryan grew paler by the second, but he said nothing, paying close attention to everything she showed him, right up to the Instagram page and the nascent campaign against them.

'I,' Bette said, coldly, 'am going to dismantle you for this. You name it, if I can sue you for it, I will. Tortious interference, malicious communications, libel – anything and everything I can. By the time I'm done with you, you'll be as bankrupt as this place.'

'Bette,' he said, shock clear in his voice, 'how could you think this has anything to do with me? It doesn't, I swear. I had no idea. You have to believe that.'

'How can I?' she demanded. 'You turn up here out of the blue, willing to work for free to get this place back on its feet? I should have known it was too good to be true – from you, of all people. I should have trusted my first instincts and kept running.'

'Bette,' Ryan said, pleading now. 'This isn't me. If I'd known this was going on, I'd have put a stop to it. I'd never do anything like this. Not to anyone, but especially not to you.'

'Oh, please,' she laughed, bitterly. 'As if I don't know for a fact just what a lying *cheat* you've always been.'

The look on his face changed. Something in his eyes folded in on itself. For a second she saw grief there, as raw as she'd felt on that day he'd called her eighteen years ago. *Beth, there's something I have to tell you . . .*

'I'm not who you think I am,' he said, his voice almost lost beneath the growing evening breeze. There was a touch of rain in the air now, and it came not from autumn but winter, with an edge of ice in it, sharp and chill. 'Bette, I lied to you.'

'I know that,' she said, voice breaking despite her attempt to steel it. 'What I don't understand is *why*. What did I ever do to you, Ryan? How could you do this to me *twice*? *Why?*'

'No,' he said, stepping nearer, as if the closer he was the more believable he would be. 'You don't understand. I didn't do this, and I didn't do what you think I did all those years ago. I didn't cheat on you, Bette, I *never* cheated on you.'

She stepped back, the wind between them. 'You're lying again. Can't you just—'

'I'm not,' he said. 'I'm *not*. The lie was what I told you in that phone call when we broke up. And I've regretted it every day since.'

Beth, there's something I have to tell you . . .

She felt a prickle of heat pass across her brow and on down her spine, followed almost immediately by a sick, underlying chill, as if a fever was gathering beneath her skin.

'Stop it,' she said, as if she could reset the world by ordering it so. 'You're still lying. *Stop.*'

'I'm not,' Ryan told her, and there was such a simple, stark gravity to his words that her heart lost its rhythm. 'The only lie I ever told you was that one. And it was the worst thing I've ever done in my life.'

'No—'

'This is what I've been trying to tell you ever since you got back,' he said. 'I should have told you years ago. I never cheated on you, Bette, and I've regretted telling you that I did every day since. I was a stupid, *stupid* teenager and at the time I thought I was doing the right thing – the *noble* thing, can you believe that?'

Bette stared at him, disoriented, sick. 'No,' she said, forcing a strength into her voice that she didn't feel. How could he be this cruel? 'I can't believe anything you say. *I* was stupid to imagine you'd changed. Now, get off my property before I call the police. You're trespassing.'

She turned and began to make her way up out of the orchard, eyes blurring, unable to breathe and not only because of the wind scouring the cliffs. Ryan followed her, quickly, reaching out to catch her by the arm. He pulled her back around to face him. They stood beside the fence, erected so many years ago in the name of someone Bette had never known.

'Bette,' Ryan said, pleading now. 'I swear, it's true. You were so homesick, that first year you were away at university. I think we spent more time on the phone or Messenger than you did going to lectures or doing coursework. You were talking about giving up, coming home to Crowdie – to me. Don't you remember? You'd worked so hard to get there, it had been everything you wanted since before we even met. It was one of the things I found so magnetic about you. You probably can't remember it, the first day we ever spent time together, but I do. I was eighteen, and the boss's daughter came to help me muck out the milking barn. I think it was a punishment for something. I can't remember what – probably another argument with Nina. You were wearing one of your dad's old red plaid shirts tied up around your waist and ripped blue jeans. You'd yanked all your hair up in a bun that looked as if it was going to fall out at any minute. You were so angry but you worked so hard that day. You had so much *energy*, like you had a pulsar right there in your chest. You had all these plans, even then. You knew exactly what you wanted. You were going to be a lawyer. You wanted to work in London, then maybe New York. You wanted to make it right to the top, and you knew just how you were going to do it. You wanted to see the world. You wanted to go everywhere – anywhere, but here. You wanted to see everything. That's what you'd *always* wanted. You were – so *bright*, in every sense. That's what I first loved about you. I think I loved it right from that first day that I had to muck out that barn alongside an angry sixteen-year-old girl I'd never spoken to before. And then – then there was *us*. And three years later, there you were talking about giving up everything you'd ever wanted. Because of *me*.'

Bette wrenched herself away from him, one hand against the fence. 'You're telling me you cheated on me for *my* benefit?' she asked, incredulous. 'Unbelievable.'

'No,' Ryan said, moving to block her way as she went to carry on up the path. 'I told you, I never cheated on you. I swear. I just made you think I did.' He rubbed a hand over his face. 'We were just kids, Bette. I was stupid and immature, in so very many ways. We both were, but me more than you. I loved you. Completely. But when I asked you to marry me, it was purely selfish. I knew it, really, even then. I couldn't deal with the idea of you leaving. I wanted you to stay here and I knew that if we got married, you would. At first I told myself it was fine, because we loved each other, that you'd come back here and we'd make a life together somewhere nearby. But that wasn't *you*, was it? It wasn't what you wanted, not really. It was just because of me. Because of,' he gestured between them, 'this. *Us*.'

Bette continued to stare at him, but she couldn't make herself speak. She couldn't move, either, she just stood there, clinging to Ophelia Greville's fence, staring at the man who had once been a boy who had broken her heart so successfully it had never really healed.

'I was never unfaithful to you, Bette. I wouldn't have done that. I *couldn't* have done that, not to you. I just made you think I was. I told you: I was stupid and immature in the worst way, because I told myself I was being an adult, making an adult decision. I've regretted it almost every day since, but actually, I don't think anything else would have worked. If we'd tried to talk it out, neither of us would have been able to end it. And we had to. Because I couldn't follow you to university, could I? What would I have done there, and then in London, for that matter? I was a farmer – this is where I belonged. This is where I *wanted* to be. I wouldn't have been happy in London, any more than you would have been happy here, not in the end. We just weren't compatible, and I realized I was going to ruin your life and make you unhappy.'

I was *unhappy*, Bette felt like screaming into the wind. *I've been unhappy ever since, you stupid, stupid—*

'It was better that you hated me, because that would drive you on and away. At least, that's what I thought at the time,' Ryan told her then. 'But I've understood for years that it was a terrible thing to do to you – and to myself. I missed you every day. I thought about you *every day*, Bette, and even though we both moved on, even though we both had other lives, *good* lives, I've always regretted what I did back then. For a long time I wanted to find you, to tell you the truth, but eventually I realized that it wouldn't help. You got the life you wanted, the life you were always meant to have. If you had stayed here you would have ended up resenting me. Maybe I got everything else wrong, but I think I was right about that. And I would never have inserted myself back into your life, but when the orchard turned up, I thought that if I helped out, it'd be *something*. Something *good* that I could do for you. I didn't cheat on you, Bette, and I've hated that I made you think I did for two decades, and I would never have brought Lucas here if I'd had the slightest idea that he would pull a stunt like this. Please believe that. I had nothing to do with this.'

Bette stared at him, numb. Her mind was refusing to process any of what he'd told her. 'I can't deal with this,' she said. 'I've got more important things to worry about. Please, Ryan, *please*. Just go.'

Chapter Forty

'None of that means anything though, does it?' Cam asked, as he listened to what Nina had told him about what Bette had found on the internet. 'He doesn't have a leg to stand on, surely?'

'It doesn't mean anything legally,' Nina agreed. She'd come to find him in the Bronagh milking barn, needing to talk everything through. Bette had shut herself away in the study, presumably working on how to get them out of this mess, and didn't seem inclined to come out any time soon. Barney was at a sleepover, for which Nina was grateful: he was just beginning to settle down again, she didn't want him picking up on more stress. 'But Bette knows what she's talking about, and she's in a mess about something, I can tell. I've never seen her so shaken. I guess she's worried about the court of public opinion? You haven't seen it, Cam. If you just looked at the Instagram posts you would absolutely assume that it's someone posting from a piece of land they own. There's no mention of us at all. It's so . . . calculated. It's scary. I'd believe it if I saw it! Anyway, since when does truth mean anything once someone's made up their mind, especially about something they've read online? And like she says, this is smart. Lucas – or whoever put him up to it – has obviously planned this out and thought it all through. He's already set it up so that if we come out now and say "Hey, look what we've found and regenerated, who wants to buy it from us?", he's got thousands of people online ready to shout that we don't have the right to sell it in the first place because it's not ours. Someone will believe it. Probably quite a lot of people. It's a nightmare.'

Nina slumped against the wall, feeling utterly defeated.

'And where's Ryan in all this?' Cam asked.

'He came up to the farmhouse earlier. He'd obviously heard about it. He looked as much of a mess as Bette, to be honest. He said he wanted me to know he had nothing to do with it. I think he really wanted to speak to Bette, but she said she was busy and had nothing to say to him. She's convinced he's involved somehow, but my gut says he wasn't. He looked really upset – grey-faced, you know? And there's nothing to connect him online, either. He's been excluded from any mention, too. I want to believe he didn't have any-thing to do with it.'

'For what it's worth, I can't imagine he did either,' Cam said. 'And look, I know this seems like the pits – and it is – but your sister's not going to be bested by a little creep like this. She'll sort it out.'

'Maybe,' Nina said. 'I really thought finding the orchard might be the turning point we needed. Especially seeing how good it looks after so much work has been done to it. But now ...'

She trailed off, weary. Two steps forward, three steps back, that's what life felt like at the moment. If they couldn't sell the orchard, or if they had to let it go for peanuts, they'd be back to square one. She'd fooled herself into believing that the orchard had put her and Barney in a more secure position, but now it turned out that wasn't even slightly true. Nina put both hands over her face, feeling for a moment as if she wanted to cry and not wanting to do that in front of her neighbour. Looking at everything Bette had shown her online had been a shock, as if she'd slipped sideways into a weird parallel universe over which she had absolutely no control.

'Hey, come on,' said Cam. The proximity of his voice took Nina by surprise and she dropped her hands to find that he'd moved closer. Cam reached out and took both her hands. 'It'll be all right.'

She looked down at their joined hands, and in a flash she remembered that unsettled dream that had included him, or someone who looked like him, a handsome mask over a nightmare that had been hiding in plain sight. Thinking about this made her eyes fill again, because she didn't want to think of him like that, but she'd been there before, hadn't she, and so had Bette, and how did anyone ever know someone else, really? She must have made some sort of sound in her dry throat, because Cam shifted slightly, looking concerned.

'Hey,' he said. 'What is it? Tell me.'

She made a face, feeling obscurely guilty. 'I can't.'

He squeezed her hands. 'Come on. You can tell me anything.'

She shook her head. If she didn't ask, would she always wonder? Would there always be doubt? It seemed important that for every uncertain aspect of her life, Cam was not among them.

'I had a dream about the orchard,' she said, sucking in a breath. 'You were there, or someone that looked like you and ... not in a good way. And I hate that I think you could have anything to do with this, but it was you who brought Ryan in ...'

'Hey,' he said. 'God, no, Nina. I'd never do that to you. Never.'

'I know,' she said, unhappily. 'You've always been there for us, there for me. But last time we talked, you said about combining the land with yours and I couldn't work out—'

'That wasn't— Nina, that wasn't what I meant.' He let go of one of her hands, touching his rough fingers to her face instead, brushing back her hair so he could trace them across the filigree line of the scar on her left cheek. 'I'm not a violent man, but I swear I'd kill the guy who—'

'Don't,' she said. 'Don't.'

'I just wish you knew you can trust me, that's all.'

'I know I can. I do,' Nina said. 'I'm sorry, I shouldn't

have said anything. I'm just messed up. I guess I always will be.'

Cam tugged her forward into a hug. Nina shut her eyes and leaned her face against his chest. For a moment she let all her weight rest against him.

'You're not a mess,' he said. 'Or at least, not any more than anyone else.'

She breathed him in, smelling the clean scent of his washed shirt below the warmth of the day's work. She tried to remember the last time she'd felt arms around her like this. It had been a while. He felt solid, secure. They stood like that for a few moments, until it occurred to Nina that this had passed beyond a friendly offer of comfort and on to something else. His hands rubbed up and down her back, and Nina pulled back a little to look up at him, and before she knew it her gaze had shifted to his lips, not so very far away at all. In the next breath and almost without either of them meaning it, Cam had leaned in and they were kissing, right there, up against the wall of his cowshed.

When it ended, Nina kept her eyes shut for a moment. When she opened them, she found Cam looking down at her, studying her carefully with a faint smile on his face.

'What was that?' she asked.

He laughed a little, tightened his arms about her a little more. 'A long time coming?'

Nina felt like crying again. 'It's not a good idea, is it? Us, I mean. We're neighbours. We see each other all the time. My son really likes you. We get on really well.'

'Hmm,' he said. 'I see what you mean. That's a whole list of terrible downsides right there.'

'You know what I mean!'

Cam smiled again. 'I do. But here's the thing, Nina. We're neighbours. We see each other all the time. Your son really likes me. We get on really well. And we're both good people. If we don't fit together as well as I'm pretty sure we've both been thinking we might, then we'll deal with it. But let's not throw away something good because of what *might* happen. Because,' he said, leaning in closer, 'what if it doesn't? What if we're really, really good together?' He hovered there for a second, their lips almost touching, waiting for her to make up her mind.

'You make a good argument,' Nina admitted, heart fluttering in her chest, letting herself relax against him, just a little.

'I'm glad you think so,' he said, and kissed her again.

Nina let herself be lost in it for a moment, in the feel of being wanted, in the sudden racing beat of her heart, in the delicious solidity of his body against hers, in the way he was so present, so focused on her. But—

'No,' she said, breaking away. 'Cam – I'm sorry. I can't. This isn't . . . I just can't.'

He stayed there for a moment, his arms around her, looking down at her, breathing fast. Then he smiled slightly and shifted, letting her go. She felt the lack immediately, the loss of warmth, of the strength she had felt in him, which was so much more than just this moment.

'Okay,' he said. 'It's okay.'

'I'm sorry—'

He stepped back, hands on his hips, head dipped. 'There's nothing to apologize for, Nina. Really.'

'I just don't think it's a good idea. Especially when—'

'I know,' he nodded, turning away. 'I know.'

By the time she got back to the dark, silent Crowdie farmhouse, and for the first time since she'd known him, Nina felt even more miserable than she had before she'd gone to talk to Cam. *But it's as stupid an idea now as it has been all along,* she told herself. *What's the point in starting something that's doomed from the start?*

The house seemed so empty. She missed her father, she missed the sound of Barney and Limpet crashing about the place like miniature elephants. For a moment Nina contemplated dragging herself up the attic stepladder and curling up in the camp bed to sleep beneath the eaves, hidden away from the reality of the world.

Chapter Forty-one

Nina barely saw Bette for the next few days. Nina didn't ask for updates, not wanting to confront whatever was going on. She kept her head down, tried to keep up a bright façade for her son, and carried on working the farm as if she were sure there would be something to hand on to Barney when the time came.

She didn't see Cam, either. Nina suspected they were giving each other space – hoped it was only that and not some deeper fracture that could not be cemented shut in time. It felt strange, though, when days went by and he did not pop into the kitchen, and when there were no pithy texts on her phone to make her laugh. She wondered how many dates he'd been on since the incident in his milking shed. She thought about those kisses, too, sometimes imagined that she hadn't pulled back the way she did. Would it be over anyway now, if so? Probably. There would still have been this awkwardness, this distance, but for a different reason. She'd be another first date that went no further, that was all.

She missed him, though, felt Cam's absence in a way that surprised her. Worse, so did Barney, who asked where both Cam and Ryan were. Without them the farm was diminished, and her son felt the lack even more than she did. He flatly refused to sleep anywhere but the attic now. He was watchful, anxious, waiting for something she couldn't fathom but nonetheless felt as keenly herself.

Allie was a saving grace, bless her. She was working ever more frantically on the walled-up door, back to trying to excavate alone, but regularly took Barney down to the ledge so that he could 'patrol'. Nina was grateful. It gave the boy both something to look forward to and a way to fulfil his need to protect his home. The costume was back, though.

Nina hated that her son felt so vulnerable again when she had tried so hard to make him feel safe. She didn't know how to feel so herself – had spent so very many years at the edge of a margin that had shrunk day by day and was angry to find herself back there again. What did it take to feel safe in this world when you owned nothing? She saw a future of dingy council flats, sandwiched amid grey concrete and endless roads, and that was if she and Barney were lucky. She missed Crowdie already, realized anew what privilege she'd been bestowed in having it for so long, regretted ever having left it when she was younger. At night she cycled through ways she might save the farm herself, an endless litany of failed schemes that served no purpose but to keep her awake. *If, if, if* . . .

Who are you kidding? she asked herself. *You're no superhero. That's what we need, isn't it? And they don't exist.*

The call came about a week later, out of the blue haze of an uneventful early evening. She'd been helping Barney with his homework. Bette was shut up in the study, or at least Nina assumed she was, and Nina expected her to appear to answer the ringing phone. When she didn't, Nina went out into the darkened hall herself, catching the call before whoever was on the other end of the line could ring off. As she picked it up, her eye was drawn to the photograph of her with Barney and Bern in the farmyard, standing in sunlight, laughing with each other. Another world, that seemed to her now. Another universe.

'Hello?'

'Hi,' said a woman's voice. 'Is Bette Crowdie there, please?'

Nina turned to look at the closed door of the study. 'Who's calling?'

'My name is Rachel Hollingwood. I'm the director of the Eveline MacDonald Women's Literature Archive in Newton Dunbar.'

This meant nothing to Nina. 'Okay. Hold on, I don't actually know if she's in.'

Nina knocked on the study door and then, when there was no answer, cautiously pushed it open. The room was empty.

'Not to worry,' said the caller, when Nina told her she had no idea when her sister would be back. 'But could I leave a number where she could get hold of me when she has time?

She emailed searching for a book by Ophelia Greville, and I'm pleased to say that I think we might have what she's looking for.'

'Who was that, Mummy?' Barnaby asked, when she went back into the living room. They had lit the first fire of the year, wood crackling warmly in the grate of the old fireplace.

'Not sure,' she told him, sitting back on the sofa beside him and taking out her phone. 'Let's find out.'

An online search turned up the information that the Eveline MacDonald Women's Literature Archive had been established two years previously. Its aim was to collect and preserve antiquarian diaries and documents written by women as a way of collating a reference library of their lives as told in their own words. In doing so, the website said, the archive hoped to preserve the lives and experiences of women from all ages and walks of life that might otherwise be lost. It was part of the James MacDonald Tower, an extraordinary structure built to look exactly like a lighthouse, but on a hill in a field, miles from the sea.

'Wow,' Nina said, as she and Barney looked at the photograph of the building, now a listed historical monument and a museum telling the story of how it had been built. 'That looks like a pretty cool place, doesn't it? I had no idea it even existed. It's got a bookshop in it, too, look – the Lighthouse Bookshop.'

Her son regarded the image carefully and for a long time.

'I like it,' he said, eventually. 'It's very clever. Everyone is so busy being amazed at the outside of the lighthouse that they don't even know that it's really a secret hideout.'

Nina was still up when Bette got back. Her sister looked tired, her shoulders slumped. It unsettled Nina, this image of defeat. She thought of her sister as upright and stalwart, always.

'Sorry,' Bette said, by way of greeting as she came into the kitchen to find Nina washing up the dinner plates. 'I had some stuff I needed to go through with the solicitor, I've been down in Dundee. I should have left you a note or something.'

'It's fine,' Nina said. 'I didn't even realize that you weren't home until you got a phone call.'

Bette shrugged off her coat and hung it with the others on the hooks beside the door. 'What phone call?'

Nina briefly explained what the caller had said. 'She wants you to phone her back.'

Her sister pulled out a chair and sat at the table, rubbing a hand over her face. 'I can't even think about that right now. There are about a million other things that are far more important.'

Nina stood the last plate on the draining board, dried her hands and joined Bette at the table. The two sisters sat together in silence for a moment.

'We're running out of time,' Bette said. 'There's only a month before I'm going to have to start paying the arrears on the mortgage. I had hoped by then that we'd have a serious buyer for the orchard, or at least one on the horizon even if the deal wasn't actually done. But there's no hope of that while this "dispute" is ongoing. Besides which, now we're going to have to deal with serious reputational damage that is going to put other buyers off, which will force the price down for the Grevilles.'

'You're not still thinking we should sell to them?' Nina asked, shocked. 'Not after what Lucas has done?'

Bette spread her hands on the table. 'If they're the only option, what else can we do?'

'What if they end up not paying enough to save the rest of the farm?' Bette looked at her, and Nina knew the answer already. 'The bank will take it. We really are back at square one.'

'I'm sorry, Nina,' her sister said, quietly. 'I should never have trusted Ryan. I should have sent him packing as soon as he turned up here.'

'It's not your fault,' Nina said, her voice thick with tears. 'For the record, I don't think Ryan had anything to do with this. I really don't. He messaged me today. He's told the Grevilles he won't work with them anymore. And he said that whatever happens we should still press the rest of the apples and begin fermenting the juice, because it's an asset that could bring us in some money. He offered to do it himself and then help find a buyer for it, and he'd make sure we knew that neither he nor the Grevilles would have anything to do with the company that bought it. And Bette – you should have seen him the night that he turned up here. He looked as if his world had ended. I don't think he'd have done this to us. I don't think he'd have done it to *you*.'

To Nina's utter shock, Bette put her hands over her face

and started to cry. For a moment Nina didn't know what to do. She'd never seen her sister sob before, but here Bette was, with all her defences down, sitting at their old kitchen table in floods of tears. Eventually she reached out and laid a hand on her sister's arm.

'Bette,' Nina said. 'What is it?'

'Everything,' Bette said, through her misery. 'Nothing. None of this should matter. It was all so long ago.'

'Tell me anyway,' Nina said, shuffling her chair closer. 'That's what sisters are for, right?'

Chapter Forty-two

'I'm looking forward to this,' Allie said, with genuine enthusiasm. 'Thanks for letting me tag along. I've wanted to visit the James MacDonald Tower ever since it hit the news a couple of years back.'

Bette watched the highland landscape pass by as they wended their way through the backroads towards Newton Dunbar with her friend behind the wheel. 'I'd never even heard of it until Nina told me about this woman Rachel's call.'

'It's a fascinating place,' Allie said. 'It just goes to show that even recent history can hold its secrets.'

Bette said nothing, still looking out of the window. *You don't know the half of it*, she thought. Even days after Ryan's revelation she couldn't seem to put it out of her mind. She hadn't slept much. The same refrain just kept revolving around in her mind. What if he hadn't done what he did? Where would they be now, two decades later? How would her life be different?

'Bette?' Allie asked. 'Are you all right?'

'Sorry,' she said. 'Just a bit preoccupied.'

'Is it Ryan?'

Bette's attention snapped back to her friend. 'What?'

Allie glanced at her. 'This is the first time in days he's going to be in the orchard, and you've chosen that very afternoon to take a trip halfway across the country. You're avoiding him.'

It was true. She'd agreed to the wisdom of pressing the rest of the apple harvest, but Bette hadn't wanted to be anywhere near Crowdie while Ryan was there. She couldn't deal with the thought of coming face to face with him around the farm.

'Did something happen between you?' Allie asked, into Bette's silence.

Bette sucked in a breath. 'No, of course not. Not in the way you mean. And anyway, he's married, Allie, and I would never—'

'What?' said her friend. 'No, he's not.'

Bette opened her mouth, but then couldn't form sounds. She tried again. 'Yes, he is. He said—'

'He *was* married, a long time ago,' Allie told her. 'For about three years. But it didn't last.' There was a pause. 'Which did not surprise me at all, to be honest.'

Bette tried to assimilate this information. She swallowed around a hard lump that had risen in her throat. 'Why not?'

Allie flexed her fingers against the steering wheel and

shrugged slightly. 'You remember how Ryan is. Always trying to do the right thing. I think he thought he was supposed to get married, so he did.'

Bette looked away again. Her eyes were too dry for more tears. 'He told me something the other day. About . . . how and why we broke up.'

There was a brief silence. Outside, the Cairngorms grew closer, craggy and eternal.

'He didn't cheat, did he?' Allie said, eventually. 'I never could believe he'd done it, when I heard all the gossip about you two breaking it off. I remember thinking it didn't make any sense. He was so utterly head over heels in love with you.'

Bette felt herself going numb. She no longer knew what to believe. She couldn't decide, this far removed from the pure rank mess of it all, whether it mattered or not. She wanted to be indifferent, for it to mean nothing either way, but couldn't shake the feeling that actually, it meant everything.

'I'm sorry,' Allie said, into Bette's continued silence. 'I should have been there for you back then. Maybe if you'd had me to talk it through with—'

'No,' Bette said. 'I should have been there for *you*, Allie. I'm the one who should be sorry.'

Allie gave a short laugh. 'Life, eh? It's all just one big circle.'

Bette let out a breath. 'Is that a good thing, or a bad one?'

Her friend reached out one hand and patted Bette's knee. 'If you work that out,' she said, 'you let me know. In the meantime, there's always wine. Hey – we're here. It's quite a sight, isn't it?'

They were crossing a bridge into Newton Dunbar and in the near distance, on a hill that rose behind the small line of houses that constituted the village, was a lighthouse. It really did look like a lighthouse, too – a tower that should be standing over the ocean, but here commanded only the gentle roll of grasses that sloped away from its white walls, a lesser foothill with the grand backdrop of the Cairngorm mountains behind it.

'That's ... impressive,' Bette agreed, as they pulled onto and along the gravel track that led past the gatehouse entrance. She found herself suddenly interested in a way she hadn't been before. 'Rachel said she'd be in the bookshop, which I think is on the ground floor of the tower.'

Allie pulled up in the small carpark and they stretched their legs before making their way inside. Within, they found a circular room crammed with bookshelves arranged around a central counter, behind which was a log-burning stove and the curve of a wrought-iron staircase that spiralled up to the mezzanine floor above, also lined with books. A collie dog appeared from somewhere, tail wagging as it sniffed at Bette's trousers – perhaps scenting Limpet amid the weave.

'Ah,' said a friendly voice, from overhead. 'Hello. You must be Bette.'

Bette looked up to see a woman beginning to descend the stairs from the upper level, her feet clanging on the steps as she moved. She was a petite woman with bobbed brunette hair, casually dressed in jeans and a blue jumper.

'Hi,' Bette said. 'Rachel Hollingwood?'

The woman smiled. 'Yes. Sorry, not quite used to that yet. We're only just married. In fact, Toby and I were away on honeymoon when your email arrived. Our head archivist thought it best to leave it until I got back – so, sorry for the delay.'

'I appreciate you getting in touch at all,' Bette said. 'This is Allie Bright. It was actually she who sent me your way in the first place.'

Allie shook hands with Rachel as she said, 'I followed the story of the tower when it all broke a couple of years ago. Very happy to see that it's still here. I'm fascinated by the archive, too.'

Rachel smiled again. 'Well, let me show you both around.'

The Eveline MacDonald Women's Literature Archive was housed not in the tower itself, but in a small building that had been constructed for the purpose on the other side of the hill. Inside were several offices, all clean and tidy, and a large, climate-controlled room containing the documents themselves.

'After the discovery of Eveline's papers, we realized there was a need for somewhere to collect, collate and preserve the similar writings of other women,' Rachel explained as she showed them around. 'Specifically diaries, but letters too, and any other ephemera. In periods gone by this is where so much of what was written by women themselves existed, and anything like that can so easily be lost if not catalogued and kept properly. We're trying to save as many accounts of women in their own words as we can, however scant. Anyway – take a seat and I'll get Ophelia out for you.'

She disappeared into the archive room and returned a couple of minutes later with a box file in one hand, on which rested two pairs of thin white cloth gloves. Rachel put it on the table in front of them and opened the file to reveal a small, leather-bound book with a tattered spine and faintly battered edges.

'Oh,' Bette said, experiencing an almost physical sensation as the recollection elbowed its way out of her deep subconscious. 'Oh. I *do* remember this.'

Allie laughed. 'Yes! Me too. Wow, that's weird.'

'Feel free to handle it, but I would ask you to put the gloves on before you do,' Rachel said. 'This one has actually been fully digitized, but I thought you might like to be re-acquainted with the book first.'

Bette pulled on the white cotton gloves and lifted it from the box. She opened the cover and there, in meticulously hand-drawn and painted type, was the title page: *The Story of Ophelia Greville*. Bette felt a strange lump in her throat.

'That's why we didn't remember it as a diary,' she murmured, turning more pages. 'She didn't call it that. Ophelia wrote it as if it was a novel.'

'No wonder we thought it was just a story when we were kids,' said Allie.

'She did have a unique style as a diarist,' Rachel agreed,

taking a seat beside Bette. 'It's interesting to consider why. It's as if she was trying to distance herself from events, to make herself an audience to her life rather than a participant. I'll email you the digital version too. That way you can read it again yourselves.'

Chapter Forty-three

They stayed at the James MacDonald Tower until early afternoon. Bette was fascinated by the tiny museum that had been established in the tower's small upper rooms, and even more so by the camera obscura hidden in its crown. *I'll have to bring Barney here for a visit*, she thought, *he'd love this as much as he loves the attic.* An email notification arrived on her phone screen as they said goodbye to Rachel, confirmation that the digital text of Ophelia's diary had arrived.

'It's a sad, fascinating story,' Rachel said, as they left. 'I'm glad someone else knows it too. I think Ophelia deserves that much, at least. That's what the archive's about, really.'

Bette opened the document as she and Allie began the drive back to Crowdie. The transcription seemed remarkably clean. But then, this was a story that two youngsters had been able to read straight off the page, so Ophelia's hand must have been incredibly neat. Bette went to the first mention of the orchard and scanned through the entry. It was all written in the third person, which added to the sense that this wasn't a diary at all but a fictionalized account of a life. It also spoke to the distance that Rachel had mentioned.

'This was the first time Ophelia met George,' she said, as she glanced over the page. 'Do you remember it? We must have read and re-read this part a hundred times.'

Bette read the scene aloud as they drove, Allie nodding along. It started with Ophelia, then only eighteen, having yet another fight with the husband to whom she'd been married for a year. She wanted to go travelling to Africa ...

'Ophelia wrote about that a lot, didn't she?' Bette broke off reading to say. 'How she'd always wanted to travel the world but Lord Greville didn't want to take her, and wouldn't let her go alone. Not surprising for the time, I suppose.'

'Yeah,' Allie said. 'Not really what a good, dutiful wife was supposed to do, especially when the whole point of the marriage was to produce an heir for the Greville line.'

'It's interesting,' Bette added, flicking back and forth through the text, eyes alighting on bits here and there that she remembered. 'Looking at this, more and more is coming back to me. I remember reading all of this with a kind of horrified detachment way back then. But now as an adult, knowing this really did happen – it brings home how trapped a woman like Ophelia would have been in this life she didn't choose. She was only seventeen when they married! She hadn't lived, and there was her father essentially selling her to Milton Greville.'

'All those the huge arguments she had with her dad before

the event,' Allie said. 'I remember cheering her on through those. She had no one to support her, did she? Her mum had been dead for years. But she wasn't shy about fighting her own battles.'

'Yup,' Bette agreed. 'She absolutely spoke her mind. I guess she knew that once she was married, what was left of her father's money would pass to her husband instead of to her and that was her last chance to carve out something for herself. That's when she made the deal with her dad.'

'Oh yes!' said Allie. 'Didn't he persuade her to "behave appropriately" by agreeing that he'd keep one per cent back of the estate for her alone? He told her he'd only consent to the marriage on the understanding that Greville would uphold that agreement, right?'

'Right,' Bette said. She looked out of the window, impressed anew at the audacity and backbone of Ophelia Greville. 'I mean, now I get how laughable the idea of one per cent of any estate is, but at the time I first read this I was – what, thirteen? I thought she was brilliant.'

'Me too,' Allie agreed. 'And I remember how much I hated Milton Greville, when one of the first things he did once they were married was to make it clear that a gentleman's agreement was exactly that – between "gentlemen" – and he couldn't be held accountable for any deal she'd had with her father.'

'Poor Ophelia. She kept pushing it, though,' Bette said. 'I admired her for that, too. She didn't let it go. She wanted to sell her one per cent of the estate to finance her trip, but there was no way Greville was going to do that. He shuts her down once and for all – and that's when it happens. She storms out of the big house, walks further than she's ever walked on the estate before and finds herself in a strange little orchard on the side of a cliff, where she meets a young man called George Crowdie.'

'Yes!' Allie exclaimed, thumping the steering wheel with the heel of one hand. 'And that's the scene that popped into my head the second you asked me about the orchard! I loved it so much, it seemed so romantic to that little thirteen-year-old me. Read it to me again.'

Bette did, picking up with the last bitter words between Ophelia and Milton and her angry tramp along the cliffs. When she got to the end she broke off, scanning the last paragraph with interest.

'What is it?' Allie glanced at her.

'Listen,' Bette said, and read out the final short passage about the orchard.

'Don't ever tell anyone this is here, George,' she said, suddenly impassioned. 'If my husband knew it existed, he would want it. He would want all of it. Keep it secret.'

A shadow passed over George Crowdie's face, and he shrugged a little, his gaze wandering past her to where the land fell into the sea. 'Tis his land, ma'am. They're his trees. The cider we make goes into his stores.'

'Not forever,' she said. 'I will make sure of it. I will.'

He looked at her, those hazel eyes curious. Ophelia didn't explain. One per cent. It was a penny in the ocean, but it was her penny, and it would be enough. Perhaps she would never go anywhere. But neither would this place. Neither would the Crowdies. Neither would this boy with the kind brown eyes.

Bette looked over at Allie, feeling as if an errant puzzle piece had finally found its correct place. 'Doesn't that sound as if that's how the Crowdies got the land from the Grevilles? Ophelia decided to use her "inheritance" to make sure George Crowdie got the orchard and presumably the farmhouse and land too as a result. That explains why the deed only dates from 1839 even though my family's history on the land goes back further.'

Allie nodded thoughtfully. 'How did she make that work, practically though? She wouldn't have had a legal recourse to force Greville to give her that one per cent.'

'No,' Bette said, the document prompting more and more memories of the story as she skimmed through it. 'But after that first visit she goes to the orchard often – it becomes her refuge, doesn't it, in a way? And . . . so does George Crowdie.'

'Right,' Allie said, nodding. 'The grand forbidden romance. God, I remember now – I was obsessed by it!'

'When Milton finds out, Ophelia promises to break it off, but only if she gets to "spend" her one per cent inheritance. Greville's had three wives by that point, but no heirs. He's in danger of becoming a laughing stock, and now his new young wife is compounding that by gadding about with a tenant farmer. He could have divorced her, which would have ruined her, but Ophelia promises to ditch the affair if he signs over the orchard and the farm to George ...'

'Hence the deed you have, written in 1839.'

'Yup. The story – this diary – finishes with George and Ophelia saying a tearful goodbye to each other. It's a tragic ending.'

'How could I forget?' Allie said. 'And now we know that Ophelia's story got even worse after that – she died the following year, in childbirth, according to what I found online.'

Bette stared out at the darkening sky. 'Exactly *when* in 1840 did she die?'

'Oh my God,' Allie said, her voice shocked. 'Not so long that the dates wouldn't work to make the baby George's rather than her husband's.'

Bette considered the implication of this. 'Wow.'

'Yeah. It'd be kind of interesting to take a look at some DNA from the current Greville line, wouldn't it?'

'That's a can of worms I have no intention of opening,' Bette said, as she considered. 'You know, in terms of our current Greville issues, I think that rather than going the legal route straight off the bat, I should go and talk to Lucas's father now that I have a clearer picture of what actually happened.'

'The current Lord Greville?'

'Perhaps if I can show him what we know about the story, he'll see that it's probably for the best if Lucas comes clean to his followers before I really get going,' she pointed out. 'None of this really puts the family in a good light, does it? And I know there's a clear argument to say that all we have

here is Ophelia's side of the story, and a deliberately fictionalized one at that . . .'

'But it's about appearances, isn't it?' Allie agreed. 'Good
idea.'

Chapter Forty-four

'You can't see him until next week?' Nina turned to look at Bette from the sink.

'It's the first appointment he had, so his secretary said,' Bette told her, continuing to chop potatoes. 'There's no point being difficult about it, it'll only cause friction. It's in our interests to make this as smooth as possible.'

'You're sure they don't have a leg to stand on?' Nina asked. 'Despite what you found out in the diary?'

Bette had now read Ophelia Greville's story in its entirety, relaying the highlights to Nina as she'd worked her way through the text. In doing so, her sister had told Nina that it seemed the Crowdies had never had to pay for the land they had received from the Greville estate. It had been gifted by Ophelia – or more precisely, by Milton Greville, presumably because his wife had no actual legal way to do so herself. Bette had mentioned to Nina that perhaps this was where Lucas's notion that the Crowdies didn't actually own the land

358

had come from. There would have been a lot of face-saving and obfuscation going on, after all. Perhaps Lucas had heard this and assumed it to be true.

'No,' Bette said, finishing the last of the potatoes and dropping them into the pot. 'The deed was signed over to us by Milton Greville himself. Even if that wasn't the case, we've been the sole occupiers of this land for close to two centuries with no counter-claim ever having been made — that has clout in itself.'

'What about that journalist, the one that turned up on the doorstep?' Nina asked. 'He's gone very quiet, hasn't he? I was expecting to see something in the paper, but nothing's been published yet, as far as I can see.'

'I think he was fishing,' Bette said. 'At the moment the only story he's got is what's on Lucas's Instagram. It might be that he's looked into it himself and realized it's all rubbish. All he'd have to do is pay for title deeds at the Land Registry, which would confirm that we own this area of land. That was probably enough to put him off. Either that or he's gathering information for a larger story. And if he's going to write with any accuracy, it will have to be in our favour unless he wants to lose a clear defamation suit, so I wouldn't worry about it.'

There came the sound of footsteps across the yard, and then a brisk knock at the kitchen door.

'Come in,' Nina raised her voice to say, and then turned to see Cam standing on the threshold.

The moment was overlaid by a sudden silence, broken

only by the bubbling of pans on the stove and the faint background tick of the clock. Nina looked at her neighbour for the first time since they'd both found themselves locked in a kiss against the wall in his cowshed, and found herself unable to think about anything else. Cam smiled, warm but a little uncertain.

'Hi,' he said. 'Sorry to appear unannounced.'

'It's fine, Cam — come in,' said Bette. 'I was thinking that we've not seen you for a while, how are you doing?'

'Oh, you know,' Cam stepped further into the kitchen but seemed uncomfortable, his hands finding their way deep into his pockets as he hunched his shoulders. 'Same old, same old.'

Nina broke herself out of her frozen state enough to heft up the dish of veg from the counter as Bette and Cam continued to talk. It gave her a chance to regain a little of her composure. *It's just Cam*, she told herself. *Sure, this'll be awkward but you can get over it and move on. He obviously has.*

'Anyway, I didn't mean to interrupt,' Cam said. 'Actually, I wondered whether I could have a word with Best Barnaby Barnacle?'

Nina, equilibrium suitably restored, turned back to him. 'Sure. I'll give him a shout, he's probably in the attic. Anything I should know about?'

Cam gave another smile, this time accompanied by a spark of slight mischief. 'Not yet. At the moment this is a job for our resident superhero. But I promise to fill you in soon. Okay?'

Nina crossed her arms for a moment, but she smiled. Maybe this was Cam's way of getting them back to normal, some scheme to get them over the hump of this discomfort and back into the routine of their friendship.

'Okay,' she said. 'It's a good thing I trust you, isn't it?'

He watched her, smile warming. 'It is.'

Nina went to call her son down from his hideout. Barney thundered down the ladder, down the stairs and into the kitchen with such excitement when he heard that Cam was there that something in her heart clenched, hard.

'Cam!' Barney said, breathless, and Nina got the impression that her son had been on the verge of running to the farmer for a hug, but held himself back.

'Hey, champ,' Cam grinned, crouching down so he was eye-level with the boy. 'Look, I need your help with something. It's not an emergency, but it is really important. Can I count on you?'

'Yes! What is it?'

Cam looked up at Nina. 'Barney and I are going to go outside to talk, is that okay? Because right now, this is top secret. We won't go far, just outside the door – but absolutely no eavesdropping. This is strictly superhero stuff.'

Nina shook her head. 'Why do I feel as if I'm going to regret encouraging this?'

Cam got up. 'You won't, I promise. At least … I hope you won't.'

The pause and his slightly cryptic statement made her frown, but Cam grinned again.

'All right, all right, go on,' Nina told them. 'But don't be long, dinner's nearly ready.'

'Can *I* listen?' Bette asked, as she crunched on a stray bit of carrot.

'Nope,' Cam said. 'Sorry.'

'Come on,' Barney urged him. 'Let's go, Cam!'

Cam looked over at Nina, still smiling. 'Ten minutes.'

He shut the door behind them and the sisters could hear the pair of them talking quietly, Cam's explanation of whatever he wanted Barney's help with punctuated by the boy's excited answers.

Nina shook her head and found herself smiling without much of an idea of why, beyond the fact that it was good to see Barney happy about something again. *He really does miss Cam,* she thought, *almost as much as I do.*

She registered this thought just as she saw how Bette was looking at her, eyes fixed in a thoughtful stare.

'What?'

'What do you mean, what?' her sister said. 'That should be my line. What's happened between you two?'

Nina turned away and busied herself with dinner. 'I don't know what you mean.'

'Oh yes, you do,' Bette said, getting up from the table and moving closer. 'The tension when he walked in was off the scale. Is that why he hasn't been round here for the past few days?'

'He's just been busy, that's all.'

'Pull the other one,' Bette advised her. 'It's got bells on. Come on, Nina, spill. I've never seen you tongue-tied around him before. Something's going on.'

'Nothing's going on,' Nina said, 'and even if there was, why would I tell you about it?'

'Because I'm your big sister, and that's what big sisters are for. Besides,' Bette added, going to the cupboard to get out the dinner plates, 'I spilled my guts on the Ryan debacle, didn't I? It's your turn.'

'All right then. Later,' Nina said. 'When Barney's in bed.'

'What do you think Cam's up to?' Bette asked, laying the table.

'No idea. Something to do with the orchard, maybe. Although I wouldn't be surprised if he's just making all this up to give Barney something to do.'

Bette smiled. 'He's good with him, isn't he?'

'Yeah,' Nina sighed. 'He is.'

For the next two days, Barney and Cam were busy with their secret project. Their neighbour would come and collect the little boy for an hour before dinner, and off they would go together. At one point she saw Cam carrying table legs and a cardboard box, but neither of them would tell her anything when she asked. She began to suspect that Bette knew what was going on too, because her sister became secretive, watching Nina when she thought she wasn't looking, eyes twinkling above a smile when Nina caught her at it. Several times she came across Bette and Barney whispering to each other, falling silent when she appeared and giggling behind their hands.

Nina found herself caught up in the game, despite not

knowing quite what it was. She had her suspicions. These were mainly sparked by the warmth she saw in Cam's eyes whenever they met, the awkwardness of that first meeting after the incident in the cowshed entirely forgotten. Now every time they bumped into each other she felt a flutter in her stomach, and although this wasn't new, she was more aware of it.

Then, on Friday morning on the way to school, Barney told her that she mustn't go anywhere or arrange to do anything else except come home after picking him up that evening.

'You need to be at home this evening, Mummy,' he said. 'Promise?'

'Where would I go?' Nina asked. 'I'm always here, bub, you know that.'

'I know, but just in case,' he said, earnestly. 'It's *important*. You have to *promise*.'

'Okay, Best Barnaby Barnacle,' Nina said, solemnly, her heart throbbing an extra beat that she did her best to ignore. 'I promise.'

You could be completely wrong, she told herself, as she kissed her son goodbye and watched him run off through the school gate. She tried to tell herself she wouldn't be disappointed if she was.

That evening, Cam came to find Barney as usual. Their neighbour waited in the kitchen doorway as Barney ran towards him with a backpack over his shoulder.

'What have you got there?' Nina called, as her son ran past her.

'Preparations!' Barney shouted back, already beyond Cam and out in the farmyard. It was only five o'clock but already getting dark, the year turning its face fully towards winter as October rode high on the calendar.

'Preparations for what?'

'You'll see, Mum!'

'We'll catch you later,' Cam said, grinning at her from the kitchen doorway.

'Wait,' Nina said, 'Barney—'

'Best Barnaby Barnacle!'

'—Best Barnaby Barnacle told me I should make sure I'm in tonight.'

'Well, you should,' Cam agreed.

'But why?'

Cam shrugged, with a grin. 'Because you've been working hard and you deserve a rest?'

'She does that,' Bette joined in, coming into the kitchen from the hallway. 'In fact, why don't you let me worry about dinner tonight? You can just chill out, put your feet up.'

Nina narrowed her eyes at her sister. 'You're in on this too, aren't you?'

'I have no idea what you mean,' Bette said, as Cam laughed from the doorway and then disappeared into the night. 'Why don't you go up and have a bath?'

Nina stared at her. 'What are you talking about? It's only just five o'clock!'

Bette shrugged. 'You can take a glass of wine. Relax for an hour.'

'Why?' Nina asked, suspiciously. 'What's happening in an hour?'

Her sister wouldn't answer that, which didn't help with the sudden, unsettled fluttering in Nina's stomach.

She did actually follow her sister's advice, because it had been a long time since she'd had time to lounge about in a bath and her back was aching. It felt luxurious to sink into the hot, perfumed water, to sip from the glass of red Bette brought her. By the time she got out it was almost six o'clock. She pulled on clean jeans and a soft jumper and padded downstairs in her socks, but there was no sign that her son had returned or that Bette had started dinner. Her sister was sitting on the sofa in the kitchen, reading, but she got up with a smile when Nina appeared.

'Good timing,' she said. 'I've just had the bat signal.'

'The what?'

In answer, Bette went to the kitchen door and opened it. Limpet was sitting on the step, ears pricked expectantly, head tipped to one side. There was a bow tie fastened to the dog's collar.

'I believe,' Bette said, 'that we need to follow him. Come on, get your boots on.'

'My *boots*? Where are we going?'

'Where do you think? Grab your coat, too. It's chilly out there.'

Bette walked with her as far as the slope and then stopped at the first dip. The orchard track had been lit with fairy lights. They'd been wound around every curlicue, every looping link, so that they threaded the entirety of Ophelia Greville's fence, glinting into the darkening night.

'Limpet will take you the rest of the way,' she said. 'It should be light enough, but watch your step anyway, you know what it's like.'

'Bette,' Nina said, stopping her sister before she disappeared. 'Is this a good idea?'

Bette sighed and shook her head, but there was a smile there too, beneath her exasperation. 'Of *course* it is.'

'But what if—'

Bette came back towards her and pulled Nina into a tight hug. 'Nina. Please. Believe me – I'm as cynical as they come. But this? Nothing makes more sense than this.'

They leaned into each other for a minute. Then Bette pulled away, looking down at the dog, sitting impatiently at their feet.

'You'd better go. They'll think you're not coming.'

The lights danced beside her, all the way down into the orchard. Barney was waiting beside the boulder at the bottom of the track. He wasn't wearing his superhero costume. Instead he had on black trousers, a white shirt, and a bow tie just like Limpet's. His hair was slicked back into a neat parting. He beamed when he saw her. Limpet ran to his side and sat adoringly at his feet.

'If madam would like to follow me?' her son said, in a comically prim voice that she didn't dare laugh at. He turned away, heading for a path through the orchard that had been festooned with more tiny, winking lights.

They followed the trail until they came to a circlet of trees sketched by more lights that had been draped along the branches to twinkle in the dark. In the centre, on a level patch of trimmed grass, Cam stood next to a table that was dressed with a white tablecloth and set with chinaware, cutlery and glasses. Beside the table stood a large wicker picnic basket, and a bucket on a stand containing a bottle of champagne. Cam was wearing the same as Barney but with an added jacket, and when he smiled at her Nina felt her eyes fill with tears.

'Hi,' he said.

'Hi.' She looked at the table, around which had been placed three chairs, which for some reason made her even more tearful. 'You made an effort.'

'Well. Someone smart told me I should.'

She looked down at herself through blurred eyes. 'I should have worn something else. Bette didn't tell me—'

'I didn't want her to,' Cam said. 'You're perfect however you are.'

He pulled out a chair for her and then for Barney, who was sparkling with more joy than Nina had seen from her son since before Bern had died.

'We did all of this together, me and Cam,' he said. 'And the second date will be on a boat because Cam's friend has got one he can borrow and the third date – well, I don't know about the third date because Cam said we shouldn't choose everything you do but I think you should go skydiving because what could be more fun than flying?'

Nina laughed, a sudden release of pressure, and looked at Cam across the table. 'You really have put a lot of thought into this. *Three* dates?'

'And four, and five, and six,' Barney piped up. 'But they are *TBD,* which is secret code for *To Be Decided* but basically Cam says there should be one a week to infinity and beyond.'

Cam smiled, but there was a serious look on his face and he glanced away for a second. 'I just ... didn't want you to assume I was only thinking about one.'

Nina's heart turned over. 'Right.'

Cam looked at her, then reached across the table to catch her fingers in his. 'Is that okay? Is *this* okay? If—'

'Yes,' she said. 'Yes. It's okay. It's ... very okay.'

They looked at each other, smiling, lost in the moment. Or at least, they were until a sudden gust of cold October wind cut through the orchard from the cliff. Nina shivered.

'Best Barnaby Barnacle, have you got a coat?'

'It's in the shed.'

'I'm sorry,' Cam said, a little ruefully. 'A picnic, by the sea, in October. Who does that?'

Nina squeezed his hand. 'I love it. I really do. I love everything you've both done. But—'

'But?'

'Will everything in the picnic keep until tomorrow?'

'Yes ...'

She grinned. 'Well then, maybe we should see if the Silver Darling has a table free?'

Chapter Forty-five

It took a particular type of person, Bette thought, to give a stately home, even a modest example, one's own name. Greville Hall stood in pristine acres of parkland that swept from the cliffs as far as the distant edge of Brechin Castle country park. At one time they might even have been one vast estate.

Inside the house, she was ushered along corridors, decorated in calm, neutral tones, by a member of household staff. Once out of the imposing main foyer, it was clear she was being taken into a wing of offices rather than the family's living quarters. At length her usher knocked at an anonymous white door, which opened to reveal a tidy woman of about fifty dressed in a red wool sweater paired with a tartan pencil skirt and warm black tights.

'I'm Adrienne Maitland, Lord Greville's secretary,' the woman explained. 'Come in, do. He'll just be a few minutes. Can I get you a beverage? Lord Greville will be having coffee presently.'

The secretary's manner was disarmingly friendly. 'Coffee would be appreciated, thank you.'

While Maitland called up to place this order, Bette looked around the office. The walls were adorned with a variety of old paintings and multiple maps of the estate demarked by different coloured lines. It was very clearly a working room, and Bette could see a second door opposite the secretary's desk – presumably the Lord's inner office. This assumption was proved right a couple of minutes later when the phone on the woman's desk buzzed and she answered, looking over at Bette with a smile as she set it down again.

'You can go in now, he's ready for you. I'll be in with the coffee shortly.'

Beyond the second door Bette expected to find another office, but although there was a desk it was more like a sitting room. There were bookcases, a picture window, a suite of richly upholstered armchairs and a coffee table set in front of an unlit fireplace. She was slightly thrown to find the room empty, but then a door in the wall behind the desk opened and a tall man who couldn't have been more than mid-fifties appeared, closing out the discreet sound of a flushing toilet as he pulled the door shut behind him.

'Ms Crowdie,' he said, striding towards her with a hand outstretched to shake hers. 'Welcome. Come in, do. I'm Graham Greville. Let's sit on the comfortable chairs – I need a break from that damned desk.'

The current Lord Greville was not at all how Bette had

imagined him, and she realized that her mental image of what to expect had been strongly influenced by reading Ophelia's diary. Graham Greville seemed astonishingly young and unstuffy in comparison with Milton Greville. He was dressed casually in jeans and a white shirt open at the neck, his sleeves rolled up on his tanned forearms. Bette felt distinctly overdressed in the work suit she'd chosen for the occasion, and a little insulted that he'd deemed that this meeting – for which she had been waiting a week – had not required a similar attention to detail from him. He seemed to register this as they sat, and was immediately full of apologies.

'I'm sorry, Ms Crowdie,' he said. 'I often find that people are intimidated by their surroundings when they visit Greville Hall, and I have found in the past that this can be somewhat mitigated by my adopting a relaxed approach. But I see now that you are unlikely to be intimidated by anything.'

Bette smiled slightly, though her tone when she spoke was cool and measured. 'No,' she agreed. 'You would be right there, Lord Greville. There isn't much that scares me. I'm here about your son, Lucas.'

Graham Greville's face darkened a little at the mention of his son, as Adrienne Maitland appeared with coffee. She set it down on the table – a cafetière and a jug of cream, elegant white porcelain cups and shortbread biscuits on a plate stamped with what Bette thought was probably the Greville coat of arms.

'Thank you, Adrienne,' Lord Greville murmured. 'We can sort ourselves out from here. Can you locate Lucas for me, please. If he's not currently at home, make sure he is on his way back. I suspect I am going to want to talk to him in the very near future.'

'Yes, sir.'

As she left, Greville poured them both coffee, took his and sat back. 'Right,' he said. 'Let's have it. What's Lucas done now?'

Bette laid it all out bit by bit over the course of the next half-hour, from their rediscovery of the orchard and Lucas's first involvement to the verified deeds to the estate and Ophelia's own account of how the transfer of lands came about.

'Ms Crowdie,' Greville said, 'not that this isn't a fascinating walk through a part of the estate's history about which I know very little . . . but so far I don't understand what the problem is.'

Bette took out her iPad and flicked to the Instagram page she already had loaded and waiting. 'This, Lord Greville, is the problem.'

She passed him the tablet and watched as he scrolled through the page's history, clicking on items here and there to read the entries. Bette watched his face, his expression growing grimmer by the second.

'This is active now?

'Yes, it was posting this morning. There's more I can show you on other sites, if you'd like to see it.'

'And you think it's Lucas?'

'I know it's Lucas, and it's not going to take much for me to prove it in court.'

He looked up from the screen, troubled by the mention of legal action. 'Then what do we do about it? What would make you happy, Ms Crowdie?'

There was a commotion behind Bette and she turned to see the door open to admit Lucas Greville. He rolled his eyes slightly as he saw his father's visitor.

'Shall I come back when she's gone?'

'Ms Crowdie is going nowhere,' Greville said, with a steel blade in his voice. 'And neither are you until you explain this.'

He held up the tablet, the Instagram page still displayed on its surface. Lucas smirked.

'You're always telling me I need to work for my living,' he pointed out. 'That's me doing that to get back what's rightfully mine. What's rightfully *ours*.'

Greville stood, incensed. 'For God's sake, Lucas! Do you have any idea what sort of law suits you've opened us up to? That's not our land – it hasn't been for several generations. Look at these deeds, for goodness's sake! That's your great-grandfather's signature, clear as day.'

'He might have signed it,' Lucas said. 'But they never paid for it. I checked. That's theft. They're thieves, and I want what they took. I want what's mine. I *want* that orchard.'

'I gave you room for this orchard of yours, right here on the estate,' Greville said, growing angrier by the second.

'I gave you funds to start up with, I even arranged for a mentor—' He broke off, realization dawning on his face. 'Is this the reason why Ryan Atkins resigned last week? He found out what you'd been up to?'

Lucas shrugged. 'I don't need him anyway. I know what I'm doing.'

Greville snorted. 'All evidence to the contrary. This is absurd. Even for you, Lucas. I trusted you enough to give you yet another chance despite all the trouble you've put your mother and I through, and *this* is how you repay us?'

Lucas threw his hands up. 'What are you talking about? I'm getting our land back!'

'Lucas,' his father said, the fury in his voice clear. 'Stop talking. Right now.'

Sullen, Lucas narrowed his eyes but subsided into silence. Graham Greville turned to Bette.

'My apologies,' he said. 'If we can find a way to settle this outside of full legal proceedings, I would appreciate it.'

'Well,' Bette said, 'in actual fact we are planning to sell the orchard. If Lucas wants it that badly, then perhaps he can pay for it, at a price that reflects the distress his attempts to destroy our family's name and livelihood has caused. If that happens, we'd be prepared to drop any charges moving forward.'

'We're not paying you a penny,' Lucas spat. 'As *if*! That shitty little farm isn't worth a thing without the orchard and that's already—'

'Lucas,' Lord Greville said, sharply. 'The only accurate

statement in that sentence you've just stated is that *we're* not paying a penny.'

Lucas cast a gloating look at Bette, but before he could say any more his father went on speaking.

'This is your mess, no one else's. If you want the orchard that badly, you can pay for it out of your trust fund,' Greville told his son, bluntly. 'I'm done picking up after you, Lucas. You wanted your mother and I to treat you like an adult – well, that starts right now. Actions have consequences. It's about time you understood that.' He turned to Bette. 'I assume you've got a figure in mind. Adrienne will give you our solicitor's details. Talk to them and we'll take it from there.'

Bette held out a hand, ignoring Lucas' apoplectic expression. 'Thank you for your time, Lord Greville.'

'No,' he said. 'Thank *you* for your patience. I appreciate that you didn't have to come and see me at all. Now, if you'll excuse me, my son and I need to have a frank discussion.'

'We're going to let *him* buy the place?' Nina asked, later, as Bette explained how the meeting with Greville had transpired. 'After everything he did to try to steal it from us?'

Bette spread her hands. 'If I had a choice? No. But Nina, if I put together a reasonable package that includes what I think we would have got for damages had we taken this to court and projected earnings for tne orchard ... we could clear every debt the farm has, including the mortgage. This really could be the answer we've been looking for. And at the end of the day, will it really matter who the orchard goes to if it means we keep the farm? If it means you and Barney get to stay, without ever having to worry about being turfed out of your home again?'

Nina sighed. 'Well, when you put it like that . . .'

They were quiet for a moment or two. The old clock ticked in the hallway, still keeping time the way it had ever since they were children. This was the Crowdie home, and the orchard had never been a part of that, not for Bette and Nina.

'What about Ryan?' Nina asked.

Bette looked away. 'What about him?'

'He thinks he's got a buyer for the apple juice. Do you want me to call him and tell him to hold off?'

Bette looked at her hands, shut her eyes for a second. 'No,' she said, eventually. 'I need to talk to him anyway. Leave it to me.'

They met in the orchard. The picnic table had been taken away, but the lights were still on the fence and in the trees. They added to the other-worldliness of the place, softened the edges of what was really there.

'I know what Lucas did wasn't anything to do with you,' Bette said, as Ryan watched her from sombre eyes. 'Graham Greville confirmed it.'

He nodded. 'I'm sorry, Bette. For everything. Truly, I am.'

They were standing by the fence, looking out over the water. It was evening, and the last light of the day was folding itself into the water, disappearing into ridges of waves that rolled endlessly into the horizon.

'What you did, back then . . .'

He dipped his head, unhappy and ashamed. 'It was wrong. I know it.'

'You took that decision away from me,' she told him. 'You treated me like a child. That *was* wrong. But the reason, and what you said about us ultimately being incompatible? You were probably right about that.'

Ryan let out a long breath. 'Still.'

'Yeah,' she said. 'Still.' They were quiet for a moment, and then Bette said, 'Nina said you've found a buyer for the juice?'

'I have,' he said, and then told her a figure far higher than she was expecting. 'I can get the deal done for you this week, unless you need to include it in negotiations with Greville?'

Bette gave a grim smile. 'No. Lucas Greville can wait an extra year for a new harvest and make his own.'

'Fair enough.'

'Are people really willing to pay that kind of money for apple juice?'

'For this apple juice they are,' Ryan told her, as he glanced around the trees. 'This is a special place, Bette. These are beyond rare, and that batch we pressed – it's all that exists.'

Bette followed his gaze. 'Then I suppose it's a good thing that we've found a way to preserve the place.'

'I just wish it could have stayed with the Crowdies, that's all.'

Bette patted Ophelia's fence. She was growing cold and it was time to move on. 'Well, I learned a long time ago that we don't always get to keep everything we want,' she said. 'But I also learned how to make people pay for what they want to take. Speaking of which, I need you to help me with a valuation for this place.'

Chapter Forty-six

Bette went in asking for £500,000, and with wrangling settled at £450,000. The Greville lawyers tried to get it down to £400,000, but Bette had missed playing hardball. She was in the mood for a fight and was more than prepared to go to court. They folded pretty quickly after that, probably at the behest of Lord Greville. The Instagram page had not been updated for weeks, and although she monitored the Reddit forums she'd found with threads about the orchard, CiderExpert001 went silent, and she was surprised to note that there was very little discussion about either the poster's absence or the orchard. She wondered whether the internet really did have that short a memory, or if Lucas would pop up again at some point with a sob story about being robbed. She doubted he'd use the word 'trust fund'. 'Inheritance' would be far more palatable. Either way, she wouldn't let him get away with twisting the narrative further. She set up alerts to monitor terms such as 'The Secret Orchard' so that she could be on top of anything that might arise in the future, although in a few months that little patch of land really would be Lucas's anyway. She could see him being smart enough to take this as a win. Because he'd got what he wanted, hadn't he? He'd had to pay for it instead of getting it for free, but no one outside of the players directly involved on the ground had to know that. None of his followers had to know anything more than that his campaign had worked, and that could only be a marketing win when he was ready to launch. As long as he never tried to paint the Crowdies as villains, she'd leave him alone. It was galling, as Nina had said, that the only consequence Lucas was having to face was a hit to his own private pot of gold. But on the other hand, the Crowdie farm was safe as a result, and that was all that mattered.

'I can't believe it,' Nina said, tearfully, on the day that Bette told her the figure was finally agreed, the deal done and the paperwork being drawn up. 'That's really it? We're really free and clear?'

'We will be. We'll pay off the mortgage first, obviously. Clear any and all outstanding debts. The rest can go into whatever improvements you need.'

Her sister hugged her hard and began to sob, months of built-up anxiety bubbling out in a sudden, shuddering tidal wave. Bette held on to her through the overwhelm, until Barney arrived at their side, he and Limpet looking up at them with equally anxious eyes.

'Mummy? What's wrong?'

381

'Oh!' Nina pulled out of Bette's arms, wiping her eyes furiously with both hands as she bent to haul the little boy into her arms. 'Nothing, bub. Nothing. It's good, I promise.'

'We do have to tell you something though, Best Barnaby Barnacle,' Bette said, glancing at Nina with a faint smile. 'It's about the orchard.'

Her sister nodded, her cheek on her son's head. The paper-work had been finalized, the signing date was just two days away. Nina had put off telling the little boy the news, but as soon as the deal was signed, the orchard and its track would no longer belong to them. It seemed appropriate that Barney was given enough time to say goodbye to the hideaway he'd adopted as his own.

He took it far better than either Bette or Nina had expected, his face solemn as he listened to what was happening with the orchard.

'We're going to have to change the map,' was the first thing he said. 'It shouldn't be on there anymore, if it isn't ours.'

'I think it's fine to leave it as it is,' Bette told her nephew. 'After all, you did look after it for a while, didn't you? We can just add a note to say that first it was taken care of by Brother Alphonse, then by Great-great-grandpa George, then by Best Barnaby Barnacle, and now it's someone else's job. That would be better than taking it off the map completely.'

Her nephew nodded, his face downcast. 'I like it down there,' he said, sadly. 'And now I won't be able to go and visit Allie, or Ryan, or help look after the trees. And we won't be able to have any more picnics and Cam really wanted to do that.'

'I'm sorry, bub,' Nina told him, gently. 'But the orchard saved us, you know. Without it we might have had to move out of the farm, and now we don't. It was a superhero just like you, in the end.'

He seemed to like that idea.

'And you know,' Nina added tentatively, 'now that you're handing over the care of the orchard to someone else, you don't need to keep a lookout anymore, do you? You don't have to sleep in the attic.'

Bette watched her nephew consider this carefully, a frown on his face. 'I have to keep staying up there for now,' he said. 'Until I know it's safe with its new owner. It's still my responsibility until then.'

Nina smiled, but Bette was pretty sure her sister was suppressing a sigh. 'Okay, bub,' she said. 'That sounds fair. Another week or so then, yes?'

Bette nodded at Nina's look. 'Everything will be signed and sealed by then.'

'All right,' Barney said. 'But I'm going to look after it extra carefully until then.'

With the farm's future secure, Bette's thoughts turned to her own. She'd let her flat for six months, a short-term lease that had gone to a banker from Switzerland working in the City for a fixed term. She thought back to the night Ryan had told her the truth about their past, what had driven him to do what he'd done. He was right: when she'd been younger she'd had a plan, and part of it was to make partner before she was forty and then move to New York. She'd missed out on the partnership by the skin of her teeth, but perhaps the notion of moving abroad wasn't such a bad one. Bette had plenty of contacts from her years in London. A fresh start on the other side of the planet would be the ideal explanation for her months away: she'd been dealing with her family's estate in preparation for the permanent move. Bette began to discreetly put out feelers, testing the waters. After all, most of her worldly goods had already been packed into storage. She was living out of a suitcase anyway. Now was the perfect time to make such a move.

Chapter Forty-seven

'Auntie Bette, can you help me with my homework, please?'

She looked up from her laptop. It was after dinner on a Wednesday night. Nina was out with the vet, tending to a sick cow, and Barney had been left in her care.

'Of course I can,' she said. 'Do you want to do it here, or in the living room?'

'It's warmer in the living room,' he pointed out.

'True. Come on, then.' She followed him out into the hall, but as they crossed it there came a hard knock at the door. She told Barney to go and get started while she went to see who it was: Lucas Greville, standing on the doorstep in the dark.

'What are you doing here?' Bette asked.

'You think you're going to take my money,' Lucas said, his young face a mask of angry outrage, 'but there's no way. *No way.*'

'You need to leave, right now,' Bette said, 'or I'm calling the police. I doubt your father would be happy about that, would he? You can't bully me, Lucas. You got what you wanted. You can have your amazing cidery, exactly as you planned.'

'It won't really be mine,' Lucas said, through gritted teeth. 'Even though you've taken half my trust fund. Everything I do has to be signed off by my father. Like I'm a *child*.'

'If you want to be treated like an adult then I suggest you start acting like one,' Bette said. 'Take this as a learning moment, Lucas. You've got the orchard. Now you get to work to make it a success. And in the future, if you want something, go about getting it the right way.'

Lucas was red-faced now, fists clenched. Bette felt no threat from him. He was a little boy having a tantrum. Though she'd never seen her nephew behave as badly as this.

'I'm not signing that deal,' Lucas said. 'I'm not paying for something that should be mine anyway. You're getting nothing from me. I don't want it.'

Bette spread her hands. 'It's a bit late for that.'

'Yeah? We'll see.'

He stalked away into the darkness. She heard the slam of his car door and saw the tail lights receding down the road. She waited until they turned the corner and disappeared before shutting the door. Bette turned to find Barney standing in the living room doorway, looking worried.

'Who was that?' her nephew asked.

'No one,' Bette said. 'Nothing to worry about, I promise. Come on, let's get your homework done. It's nearly time for bed.'

As they settled once more in front of the fire, though, Bette thought about what Lucas had said. Would Graham Greville go back to the drawing board to renegotiate the settlement this late in the day, or even dump it entirely if his son managed to convince him? Maybe. He certainly could from a legal standpoint – it wasn't signed yet, after all. She looked at her watch with a silent sigh. It was too late to do anything about it now, but tomorrow morning she'd have to make sure she was prepared for such a move.

Chapter Forty-eight

Nina was exhausted by the time she'd finished with the vet and the sick heifer. When she eventually got back to the farmhouse, it was almost ten o'clock. Bette had put Barney to bed, Nina calling him from the cowshed to say goodnight. She went up as soon as she came in and stood at the bottom of the attic ladder. Limpet was in his usual place at the edge of the hatch, and pricked up his ears when he saw Nina below him. Nina listened for a moment, but Barney was obviously fast asleep.

'Good dog,' she whispered to Limpet, and then went back downstairs to the kitchen.

'Do you want a glass of wine and a bowl of soup?' Bette asked her. 'Or are you more in favour of a shower and bed?'

'I can't go to bed. I'll have to check on the cow again in a few hours. And actually, Cam's made me some food over at his place,' she said, as her phone pinged with an incoming text. She looked at the message and smiled. 'Speak of the devil. He's asking if he should run me a bath.'

She looked up at Bette to see her sister smiling at her over her wine glass. 'You two seem to have hit the ground running.'

Nina made a face, a little embarrassed. 'Not really. I mean we haven't— well, we haven't. But we've been friends for years now, so it's not like we need to get to know each other, is it? I guess things are moving more quickly as a result.'

Bette held up a hand. 'Hey, I'm not knocking it,' she said. 'I think it's great.'

'Really?'

'Yes, really. Cam's a good guy, and perfect for you. I mean, how many men would want a woman coming over straight after dealing with a stinky cow and not even expect her to shower first?'

Nina laughed. 'I suppose there is that.'

'Go on then,' Bette said. 'You'd better get over there. Don't want that bathwater getting cold.'

'Are you sure?'

'Of course I'm sure. Barney's fast asleep. And,' Bette added, 'you'd best make the most of it. I'll not be here to babysit for much longer.'

Nina thought about what it would be like when Bette moved out again. It was strange, given how adamant she'd been that she hadn't wanted her older sister to stay there in the first place, that the thought wasn't a happy one.

'Have you got any idea of where you're going to go?'

Bette tipped her head on one side, her hair falling into her eyes. It had grown longer since she'd been living back at Crowdie, and as Bette pushed it back Nina realized that she'd stopped straightening it, too. 'Well, I've put feelers out in New York. But today I contacted an old client of mine. He's not my ideal employer, but before I left London he mentioned he might have something for me. Turns out he needs someone in his Sydney office.'

'Sydney?' Nina said, shocked. 'Australia?'

'Yes.'

'That's such a long way away.'

Bette smiled. 'You could bring Barney to visit. Soak up some of that southern hemisphere sunshine.'

Nina wondered how Bette thought she could leave the farm for the time it would take for such a trip, but didn't voice the thought. 'Maybe.'

'Go on,' Bette told her. 'Get over to Bronagh. Cam's waiting. Barney and I will be fine.'

'I can't help thinking she's running away again,' Nina told Cam, a little later. She was sitting with him at his kitchen table with a glass of wine, feeling revived after a soak in a deliciously hot bath and some expertly made cheese on toast. 'It's because of this thing with Ryan – I honestly think that experience shaped her whole life, and now she's found out that it wasn't at all as she'd thought and she's having the same reaction – except this time she's running all the way to the other side of the world.'

Cam touched her hand lightly. 'Your sister's got her head screwed on pretty tightly,' he said. 'Whatever she decides to do, I'm sure she'll be fine.'

'But Australia is so far away,' Nina said, repeating what she'd said to Bette earlier. 'I never thought I'd say it, but I'd *miss* her, Cam. Barney would, too.'

Cam shuffled his chair closer and kissed her on the forehead. 'I know you would. But look on the bright side – it'd be a great excuse to visit.'

'That's what she said. But how could I leave the farm?'

'Ah, well,' he said, wrapping an arm around her and tugging her closer. 'That's where I come in. Because let's not forget – you'll still have *me*.'

Nina rested her head against his chest, hearing his heart beat. She sighed. 'I'd just like to see her happy. All this time I thought she was living her life to the max and loving it. But now ... now I'm not sure she ever has, really.'

'She'll find her way,' Cam said. 'Look how she managed to sort out Lucas, the orchard and the mess Bern left behind, all in one go.'

'I know,' Nina agreed, pulling back to pick up her wine glass. She was so tired that it had gone straight to her head. If she leaned against Cam much longer she'd probably fall asleep right there on her chair. 'By this time next week we should be free and clear. It feels as if things might be okay after all. For a long time I wasn't sure they would be.'

'How's Barney dealing with the loss of the orchard?' Cam asked.

'He's upset about it, but he'll be all right. He's a good boy. All he really wants is to make sure Brother Alphonse's trees survive and are looked after.'

Cam looked thoughtful. 'Maybe there's a way he can still feel as if he's doing that, even once the Grevilles have got their hands on it.'

Nina snorted. 'I doubt Lucas Greville will have any patience for a six-year-old kid hanging about.'

'No, but . . . maybe you don't have to give up *all* the trees. Why don't we graft a few buds onto some rootstock and plant one here? I'll give him a corner to set it in. That way Barney can check on it anytime he likes, and he'll know that whatever happens, Brother Alphonse's trees will live on. There's no need for Lucas Greville to ever know about it.'

Nina watched him, moved by Cam's thoughtfulness. 'That's a lovely idea. Thank you.' A sudden yawn overtook her and she put a hand over her mouth. 'Oh God. Sorry. It's been a long day.'

'Why don't you lie down for a bit?' Cam asked.

Nina looked at her watch. 'I can't. I need to go and check on this cow. Thank you for pampering me. You'd better be careful or I'll get used to it.'

Cam pulled her to him and kissed her. 'That would not be a problem.'

Nina groaned. 'You're not making it easy for me to leave.'

'It's okay. You can always come back. I'll leave the door open. Or shall I come with you?'

'Nope,' Nina said, finally pulling away and forcing herself out of her chair. 'You've had just as long a day as I have. Get to bed.'

'Yes, ma'am.'

Nina was shoving on her boots by the back door when she stopped. 'Do you hear that?'

Cam paused in the process of collecting up their dinner plates. 'What?'

She listened again. The kitchen clock ticked its regular rhythm, the fridge buzzed its low electrical hum, and—

'Is the radio on? Or a TV somewhere?'

Cam frowned. 'I don't think so . . .'

Nina opened the door, expecting to see rain that would explain the low, burbling roar. But the night was dry and clear, stars out overhead. She stepped out into the farmyard and heard a strange semi-distant bellow – animal, not human. It came again, followed by a frantic thumping and pounding, more animal bellows echoing into the night.

'Cam, something's wrong. I think it's the horses . . .'

She stepped out into the farmyard and the roar grew louder. Nina turned towards a light she didn't recognize and screamed as she saw the ragged, orange-yellow flicker of flames.

Chapter Forty-nine

The sound jolted Bette from an unsettled sleep and for a moment she couldn't work out what the noise was. Turning over, she saw her mobile, ring silenced but still skittering slightly on the bedside table as it vibrated with an incoming call. She reached for it and saw Nina's name and the time – well after midnight.

'Nina?' Her voice was bleary in the darkness.

'Bette? Bette!' Her sister was shouting, frantic. There was something going on in the background. *'Are you there?'*

'Nina?' Bette was suddenly wide awake. 'What's wrong?'

'There's a fire,' Nina said, voice a shouted sob. *'Cam's barns. We've got the horses out, but—'* There was a muffled shout from off, then the sound of crackling as her sister's hand covered her phone's mic.

'Nina?' Bette scrambled to pull her clothes on. 'Nina!'

'I'm here,' she said, breathless but a little clearer. *'It's bad, Bette, really bad.'*

'I'm coming,' Bette said, juggling the phone from one ear to the other as she dragged on her shirt.

'*No!*' Nina said. '*I just want to know that Barney's okay.*'

'He's fine – he's upstairs, fast asleep in the attic.'

'*Can you check?*' her sister said, her voice rising again. Bette realized that the rush of sound in the background must be flames.

'He's fine, I promise,' Bette said. 'I'd have heard Limpet jumping down the ladder if he'd come down.'

'*Just make sure he's okay,*' Nina said. '*I don't want him to be scared.*'

'I am, right now,' Bette said, already making for the door. 'Don't worry.'

There was a commotion down the line, another shout.

'*I've got to go.*'

'Be careful,' Bette begged her sister. 'Nina—'

But Nina had gone. Bette ran to the bedroom window. It looked out over the front of the house and as she squinted in the direction of the Bronagh farm she could see an uncanny orange glow in the darkness above the treeline that separated the two properties. How long would it take for the fire brigade to arrive?

She went out into the hallway. The house was silent, dark. The stepladder up to the attic stood in the corner beside the bathroom, undisturbed since her nephew and his faithful hound had climbed it to bed earlier. Bette had checked on him as she'd gone to bed herself, silently negotiating the rungs with bare feet to stick her head up through the hatch.

He'd dragged the old camp bed right beneath one of the windows that faced the rear of the house and the cliff, but had been fast asleep, the moonlight washing his small face in silver. She'd watched Barney's chest rise and fall for a moment, before reaching out to pet Limpet, curled in his familiar position beside the hatch. The collie thumped his tail twice, before settling back down. Bette was convinced this was how she would find them both now as she climbed back up the ladder. The window Barney had chosen to sleep beneath looked out to the east, over their farmyard, not northwest, which is the direction he'd need to be looking to see the fire. Even if he'd woken and happened to look out of the window, he would have seen nothing. She was sure that in any case, Barney would have woken her if he'd seen something that worried him and had realized his mum wasn't in her room. He knew where his aunt was and that he could come to her for anything he needed.

Bette made her way up the ladder's narrow rungs as quietly as possible, thinking that the best thing to do was hope that her nephew would sleep right through until morning and whatever aftermath it brought.

The first thing she saw as she looked through the hatch was that Limpet wasn't where she'd expected him to be. He'd moved from his guard post to sit beside the camp bed, alert, ears pricked. He yipped a little and then gave a short whine as she appeared.

'Ssh,' Bette whispered. 'Good boy. Come here.'

Limpet immediately came to her and as the dog moved

Bette's heart gave a strange double-beat of fear. The sleeping bag was pushed back and empty, the pillow askew. Barnaby was not in the bed.

'Barney?' she climbed fully up into the dark attic, reaching for the light and pulling the cord so that the bare bulb shone, making her blink in the sudden brightness. 'Where are you?'

Limpet sat at her feet and whined again.

'Where is he? Where's that Best Barnaby Barnacle?' she asked the dog, thinking her nephew must be hiding, probably because she hadn't used his 'proper name'. Maybe he'd slipped under the camp bed when he'd heard her climb the ladder into the attic. *The dog's here, though. He never goes anywhere without Limpet. He's here somewhere.* 'Where is he, Limpet?'

The dog pricked up his ears and went to the window, jumping onto the camp bed and looking out into the night. Bette followed, bracing her hands against the sloping walls as she ducked her head to look out, heart jumping again because she expected to see her nephew sitting on the roof tiles, staring at the stars, just as she'd stupidly told him she used to do herself.

No sign of him.

Bette looked down at the dog. Limpet whined again, gaze fixed on whatever he could see out of the window that she couldn't. She fumbled for the light cord again, plunging the attic back into darkness. She looked out of the window again and this time what she saw made her heart plummet into her toes.

There was a glow on the horizon, sickly orange and flickering. For a second she thought it must be some kind of reflection of the flames burning at Cam's farm, but how? Surely it was too far away for that? The glow was coming from the direction of the cliff. There must be another fire.

Bette drew in a sharp breath. The *orchard!*

She gave an unintelligible shout and pulled her phone from her pocket, scrambling to call for help. Then a terrible dread washed over her. Where was Barney's superhero costume? He'd finally agreed not to sleep in it, but he always kept it by the bed, just in case—

'Oh, *God!*'

Bette made for the hatch, trying to work her phone at the same time.

'Limpet! Here boy,' she shouted, and the collie scrambled past her before she'd even reached the top rung, bumping against her in his eagerness to get down. Bette almost fell straight down the ladder, letting go of her phone to catch herself. It fell, smacking hard onto the landing below, then bouncing straight through the bannisters. She heard it smash as it finally crashed to a stop at the bottom of the stairs.

Limpet had already reached the back door, barking frantically as she rushed to catch up. She snatched up her phone but it was clearly damaged beyond use. Bette threw it down and ran on, grabbing up the cordless house phone from the hallway and running with it into the kitchen, dialling as she stuck her feet into the first pair of boots she came to. When the operator answered she tried to tell them what was happening, but all she managed to get out was *Crowdie Farm, Arbroath*, and *Orchard, there's a fire in the orchard* because it was taking too long, too long. She dropped the handset and yanked open the door, the operator still trying to get her attention. Limpet plunged out into the darkness, barking, heading for the barn and disappearing into the thick darkness beyond, heading straight for the orchard because he, like Bette, knew exactly where his beloved owner had gone.

She ran after him, panicked and unsure, because she didn't have a phone and should she have stayed on the line? Should she have called Nina? Except she couldn't because she didn't have her sister's number memorized, it was just a contact in a phone that was totally dead, and besides there was *no time*.

The boots were too big – *her father's?* – and she had to fight to keep her footing on the uneven ruts of the track, struggling to see where she was going in the dark. She took two lunging steps and screamed as her ankle turned, going down hard on her knees. Limpet was barely even a shape in the darkness ahead of her as he raced for the orchard fence. Bette struggled up. She could hear the flames now, crackling, roaring. The dog careened away through the gorse and down the path, vanishing into a belch of smoke as Bette stumbled on in his wake.

'Barney!' she shouted, coughing as the first wreaths of smoke twisted around her in the scarred night. '*Barnaby!*'

She reached the boulder at the bottom of the slope and shock brought her to a standstill. The fire was eating its way through the dry old trees with stunning speed. Bette watched as one ignited in a burst of flame that engulfed it in an instant. It went up like a burning torch, branches crackling as red-hot embers plumed into the air.

Bette heard Limpet barking and fought her way onward, eyes stinging, almost blind.

'*Barney!*'

She saw him through the smoke, a tiny figure all in black. He was trying to haul a bucket of water from the tank towards one of the burning trees. Limpet had given up barking and had grabbed the tail of the boy's cape instead, trying to drag him back towards Bette and the path out of the orchard. Bette reached them in two struggling steps, tripping as her ankle turned again in the loose boots. She crashed to her knees beside her nephew, grabbing him by both arms as water sloshed over the side of the bucket.

'What are you doing?' she screamed over the roaring fury of the flames, trying to prise his fingers from the bucket's handle. 'We've got to *go*!'

'No!' He was sobbing real tears, rasping breaths sucking in smoke, 'We've got to save the trees, Auntie Bette, look at the trees, they're burning—'

He tried to struggle away from her, but she yanked him closer, forcing him to drop the bucket. Bette wrapped both arms around him and lifted him, but as she tried to get to her feet her ankle gave way. She muffled a scream, stumbling as she turned for the path, still trying to hold on to her nephew. Limpet was barking, barking, barking – at them, at the fire, at the smoke. It had worsened even in the brief minutes since she'd arrived and Bette saw with a consuming horror that the flames were in danger of cutting them off. If they didn't get up the path before the flames reached it, they'd be trapped with no way to get out.

Bette set Barney down and knelt, grabbing him by the shoulders.

'Run,' she begged him, giving him a little push towards the path. *'Limpet!'*

The dog knew exactly what to do. Before Barney had even had a chance to find his footing, the collie had the black cape in his teeth and had got behind the boy, pushing him forward with his black-and-white head at his back, forcing him into a run with no time to pause or think.

Barney tried to twist around to see where she was. 'Auntie Bette!'

Bette began to stumble after them but knew there was no way she would make it. Neither would they if she didn't do something. She turned back instead, snatched up the bucket of water, lurched two painful steps to douse the flames licking too close to the fleeing boy.

'GO!' she screamed, 'Don't stop!'

The smoke was blinding now, acrid, and it brought with it an unbearable heat. She saw the dog and his boy on the slope, glimpsed them climbing higher, her nephew now running of his own accord.

'Keep going!' she screamed, though they probably couldn't even hear her over the conflagration. 'Don't stop! Keep running until you get home!'

A gorse bush went up, igniting her only way out. *Let them get away*, she prayed in silent horror. *Please just let them get away.*

She was trapped, cut off inside the burning orchard, her circle of safety growing smaller with every second. She searched for a way out, but there was none. She couldn't even climb over the fence and leap down the cliff. Everything was ablaze now, everything. But no – that wasn't quite true. Through the smoke her gaze fell on one of the new trees they had planted just days ago, the fresh rootstock with Ryan's grafted buds. The sapling was backlit by the blaze, haloed in a hell of flames, but it hadn't yet caught fire. Bette's fear turned to rage. Because this was deliberate, wasn't it? It had to be – two fires so close together, in one night? Someone had wanted to destroy this place, to raze every trace of this ancient orchard, because nothing would be left after this fire. Without the growth of the old trees it would be lost, finally and forever. There would be no way to propagate any more salt apples once the last of these trees went up in flames.

Bette lurched forward, wrapping both hands around the sapling's thin trunk and yanking it from the ground with the full force of her fury. She couldn't make it down the cliff, but maybe the tree would. Maybe someone would see it once this had all burned out, or if not maybe it would still find a way to live on, to bury its roots in the sparse rivulets of earth in the cliff and thrive despite the odds. Five hundred years, this place had survived. It couldn't die now.

She turned back towards Ophelia's fence. As she did so Bette caught sight of something that for a moment she couldn't understand. It looked like a black bedsheet, caught against one of the curlicues of wrought iron. Then she realized that it was the tarp that Allie had secured over the hole she had excavated in Brother Alphonse's ancient walled-up door. The raging heat of the fire must have flapped it loose.

Bette looked back at the fire. Would it find its way into that passageway carved into the cliff? How far back did it go? Far enough to keep her out of the flames? Would the ceiling hold? What chance was there of a cave-in?

What choice did she have but to find out?

Bette started hobbling towards the cliff, coughing and choking in the smoke. By the time she made it to the rock-face she could barely see, counting off the bee boles as she felt the wrath of the fire moving ever closer. She could hardly put weight on her ankle, the pain was so great.

When she reached the walled-up door she pushed the sapling through the gap first. Hauling herself through was far harder. By the time Bette had dragged herself through the hole, her hands were raw. She dropped through the gap, collapsing in a heap on the rough rock floor beyond. She forced herself up. She couldn't stop. The fire outside roared closer by the second. Bette felt her way forward into pitch black.

Chapter Fifty

Nina wiped a shaking hand over her face. It came away covered in soot and sweat. She tried to make out the time on her watch, her eyes so dry she could barely blink. She thought it was after 1.30am. She looked across to the firefighters. Half of them were still trying to damp down the conflagration, the others were training their hoses on the outbuildings that connected the barns to the main farmhouse in an attempt to stop the fire from spreading. The damage was already bad enough. Cam's horse barn had gone, the milking parlour was in flames. He'd lost one John Deere, the skeleton of the tractor still lit up like a horrifying carnival hulk in the shadows of the billowing smoke.

They'd saved the two horses and the donkey, at least, though the poor things were traumatized. Nina hadn't even tried to get a harness on the grey, just opened the gate and let her run, the other two following in her wake. They'd be in one of the pastures on the cliff. Safer there than in the smoke and havoc. The cows had been trickier, dangerous in their fear, especially with most of them with their calves still at heel. They'd been in the field that abutted the milking barn and moving them, with the heifers all pressed up close against the furthest fence, would have taken both Cam and Nina away from the battle to stop the fire. They'd had to wait until the fire engines arrived – two of them, roaring up the gravel road with their sirens blasting, adding to the general terror. Nina couldn't imagine that her son had slept through it all, hoping instead that Bette had the good sense to keep him away from the windows, preferably in the kitchen with the distractions of a superhero film, a blanket and hot chocolate.

Now that she'd stopped for a second, her limbs felt like lead. Nina stood in the wick and flicker of the fire, exhausted, spent, not knowing what to do now that someone else was in charge. As soon as the fire brigade had arrived they'd been told to stand back, let the professionals do their jobs, but how could anyone do that? Cam was still hovering close, ready to dart in and help. She wondered if she should go into the house despite what they'd been told, start grabbing whatever of his she could. The flames didn't seem to be diminishing.

Nina saw him turn and look for her, perhaps as if he'd read her mind. He came towards her, haggard beyond belief, and then he looked past her for a moment, his footsteps faltering.

She heard the screaming cry as she turned, and there was her son, her Barnaby, her baby, running towards her with his daft-as-all-hell collie dog at his side, all dressed in black.

For a second she couldn't fathom his presence, and then she was running at him, too, with Cam behind her.

'Mummy,' Barnaby was crying, sobbing, sucking in breath as if he'd run a marathon. 'Mummy, Mummy!'

'What are you doing here?' Nina gasped, when she reached him. She pulled him up into her arms and found herself clutching a child who reeked of smoke. She lent away far enough to pull off his mask and beneath his face was sweaty and red apart from the caked black charcoal stains around his mouth, nose and his red, streaming eyes.

Cam reached her side and placed one large hand on the boy's head. 'What happened? *Paramedic!* Over here!'

Barney was sobbing so hard he could barely speak. Nina tried to turn towards the ambulance that was parked at the farmyard gate and found Limpet bumping into her, his jaws still clamped around a mouthful of the boy's cape as if he was determined to never let go. As the paramedics ran towards them, she looked fearfully back towards Crowdie farmhouse, as if somehow that would also be alight, but there was no sign of fire from above the treeline. And then her son said:

'It's the o-o-orchard. I saw a burglar and I followed and it's on fire and Auntie Bette—'

His words were lost under the wail of another fire engine screaming to a stop at the farmyard gate. Cam ran towards it as the two paramedics took charge of Barnaby.

'Mummy!' the boy said, still crying.

'I'm here,' she said. 'Don't worry, baby, I'm here.'

'No,' Barnaby said, shaking his head violently, trying to

struggle away from the medics. 'You've got to save Auntie Bette!'

She looked at the paramedics, hesitating. How could she leave her son with strangers at this moment, however capable they were?

'Please, Mummy,' Barnaby said, with a desperation too bright for his few years. 'Take Limpet with you – he saved me, he can save her too! You *have* to help Auntie Bette!'

Nina looked over to where Cam was directing the engine. She kissed her son, and she ran, with Limpet at her heels. It was dark, but once she'd put one fire behind her Nina could clearly see where the second was burning against the night sky. She crossed the ragged boundary between the two farms and turned onto the track that separated the pastures. The fire engine followed and the artificial blue glare from its headlights threw her into shadow, stretching her into a weird, spindly form across the pocked dust ahead. It bumped and growled behind her as she curved with the track, running, running. When she reached the pasture she swung open the gate, heading straight for the fence.

She was only halfway to the dip when Limpet stopped. Nina went two more steps and then realized why – the entire path was alight. The crackle of the fire was immense. It had consumed the gorse bushes, lighting them up like tinder torches. There was no way into the orchard. There was no way out, either.

'Bette,' she screamed. 'Bette, Bette, *Bette*!'

Behind her the fire engine had ground to a halt again,

doors slamming, shouts and instructions being issued. In seconds they had unwound a hose and water was slamming towards the burning brush. Nina was numb. What could she do? There was nothing she could *do*. She felt someone appear at her side – Cam. She made her way along the cliff edge, Limpet still with her as she tried to find a place where the bushes were less dense.

'Nina—' Cam tried to pull her to a stop, but Nina kept going.

She found herself back at the broken fence that divided the Crowdie farm from the Bronagh land. Nina wove through it, then tried to come at the orchard from a different angle. Back in her own pasture, one group of firemen angled the jet of water from their hose straight over the cliff edge and onto the flames while the others battled their way down the path.

'Nina,' Cam shouted. 'Wait! You can't get too close.'

'I have to see,' she shouted.

She picked a spot where the scrub at the cliff edge seemed less dense and pushed into it. The smoke blurred everything, clogged her eyes, her nose, grimed against her skin along with a blunt heat that seemed all-pervading now, every-where. Somewhere behind her Limpet had started barking, adding to the disastrous, discordant cacophony of the night. Nina cleared the last bush and almost plunged straight over the edge and down into the burning orchard. Cam grabbed her shoulder to pull her back, anchored her against him. Limpet barked on and on as they stared at the horror below, a sea of burning trees obscured by billowing black smoke and hot steam as the jets of water from the fire hoses joined the fray.

'There's nothing we can do,' Cam said, pulling her back. 'I'm sorry, Nina. This isn't safe. Come on.'

She let him lead her back away from the cliff edge. The whole night seemed unreal, a fever dream. *Mum. How am I going to tell Mum? And Barney, how do I—* Limpet was still barking, terrified or perhaps only desperate to get back to Barney, which was where she should be too. Cam was right, there was nothing she could do here. Her son would need her, and Limpet. Nina looked around for the collie but couldn't see him. Still his bark echoed into the fractured night.

'Limpet,' she shouted, throat dry, voice cracked. 'Here, boy!'

The dog kept barking, but didn't appear.

'Limpet!' Cam tried. 'Come!'

The barking went on and on and Nina was suddenly afraid that Limpet had followed her too close to the edge, had fallen down into the burning orchard. But the barking wasn't pained – it was frantic in a different way, urgent, determined. She tried to locate it, to pinpoint its direction, and realized it wasn't coming from the cliff edge, but further inland, across the field.

She followed the sound, stumbling on the uneven ground of Cam's disused clifftop pasture. Everything was suddenly thrown into stark relief: Cam had flicked on his torch, light pouring across the hillocky grass. There ahead of them was the dog, standing in a shallow dip beside a collection of rocks, barking as he pawed at the ground.

'Limpet!'

The collie kept digging. She went to grab his collar, sliding down the slight incline towards him, then lost her footing and fell forward, her knees crashing into metal that rang with an echoing clang. Nina scrambled backwards as Cam reached her. The soil where she'd fallen had given way, falling into a rusted grille lodged in the ground.

Limpet stopped barking and in the relative silence echoed a new sound: a distant voice, shouting from beneath the soil, hoarse with spent effort.

'*Help!* Is anyone there? Limpet, go get help. Go get *help*, Limpet!'

'Bette?' Nina screamed, into the hole. '*Bette?*'

'I'm here!' her sister shouted. 'Nina! I'm here, I'm *here*!'

With her hands Nina began to scrape away the soil, trying to rip out handfuls of the grass that had grown over and through the hatch on which she knelt.

'Cam, go and get help,' she shouted. 'We need shovels, we need people to dig.'

'Wait,' Cam said. 'Nina – wait, we don't want to risk a cave-in.' He knelt beside her, leaning down to shine his torchlight into the hole. It was narrow, mainly earth with a small gap, through which they had heard Bette's voice. 'Bette? Where are you?'

'In a passageway. There are steps, but they're partially buried – soil, I think. I can't climb anymore.'

'You've got decent air?'

'Yes. It's stuffy, but yes.'

'Are you hurt?'

'My ankle, that's all. Get me out of here, *please*. I haven't got a light, I can't *see*—'

'We're coming,' Nina promised. 'We'll get you out, Bette. We will.'

Chapter Fifty-one

It felt like hours before they'd managed to dig out the passage entrance, but later Nina told her it was less than thirty minutes. Funny how time passes so slowly in darkness. The fire in the orchard was still smouldering as Bette crawled her way over the last of the earth that had tumbled down Brother Alphonse's lost steps. In the end she'd been shovelling soil with her hands. Nina had been the first person she'd seen when she'd made her way out, her younger sister grabbing her in a bear hug as if she'd never let go, despite how filthy Bette was by that point. When Nina did release her, it was Bette's turn – she hugged Limpet, his tail wagging furiously, long tongue lolling out of a wide doggy grin.

'You,' she told him, still breathless, 'are a certifiably good boy.'

Bette had been convinced that the fire would follow her into the passageway – she'd been able to hear it roaring behind her, the sound echoing off the stone walls, multiplying in the confined space into a fiery fury she couldn't escape. Bette had crawled her way along the passageway and then come upon a step, then another, and another. She'd climbed them on hands and knees, the air around her old and mouldering but mercifully free of smoke. As she'd got higher she'd gradually become aware of a fresh eddy of air washing across her face from above. She followed it until her knees hit earth instead of stone and the passageway had narrowed into a gap only wide enough for her voice to pass through. She shouted herself hoarse until finally, finally, she'd been answered by Limpet.

The paramedics insisted on taking both her and Barney to A&E. Nina went with them in the ambulance. Nina sat with Barney on her lap, arms wrapped around her son.

'Is it bad?' Bette asked, of the orchard.

Her sister looked at her over her son's head, tightened her grip on him. 'Could have been worse,' she said.

Bette couldn't argue with that.

Her ankle was badly sprained, but not broken. It was bandaged and the scrapes on her hands were treated, but Bette counted herself lucky to have escaped as she had. She gave a statement to the police, told them the history of Lucas's involvement with the orchard, of his recent threatening visit. It wasn't evidence, but it was suggestive. No, Bette couldn't think of anyone else who would want to cause this much damage, especially not to both farms. Presumably the burning of Cam's barn had been meant as a distraction, so that the fire services would be too busy to save the orchard until it was far too late. Bette still hadn't got a straight answer from anyone about whether that part of the plan had worked.

'I need to get Barney up to bed,' Nina said, when they finally got back to the farm. 'He's exhausted.'

'You should rest, too,' said Cam, who had been waiting for them when they'd got back to Crowdie. The fire at Bronagh was finally out. He looked grey with exhaustion, but there was still so much for him to do.

Nina kissed him. 'What about you?'

'I'll be fine,' he said. 'Ryan and Allie are both coming up to help with the animals. You just rest for a while.'

Bette went over to kiss her nephew goodnight. The little boy wound his arms around her neck, holding on tightly. 'I'm sorry, Auntie Bette,' he mumbled, into her ear. 'It's my fault you got hurt.'

'Hey,' Bette said, lifting him out of his mother's arms to hug him close. 'It's not. Okay? I just wish you had woken me up when you saw something, that's all.'

'I didn't see the fire, not to begin with,' he said. 'I just saw the burglar. Limpet heard him and woke me up so I saw him sneaking through the farmyard. I was just going to follow him and I didn't want Limpet to make a noise so I told him to stay where he was. But then I saw the fire.'

Bette looked over at Nina, who smiled grimly. 'He's told the police everything he saw. They've taken prints of footprints and tyres but they're not sure it'll do much good. There's so much traffic through the farmyard.'

'I wish I hadn't lost my phone,' Barnaby said. 'If I had it we would be able to see who it was.'

'Did you take photographs?' Bette asked. 'Of the burglar?'

The boy sniffed. 'Yes. But it was dark and I dropped it when I was trying to throw water on the fire. It'll be all burned up.'

Bette kissed her nephew on the forehead. 'It doesn't matter, Best Barnaby Barnacle. It's just a phone. You really were a superhero tonight. And now you need to go to bed.'

She tried to sleep, but couldn't. Bette lay in bed staring at the ceiling of the guest room instead, cycling through terrors both real and imagined. She could still hear the crackle of the flames, feel the heat of them eating their way towards her through the ancient orchard. Eventually she gave up on the idea of sleep and got up again.

Downstairs, she found Nina in the living room. Despite the morning light outside her sister had lit the fire and was huddled under a blanket on the sofa. There were huge dark rings under her eyes, her face pale as milk.

'I can't get warm and I can't sleep,' she said, when Bette came in. 'I'm lying here shivering, thinking about what would have happened if you hadn't found Barney when you did. And you, stuck down there—'

'Hey.' Bette went to the sofa and squeezed onto it, burrowing under the blanket beside her sister. 'Everything's okay. I think you're in shock and it's only coming out now. Maybe you should see a doctor?'

'I'm fine,' Nina murmured, watching the flames again. She shivered. 'I wasn't the one caught up in it all really, was I?'

Bette rubbed Nina's arm. 'Close enough. And that's probably worse. I was so full of adrenaline I'm not even sure I knew what I was doing.'

Nina shifted to rest her head on Bette's shoulder. 'You knew exactly what you were doing,' she said. 'You always do.'

They sat like that for a while, quiet, both of them watching the fire.

'What are we going to do?' Nina whispered. 'The orchard's gone. Hasn't it?'

Bette turned her head to press her lips into her sister's hair, thinking again about those flames. 'I think so, yeah.'

'Then we don't have anything to sell. How will we—'

'Don't think about that now.'

'But—' Nina's phone pinged with an incoming text. She flicked open the notification, sitting up as she read it.

'What is it?' Bette asked.

'It's Cam. The police have finished going through his CCTV footage and they've got images of a car passing back and forth on the main road several times before letting someone out at the bottom of the track. Then, about forty minutes later the same car comes back and picks up what looks like the same person again. They're trying to enhance the image enough to get a licence plate.'

'I didn't know Cam had CCTV.'

'He got it last year, after a bit of petty theft. I asked Dad if we could install it too but I guess we couldn't afford it. The cameras Cam's got only cover the farmyard, the house and that part of the road.'

'Well, it's something. And it sounds as if the arsonist had an accomplice. They can't see who it is that gets out?'

Nina examined the text again and then shook her head. 'Too dark, and he had a hood.'

Something about this niggled at Bette's tired mind. Was it the CCTV? She wondered if Lucas has known it was there. The figure had worn a hood, which suggested he might.

'How long does Cam keep his CCTV tapes for?' she asked. 'Lucas must have planned where to set the fire in his barn. He might have been caught on camera doing that at an earlier time.'

'There aren't any tapes,' Nina said. 'I was there when Cam gave them access – everything uploads to a cloud server, so the police could just log into it.'

The niggle grew more insistent. Bette got up and went out into the hallway. Her eye was drawn to that photograph again, the slightly shaky one of Nina, Barnaby and Bern in the farmyard. She took it from the wall and looked at it for a moment before taking it back in to show Nina.

'I keep meaning to ask about this photo,' she said. 'Who took it? Was it Cam?'

'No,' Nina said. 'That was Barney. Dad had only just given him his old phone. He was still learning how to use it and he wanted to test out the timer. Dad insisted that he print it out and put it up on the wall, even though it's a bit blurry.'

'How did he send it to the printer? Did Barney email it to Dad and get him to do it?'

'No, it was already connected to the cloud, so it uploaded

automatically. Dad just printed it from there. Why are you asking about this now?'

'Because,' Bette said, 'I'm guessing that Barney's phone was still connected to the cloud when he followed the "burglar" down to the orchard last night, wasn't it? And if it managed to back up before the fire got to it . . .'

Nina stood up, face flushed. 'Get the laptop!'

They trawled through the photographs together. The phone had uploaded, but most of the images were dark and blurred. They started in the attic, where Barney had obviously tried to take photographs of the figure he had seen through the window. Then there were some snapped as he'd tried to catch it up – shaky images taken at night. None were any use for what they needed, although there was a least a time-stamp that would match up with the images from Cam's CCTV.

'If nothing else, that's a clear link between the two crime scenes,' Bette pointed out, as she clicked onto the next image. 'And also indicates that whoever it is knew exactly where they were going. It can't hurt for the investigation to—'

She fell silent as the next photograph opened. Bette stared at it, her heart thumping.

'Bloody hell,' Nina said.

It was the figure again, snapped seconds after climbing over the fence that led to the orchard path. Barney had managed to snap a photograph at the exact moment that one of the encroaching bushes had caught on his hood, pulling it back. The moonlight was bright enough to illuminate the face beneath.

It was clearly Lucas Greville.

'Best Barnaby Barnacle,' Bette said, in disbelief. 'The Peter Parker of Arbroath. Crowdie's own little crime-fighting superhero.'

Nina laughed, and then clamped a hand over her mouth, tears in her eyes.

Chapter Fifty-two

Nina finally drifted off. Bette slipped out from beneath the blanket and tucked it around her sister, pausing to smooth a curl of Nina's long hair from across her face. Asleep, she looked so much like the little girl she had once been, and Bette's heart clenched slightly at the thought. She went out into the kitchen, pausing at the bottom of the stairs to listen out for her nephew, but the house was silent. In the kitchen, Bette poured water into the kettle for tea, but hesitated over flicking on the switch. Outside, the early winter sun was low and thin, gleaming against the wet concrete of the farmyard. It must have rained since they got back. She thought of the ruined orchard and had to see it for herself.

Her ankle was smarting even before she'd reached the polytunnel, the painkillers beginning to wear off. For a moment she contemplated turning back to retrieve her father's walking stick, but pushed on instead. Despite the downpour there was still the lingering stench of smoke on the breeze, which only grew stronger as she crossed the track and went into the clifftop pastures. Even from the meadow she could see the beginnings of the damage – not just the charred bushes at the cliff edge, but the way the fire engines had churned up great clods of turf, too, leaving deep ruts in the soft earth.

There was police tape across the fence, a blue-and-white warning that she should go no further. Bette leaned against the barrier, the throb in her ankle nothing compared to the one in her chest as she took in the destruction. Even the little she could see from where she stood was devastating. What was left of the gorse resembled spindly black fingers clutching at the damp air. The heather hung in charcoal tatters, the bracken and grasses razed to ragged stumps.

It was gone. Five hundred years it has stood, but now it was gone, and with it the last chance she'd had to keep Crowdie in her family.

'Bette?'

She didn't realize she was crying until she turned and saw Ryan striding towards her across the ruined pasture. When he was close enough he reached out and pulled her to him, wrapping his arms around her, his face against her neck.

'I'm so glad you're all right,' he said, his voice hoarse. 'When I heard what happened – what *nearly* happened . . . My God, Bette—' he hugged her tighter.

They stood like that for a long time, his grip on her not lessening, until she thought she might not be able to breathe. When Bette pulled away Ryan took her hand, as if he were worried she might disappear into the dissipating smoke if he let her go. Bette looked down at their joined hands, at their interlaced fingers, and thought about her little sister's sleeping face. If only she could turn back time, she thought, then. If only she could do things differently from the start.

'This is my fault,' she said.

Ryan's fingers flexed around hers. 'What? Of course it isn't.'

She turned to look at the destruction behind her. 'I couldn't do it,' she said. 'My dad only asked me for one thing. To save the farm. To keep it in the family. And I couldn't do it. I failed, Ryan, and now we're going to lose everything. It's *over*. This place won't ever be Barney's. And that matters, doesn't it? It *matters*.'

Ryan squeezed her hand. 'This wasn't your fault,' he said again. 'None of it.'

'Wasn't it? Are you sure about that?' she demanded. 'What if I had never gone away to university? What if I'd stayed here and helped with the farm, instead? If I hadn't been so selfish back then, maybe things wouldn't have got as bad as they did in the first place. What if—'

'You weren't selfish,' he said. 'You were young and you had things of your own you wanted to do. You can't think about what ifs, Bette.'

'Why not?' she said. 'Don't *you* ever think about it?'

He looked at her, his expression so eloquent that it turned her heart inside out. 'I did,' he said. 'Every day, for a very long time. "What if?" It's a phrase to mire yourself in and it does no one any good. All it does is stop you moving forward. And being stuck in the past is the only sure way to ruin your future.'

She sucked in a breath, the tears on her cheeks cold in the wind from the cliff.

'I should have stayed,' she said. 'I should have—'

'Bette.' He reached out and pulled her to him again, tucking her head beneath his chin. 'Don't. Even if you had, you don't know that anything would have been different.'

'*We* would have been different,' she said.

He was silent for a moment, and when he spoke his voice was sad, but resolute.

'You would have been staying for the wrong reasons. It would have caught up with us both eventually, one way or another.'

She let herself be still for a moment, breathing him in. Bette wanted to believe that what he had said was true, that she hadn't taken a wrong step back then. But how would she ever know? If she'd stayed, she would have had this. She would have had Ryan, a home, maybe a family, and who was to say that wouldn't have made her just as happy, just as fulfilled? Who was to say it wouldn't have lasted, that the Crowdie farm would never have reached this point of no return? She'd convinced herself that what she had left behind had never been real in the first place, but perhaps she'd been lying to herself. Perhaps what she'd left behind was the only real thing she'd ever had.

'Anyway,' Ryan said, 'there's no way Lucas Greville gets away with this, is there? There'll be a police investigation.

And Cam and Allie and I were talking about suing for damages in the civil courts, too. You're more than capable of making him pay for this.'

Bette thought of Lucas's face on that photograph. Ryan was right. There was no way she couldn't nail that boy for every penny he had for what he'd done. Bette knew that was what Nina would be counting on: her big sister, making everything right for her in a way she'd never done when she was a kid. But—

'It'll take too long,' Bette said. 'The criminal investigation will come first, and that could take months – years, even. The civil courts will want it out of the way before scheduling their own proceedings. That will be too late for us. The bank won't wait any longer. It was hard enough to get them to delay recalling the debt over these past months. My flat won't be enough to cover everything. The orchard sale was our last hope of holding on to the farm. And that's gone, Ryan. It's all gone.'

He stroked one thumb across her cheek. 'Not all of it,' he said. 'Not quite.'

'What are you talking about?'

Ryan looked down at her bandaged ankle. 'How far can you walk? I've got something to show you.'

She hadn't expected to find herself in the stone passageway again so soon. Bette hesitated beside the ancient iron grille that her rescuers had prised up to pull her out of the underground hideaway.

'We don't have to go down if you prefer not to,' Ryan said. 'But it's a way to see the orchard without breaking the police cordon. Allie and I went down there with Cam and it seems very safe. Allie thinks it's a natural tunnel in the rock that has been further carved out over the centuries. She thinks it means that the monastery was here,' he added, looking around at the windswept pasture, 'on Cam's land. The tunnel was a way to get straight into the orchard from inside the monastery walls.'

In the end, Bette's desire to see the damage for herself outweighed her reticence. Ryan handed her a small torch and then went ahead of her down the stone steps with his own. The smell of smoke became more pungent the lower they descended. By the time they reached the last step the stench of charred wood was overwhelming, but there was no sign that the flames had breached the walled-up doorway. Morning light filtered through the ragged gap that Bette had dragged herself through just hours before. Ryan stepped up to the hole and looked out before turning to her.

'Have a look,' he said, and shifted so that she could stand in front of him.

There was still smoke drifting through the carcasses of the desiccated trees. Some had gone completely, nothing left of them but burned stumps. Others were still standing but were clearly scorched, most of their branches reduced to cinders. The earth beneath was black, coated with a layer of wet ash where the firefighters had put out the flames. It looked like a scene from a post-apocalyptic blockbuster, a ruined landscape of scorched earth and devastation.

'Oh,' Bette said, shaken to think that she'd been in the midst of what had raged through this hidden patch of ground. 'It's even worse than I thought.'

'No,' Ryan said, resting a hand on her shoulder and squeezing before pointing past her. 'Look.'

She searched through the wisps of smoke tangling around the tattered remains of trees. It was hard to make out anything in the incessant palette of black and grey, but then she saw what he was pointing at.

'Is that . . . my grandmother's tree?'

Ryan puffed out a little laugh. He was standing so close that it ruffled her hair. 'Yes.'

She was stunned. 'But . . . it doesn't look burned.'

'There are others too, look,' he told her. 'I can count three, maybe four. I think the firefighters got to them before the flames did.'

Bette felt a prickle shift across her skin. Could it be true? 'They might not be burned, but they don't look very healthy.'

'It's just ash,' Ryan told her. 'I can wash them down. Bette, if I'm right, they'll survive.'

Bette let out a long breath. She felt giddy, the exhaustion of the past night suddenly catching up with her all at once.

'Good,' she said, faintly. 'That's good.'

They stood there for another minute or two, taking in the state of the orchard. Then Bette turned away, shining her torchlight back the way they had come.

'What's this?'

Bette turned to see Ryan studying something on the floor

426

of the passage, illuminated by the beam from his torch. As he crouched down and picked it up, she realized what it was.

'It's one of the saplings,' she said. 'I pulled it up, thinking I could save it, but I couldn't carry it and crawl up the stairs so I left it behind. I completely forgot about it.'

Ryan stood, examining the grafts he'd made in the small tree. 'I need to get this back into soil as soon as possible.'

'Do you think you can save it?'

'I can try. Even if the rootstock doesn't survive, I might be able to remove the grafts and transfer them to another sapling. With this, and those trees out there? Maybe this isn't the end of the orchard after all. That's something, isn't it?'

Yes, Bette thought wearily, it was something. Even if this land was no longer theirs, it would be good to know the orchard at least would survive in some form.

By the time they reached the top of the steps again, Bette was about ready to drop, she was so tired. Her ankle was throbbing painfully, making her hobble so badly that she had to lean on Ryan at every step. They'd made it to the Crowdie track when her phone beeped with an incoming text. She wrested it from her pocket and saw that it was from Roland Palmer.

JUST SEEN WHAT HAPPENED, it said. *PLEASE CALL AS SOON AS CONVENIENT. I HAVE NEWS.*

Chapter Fifty-three

The next few days were a whirlwind of 'hurry-up-and-wait'. Nina began by keeping Barney off school, but soon realized that it was better for him to be elsewhere and occupied rather than continually wanting to see how the police investigation was progressing. She wondered whether she was seeing the beginnings of a future career for her son. If he couldn't become an actual superhero, perhaps he'd end up being the first detective in the Crowdie family, instead.

Bette had been largely absent since the day after the fire. Nina wasn't sure what was going on, but intuited that it had a lot to do with the bank, as her sister had made frequent trips to Dundee and back. She was afraid to ask, knowing that the inevitable was coming and wanting to delay it for as long as she could. Her certainty that they'd soon have to leave Crowdie had been softened by Cam, who despite the ongoing clean-up at his place had been keen to reassure her on one particular point.

'You don't need to worry,' Cam had told her. 'You and Barney won't have to go far. You can move in with me.'

She'd laughed when he'd first said it, for two reasons. The first being that she couldn't believe he was serious and the second being that against all her better judgement and experience, she really hoped he was. 'Don't be ridiculous,' she said. 'We've barely been dating two months.'

He'd kissed her then. 'When you know, you know. And maybe we've only been dating for two months, Nina, but I think we've both known for far longer than that. Haven't we?'

Still, Nina worried. Would she be saying yes for the wrong reasons? And it was too soon, wasn't it? It had to be. But when did timings ever really align in this world?

She didn't raise the issue with Bette, who had enough on her plate already. Besides, if Nina brought it up herself she'd be instigating a conversation that she'd like to delay as long as possible. She went on working the farm as always while the days shortened, the light frozen from the sky by the approach of winter.

The day was coming, though. She would have felt it, even without knowing that the three-month deadline Bette had agreed to with the bank was almost upon them. The leaves had gone from the trees and Nina missed the old oak tree waving at her as she stood at Crowdie's kitchen door. Perhaps by the time the season turned she'd be gone from here, her chances to finally decipher what elusive words the leaves were spelling out for her spent.

'The police have finished down in the orchard,' Bette said, one morning. 'I'm going to go and see it. Will you come with me? There are some things we need to talk about.'

'Do we have to go down there?' Nina asked. 'I'm not sure I want to, Bette. Not knowing what nearly happened to you and Barney there.'

Bette reached out and squeezed her hand. 'That's exactly why I want you to come,' she said. 'It'll help, Nina. I promise. Please?'

Nina wasn't convinced, but agreed all the same. They wrapped up against the cold of the north wind and made their way to the clifftop. As they crossed the pasture and neared the dip, she saw that the fence had been opened up, the bars that they'd previously had to climb over to get to the orchard path removed. The firefighters must have done it, she thought, to make their access easier. Beyond, the charred overgrowth hung in black tatters, desiccated by the fire and ragged by the wind. Nina hesitated, her stomach turning, but her sister took her hand with a smile. 'It's okay,' Bette said, fingers interlaced with hers. 'I promise.'

They walked on like that, making their way carefully down the path, which Nina was surprised to see looked as if it had been swept clear of ash. She thought the wind must have carried the worst away, except that Ophelia's fence was clean, too, soot wiped away as if with careful intention.

Bette paused at the bottom of the track, beside the huge boulder that had stood sentry over this place for who knew how long. For a moment the two sisters stood still, contemplating the ruined land before them. Everything was black and grey, even the sky, even the waves. The lights Cam and Barney had strung through the trees had burned in the fire, and besides, they would have nothing to hang from now, nothing to illuminate. It was all dead.

'Oh,' Nina said, though it was more a sob than a word.

Bette squeezed her hand again. 'There's something I want to show you.'

Nina tried to pull away. 'No,' she said. 'Please. I want to go, Bette. I can't—'

'Trust me,' Bette said. 'Please?'

And so Nina let her sister lead her into the broken orchard. She wanted to shut her eyes, to close out the sight of all the ravaged, dead trees. The smell of charcoal was heavy around them, rising in pungent drifts every time their feet crushed a burned branch.

'Bette,' Nina tried again. 'Really, what's the point—'

'Look,' Bette said, and stopped.

For a moment, Nina couldn't take in what she was looking at. It was a tree. Not a charred stump, but an actual tree. Its branches were as tangled as they had ever been, but they were whole. There were even still a few leaves still clinging on against the season, dried but still yet to fall. Nina let go of Bette's hand, overwhelmed with an emotion she couldn't name. She reached out to touch the bark, then hesitated.

'It's okay,' Bette said, with a laugh. 'It's real. It won't disappear if you touch it.'

Nina traced her fingers down the little tree's trunk, then

looked at her hand. It came away clean, no trace of soot or ash. She looked at Bette. 'What? But how—'

'Ryan,' her sister said. 'He's washed the trunks of the trees that have survived.'

Nina felt her eyes widen. 'There are others?'

Bette wasn't sure she'd ever seen her sister look so purely happy. 'Come and see.'

Bette saved the best for last. Their grandmother's tree. It still stood against the cliff, where it had been since long before either of them were born. Nina blinked and felt tears on her cheeks, and then Bette wrapped an arm around her shoulder and pulled her close. They stood like that for a long time, two sisters looking at their family tree.

'Ryan thinks the orchard can be saved,' Bette said, eventually. 'It'll take time, but he's convinced.'

Nina wiped her hand over her face. 'Well, that's good. Isn't it? That this isn't the end of it. I'm so glad.'

'There's something else,' Bette said. 'It turns out that Dad had an insurance policy on the farm. Not just on the house, or the equipment. But on the land, too. All of it. Including the orchard. He'd taken it out years ago, when the farm was doing well.'

'What?'

Her sister laughed. 'Roland Palmer found a renewal from last year in one of the piles of paper Dad had left unfiled. He thought it was worth checking to see if Bern had kept up with the payments – if it was still valid. And it was. Dad might have let everything else slide, Nina, but he always made sure that was paid. Roland and I have spent the last week sorting out the policy and talking to the underwriters.'

'And . . . what does that mean?'

'It means,' Bette said, 'that we're going to get a hefty payout for this place after all. It's not enough to clear everything with the bank, but that's okay. Because yesterday I accepted an offer on the London flat, and the two combined will be more than enough.'

Nina stared at Bette. 'Then . . . you're really going? To Australia?'

Bette smiled again and looked down at her hands. 'Actually, something else has come up.'

'Oh?'

'Roland's looking to retire in a couple of years,' Bette explained. 'We've got to know each other from working together over the past couple of months. He's offered me a place in the company, with a view to taking it over when he finishes up.'

'In *Dundee*?' Nina asked, astonished.

'Yep.'

'And you're thinking about it?'

'I am,' Bette said. 'It would mean I could see the Greville case through myself, for starters. Can't do that from the other side of the world, however good the internet is. And besides . . .'

'Besides?'

Bette let her gaze rove over their grandmother's tree. 'I don't want to run away this time. I want to stay and help set everything right. Including the orchard. This place made amazing cider, once. Let's help it do that again.'

Nina considered. 'You think *we* should make cider? Do you think we *can*?'

'I do, and I do,' Bette said. 'We can ask Cam if he wants to invest. Ryan, too.'

'Ryan?'

Bette looked away. 'He's a good guy. He knows what he's doing in the orchard, and with cider,' she said. 'There's no point in letting the past damage the chance for a better future, is there?'

Nina threw her arms around her sister, pulling her into a bear hug that made Bette laugh and gasp for breath.

'I hated the idea of you being so far away,' Nina said, her chin on her sister's shoulder.

'Hmph,' Bette muttered. 'That's not what you said to Mum a few months ago.'

'Yeah, well. You've grown on me.'

'It's not going to be easy to get this place back on its feet,' Bette warned.

'I know,' Nina said. 'But it'll be fine.'

'It's going to need so much work and neither of us know what we're doing . . .'

'Trust me,' Nina insisted. 'It'll work. It has to. Because I have the *perfect* name.'

'Yeah?'

'Yup,' Nina said, pulling back. 'Right here is where we'll be making Salty Sisters Cider.'

Bette laughed. 'I like it.'

'Of course you do. Because it's perfect. Like me.'

Bette shook her head. 'You're such a brat.'

'Yeah, well. You're a diva. What are you going to do about it?'

They started to walk back through the ruined orchard, bickering and laughing, sharing dreams about the future. Nina looked back at their grandmother's tree before it disappeared from view. She raised one hand in a wave, and she was pretty sure the tree waved back.

Acknowledgements

All books require an entire army of support behind the scenes, but for me none more so than when I was writing *The Secret Orchard*. Huge thanks to my editors, Louise Davies and Clare Hey, for their support, patience and expertise as this story came together. The same goes for my brilliant agent Ella Kahn, who continued to be there for me while having a rather momentous year of her own, and also her colleagues at DKW, Bryony Woods and Camille Burns, for stepping in with such expertise when needed. Thank you to Pip Watkins for creating a beautiful cover that sits so well beside my previous books and yet still has its own unique character. Thank you as always to the indefatigable Sara-Jade Virtue for her genius at brand direction, Sabah Khan and Laurie McShea for marketing, Moria Eagling for the copyedit and Gabriella Nemeth for proof reading, Maddie Allen and Kat Scott for their sales efforts, and production controller Isabelle Gray for keeping everything running smoothly for distribution.

Last but never least, thank you to my wonderful husband, Adam Newell, both for his endless support and for using his skills as an international book-hound to find me the best on-topic research material. By the time this book comes out, I very much hope we are enjoying the fruit from our own tiny (though not so secret) orchard.

Discover more uplifting reads from Sharon Gosling ...

The Forgotten Garden

**A novel of second chances and blossoming communities
from the author of *The Lighthouse Bookshop*.**

Budding landscape architect Luisa MacGregor is stuck in a rut – she
hates her boss, she lives with her sister, and she is still mourning
the loss of her husband many years ago. So when she is given the
opportunity to take on a parcel of land in a deprived area, she sees
the chance to build a garden that can make the area bloom.

Arriving in the rundown seaside town of Collaton on the
north-west coast of Cumbria, she realises that her work is
going to be cut out for her. But, along with Cas, a local PE
teacher, and Harper, a teen whose life has taken a wrong
turn, she is determined to get the garden up and running.

So when the community comes together and the garden starts to grow,
she feels her luck might have changed. Can she grow good things
on this rocky ground? And might love blossom along the way ...?

Available now in paperback and ebook

**SIMON &
SCHUSTER**